Annie O'Neil spe... draped over the fa... hand. Novels, bak... angst poetry ate ... splits her time be... helping her with their cows, listening ... whilst weeding and spending some very happy hours at her computer writing.

Cursed with a poor sense of direction and a propensity to read, **Annie Claydon** spent much of her childhood lost in books. A degree in English Literature followed by a career in computing didn't lead directly to her perfect job—writing romance for Mills & Boon—but she has no regrets in taking the scenic route. She lives in London: a city where getting lost can be a joy.

Kate Hardy has been a bookworm since she was a toddler. When she isn't writing Kate enjoys reading, theatre, live music, ballet and the gym. She lives with her husband, student children and their spaniel in Norwich, England. You can contact her via her website: www.katehardy.com

Once Upon a Christmas Night

ANNIE O'NEIL

ANNIE CLAYDON

KATE HARDY

MILLS & BOON

First Published in Great Britain 2021
By Mills & Boon, an imprint of HarperCollins*Publishers* Ltd
1 London Bridge Street, London, SE1 9GF
www.harpercollins.co.uk

HarperCollins*Publishers*
1st Floor, Watermarque Building,
Ringsend Road, Dublin 4, Ireland

ONCE UPON A CHRISTMAS NIGHT © 2021 Harlequin Books S.A.

The Nightshift Before Christmas © 2016 Annie O'Neil
Once Upon a Christmas Night... © 2013 Annie Claydon
Christmas with Her Daredevil Doc © 2017 Pamela Brooks

ISBN: 978-0-263-3026-60

MIX
Paper from
responsible sources
FSC™ C007454

This book is produced from independently certified FSC™ paper to ensure responsible forest management.

For more information visit: www.harpercollins.co.uk/green

Printed and bound in Spain
by CPI, Barcelona

THE NIGHTSHIFT
BEFORE CHRISTMAS

ANNIE O'NEIL

This one's for my guy. You're my Christmas, birthday and HEA all wrapped up into one handsome, blue-eyed Scottish package.

Wifey xx

CHAPTER ONE

"OKAY, PEOPLE! LISTEN UP, it's the start of silly season!"

"I thought that was Halloween?"

"Or every full moon!"

"First snowfall?"

"Hey, Doc? Is that where your locum tenens is? Stuck in one of the drifts?"

"He won't last long in Copper Canyon if that's the case. A man needs snow tires."

"A *woman* just needs common sense! I follow the snow-plows! Got them tracked on my phone!"

Copper Canyon's Emergency Department filled with laughter. Impressive, considering they were down to a quality but skeleton staff. Never mind the fact it was almost always one of the busiest weeks of the year. The town was full of holiday visitors and the ski resort up the hill always had an emergency or six their small clinic couldn't handle.

Katie scanned the motley crew who would see her through Christmas Eve and, for some double-shifters, into the Big Day itself. Valley Hospital was no Boston General, and that was just the way Katie liked it. The facility was big enough to have all the fancy equipment, small enough to be able to give the personal touch to just about every-one who walked through those doors. And if they needed an extra hand, there were always the emergency services guys up on the mountain, willing to lend a hand. It wasn't home yet…but she'd get there.

"Thank you, peanut gallery. Time to focus." Katie tried her best to smile at the small but vital crew, all visibly buzzing with Christmas cheer. It wasn't their fault she wanted to rip every bauble, snowman and glittery snowflake from the walls. Someone else took that prize. "Thanks for wearing your red and green scrubs, by the way—you all look very…festive."

"Who doesn't love Christmas, Doc?" a tinsel-bedecked RN quipped.

Me.

"Right!" Katie soldiered on. They were used to her grumpy face—no need for Christmas to morph her into a jolly, stethoscope-wearing elf. "Just in time for the lunchtime rush, I've got our first Christmas mystery X-ray!"

A smattering of applause and cheers went up as she worked her way through the dozen or so staff and slapped the X-ray up on the glowing board with a flourish.

"Any guesses?"

"Why would anyone stick one of those up their—?"

"I know! Especially at Christmas."

"At least it's not a turkey thermometer. We had one of those last year. Perforated the intestine!"

The group collectively sucked in a breath. *Ouch.*

"C'mon, Dr. McGann, that's too easy. Give us a hard one!"

"All right, then." She turned to face the cocky resident. "If it's so easy, what's your guess?"

"Cookie cutter?"

Katie winced and shook her head.

"Nope. Good guess, though. Try again."

She joined the staff in tipping their heads first in one direction then the other. It wasn't that tough…

"Tree decoration. Six-pointed snowflake. My Gramma Jam-Jam used to have one. It was my wife's favorite."

Katie's body went rigid with shock as the rest of the staff turned to see who the newcomer to the group was. She didn't need to turn around. She didn't need to imagine who or what Gramma Jam-Jam's tree was like. She'd helped decorate a freshly cut fir in her old-fashioned living room as many times as she had fingers on a hand.

As her thumb moved to check that the most important finger was still bare, waves of emotion began to strike her entire body in near-physical blows. She willed her racing heart to still itself, but every sensory particle within her was responding to the one voice in the world that could morph her by turns into a wreck, a googly-eyed teen, a blushing bride...

Dr. Joshua West. Her ex-husband.

Well. He would be her ex if he would ever sign the blinking divorce papers!

She couldn't even manage to turn around and look at him, and yet her body was already on high alert to his presence. He was close. Too close.

She heard a shifting of feet. Maybe it was one of the nurses... Maybe it was... Her eyes closed for a moment.

Yup. There it was. That perfectly singular Josh scent. The man smelled of *sunshine.* What was *up* with that? It was the dead of winter. Freezing-cold, snowing-right-now *winter.* And yet she could smell warm sunny days and the rural lifestyle only her husband—her *ex-husband*!—could turn into something delicious. Talk about evocative! One whiff of that man had never failed to bring out her inner jungle cat. From all the excitement swing-dancing around her chest cavity in preparation for a high dive down to her...*nethergarden*...it was clear the cat had been in hibernation for some time.

Her spine did a little shimmy, as if she already didn't get the point.

She did a laser-fast mental scan of her medical books. Maybe her body was trying to tell her something different!

Frisson or *fear*?

Her tongue sneaked out and gave her lower lip a surreptitious lick.

Guess that answers that, then.

How could that rich voice of his still have a physical effect on her? Hadn't two years apart been enough to make her immune to the sweet thrill twirling along her insides every time she heard him whisper sweet—?

"Nice to see you, Katiebird."

Don't even start *to go there!* She took a decidedly large step away from Josh. *Sweet or not, they'd been* nothings *in the end.*

"Right, everybody! Let's get these patients better."

Katie clapped her hands together—more to prove to herself that she had her back-to-work hat on than anything else. That, and she didn't want anybody around to witness the showdown she was certain was coming.

The group dispersed back to their posts, with a couple of interns still marveling over the human body's ability to deal with the unnatural. Precisely what Katie was experiencing at this exact moment. Fighting a natural instinct. Every time she laid eyes on Josh it was like receiving a healing salve. Her eyes were still glued to the X-ray, but she knew if she only turned her head she was just a blink away from perfection.

She sucked in a breath. Not anymore! No one and nothing was picture-perfect. Life had a cruel way of teaching that lesson.

"Are you ever going to turn around?"

His words tickled her ear again. The man clearly didn't believe in personal space when his wife was trying to divorce him.

"Are you going to tell me what you're doing here?" Katie wheeled round as she spoke. Her breath was all but sucked straight out of her as she met those slate-blue eyes she'd fallen so deeply in love with. It had been a long time since she'd last seen them up close and personal. A really long time.

She fought the sharp sting of tears as she gave a quick shake of her head and readjusted her pose. She could do nonchalant while her world was being rocked to its very core. She was a McGann, for goodness' sake! McGanns were cool, analytical, exacting. At least that was what she'd told herself when her parents had swanned off to another party in lieu of spending time with their only daughter. McGanns were the polar opposite of the West family. The Wests were unruly, wayward, irresponsible! Invigoratingly original, passionate, loyal...

Her teeth caught her lower lip and bit down hard as her brain began to realign the Josh in her head with the one standing in front of her. Thick, sandy-blond hair, still a bit wild on top and curling round his ears, softening the edges of his shirt collar. No tie. *Typical Josh*. He rarely did formal, but when he did...

She swallowed and flicked her eyes back up to his hair to miss out on the little V of chest she knew would be visible. No hat. *Natch*. Why follow the same advice you'd give your patients? There were a few flakes of snow begging to be ruffled out of the soft waves. Her fingers twitched. The number of times she had tucked a wayward strand back behind one of his ears and given in to the urge to drop completely out-of-character sultry kisses along his neck...

No! And double, triple, infinity no! No Josh West. Not anymore!

"Didn't the agency tell you?"

The expression on his face told her he knew damn well it hadn't told her. The twinkle in his eye told her he was enjoying watching the steam beginning to blow out of her ears. Typical. He always had been spectacular at winding her up and then bringing her to a whole other plane of happy—

Stop it, Katie McGann. You are not falling under his spell again.

"Tell me what?"

"No need to grind your teeth, darlin'." He tsked gently. "It'll give you a headache."

"Headache?" Maddening and headache-inducing didn't even *begin* to cover the effect he was having on her. "Try migraine."

"Good thing I'm around, then."

He gave her one of those slow-motion winks that had a naughty tendency to bring out the…the *naughty* in her.

"Those things can knock you out flat."

An image of a shirtless Josh slowly lowering himself onto her…into her…blinded Katie for an instant. The muscled arms, the tanned chest, slate eyes gone almost gray with desire and lips shifting into that lazy smile of his— the one that always brought her nerves down a notch when she needed a bit of reassurance.

She scrunched her eyes tight and when she opened them again there it was in full-blown 3-D. The smile that could light up an entire room.

"Josh, I can't do this right now. Our locum hasn't bothered to show, and as you can see—" her arms curled protectively around herself as the sliding doors opened to admit a young man with a child "—I'm busy. Working," she added, as if he didn't quite get the picture.

Never mind the fact he'd come top in the class above hers at med school, so clearly had brains to spare. Or the little part about how she was standing there in a lab coat in the middle of an ER. A bit of a dead giveaway. *Urgh!* If she used coarse language, a veritable stream of the colorful stuff would be pouring forth! Why was he just standing there? *Grinning?*

"What's the game here, Josh? Yuletide Torture? Our last Christmas together wasn't horrific enough for you?"

His expression sobered in an instant. She'd overstepped the mark. There was no need to be cruel. They'd both borne their fair share of grief. Grinding it in deep wasn't necessary. They would feel the weight of their mutual loss in the very core of their hearts until they each stopped beating. Longer if such a thing was possible. Forgetting was impossible. Surviving was. But only just. Which was exactly why she needed him to leave. *Now.*

"Sorry, Kitty-Kat. You're stuck with me. I'm your locum tenens."

To explain why he was late for his first shift, Josh could have told Katie how his car had spun out on some black ice on the way in, despite it being a 4x4 he drove, and the all-weather tires he'd had put on especially, but from her widened eyes and set expression he could see she had enough information to deal with. The latest "Josh incident," as she liked to call his brushes with disaster, could be kept for another time.

"No. No, I'm sorry, Josh—that's not possible. We can't…"

He heard the catch in her voice and had to force himself to stay put. In his arms was where his wife belonged when she was hurting, but it was easy enough to see it was the last place she wanted to be.

He flexed his hands a few times to try and shake the urge. With Katie right there, so close he could smell her perfume… It would be futile, of course, but one thing people could always say about Josh West—he was a man who never had a problem with attempting the impossible. How else could he have won Katie McGann's heart? Cool East Coast ice princess falling in love with the son of a Tennessee ranch manager, scraping his way through med school with every scholarship and part-time job he could get his callused hands on? It was when he'd finally got his hands on her—man, they'd shaken the first time—he'd known the word "soulmates" wasn't a fiction.

"Dr. McGann?"

Both their heads turned at the nurse's call, and the strength it took to keep his expression neutral would have put a circus strongman out of work.

So. Katie had gone back to her maiden name.

Another nail in the coffin for his big plan, or just another one of Katie's ways of ignoring the fact they belonged together? That everything that had happened to them had been awful—but survivable. Even more so if they were together.

"Can you take this one? Arterial bleed to an index finger. He says it's been pumping for a while. Shannon's in with him now." The nurse held out a chart for her to read.

"Absolutely, Jorja. How long's a while?" Katie asked, taking the three strides to the central ER counter while scanning the chart, nodding at the extra information the charge nurse supplied her.

Josh took the chance to give his wife a handful of once-overs—and one more for good measure. It had been some time since his eyes had run up those long legs of hers. Too long. He'd been an idiot to leave it so long, but she had been good at playing hide-and-seek and he'd had his own dragons to slay. A small flash of inspiration had finally led him to Copper Canyon—the one place he'd left unexplored.

He stuffed his hands into the downy pockets of his old snowboarding coat, fingers curling in and out against the length of his palms. Laying his eyes on her for the first time in two years was hitting him hard. She'd changed. Not unrecognizably—but the young woman he'd fallen in love with had well and truly grown up. Still beautiful, but—he couldn't deny it—with a bit of an edge. Was this true Katie surfacing after the years they'd spent together? Or just another mask to deal with the disappointments and sorrows life had thrown at them in the early days of their marriage?

Gone was the preppy New England look. And in its

stead... He didn't even know where to begin. Was this Idaho chic? Since when did *his* Katie wear knee-high biker boots, formfitting tartan skirts in dark purple and black with dark-as-the-night turtlenecks? Yeah, they would be practical in this wintry weather, but it was a far cry from the pastels and conservative clothes she'd favored back in Boston. The new look was *sexy*.

A hit of jealousy socked him in the solar plexus. She hadn't... He suddenly felt like a class-A *idiot* for not even considering the possibility. She hadn't moved on. Not his Katie. Had she...?

His eyes shot up the length of her legs to the plaid skirt and then up to her trim waistline, irritatingly hidden by the lab coat. His eyes jagged along her hands, seeking out her ring finger. Still bare. He would never forget the moment she'd ripped off her rings and slapped them onto the kitchen counter. Throwing had been far too melodramatic for his self-controlled wife. The word "Enough!" had rung in his ears for weeks afterward. Months.

He exhaled. Okay. The bare finger wasn't proof positive she wasn't seeing someone else, but it was something. He scraped a hand through his mess of a hairdo, wishing he'd taken a moment to pop into a barber's. But he hadn't worried a jot about what he'd looked like over the past two years, let alone worried about impressing another woman. From the moment he'd laid eyes on Katie to the moment she'd hightailed it out of his life—*their* life—he'd known there was only one woman in the world for him. And here she was—doing her pea-pickin' best to ignore him.

His eyes traveled up to her face as she scanned the chart, listening to the nurse. He knew that expression like the back of his hand. Intent, focused. Her brain would be spinning away behind those dark brown eyes of hers to come to the best solution—for both the patient and the hospital, but mostly the patient. One of the many traits he loved about her. Patients first. Politics later. Because there were *always* politics in a hospital. He knew that more than most. It was why staying at Boston General hadn't worked out so well. Why a new job in Paris just might be the ticket he needed to wade out of that sorry old pit of misery he'd been wallowing in.

But he wasn't going anywhere until he knew Katie was well and truly over him. He checked his watch. Seven days to find out if she was cold- or warm-blooded. It ended at the stroke of midnight on New Year's Eve. He'd either hand her a plane ticket or the divorce papers. He sucked in a fortifying breath of Katie's perfume. *Mmm...* Still sweeter than a barn full of new summer hay.

Well, then. He gave his chin a scrub and grinned. *Best get started.*

CHAPTER TWO

"WHAT YOU GOT THERE?" Josh stepped up to the desk, shrugging off his jacket as he approached. Out of the corner of her eye Katie could see Jorja's lips reshape into an O. Josh—or rather his body—had that effect on women. It was why she'd never thought she'd stood a chance. People always mistook her shyness for being stuck-up. But Josh had seen straight through the veneer and gone directly to her heart.

He turned his Southern drawl up a notch. He could do that, too. Pick and choose when to play the Southern gent or drop it if he saw it detracted from his incredibly sharp mind.

"Dr. McGann, may I help keep you out of the fray while you sort out the big picture?"

Katie eyed him warily for a second, then made a decision. By the hint of a smile that bloomed on his lips she could see it was the one he had been hoping for.

He would stay.

Never mind the fact that showing up on Christmas Eve when they were a doctor down wasn't giving her much of a choice. She had it in her to kick him the hell outta Dodge, if that was where he needed booting. But right now there were patients to see, and pragmatism always trumped personal.

"Twenty-five-year-old male presented with an arterial

cut to the bone on his index finger." She tapped the chart with her own.

"Turkey?"

"Ham. Too easy for the likes of you."

She pressed the chart to her chest, claiming it as her own. Katie let her eyes travel along all six feet three inches of her ex. Josh had always been a trauma hotshot. And he'd always looked good. She'd steered clear of the Boston General gossip train, so didn't really know what path he'd chosen professionally after she'd left, but personally nothing had changed in the looks department. He still looked good. She looked away.

Too good.

"You're the next one down." She pulled the X-ray down from the lightboard and passed it to him with a smirk. "Make your Gramma Jam-Jam proud. You can put your stuff in my office for now—the staff lockers are further down the corridor and this patient's been waiting too long as it is."

She tipped her head toward a glassed-in cubicle a few yards away. Josh took advantage of the broken eye contact to soak in some more of the "New Katie" look. Her super-short, über-chic new haircut suited her. It sure made her look different. *Good* different, though. No longer the shy twenty-one-year-old he'd first spied devouring a stack of anatomy books in the university library, a thick chestnut braid shifting from shoulder to shoulder as she studied.

He cleared his throat. Whimsical trips down memory lane weren't helping.

"Green or red scrubs," she added, pointing to a room just beyond her office.

"You always liked me in blue."

The set of her jaw told him to button it.

"Green or red," she repeated firmly. "The patients like it. It's *Christmas*." She handed him the single-page chart with a leaden glare and turned to the nurse. "Jorja MacLeay, this is Dr. West, our locum tenens over the next few days. See that he's made welcome. His security pass should expire on the first of January."

"At the end of the day?" Jorja asked hopefully.

"The beginning. The very beginning," Katie replied decisively, before turning and calling out her patient's name.

He flashed a smile in the nurse's direction, lifted up his worn duffel bag to show her he was just going to unload it before getting to work. The smile he received in return showed him he had an ally. She shot a mischievous glance at his retreating wife and beckoned him toward the central desk.

"Don't mind her," Jorja stage-whispered. "A kitten, really. Just a grumpy kitten at Christmas." She shrugged off her boss's mysterious moodiness with a grin. "As long as she knows you've got your eye on the ball, she's cool."

Josh nodded and gave the counter an affirmative rap. "Got it. Cool. Calm. Collected. And Christmassy!" he finished with a cheesy grin.

"Says here you're double-shifting."

"You bet. Where else would a fellow want to see in Christmas morning?"

Jorja laughed. "Cookies are in the staff room down the hall if you need a sugar push to get you through the night. Canteen's shut and the vending company forgot to fill up the machines, so there might be a brawl over the final bag of chips come midnight!"

"Count me in! I love a good arm-wrestling session. Especially if the chips are the crinkly kind. I love those."

"I can guarantee you'll have a fun night…at least with most of us." She shot a furtive look down the corridor to ensure Katie was out of earshot and scrunched her face and shoulders up into a silent "oops" shrug when Josh raised his eyebrows in surprise.

"You two don't know each other or anything, do you?"

"We've met." It was all Josh would allow.

It was up to Katie if she wanted to flesh things out. He'd been the only crossover she'd allowed between personal and professional and he doubted she had changed in that department. She was one of the most private people he had ever met, and when news of what had happened to them had been all but Tannoyed across Boston General, it had been tough. Coal-pit-digging tough.

Jorja giggled nervously and flushed. "Sorry! Dr. McGann is great. We all love her. The ER always runs the smoothest when she's on shift."

Josh just smiled. His girl always strove to achieve the best and ended up ahead of the game at all turns. Except *that* night. She'd been blindsided. They both had.

He shook off the thought and waved his thanks to Jorja. First impressions? Young to be a charge nurse. Twenty-something, maybe. She struck him as a nurse who would stay the course. Not everyone who worked in Emergency did. She was young, enthusiastic. A nice girl if first impressions were anything to go by.

He'd gone with his gut when he'd met Katie. Made a silent vow she would be his wife one day. It had taken him a while, but he'd got there in the end. And today the vow still hit him as powerfully as the day they'd made good on a whim to elope. Five years, two months and fourteen days of wedded… He sighed. Even he couldn't stretch to "bliss." Not with the dice they'd been handed.

He thought of the divorce papers stuffed inside his duffel bag. There was only one way Katie could ever convince him to sign them. Prove beyond a shadow of a doubt that she felt absolutely nothing for him anymore. He gave a little victory air punch. So far he'd seen nothing to indicate she would be able to get him to scrawl his signature on those cursed papers tonight.

Just the shift of her shoulders when she'd heard his voice had told him everything he needed to know. She could change her name, her hair and even her dress sense if she wanted to—but he knew in his soul that time hadn't changed how his wife felt about him. No matter how bad things had become. She couldn't hate without love. And when she'd finally turned round to face him there had been sparks in her eyes.

Katie stuffed her head into the stack of blankets and screamed. For all she was worth she screamed. And then she screamed some more. Silent, aching, wishing-you-could-hollow-yourself-out-it-hurt-so-bad screams. There was no point in painting a pretty picture in these precious moments alone.

Seeing Josh again was dredging up everything she had only just managed to squeeze a lid on. *Just.* In fact, that lid had probably still been a little bit open because, judging by the hot tears she discovered pouring down her face when she finally came up for air, she was going to have to face the fact there was never going to be a day when the loss of their baby didn't threaten to rip her in half.

What was he thinking? That he could saunter into her ER as if it were just any old hospital on any old day? With that slow, sweet smile of his melting hearts in its wake? She'd not missed the nurses trying to catch his eye. Jorja's giggles had trilled down the hallway after she'd stomped off. Josh did that to people. Brought out the laughter, the smiles, the flirtation. The Josh Effect, she'd always laughingly called it. Back when she'd laughed freely. Heaven knew, *she'd* fallen under his spell. Hook, line and sunk. If only she'd known how far into the depths of sorrow she'd fall when she lost her heart to him, she would have steered clear.

She swatted away her tears and sank to the floor of the

supplies cupboard, using her thumbs to try and massage away the emotion. Her patient was going to be wondering where she was, so she was going to have to pull herself together. Shock didn't even begin to cover what she'd felt when Josh had walked into her ER. Love, pain, desire, hurt…those could kick things off pretty nicely.

"Of all the ERs in all the world, he had to walk into this one."

Talking to herself. That was a new one to add to her list of growing eccentricities. Maybe she should have fostered some of those friendships she'd left behind in Boston.

"Sounds like the start of a pretty good movie." Josh's legs moved into her peripheral vision as his voice filled her ears.

"More like the end of one."

"No, that's the start of a beautiful friendship."

"Well—well…" She trailed off. Playing movie quotation combat with Josh was always a bad idea.

She huffed out a frustrated sigh. Couldn't she just get *a minute* alone? She should have gone to the roof. No one went there in the winter, and she relished the moments of quiet, the twinkle of Copper Canyon's Main Street. She swiped her hands across her cheeks again, wishing the motion could remove the crimson heat she felt burning in them. Against her better judgment she whirled on him and tried another retort.

"Should I have said 'of all the *stalkers* in all the world'?"

"Oh, so going to the supplies cupboard to track down some mandated holiday scrubs has turned me into a stalker, has it?" he asked good-naturedly.

The five-year-old in her wanted to say yes and throw a good old-fashioned tantrum. The jumping-up-and-down kind. The pounding-of-the-fists kind. The *Why me? Why you?* kind. The Katie who'd shored up enough strength to finally call their marriage to a halt knew better. Knew it would only give Josh the fuel he wanted to add to a fire she could never put out.

She wasn't going to give him the satisfaction of knowing how much she still cared. That had been his problem all along. Too trusting that everything would be all right when time and time again the world had shown him the opposite was true. Who else had become an adrenaline junkie after their daughter had been stillborn? Hadn't he known how dangerous everything he'd been doing was? And she'd always been the one who'd had to pick up the pieces, apply the bandages, ice the black eyes, realign the broken nose... Trying her best to laugh it off like he did when all she'd wanted to do was curl up in a corner and weep.

Couldn't he see she had to play it safe? That losing their daughter had scared her to her very marrow? If she were *ever* to feel brave enough to move forward—let alone try and conceive again—he needed to call off his game of tug-of-war with mortality.

She scratched her nails along the undersides of her legs before standing up, using the pain to distract herself from doing what she really wanted.

"Large or extra-large?" she bit out.

"Guess that depends on if you need me to play Santa later." He grabbed a pillow from a shelf and stuck it up his shirt.

Without bothering to examine the results, Katie yanked a pair of extra-large scrubs from a nearby shelf. Not because she needed a Santa but because she didn't need to see how well he filled out the scrubs. The first time they'd met—*woof!* And she was no dog owner.

The first time they'd met... He said it had been in the library, but she was convinced to this day that he'd made it up. The day she'd first seen him—easily standing out in a crowd of junior residents, all kitted out in a set of formfitting scrubs—his eyes had alighted on her as if he'd just gained one-on-one access to the Mona Lisa herself... Mmm... That moment would be imprinted on her mind forever... She'd never let anyone get under her skin—but she'd been powerless to resist when it had come to Josh.

"Green! Good to see you remember red always makes my complexion look a bit blotchy."

Katie blew a raspberry at him. She wasn't playing.

"Or is it that you remember green always brings out the blue in my eyes?" He winked and took hold of the scrubs, trapping her hand beneath his.

Just feeling his touch reawakened things in Katie she had hoped she'd long-ago laid to rest. Her eyes lifted to meet his. Stormy sea-gray right now. Later... He was right. Later they'd be blue, and later still the color of flint. She had loved looking into his eyes, never knowing what to expect, trying to figure out how to describe the kaleidoscope of blues and grays, ever-shifting...ever true.

As the energy between them grew taut, the butterflies that had long lain dormant in her belly took flight, leaving heated tendrils in their wake. She tugged her hand free of his and gave him a curt smile. Physical contact with Josh was going to have to be verboten if she was going to keep it together for the next eight days. It was bad enough he'd seen her red-rimmed eyes.

She glanced at her watch.

T-minus...oh, about one hundred and ninety-two hours and counting!

"Twenty-four hours."

"Beg pardon?" Josh shook his head.

Hadn't he been riding the same train of thought she had? If she'd gone off on a magical journey down memory lane, the chances were relatively high he'd done the same thing. Different tracks—different destinations.

She cleared her throat. There was about half an ounce of

resolve left within her and she needed to use it. "I'm giving you twenty-four hours."

He raised his eyebrows and gave her his *What gives?* face.

"Oh, don't play the fool, Josh. You've ambushed me. Pure and simple. And on—" She stopped, only just missing having her voice break. "It's the minimum notice I have to give the agency if I want a replacement."

"What are you on about, Kitty-Kat?" He pulled himself up to his full height. Josh always played fair and he could see straight through her. This was a below-the-belt move.

She jigged a nothing-to-do-with-me shrug out of her shoulders, her eyes anywhere but on his. "If it's quiet enough we might be able to let you go earlier without telling the agency."

She might not want him here, but she didn't want to tarnish his record. He was a good doctor. Just a lousy husband. She squirmed under his intent gaze, pretty sure he was reading her mind. A sort of, kind of lousy husband.

"Don't be ridiculous. Christmas is always busy! You're going to need me. What kind of man would I be, leaving you to deal with a busy ER all on your own?"

"That's terribly chivalrous of you, Josh. I'm going to need a doctor—yes. But I don't need *you*." She looked at her watch again, not wanting to see how deep her words had hit. Laceration by language was *way* out of her comfort zone—but tough. Josh had pushed her there—and she had an ER to run.

"Sorry, I've got to get to this patient."

"Yup! I'm certainly looking forward to mine!" He mimed snapping on a pair of gloves with a guess-it's-time-to-suck-it-up smile.

If she was feeling generous, she had to give it to him for keeping his cool. Assigning him a rectal examination as a "welcome gift" was not, she suspected, the reunion he had been hoping for. Then again, finding out her estranged husband would be her locum for the next week wasn't much of a Christmas present for her, so tough again! Hadn't two years' worth of sending him divorce papers given him enough of a clue?

"Uh... Kate?"

"Yes?"

"Are you going to move so I can get my patient's Christmas ornament back on the tree?"

"Yes!" she blurted, embarrassed to realize she'd been staring. "Yes, of course. I was just..." She stopped. She wasn't "just" anything. She stepped back and let him pass.

"I'm happy to see you, too, Katiebird," he said at the doorway, complete with one of those looks she knew could see straight through to her soul.

She rubbed her arms to force the accompanying goose bumps away.

"Me, too," she whispered into the empty room. "Me, too."

"Hello, there... Mr. Kingston? I understand you've got a bleeding—" Katie swiftly moved her eyes from the chart to the patient, instantly regretting that she'd wasted valuable time away from her patient.

Unable to resist the gore factor, the young man had lowered his hand below his heart and tugged off the temporary tourniquet the nurse had put in place. Blood was spurting everywhere. If he hadn't looked so pale she would have told him off, but Ben Kingston looked like he was about to—

Oops!

Without a moment to spare Katie lurched forward, just managing to catch him in a hug before he slithered to the floor.

"Can I get a hand in here? We've got a fainter!"

Katie was only just managing to hold him on the exam table and smiled in thanks at the quick arrival of— Oh. It was Josh. *Natch.*

He quickly assessed the situation, wordlessly helping Katie shift the patient back onto the exam table, checking his airways were clear, loosening the young man's buttoned-at-the-top shirt collar and loosening his snug belt buckle by a much-needed notch or two as she focused on stanching the flow of blood with a thick stack of sterile gauze.

"Got a couple extra pillows for foot elevation?"

"Yup." Katie pointed to the locker where they stored extra blankets and pillows. "Would you mind handing me a digital tourniquet first? I'll see if I can stem the bleeding properly while he's still out."

"Sure thing." Josh stood for a moment, gloved hands held out from his body as they would be in surgery, and ran his eyes around the room to hunt down supplies.

"Sorry, they're in the third drawer down— Wait!" Her eyes widened and dropped to Josh's gloved hands. "Weren't you in the middle of…?"

She felt a sharp jag of anger well up in her. *Typical, Josh!* Running to the rescue without thinking for a single moment about protocol! Was simple adherence to safe hygiene practices too much to ask?

"Done and dusted." He nodded at the adjacent exam area. "He's going through the paperwork with Jorja." He took in her tightened lips and furrowed eyebrows and began to laugh. Waving his hands in the air, still laughing, he continued, "You didn't think…? Katie West—"

"It's McGann," she corrected quietly.

"Yeah, whatever." The smile and laughter instantly fell away. "I always double-glove during internal exams. These are perfectly clean. You should know me better than that." His eyes shifted away from hers to the patient, the disappointment in his voice easy to detect. "You good here?"

She nodded, ashamed of the conclusion she'd leaped to. Josh was a good doctor. Through and through. It was the one thing she'd never doubted about him. He had a natural bedside manner. An ability to read a situation in an instant. Instinctual. All the things she wasn't.

She slipped the ringed tourniquet onto the young man's finger and checked his pulse again. It wasn't strong, but he'd be all right with a bit of a rest and a finger no longer squirting an unhealthy portion of his ten pints of blood everywhere. He'd need a shot of lidocaine with epinephrine before she could properly sort it out, so she would need to wait for him to come to. Being halfway through an injection wasn't the time when a patient should regain consciousness. Especially when Josh was leaping through curtained cubicles, coming to her rescue. She jiggled her shoulders up and down. It wouldn't happen again.

"Are you nervous, Doc?"

"Ah! You're back with us!" Katie turned around in time to stop the young man from pushing himself up to a seated position. "Why don't you just lie back for a while, okay? I have a feeling your finger didn't start bleeding half an hour ago, like it says in your chart, Ben."

He looked at her curiously.

"Is it okay if I call you Ben?"

"You can call me what you like as long as you stitch me up and get me outta here, Doc! It's Christmas Eve. I've got places to go…things to do—"

"Someone to drive you home?" Katie interrupted. "After your fainting spell, I don't think it's a good idea for you to get behind a wheel."

"And I don't think it's a good idea for *you* to boss someone around on Christmas Eve!"

Katie backed away from Ben as his voice rose and busied herself with getting the prep tray ready. Emotions ran high on days like this. Especially if the patient had had one too many cups of "cheer." Unusual to encounter one on the day shift, but it took all kinds.

"Cheer" morphed into cantankerous pretty quickly, and

Ben definitely had a case of that going on. She stared at the curtain separating her from her colleagues, knowing she'd be better off if there was someone else in the room when she put in the stitches.

She sucked in a breath and pulled the curtain away. "Can I get a hand in here?" She dived back into the cubicle before she could see who was coming. Josh or no Josh, she needed to keep her head down and get the work done.

"Everything all right, Dr. McGann?"

At the sound of Jorja's voice, Katie felt an unexpected twist of disappointment. It wasn't like she'd been hoping it would be Josh. Her throat tightened. *Oh, no...* Of all the baked beans in Boston Harbor... Had she? *Clear your throat. Paste on a smile.*

"Yes, great. Thank you, Jorja. Nothing serious, just thought we could do with an extra pair of hands now that Mr. Kingston here has rejoined us."

Josh tried his best to focus on the intern's voice as he talked him through how he saw things panning out on Christmas Eve based on absolutely zero experience, but he couldn't. All he could hear was Katie, talking her patient and the nurse through the procedure in that clear voice she had. The patient had definitely enjoyed a bit of Christmas punch before he'd arrived, and Josh didn't trust him not to start throwing a few if he was too far gone.

"Hey." He interrupted the intern. "What did you say your name was again?"

"Michael," the young doctor replied, unable to keep the dismay from his face. He'd been on a roll.

Tough. Fictional projections weren't going to help what was actually happening.

"Michael, what's your policy on patients who've had a few too many?" He mimed tossing back some shots.

"Oh—each ER head is different, but Katie usually calls

the police." He looked around the ER as if expecting to see someone stagger by. "Why?"

"Just curious." He gave Michael's shoulder a friendly clap with his hand, hoping it would bring an end to the conversation. "Thanks for all the tips," he added, which did the trick.

He tuned his hearing back into the voices behind the curtain where Katie was working. The patient was young and obviously a gym buff. As strong and feisty as she was, Katie was no match for a drunk twenty-something hell-bent on getting more eggnog down his throat. Drunk drivers on icy roads were the last thing the people of Copper Canyon needed on Christmas Eve. Or any night, for that matter.

"Okay, Ben, you ready? I'm just going to inject a bit of numbing agent into your finger."

"What *is* that?"

Josh inched a bit closer to the curtain at the sound of the raised voice.

"It's a small dose of lidocaine with epinephrine," Katie explained. "It will numb—"

"Oh, no, you don't!" The patient—Ben, that was it—raised his voice up a notch. "I've been on the internet and that stuff makes your fingers fall off. No *way* are you putting that poison in me!"

Josh only just managed to stop an eye roll. Self-diagnosis was a growing epidemic in the ER…one that was sometimes harder to control than any actual injury.

"I think if you read all of the article you'd find that's more myth than reality."

Always sensible. That was his girl!

Ben's voice shot up another decibel. "Are you telling me I'm a *liar*?"

"No, I'm saying digital gangrene is about the last thing that's going to happen if I—"

"You—are—not—putting—that—sh—"

"Hello, ladies." Josh yanked the curtain aside, unable to stay quiet. "Need an extra pair of hands?"

"No," Katie muttered.

"Yes," Jorja replied loudly over her boss.

"They're trying to give me gangrene!"

"Really? Fantastic." Josh rocked back on his heels and grinned, rubbing his hands together in anticipation. "I haven't seen a good case of gangrene in ages." He flashed his smile directly at Katie. "Are you trying to turn Mr. Kingston here into *The Gangrene who stole Christmas*?"

Everyone in the cubicle stared at him for a moment in silence.

"The Grinch!" Josh filled in the silence. "Get it? Gangrene? Grinch?"

There was a collective headshake, which Josh waved off. "You guys are hopeless. They're both green!"

Jorja groaned as the bad joke finally clicked.

"Well," he conceded, "one's a bit more black and smelly, and isn't around for the big Christmassy finish, but, Ben, my friend..." Josh took another step into the cubicle, clapping a hand on the young man's shoulder from behind and lowering himself so that he spoke slowly and directly into the young man's ear. "I've known this doctor for a very long time, and if she needs to stabilize the neuronal membrane in your finger by inhibiting the ionic fluxes required for the instigation and conduction of nerve impulses in order to stem the geyser of blood shooting from that finger of yours, she knows what she's talking about, hear?"

Ben nodded dumbly.

"Right!" Josh raised a hand to reveal a set of car keys dangling from his fingers.

He saw Katie's eyebrow quirk upward. He would have laid a fiver on the fact she was thinking he'd taken up pickpocketing to add a bit more adrenaline to his life. He'd win the bet and she'd be wrong. He'd just seen enough drunks in his Big City ER Tour. The one where he had done everything but successfully forget the brown-eyed beauty standing right in front of him.

He cleared his throat and stepped away from Ben. "You owe Dr. We—Dr. McGann an apology. And while you do that—" he jangled the keys from his finger "—I'll just be popping these babies over to Security until we get someone to pick you up."

Ben opened his mouth to object, his eyes moving from physician to nurse and back to Josh before he muttered something about being out of order, his mother's stupid car, and then, with a sag of the shoulders, he finally started digging a cell phone out of his pocket.

"Excellent!" Josh tossed the keys up in the air, caught them with a flourish, gave Jorja a wink and tugged the curtain shut behind him before anyone could say *boo*.

"Well..." Josh heard Jorja say before he headed off. "He's certainly a breath of fresh air!"

Katie muttered something he couldn't quite make out. Probably just as well.

Josh grinned, his shoes glued to the floor until he was sure peace reigned behind Curtain Three. He heard Katie clear her throat and put on her bright voice—the one she used when she was irritated with him.

"Now, then, Ben, if you can just show me that finger of yours, we can get you stitched up and home before you know it. Jorja? Could you hand me some of the hemostatic dressing, please? We need to get the wound to clot."

Josh began to whistle "Silent Night" as he cheerily worked his way back toward the main desk. Job. Done.

"How long do you intend to continue this White Knight thing?"

Josh's instinct was to smile and tell her he would wield his lance and shield as long as it took for her to see sense and come back to him. Longer. Until the day he died, he would protect Katie. He'd taken a vow and had meant it.

He had broken part of it, and he was going to spend the rest of his life making good on it. Even if that meant walking away, no matter how hard it hurt.

But this was work. Personal would have to wait.

"Where I come from, people stick around to help one another when the going gets tough." He laid the Tennessee drawl on as thick as molasses. It always got to her and this time was no different.

He watched as her hands flew to her hips in indignation, then shifted fluidly into a protective, faux-nonchalant crossing of the arms. Her eyes widened, the lids quickly dropping into a recovery position. One of her eyebrows arched just a fraction before her face became neutral again. But she couldn't keep the flush of emotions from pinking up her cheeks.

He shifted his stance, ratcheted his satisfaction down a couple of notches. He wasn't playing fair. He knew more than anyone that teamwork in an emergency department was something Katie valued above all else. Unless, it seemed, it came from him.

He stood solidly as she gave him the Katie once-over. He wouldn't have minded taking his own slow-motion scan over the woman he'd dreamed about holding each and every night since she'd told him in no uncertain terms she'd had enough of his daredevil ways. He'd have to play it careful. Divorce rules shifted from state to state, and he hadn't checked out Idaho. If she'd moved to Texas he would have shown up a lot earlier. No need to wait for a signature there. As it was, he thought two years had given them each more than enough time to know they were meant for each other. Given *him* enough lessons to know she'd been right. He'd suffered enough loss to know it was time to change. Move forward—whatever shape that took.

"Where are you staying?"

Unexpected.

"Here." He pointed at the hospital floor.

There went that eyebrow again.

"Locum tenens wages aren't enough to get you a condo?"

He shook his head. "I didn't know how long I'd be staying."

She refused to take the bait.

"Usually housing comes with the contract."

What *was* she? The contract police? Or... A lightbulb went off... Was she trying to figure out where he'd be laying his sleepy head? Was she missing being held in his arms as much as he had longed to hold her? Truth was, he never bothered with separate housing on these gigs. Hospital bunks suited him fine... Friends' sofas sufficed when he was back in Boston. Home was Katie, and it had been two long years...

He heard the impatient tap of her foot. Fine...he'd play along.

"Not this time of year. And it was too short a contract for me to put up a fight."

Katie's jaw tightened before she shifted her chin upward in acknowledgment of the obvious. She knew what he meant. The locals had dibs on all the affordable properties. Everything went to the top one hundred highest-paid, most famous, with the biggest bank account, et cetera, et cetera. Life in Copper Canyon was a heady mix of the haves and those who *worked* for the haves.

Mountain views, private access to the slopes, sunset, sunrise, heated pools, wet bars, ten thousand square feet minimum of whatever a person could desire—you name it, they had it. Copper Canyon saw most of America's glitterati at some point, on the slopes or at one of the resorts... if, that was, they didn't have a private pad.

"You staying at your parents'? I remember them having a pretty plush pad out here and not using it all that much."

Risky question, but he couldn't imagine why else she would have moved here. She walked over to the board and began erasing patient names and rearranging a few others.

"They're usually at the Boston brownstone or in the Cayman Islands, right?"

"Jorja? Could you make sure the tablets are all updated to reflect what's on the board? We've got quite a few changes to note," Katie called over her shoulder to the main desk.

"Sure thing, Dr. McGann. On it!"

Josh leaned against the wall, one foot crossed over the other, hands stuffed in his pockets, happy to just watch her play out her ignoring game. He threw in an off-key "Rudolph the Red-Nosed Reindeer" whistle for good measure.

"And let's pop something different on the music front, Jorja. Some *nice* carols."

Josh grinned at Jorja, dropped her a wink and dropped his whistle simultaneously.

"They just don't stop, do they? Your parents?"

Only the squeak of the whiteboard pen could be heard over the usual hospital murmur.

Wow. Having a conversation with a brick wall would have yielded more return.

"The indefatigable McGanns! That's how I always thought of them."

Katie's lips tightened. She didn't do chitchat. Especially when it came to her parents. They were the source of any well-packed baggage Katie had hauled around through the years. Parents who'd discovered they hadn't really been up to parenting so had handed it over to nannies and boarding schools to do the work for them. They were harmless enough folk at a cocktail party, but he knew their lack of interest as parents hurt Katie deeply.

"I'm not staying there this week."

Interesting.

"I always stay at the hospital over Christmas," she volunteered hastily, with a quick pursing of her lips. "My parents have come in to ski for the week—"

Josh snorted and was relieved to see Katie join in with an involuntary snigger.

"Well…at least they'll look fabulous in their ski gear before they hit the cocktail circuit."

Her eyes flicked away with a shake of her head. She must have remembered she'd told herself not to enjoy being with him.

"It's easier not to get stuck in a storm if I'm here."

Wow! Two whole sentences! They were on a roll. He kept his ground. Nodded. Tried not to look too interested. He'd learned long ago that it took a lot to get Katie talking, but once you opened the floodgates…

"So…where are you really staying?"

Bang goes that theory.

"Honestly, Kit-Kat. My plan was to just stay here."

Her brown eyes were briefly cloaked by a studied blink. Then another. Her lips twitched forward for a microsecond in a moue. Was that a response to his being there? Had an image of the two of them wrapped together as they'd always been in bed flashed across her mind's eye as it had his?

He cleared his throat and shifted his stance. "Casual" was getting tough to pull off. What he wouldn't give to take the two steps separating them and start to kiss those ruby lips of hers as if each of their lives depended on it. It felt as though his did, and standing still was beginning to test his fortitude.

"I see." She abruptly turned to face the main desk, where Jorja was checking in a new patient. "We'd best get you to work, then."

Fair enough. *She wasn't saying no.*

And… A smile began to tug at the corners of his mouth. Depending on how you looked at it, Katie was saying *yes*. Yes to his staying. Yes to his being in the hospital. Yes to their being together.

Okay, it was a bit of a leap, but he was willing to take the risk. In for a penny and all that…

He pushed away from the wall and took a step behind her when she turned back to face the board, unsurprised to see her shoulders stiffen…then relax when he kept just enough space between them for her to know he wouldn't do what he'd always done before their lives had been ripped in two.

He closed his eyes and pictured the scene. She'd be studying something—anything—an X-ray, a chart, the wall—it didn't matter. He'd step right up behind her, arms slipping round her waist, hands clasped against her belly, his chin coming to a rest on her pillow of chestnut hair or slipping down alongside her cheek for a little illicit nuzzle or to drop a kiss on her neck…

He heard her sigh at the exact same time he was blowing out a long, slow breath between his lips. *Oh, yeah.* They were on the same page all right. It just hadn't been turned for a while.

"Hey, you two—you're in for the Secret Santa, right?"

Josh and Katie both whirled round to see a grinning Jorja holding out a Santa hat with folded pieces of paper being rapidly jiggled around.

"Count me in." Josh reached into the hat and grabbed a bit of paper. If he was going to show Katie he knew how to settle down, enjoy small-town life… "Who doesn't love a bit of Secret Santa action?" He turned to Katie. "That is if it's all right with the boss lady?"

"Who am I to curtail your holiday cheer and our small-town ways?"

And they were back in the ring! Three years ago the idea of going back to his small-town roots would have made him run for the hills…or the bright lights of Manhattan, more like it. But after he'd quit Boston for Manhattan, Chicago, Miami, none of them had stuck. Not one had sung to him. Nothing worked without Katie.

"I'm just a small-town boy, and nothing says home

like…" His eyes sought hers and in that instant he was sure each of them knew what he might say.

"Like what, Dr. West?" Jorja pressed.

Katie. It had always and only been Katie.

"Like having an opportunity to put down roots! In the form of a Secret Santa. I just love a good old-fashioned round of Secret Santa."

Too emphatic?

He felt Katie giving him a curious glance. *Good.* He wanted her to see the changes. Maybe not all of them. The pins in his leg could wait. And the scars along his hip and spine. It wasn't looking like she'd be ripping off his clothes for a moment of unchecked ardor anytime soon, so he was good with that. But he'd been careful that she didn't see him walk too much. She'd know. She'd definitely know. And she'd never come back to him then.

"Dr. McGann? Are you taking part in the draw?"

Jorja waggled the hat in front of his wife's face. She might be a good nurse, but that girl sure didn't read body language all that well.

He watched Katie put on her bright face and return her focus to Jorja. "Of course. In for a penny…"

Josh felt Katie's eyes land on him as the words came out of her mouth, her hand plunging into the hat blindly to grab a bit of crumpled paper.

She remembered. They'd both said it. A lot. Especially in the early days of their marriage, when they'd needed every penny to repay their medical-school bills, making their own way after just about the best elopement a couple could ever have had when Katie had decided her parents didn't deserve to put on a society wedding. A church full of her parents' business associates and bridge pals mixing with his ruckus of a family, who would show up to a black-tie event wearing their funeral clothes? No, thanks.

His lips twitched as her eyes stayed locked on his.

They'd spent just a few hundred dollars on rings, the honeymoon, and a huge chocolate cream pie that they'd set between them at a roadside diner and eaten in one go... Then, not too long after, they had been putting down deposits on cribs and—

Josh raked a hand through his hair and looked away first. It was still hard to go there. Still impossible to believe they'd really lost their little girl. That sweet little baby who'd never even had one chance to look into her parents' eyes...

"Right! You said you wanted me to get to work." He craned his neck to look around at the waiting room and stuffed the bit of paper into his lab coat pocket. "Who's next?"

Katie had to shake her head for a minute before she could think clearly. Having Josh here was like receiving a physical assault of emotions she hadn't wanted to feel again.

Pain...

She unnecessarily scrubbed her hands through her super-short hair, having forgotten, just as her eyes connected with Josh's, that she didn't have a ponytail to curl her fingers through anymore. *Yup.* The pain she could certainly do without.

Fear.

That Josh would be safe. That he'd come home from his latest escapade unscathed. That he would come home at all. Bearing another loss in the wake of their stillborn baby girl...wondering if he'd well and truly be there for her if they decided to try and conceive again... No. She just hadn't been able to do it.

Desire.

The desire felt good. *Too* good. And it was too much of a link to the pain and the fear. A trilogy of Josh, all wrapped up in a gorgeous sandy-haired, blue-eyed package she had never been able to resist. But she had to. For her sanity, first and foremost. For her heart.

"What do you think? You happy to let me go with the photocopy girl?"

"Beg your pardon?" Katie forced herself to focus on the words coming out of Josh's mouth about a patient newly arrived from an office party gone wrong. Photocopies. Bottoms. Broken glass.

His front tooth was still crooked. She'd always liked that. The imperfection made him more…perfect. Hmm… Maybe she shouldn't focus on his mouth. His eyes—definitely blue-gray in this light. Flinty? Steel-blue. Was there such a thing? And with little crinkles round the edges. Those were new. Sun, maybe? Or just the passage of the two years they'd put between them?

It might have felt like an eternity, but two years wasn't really that long. Then again, they'd been through a lot. But Josh had always seemed impervious to it all. Definitely a glass half-full— That was it! *Glasses.* He probably just needed glasses. Typical Josh to put practical needs like getting his eyes checked on hold. She tilted her head to the side. They *were* kind of sexy. The crinkles…

Nope. *Nope.* Still not hearing words. Still not focusing. What about the little bridge between his eyes? That was just like anyone else's. Just part of someone's face. A plain old face just like any other doctor in any other hospital. With a nose and high cheekbones and two perfectly formed… *Argh, no!* And she was back to his lips.

"Apologies, Dr. West." She put on her best interested face. "I didn't quite catch that."

A low laugh rumbled from his chest. Josh knew damn well she'd been ogling him and he was loving it. From the first day he'd draped a stethoscope round her neck, he'd known he had the power to cut straight through her prim-and-proper exterior and bring out the hidden tigress in her. The one she hadn't known existed. Bookish only children who preferred the company of their elderly nannies weren't obvious contenders for being horny minxes aching to see how it felt to be scooped up in a single swoop, her legs wrapped round his waist, his hands cupped on her—

"…derriere."

"Beg pardon! What was that again?"

This time Josh didn't even bother going for subtle.

"Katie, do you just wanna sneak off and make out for old times' sake while the anesthetic gets to work?"

"What? *No!*" She shook her head, sending a horrified look over her shoulder to see if anyone had overheard him. "No!" she added, with a look. She didn't *make out* with people. Let alone with the one man on the planet she needed statewide clearance from if her brain was ever going to work properly again.

She forced herself to play a quick game of catch-up.

"You say she broke her office's copy machine by sitting on it? Why on earth was she doing *that*?"

"You never butt-copied—?" Josh stopped himself, his smile shifting from astounded to tender. "It's something that happens when an office party gets out of hand. This gal clearly likes to get her cray-cray on."

"I have *no* idea what crayfish have to do with it."

"Crazy!" Josh laughed. "Cray-cray is crazy, if you're down with the kids—know what I mean?" He struck a pose for added emphasis.

Katie sniffed. She could do zany. If she put her mind to it. But photocopying her butt? That was just ridiculous. The germs on one of those things should be off-putting enough!

"Well, you two sound perfect for each other."

Katie saw the sting of hurt her words caused and wished she could yank them straight back. Josh might do wild but he also did wonderful. If only he hadn't kept pushing the boundaries after their loss. If only he'd convinced her he could play things safe—even for a while—they might…

"I best get on, then."

Katie watched as Josh turned and made his way toward the curtained cubicle where his patient was waiting. There was something…different about his gait. Something different about *him*. He'd changed. Really changed. Her teeth caught hold of her lip and gave it a contemplative scrape.

Changed enough to hear what she had to say?

A series of loud guffaws burst from the curtained area where Josh was de-sharding his patient's booty.

No. Same ol' Josh! Some stray Christmas spirit must have sneaked into her coffee that morning. No one changed *that* much. She would just see through the time they had to work together as professionally as she could. No point in reopening old wounds. She'd borne enough hurt for a lifetime.

She scanned the board and picked a good old-fashioned broken arm. Some enthusiastic decorative touches to a snowy rooftop, no doubt. Fixing. Setting. Repairing. That was what she did. It was how she survived.

Once again she shook on her bright smile and pulled open the curtain.

"Right! Mr. Dawsen, I understand you've broken your arm?"

CHAPTER THREE

"I'LL JUST BE in the residents' room—cool?" Josh popped a finished chart onto the RNs' central desk, flashing a smile to the two nurses trying to untangle a set of twinkling lights. A patient's or some late decorating? They paid him no attention, so he hightailed it down the corridor, hoping for a few moments to regroup. It was time to pull up his socks and tell Katie the truth. The real reason he was there.

She'd yanked six of his safety-net days out from under him, unwittingly putting all his partridges in the one pear tree. It was do-or-die day *now*. For a man who didn't plan much, he had definitely planned this out. A whole week to gauge her mood…time to maybe inject a bit of romance into snatched moments alone. But with this stupid twenty-four-hour thing she showed no sign of shifting from, he had to get a move on. They were just a few hours away from midnight, and once that clock pinged upon the Christmas star, his time would be well and truly running out. Josher-ella was going to have to get a move on.

He looked at his backpack, slung on the back of the lone chair parked across from the bunk he'd thrown himself on for a catnap. He wouldn't have been surprised if the sheaf of official papers lurking in the side pocket had taken on a life of their own, unzipped the bag and come out and danced at him like an evil sugarplum fairy…or whoever the evil one was in *The Nutcracker*.

He cursed silently. He'd once loved Christmas and all the schmaltzy, cheesy, sentimental stuff that went along with it. When they'd lost their daughter just a few days before the holiday, it had sucked the season dry of any good feeling. He wanted that back—and the only way to get it was to woo his wife back into his arms. And if this was the season for miracles he was a first-rate candidate.

Otherwise…? Otherwise he would have taken the job in Paris when he'd got the offer. Moved to France to study with the most elite team of minimally invasive fetoscopic surgeons? Hell, yeah! It would have been a gargantuan leap forward for his career. He'd spent the past two years doing locum residencies in every single obstetrics unit he could. He would never know why his little girl had been stillborn—but if he could help other women he'd be there.

But his heart wouldn't be. And to end up in the City of Love without the woman he adored by his side would have been pointless. Not to mention the fact that Dr. Cheval insisted on total focus. No distractions and no demons. Right now Josh was hauling those things around big-time.

When the job offer had come, he'd seen it as life's way of grabbing him by the scruff of the neck, giving him a right old shake and demanding, for once, that he take responsibility for everything he had done. Own up to how his behavior had driven his wife away. And after she'd gone he'd pushed at life a bit more. A *lot* more. Life had pushed back, and now he had the metal infrastructure to prove he hadn't come out the winner.

He gave his head a good old scratch, shooting a look up to the heavens to see if there were any clues there.

Mistletoe.

Of course. *Love.* The high-voltage current he'd felt the first, second and every other time he'd laid eyes on his wife was electric. But going to the city where hand-holding and kisses on bridges and feeding each other delectable morsels of…

Hey! Now, *there* was an idea. He and Katie had always enjoyed a good picnic. Out on the common—or on a bench if it was pouring down—regardless of the sideways glances they'd received from passersby. It was what supersized umbrellas were made for, right?

A smile lit up his face. He'd do a Christmas dinner picnic! The smile faded just as fast. The canteen was closed. The way the snow was coming down meant leaving the hospital would be a challenge. Or just plain stupid. He'd already done stupid…

"Hey, Dr. West." Jorja poked her head round the corner with an apologetic expression. "Sorry to ruin your break, but we've got mass casualties coming in!"

Adrenaline shot through him and he was up and out of the bunk before Jorja had even removed herself from the door frame.

"What happened? How many? Do we have enough on staff? Is there any chance of diverting any of the patients to another hospital?"

Jorja's eyes widened, along with her mouth. Streaks of red began to color her cheeks.

"Uh…" She pushed at the floor with the stub of her toe.

"Sorry, too much television! I forget Copper Canyon is totally different from what you get out east."

"There are two. Patients, that is. With gastro. Dr. McGann is already down there."

Josh's heartbeat decelerated and he tried not to laugh. Much. The poor girl looked mortified. He slung an arm around her shoulders and tugged her in for a half hug as they made their way out into the main corridor. "Hey, Jorja, don't you worry. I can adjust my big-city ways…"

The words stopped coming. What the heck was he doing, bragging about his big-city machismo when he'd grown up in a town with two unlit junctions? Junctions where he'd been guaranteed to see his math teacher or his father heading off to the cattle markets. There was no hiding anywhere in that place if you stuck around—which was why he'd loved losing himself in the big city. And then he'd met Katie…like an angel he hadn't known he'd needed to meet. Found him. That was what she'd done. She had found him. Shown him how important it was to be grounded.

He looked straight up, silently cursing the invisible heavens. She was his lighthouse, his beacon, his…whatever analogy best fit the scene. She was his heart. His soul. And if he didn't get a move on he was going to lose her for good.

"Uh… Dr. West? Are you trying to…?" Jorja was shifting underneath his arm, turning toward him, shifting her gaze upward as well.

Damn. Mistletoe.

Katie heard them, then saw them. A twist of nausea squirled around her stomach as she took in the nervous laughter, the awkward shuffle of feet and the chins tipping up toward the ceiling. Jorja had practically covered the hospital in mistletoe, so it was hardly surprising that the one person who would find a way to put it to use was Josh. He had always been a flirt. It was his nature. To charm, to delight, to dazzle.

She turned away quickly, not wanting either of them to see the hurt in her eyes, the sheen of tears she'd only just managed to check when she'd spotted them. The last thing she was going to do was stick around and watch her husband kiss someone he'd only just met!

At least she knew Josh showing up out of the blue wasn't some clever plot to see *her*. It was a fluke. A needle-in-a-haystack chance of Yuletide torture. *Just terrific.* She'd spent two entire years patching the shredded remains of her heart together, and just when she'd come to terms with her play-it-safe, hiding-out-in-Idaho lifestyle, Josh had parachuted in and undone years of exacting damage control.

Adrenaline began to surge through her. She tugged at the high ribbing on the neck of her sweater, suddenly wishing she had scrubs on. Why hadn't one of her patients thrown up on her? Then she could have missed this nauseating scene of mistletoe magic. She checked herself. Wishing patients ill wasn't her style, and thankfully the two gastro cases had turned out to be overindulgence rather than food poisoning.

Who ate massive portions of something called Chocolate Decadence and *didn't* expect a sore stomach? People who weren't careful. People who were reckless. People who made decisions on a whim—like Josh.

She made a beeline for the doctors' locker room and grabbed her winter coat before pushing through the heavy door into the stairwell and pounding up step after step toward the roof, letting out an involuntary wail of relief when she found it was empty.

Silent screams into blankets while trying to retain her control were one thing—but seeing Josh with another woman... Words couldn't even describe how much it had hurt. Throat-scraping wail after howl poured out of her throat as the snow bit at her cheeks and the wind swirled through her hair and into her tear-blinded eyes. Why had Josh—of all the people in the world—had to show up? Hadn't he done enough harm? It was worse than shock. It was Shock and Awful.

Chest heaving from the effort of purging her sorrow, Katie forced herself to take more level, steadier breaths. Knowing a chill could turn into pneumonia in the blink of an eye at this time of year, she excavated a woolly hat from the depths of her pocket. She hadn't let those Girl Scout sessions go to waste.

Prepared at all times. Self-contained at all times. She tugged on her hat and scowled. Which one had she left out?

"And a smile in the face of adversity."

Katie's frown deepened. She turned this way and that, taking in the roof as though she were a child stuffed into an over-thick snow outfit. The urge to throw a tantrum was welling within her again. Twice in one day? Must be a record! Maybe she should have gone the bad-girl route as a kid. It might have garnered her a bit more attention from her parents.

She harrumphed. Unlikely.

She pulled out her phone and trawled a finger along the not-very-long list of names to see if there was anyone on there she could talk to. Colleague. Colleague. Colleague. Mentor. Nanny.

Alice Worthing! Her shoulders softened. She had absolutely *loved* her Irish nanny. Alice was the only person she'd told in advance of her elopement, and the second she'd seen the twinkle in the dear woman's eyes, she'd known she was doing the right thing.

Wow—had they both been wrong!

She pushed at the phone symbol anyhow. It would be nice to hear a friendly voice on Christmas Eve.

After a couple of rings she heard laughter and then the lilted *hello* she knew so well. Fifteen years in the US, married to an American for ten of them, and her accent hadn't changed a jot.

"Hello? Is anyone there?"

Katie started. "Sorry, Alice. It's me, Katie Wes—Katie McGann."

"Katie! My sweet Katie. Darlin', how the devil are you? It's been so long. *Too* long! What is it? Over a year now since you went out west. Are you all right, love? Is everything okay?"

"Yes. Fine." She kicked her boot into the thick roof-top snow.

"Well, that's a lie and we both know it."

Katie smiled at the phone, double-checking that she hadn't video-dialed her friend by accident.

"It's just—I—um—wanted to wish you a merry Christmas."

"Well, that's a lovely sentiment, Katie, but why not tell me the real reason you called?"

"I'd forgotten how quickly you see through me." Katie grinned, now wishing she *had* video-called Alice.

"Well, you and I both know how precious life is, so come on—spit it out."

"Josh."

"Oh, Katie, no—nothing's happened to Josh, has it?"

"No! God, no!" Katie felt surprised at how glad she was that was true. She might not want to be married to him, but she couldn't bear the thought if… "He's shown up at the hospital as my locum."

Another round of laughter followed as Alice called out to her husband, saying Josh had found Katie. She heard the click of the receiver as Alice's husband got on the line.

"So he finally tracked you down, did he?" James's deep voice rumbled down the line. "He tried to plumb us for info but we didn't breathe a word. We knew you wouldn't want us getting involved. Want me to come out and beat him up for you?"

Katie knew he was joking, but James had always been very protective of her. Her relationship with her own father had never been a close one, so she liked James's concern.

"What sort of nonsense are you talking, man?" Alice hushed him. "Josh's dead romantic. Always was. A bit wild, but showing up on Christmas Eve and all…"

"It wasn't exactly as if they left things on a good note," James riposted.

"Yeah…well…" Katie's mind whirred, trying to catch up with everything as Alice and James bantered. "He came and asked you where I was?"

"Course he did. The boy's mad for you. Always was."

Then why was he trying to kiss Jorja?

Katie and Alice talked for what felt like hours. They had a lot to catch up on. But as the roar of doorbells and barking dogs started to drown out their voices, Katie knew she had to let Alice get back to her own life. She tipped her head to see if she could differentiate between clouds and the falling snow.

"Sorry, Katie. Our little girls' choir has just shown up to sing carols. Please forgive me but I need to go. You'll sort it out for the best. You always do. Lots of love."

"Oh! How is Catherine?"

"She's grand, darlin'. Must dash, but call again soon!"

And the line went dead.

Katie didn't know if she felt better or worse for having made the call. A thousand questions and no answers added to her frustration. She kicked a satisfying lump of snow up into the glowering sky and watched it float back down to the rooftop.

The helicopter hadn't been used in a while, and from the looks of things, the crew hadn't been up yet with the blower. The snow was a good foot deep where she was standing. The drifts were deeper over by the edges. A good three feet by now. Maybe deeper. Winter had started early in Copper Canyon, and no matter how hard they tried to stay on top of the accumulating snow, they couldn't. Which, in this case, was all right. Because it was…beautiful.

She felt the fight go out of her. Maybe that had been her problem all along. Trying too hard to control things. Josh. Herself. She'd even broken down the seven stages of grief, giving herself a month to go through each stage, fastidiously identifying and eradicating anything that would hold back her progress to—to what, exactly?

Josh's angry words came back to her in echoing anvils

of self-recognition. *Micromanager. Risk-averse. Exacting perfectionist! Control freak.*

The last one wilted her shoulders into a hunch against the buffeting wind. She looked around the roofscape again, as if it would conjure Josh up from the lower reaches of the hospital so he could call her out himself. Except the only voice she heard those words in was her own. *She* was the one who had shaken off the rest of the words he'd said and turned those remaining into insults. The words she wouldn't let herself remember?

Gorgeous. My love. Sweetheart. Angel. Darlin'.

She blinked away the sting of tears. When things had been good between them, they had been, oh, *so* good. Josh had given her reserves of strength she hadn't known she had. Lit her up like a…oh, the irony…lit her up like a Christmas tree!

She blinked again, feeling a tear drop this time. She swiped it away and tried to shake off the memories. She was in a new place now, and up until the start of this double shift on Christmas Eve, things had been pretty good. Well… She tugged a foot through the snow and stomped toward the roof edge.

Neutral.

How pathetic was that? Even *she* had to snicker at herself. To aspire to have a *neutral* day? Wow! That elite education she'd aced had *really* prepared her for life. She scrunched her eyes tight and forced herself to open them with the promise of seeing something that made her smile.

Not too far away the twinkling lights of Copper Canyon's main street were glittering away like a perfectly decorated window display. The town council always did well. Never too opulent, never mistaking the decor for any holiday other than Christmas. At the far end of Main Street, where the two-lane road split and circled round the town's green, an enormous evergreen twinkled and shone like a bejeweled Fabergé egg through the fat snowflakes swirling around it. At the base of the tree, Katie could make out the lit outline of the bandstand, its columns rising in twisted swirls of red and white lights.

She reached the edge of the roof and eyed the drift. Higher than she'd thought. Enough snow to cloak the thick safety barriers she knew ran around the edges. She should make a note to hospital admin that they really must be raised—

She checked herself. As far as she knew, she was the only one who was mad enough to come up to the roof in the middle of a snowstorm.

See, universe? Katie McGann can be just as much of a nut burger as the rest of them!

She gave the elements a satisfied grin as she pulled her emergency pair of waterproof mittens from the inner pocket of her down jacket.

Well...pragmatism *was* useful. And it was hardly a storm. A bit of wind. Thick latticed snowflakes big enough to catch on her tongue. She eyed the split-level roof just below her. The empty administrative offices...

She pushed her lips in and out as she considered. Without snow...? Maybe a six-foot drop. With snow...? Hmm...two feet of emptiness before she hit several feet of fluffy virgin snow. Her mind shot back to the rare trips up to her late grandparents' cabin in Vermont, where she, Alice and her grandmother had made endless snow angels.

"Always room for more angels to look out for us." That was how her grandmother had put it. So when she was upset and there was some snow to hand...snow angel. Magic recipe for a better mood.

Would it be fluffy enough to...? *Yeah...why not?* She could throw caution to the wind as easily as the next person...right?

She opened her arms wide, eyed the tilt of the snowdrift, turned around and began to press her weight into her heels. She wobbled for a moment…regained her footing…then reasoned with herself that this was precisely the sort of litmus test she needed to pass in order to prove she could well and truly survive without Josh…beyond *neutral*.

She sucked in a breath and smiled—at the world for just being there and being all snowy and twinkly so that she could make a snow angel when she sure as hell needed one.

As she shifted her heels along the edge again and raised her arms, the door to the stairwell burst open. Josh was calling out her name at ten decibels. His face was a mix of horror and fear when his eyes lit upon her. He called her name again, the vowels bending and elongating in the wind.

"Kaaa-tieee!"

Their eyes connected in a way they never had before. For the first time she saw he had been through it, too. The harrowing, mind-numbing pain of loss. And in that moment she wished back the two years they had spent apart.

Josh watched in horror as Katie's arms windmilled for balance. His eyes raced down her legs as she shifted her heels to regain traction on the icy ledge. Each micro-move she made became overexaggerated with her fruitless efforts to stay upright. Their eyes stayed locked as she completely lost her footing and fell helplessly back into the void.

Never in his life had he felt such searing pain. He had thought the grief at losing his daughter was the worst thing he could have lived through, but losing Katie as well would kill him.

An infinity of darkness spread out before him as he shouted and stumbled toward the edge, not even sure he was making a single sound above the howling in his skull.

Katie's comprehension of the world shifted as her body lost its fight with gravity. Apart from the terror she'd seen in her husband's eyes, she suddenly understood what he meant about the freedom in letting go. Just the release of falling backward was exhilarating.

She opened her throat and screamed as sensations hit her in surreal hits of slow-motion recognition. The breeze swept past her cheeks. She blinked away a snowflake. With the surprise of the fall she'd lost her sense of where she was actually falling. It might have gone on forever.

The sky was astonishingly textured with clouds and the odd hit of stars… When was the last time she'd just looked up and enjoyed the sky?

Before she could take it all in, she hit the powdery snow with a fluffy *ploof!* and lay utterly still as her breath came back to her.

A dim awareness of sound came to her. A male voice. *Josh!* It had to be Josh. Her mind whirled into catch-up mode, her eyes widening as she realized what she was hearing.

"Katie! No!"

Ragged. Rough. Grief-stricken. Why was Josh so upset? She was just making a snow angel, for heaven's sake.

His face appeared over the edge, his features etched with anxiety.

"I fell."

"Yes!" The air came out of his mouth in thick, billowed huffs of breath. "Yes, you did."

"It's nice down here." She saw the sheen of tears rise in his eyes before he had a chance to disguise it as something else. Josh had never been a weeper. He swiped at his eyes with his sleeve. Maybe she'd been mistaken.

"Are you all right?"

Katie could tell Josh was trying to keep his voice under control. Behave as if he saw his estranged wife fall off the edge of a building every day. It suddenly struck her that his reaction was utterly different from what she would have expected. The old Josh would have just leaped over the edge and joined her. Pulled her into his arms and then, after a deep, life-affirming kiss, would have made snow angels with her. Right?

"Katie?" Josh knelt on the ledge and began to scan her acutely for injury. "Are you okay?"

"Pretty good." She moved her arms and legs just a little bit, suppressing a surprise hit of the giggles as she did so. Nothing hurt. She'd landed on an enormous pillow of snow, for heaven's sake! "Actually..." She met his eyes properly this time. "It was pretty fun."

"Fun, huh? Is that what you think? Near enough giving me a heart at—?"

He stopped himself and she watched silently as Josh re-arranged his features into a long, studied look before visibly deciding to swallow whatever lecture he'd been about to give. She knew the expression well...and it gave her a hit of understanding she hadn't known she needed. It was the look Josh must have seen on *her* face time and again after they'd lost their baby girl and he'd come back from yet another high-octane experience.

Josh looked away from Katie and gave the vista a scan. The early-evening gloaming left hints of light on the tips of the mountains...gave the glittering Main Street more of a festive punch. His lips thinned as he slowly inhaled and exhaled, trying to get his racing heart under control.

His relief at finding Katie alive and well was morphing into anger. How *dare* she do this? Take such a huge risk? Didn't she know how precious she was to him? His anger welled up further into his chest, searing him from the inside out. *How dare she?*

"A thank-you for stopping you killing yourself might be nice."

"Killing myself?" She pushed herself up to sit and squinted at him through the falling snow. "You think if I—Katie West—Katie McGann," she corrected herself, annoyed, "was going to do something so stupid as to kill myself I'd do it by jumping two feet into a snowdrift?"

"That was difficult to see from the doorway." Josh cleared his throat again and swore under his breath. "So you weren't—?"

"Of course I wasn't. I was just…" She let herself plop back into the lightly compacted drift. "I was just trying to make a snow angel."

She spoke softly. More truculent than apologetic, but, hell, he'd take it. She was alive. That was good enough for now.

He tipped his head to the side and eyed her. "You only make snow angels when you're upset."

"No, I don't!" she shot back, her eyes anywhere but meeting his.

Yup! She was upset. He knew his arrival had upset her, but he hadn't thought launching herself into a snowdrift four floors off the ground would be her response. Maybe he should have called. Scheduled lunch. Done something normal, like she'd been begging him to do all along.

He knelt on the ledge and hitched up his bad leg before slipping over into the snow mattress Katie was pillowed in. He winced. The old-timers were right about feeling the cold differently once your body had proved itself fallible.

He gave her a grumpy glare and flopped down onto the snow beside her, where they lay in silence for a few moments. He'd thought he'd lost her just now. Lost the love of his life.

Okay, firebrand…cool your jets. You've both had a shock.

He shot a sidelong glance at Katie and saw her all wide-eyed and… *Seriously?* Was she *grinning*? That grin near enough sucker punched the rest of the breath out of his chest and he only just managed to reel in the angry words.

His emotions were running so wild it was impossible to tell if he should just whip out those stupid divorce papers and give her his signature right now. Then maybe they could both get on with their lives.

He swiped at the snowflakes clustering on his lashes. There was no way he could move on. Not like this. Not yet. And if Katie didn't give a monkey's about him she wouldn't be flinging herself off the sides of buildings on Christmas Eve. So…it was a silver-linings moment. A weird one. But a moment to count himself lucky. Blessed.

It didn't stop him from needing to expunge a bit of "grumpy," though.

Eyes rigidly glued to the heavens, he leveled his voice before starting. "Well, isn't *this* cozy?"

"That's one way of putting it," Katie grumbled.

"This a new Idaho thing? Hurling yourself off the side of buildings without an audience?"

"Something like that."

"Any reason in particular, or did whimsy just overtake you?"

"Yeah," she bit back drily. "That's how I roll. Got it in one, Josh. Crazy Katie West, hitting the fast lane again!"

"West?" He tried not to sound hopeful.

"Whoever."

He let the words settle for a moment. It took one to know one, and she was calling him out. She always read life's instruction book. He barely looked at the book's cover before flinging it away and just going for it. Especially once he'd met his wife. With Katie by his side he had felt invincible.

"It was pretty reckless." He couldn't stop the words choking him as they came out. He sounded like his dad.

"Yeah? Well, the fact you couldn't see the four-foot-deep drift of snow I was aiming for probably gave you the wrong idea. I calculated the risk in advance and determined there was little to no damage that could come to a girl trying her best to have a little *alone time* and make herself a blinking snow angel! And if you want to talk about reckless, you'd better be careful with Jorja. She's got a reputation."

Josh pushed himself up on his elbows and gave her his best *what are you talking about?* look. "Jorja?"

"Yes. Jorja." Her voice went singsong as her hands started to make the beginnings of angel wings in the snow. "Josh and Jorja, sitting in a tree..."

"What are you talking about?"

"The mistletoe?" Her arm movements widened and her legs joined in, occasionally giving his own hand or leg a bash as she worked out her frustration on her snow angel.

"You think I made out with Jorja under some mistletoe?" His voice rang with pure incredulity.

"I *saw* you!" Katie all but snarled.

"No, you did *not*!" Josh retorted, dredging up his best five-year-old's retorts. "You might've seen me standing there—but dodging mistletoe in that hospital of yours is as easy as avoiding patients!"

"Which—by the looks of things—you're doing a pretty good job of. You were hired to work—not to gallop round like an errant King Arthur, swooping up damsels in distress at every hint of a berry! You're a doctor, if my memory serves me correctly! Shouldn't you be behaving responsibly for once? *Doctoring?*"

Katie's words hit him with rapid-fire precision—her body was moving as quickly as she could speak. Josh had never seen her like this—in full flow. Her arms and legs swinging hither and yon. It was going to be one hell of a snow angel.

He couldn't let her words go. Wouldn't stay silent. He was hurting, too. Always had. Putting on a brave face had been the hardest thing he'd done, but he'd thought that was what she'd needed from him.

"You're the one in charge, Katie. Shouldn't you be down there, bossing people around? Making sure everything's in order? Everything in its right place?"

Again and again he'd bitten back words like these in the depths of their grief. But this was Last Chance Saloon time.

Despite the widening shock in her dark eyes, the words continued to fly, unchecked, past his lips.

"C'mon, Katie—you always seemed to know what was best for me. What would you advise? What would you suggest I do now?"

"What—what do you mean?" She pushed herself up to stand, distractedly brushing the snow off her clothes, discomfort taking the place of fury.

"You're really good at laying down guidelines. Heaven knows how they're getting on down there without little Miss Perfect dotting the 'I's and crossing the 'T's. How would you *recommend* I comfort myself after seeing my wife take a swan dive off of a building?"

He was all but shouting, rising to his full height before they both awkwardly swung themselves over onto the roof, then stood for who knew how long like two cowboys frozen in a standoff.

"I wasn't—" Katie finally broke the silence then stopped herself, unable to resist glaring at him while she tried to regain her composure. Her common sense.

They'd had a variation on this fight a thousand times and she didn't have it in her to have it again. Didn't want to. She'd seen the fear in his eyes and she'd never meant to be cruel to him. Not then. Not now. But this very moment was proof positive that they couldn't be together. Not when they couldn't even bring a bit of good out of the other as they had once done. They needed to wrap this up. It was the only way to go forward.

"Why are you here, Josh? What exactly is it that you want?"

"You," he answered. "I came here because I want *you*."

The air between them grew electric. With unspoken words. Unspent desire.

His blue eyes told her a thousand things at once. Gone was the recrimination. The anger. In their place was the heady, crackling energy that had never failed to draw them together. Katie hadn't realized how much she missed Josh on a physical level.

He didn't wait for an invitation.

Two of his long-striding steps and he'd pulled her up and into his arms. All thought was gone. She was reduced to sensation only, such was the power of his touch. She felt his lips against hers, both urgent and tender. Her every pore ached with the immediacy of her body's response to his touch. Winter jackets, woolen hats, leather gloves—none of the clunky gear of the season detracted from the pure, undiluted hunger Katie was experiencing.

Somewhere out there in the far reaches of her mind she knew she should be pushing him away. Knew she shouldn't be returning hungry kiss after kiss, each one filled with two years' worth of need. His hands cupped her jaw as the kisses grew deeper still. A low moan met one of his as they pressed tightly against the other. Everything felt familiar and new—as it always had—but their connection was… It felt unbreakable. Timeless.

Had she been wrong to send him away?

A vibration jostled at her waistline. Her pager.

Another one sounded. Josh's.

She pulled back, wondering if her mouth looked as bruised with kisses as Josh's did. Her fingers fumbled with the pager, her eyes still glued to her husband's face.

He was part of her. She knew that now. Making him leave had been ridiculous. No amount of time or distance could sever the ties between them. But what they had wasn't healthy. Wasn't meant for long-term—especially if she were ever, one day, to hold a baby of her own in her arms.

"Multiple injuries. We'd better get down there."

"What?" Katie shook her head clear of the "Josh and baby" fog.

"Read your pager. Ambulances are due in a few minutes."

"Right. Yes." She grabbed her phone from her pocket, relieved it hadn't been lost to the snowdrift in her snow-angel frenzy, and punched out the numbers of the ER desk. "It's Dr. McGann. Are the teams setting up the trauma units?"

Josh watched as Katie listened, responded, thumbed away the stray wisps of lipstick from around her mouth and tugged her clothes back into place. Moment by moment she became Dr. McGann again. This reinvention of herself who was all business. The Katie he'd first met. Not the one who came alive each time they touched or when their eyes lit upon the other. *This* Katie's eyes were near enough devoid of life. His heart ached to put back each and every spark he knew lay dormant within them. Now wasn't the time.

He shifted his hips. His body was trying to fight down the force of desire kissing Katie had elicited in him. She felt good. Ridiculously good in his arms. It made the idea of Paris even more insane if she weren't by his side.

The peal of ambulance sirens became faintly audible.

If he'd had a spare half hour he would have made a snowman up here and then kung fu'd its head off. It would have been satisfying. For about a second.

He shook his head and took up the pace Katie was setting to the roof door. At least he knew work would keep him distracted for the next hour or five, depending upon how bad the traumas were. Snow and automobiles? The onset of darkness on Christmas Eve, when everyone's expectations were just a little bit higher than any other time of year…? Yeah. It wasn't going to be pretty. Not in the slightest.

CHAPTER FOUR

KATIE STOPPED IN her tracks. Now, *this* she certainly hadn't expected. The first ambulance had pulled into the covered bay with a horse trailer attached to it, and the crew, along with the help of a teary girl dressed up as the Virgin Mary, were unloading a donkey.

"Can you help Eustace, please?" the girl wailed when her eyes lit on Katie.

Eustace the donkey?

"Ooh! A nativity donkey!" Jorja appeared alongside Katie, rubbing her hands together and blowing on them as her feet sashayed her from side to side.

"I think we'd better take a look at *you* first." Katie's eyes were on the girl who, through the folds of her costume, was clutching her side. "What's your name, hon?"

"Maddie."

"What a lovely name! Is there anyone you can leave in charge of the—Eustace—while we bring you inside?"

"No!" The girl's eyes widened in fear, and as she and the donkey stepped into the bright light of the ambulance bay outside the ER, Katie could see she also had a cut on her forehead over what appeared to be a growing lump. "I am not leaving Eustace. He is my best friend and we have to get to Bethlehem tonight!"

"Maybe we can find a hitching post for Eustace."

"But he's bleeding!"

"What have we got here?"

Josh's voice shot along Katie's nervous system as she approached Maddie. Her fingers flew automatically to her lips, and she wished the remembered pulse of their kisses weren't so vivid. She pushed down the thoughts and forced herself to focus. A Mary intent on getting to Bethlehem and a donkey with quite a serious cut to his haunch. Hospital protocol to adhere to…

A lightbulb went off. Josh's passion for medicine had come about by fixing the local wildlife and working under the wing of the country vet on the ranch his father had managed. It wasn't really playing by the rulebook, but… Were there different rules at Christmas? Or at least a bit of Yuletide flexibility? The emergency vets were on the other side of town, and using ambulances to tow livestock trailers had already been done—

"What do you say we pop you on a gurney, Maddie? Out here? That way Dr. McGann can take a look at you and I can stitch up… What did you say your pal's name was?"

Mind reader.

"Eustace!" Maddie replied with a broad smile, then another wince.

"Eustace! I had an Uncle Eustace, and he was as stubborn as a mule. Did you say your Eustace was a mule or a donkey?"

"A donkey! Can't you tell the difference?" Maddie giggled through her pain.

Katie couldn't fight the smile his words brought. Josh's way with patients—especially children—had always been second to none. He still had the magic touch. Something she'd worked hard at and never fully achieved. Especially after the baby.

The thought instantly sobered her. They had two or even three more ambulances due in from the same crash, so they needed to get down to business, bedside manner or no. Maddie's parents, or whoever had been driving the truck pulling the trailer, must be incoming. Otherwise they surely would have shown up with Maddie and Eustace.

"Jorja, can you—?"

"Already on it!" the nurse called, halfway through the electric doors.

"Hey, fellas!" Josh was signaling to the ambulance drivers to move the livestock trailer outside of the bay so the other ambulances would have room to pull in when they arrived.

Katie's two interns had appeared, with a gurney each, and Jorja had shouldered an emergency medical kit.

"Where would you like this one, Dr. McGann?" asked Michael. She smiled gratefully at the curly-haired intern and pointed over to a well-lit spot by the sliding doors. He was quiet—very committed and ultraserious. Birds of a feather. They got on well.

"Make sure those brakes are on." She pointed at the gurney wheels. If they needed to whisk Maddie inside for any reason, they could—but out here they needed to be as safe as possible.

"Where are your parents, honey?"

"Be careful with his halter." Maddie's eyes were glued on Josh as he expertly knotted Eustace to a pillar, petting and soothing the donkey, who seemed also to have fallen under Josh's spell. *Dr. Doolittle strikes again!*

Maddie threw tips at Josh for keeping Eustace happy, her fears about his welfare quelled by his verbal updates. Katie gave an internal sigh of relief. If Maddie had been in that livestock trailer when the crash happened, she was bound to have had a heck of a knock, and inspections for broken ribs were less than fun. If she was properly distracted that would help.

"We're going to put a little numbing agent on Eustace's rump, here. Is that all right, Maddie? Do we need your parents' permission to go ahead and give him stitches?"

Katie shot him a look. She received a nod of response.

One that said he knew what was going on and was playing the Distraction Whilst Gathering Information Game.

"Michael," she whispered, "can you get me some scissors, please? We need to cut these off." Katie needed to get the layers of robes off Maddie without moving her ribs. If she lifted the robes off over the girl's head and there had been any acute breaks or internal injuries, the movement might make things worse. Broken ribs were one thing... Punctured lungs were a whole new kettle of fish.

"Dr. McGann." Shannon, her other intern, tapped her on the shoulder, magically appearing with a pair of scissors in hand. "A second ambulance is five minutes out. They've got a male patient presenting with suspected fractured wrist and extensive leg injuries and another young adult male presenting with a broken nose and other minor injuries from an air bag."

Katie nodded whilst deftly dividing the robes of Maddie's costume. The girl's face was growing paler, and the sooner she could get her lying down for an examination the better. "Want to give me a hand here, Shannon?"

"Sure, but don't you want me to do the incoming—?"

Shannon was always keen to be first on scene for whatever "A-list" injuries came through the emergency room doors, but Katie had been very careful to divvy them out between her gore-hungry intern and Michael, whose "ladies first" attitude Katie hadn't quite figured out. Nervous or just genuinely polite?

Tonight wasn't about politics, though. It was about priority.

"If you could help me get Maddie out of these robes and then make sure there are two triage areas prepped, nurses on standby with gurneys and a couple of wheelchairs, that would be great. There doesn't sound like much the EMTs won't be able to handle in terms of stabilizing. Let X-Ray know someone will be on the way up."

Shannon's lips pursed in disappointment, and Katie

knew better than to think the evening would run smoothly. If you relaxed, things went south. That was how it worked in an ER. That was how it worked in life.

"Ouch!" Maddie gasped and wobbled.

Katie and Shannon each reached for an elbow as the last of the biblical robes dropped away. Maddie's hands flew to her side, where blood was seeping through her shirt, and Eustace brayed softly, as if he knew his owner was in pain.

"You cut my robes?" Maddie was properly tearful now.

"Easy there, boy. I just need you to stay steady," Josh was saying.

"It's all right, honey. We can get those stitched back up for you—no problem."

Katie's eyes flicked back to Josh as he made a general callout for an electric shaver. The donkey's winter coat was making the topical numbing agent less effective, and she could tell he was trying to play by the rules as much as possible. They could use xylocaine without too many questions. But proper injectable painkillers…? Less easy to explain where vials of lidocaine were—much less to write up a chart for Eustace. Off the books was best—even if it bent the rules.

Katie thought for a second of stopping him. This was how doctors got fired. Risks. She never took risks. Josh never needed to think twice about it.

"Nurse!" he called, without looking up from what he was doing.

Katie flinched infinitesimally as Jorja appeared by Josh's side in an instant. He had said it was all a mistake. The mistletoe mishap…

She pulled her gaze back to Maddie, whose eyes were widening at the sight of the blood on her white shirt.

"It's all right, Maddie. Let's get you up on the gurney, honey." She looked at Michael, who had arrived back at Maddie's other side. "On three." They eased Maddie up and onto the gurney on her count. "Right! Let's check you out. I'm going to have to lift up your shirt, and it's pretty cold out here. Are you sure you don't want to go inside?"

"No!" There was no mistaking the determination in the girl's voice. "Where Eustace goes, I go." She twisted suddenly, trying to get a better look at her pricked-eared pal. Her eyes tightened with pain. "It hurts to breathe."

Fear suddenly entered the little girl's eyes. She couldn't be more than eleven...but Katie was sure an old soul was fueling her.

"Lie down again, hon. I think you might've bruised a couple of ribs. Michael, could you get me a couple of blank—?"

"Already on it, Doc."

Katie rucked up Maddie's shirt, relieved to see the bleeding was from a gash and nothing more. But in a dirty livestock trailer? They'd have to put a booster tetanus shot on the girl's tick-list as well.

She tried to go for Josh-casual. "Say, it looks like you and Eustace are both going to be getting stitches tonight."

A grin lit up the girl's face. "Really?"

Hmm... Josh-casual obviously works.

A sting of guilt shot through her at the words she had flung at him when things had seemed too dark to continue. *Reckless. Unthinking. Careless.* Maybe his laissez-faire attitude had been to soothe her. To comfort her in a time of great sorrow.

She swallowed hard and continued her examination of Maddie.

"That hurts!" Maddie yelped.

"That's your rib cage acting up. Where exactly were you when the accident happened?"

"With Eustace."

Katie's eyes widened, her suspicions confirmed. *Well, that was just about as health and safety unconscious as things got.*

"And your parents let you ride in there?"

Maddie's eyes began to dart around the covered area. "Not exactly…"

"Who was driving the tow vehicle?"

"My bro—" She reconsidered giving the information, swallowing the rest of the word. Tears sprang into her eyes. "Am I going to get in trouble?"

"No, honey. Of course not. But riding in trailers with live—with Eustace—isn't really legal."

"Are my brothers going to jail?"

Katie's eyes shot across to meet Josh's, but he was one hundred percent focused as stitch after stitch brought the sides of the cut on Eustace's rump neatly together. She had always loved watching Josh's hands at work. They were large, capable hands. The intricate work they completed with skillful dexterity always surprised her.

Just as easy to picture him whipping a lasso into action as he had when he was a boy as it was to see him deftly tying a miniature knot at the end of a row of immaculate stitches as he was now.

"Probably best if you keep pneumonia out of the symptoms…"

Josh didn't look up as he spoke, but he had always had a second sense for when Katie's eyes were trained on him. She stiffened. It wasn't often he had to remind her to keep her eye on the ball. The role reversal didn't sit well.

"Maddie?" Josh raised his voice a bit. "Eustace is doing pretty good, here. Mind if I snaffle him some carrots from somewhere, then let him have a bit of a lie-down in the trailer?"

"That would be nice." Maddie sniffled, her fear and pain visibly kicking up a notch. "There are carrots already in the trailer."

"Michael." Katie snapped into action. "Let's tuck these blankets round Maddie and get her a tetanus shot before bringing her up to X-Ray, please, to check on her ribs. Maddie, honey, Michael's going to need your parents' phone number so we can get in touch—just to okay any treatment you're going to need, all right?"

"You're not going to let them arrest my brothers, are you? We just wanted to get to the nativity early!"

Tears began to pour out of Maddie's blue eyes and Katie's heart all but leaped to her throat. There was such love and protectiveness in her words. "Why don't we take things one at a time? We'll call your parents, sort you out, and then deal with everything else as and when it happens."

"Do you think there will be an angel looking after my brothers?"

"Dr. McGann?" Jorja stuck her head through the sliding doors. "That second ambulance is incoming."

"I sure do, Maddie," said Katie. And she meant it. "This is Michael—Dr. Rainer. He's going to take you up to X-Ray. We'll see you in a little bit, all right?"

"Okay…" The young girl snuffled. Her head turned to find Josh within sight. "Thanks for looking after Eustace."

"You bet, kiddo. It was my pleasure." Josh flashed her one of his warm smiles and gave her arm a quick squeeze before Michael and a nurse wheeled her off to the ER.

The wail of the sirens grew louder and Katie ripped off her protective gloves, quickly wiggling her fingers into the fresh pair one of the nurses handed her. If she'd thought things had been busy earlier, they were going into full-time Christmas Eve Crazy now the sun had set.

"Teenage male, presenting with multiple leg injuries and compound fracture to the wrist."

"Got it." Josh helped unload the gurney along with the EMT. This was Chris, Maddie's older brother.

Josh took in the EMT's rattle of information as he scanned the teen's face again. Chris couldn't have had his first whiskers for long, let alone gained much experience behind the wheel in a snowstorm.

A nurse met him at the doors and took over as the EMT

finished reeling off the treatments Chris had already received. His injuries were severe. Compound fracture to the femur. Possible compression to the ankle. Severe dislocation of the knee. And who knew what muscles and ligaments might have been torn or burst? He'd be off that leg for months. Minimum. From the looks of the blood loss and extensive damage, the boy would need to be in surgery sooner rather than later. No time to wait for parental consent.

"Right, we'd better take a look at the mess you've made of yourself."

"Where's Maddie?" The boy's eyes were wide with panic.

"It's all right, buddy. Maddie is up in X-Ray. Looks like you messed your leg up pretty well."

"Where's my brother? Have you seen Nick? Where's Maddie? Is Eustace all right?"

A gurney went past with one of the interns at the helm. The keen one. Shannon…? Didn't matter.

"Hey, bro!"

Another teenage boy called from a gurney as he was wheeled past. Blood was smeared all over his face and winter coat. This was obviously the one with the broken nose.

"You haven't given them Mom and Dad's number, have you?" he shouted, before his gurney turned the corner to one of the triage areas.

"No way—what do you think I am? An idio—? *Ow!*" The scream Chris emitted filled the corridor, and just as quickly as the howl of acute pain had taken over the soundscape, it disappeared as Chris lapsed into unconsciousness.

"Anyone think to check on the femoral artery?"

Josh didn't know why he was asking. There was blood everywhere, the EMTs were long gone, and the nurse had been with him for no more than a few seconds.

"Let's skip triage and get straight up to surgery—"

"Only for a handover." Katie's voice broke in.

"This guy's going to bleed out if we don't get him on a table fast. And who knows what sort of filth is in that leg? Time's against us, Katie."

"Yes, it is. And that's why we're going to let one of the orthopedic surgeons cover this one. They're already prepping the room."

Josh nodded curtly. He thrived on make-or-break surgery, and if there was one person in the world who knew that was true of him, she was standing right there looking the picture of officiousness.

"We need you in Trauma, Josh. There are more patients incoming. The rescue crews only just opened up the car that got hit by the snowplow."

"Understood."

And he did. Katie did prioritizing. He did gut instinct. It was why they had always worked together so well. The yin to the other's yang. Sure, there were fiery moments—but balance always won out in the end.

Well... He watched as she flew past him into one of the cubicles, where a patient could be heard arguing with one of the nurses. He scrubbed his jaw hard. Balance hadn't *always* won out in the end.

He gave the nurse on the other side of the gurney a tight smile.

"Let's get this whippersnapper up to surgery so we can get back for the incomings."

"You bet, Dr. West."

"Mrs. Wilson goes into Three and Mr. Wilson into Four." Katie was issuing directions faster than a New York traffic cop in rush hour. She was in a fury. The Wilsons had been the hardest hit but had been the last to be brought in.

"It took the fire crew a while to dislodge their car from the snowplow."

"One more patient incoming!"

Michael was hurtling down the corridor with a gurney. Gone was his quiet, serene demeanor. He looked near wild with panic. For an instant Katie thought the gurney was empty and that her reliable intern had all but lost the plot entirely—until she saw the tiny figure lying on the gurney. A little girl. She looked about three.

The same age her daughter would have been if she had lived. The hollow ache of grief began to creep into Katie's heart. Josh appeared on the other side of the gurney. *Great. Just what she needed.* The one person in the world who could make these feelings multiply into Infinityville.

"What have we got here?"

"Three-year-old girl presenting with abdominal bruising and pain, blood in the urine, internal bleeding—suspected trauma to the left kidney."

Michael rattled out a few more details as they raced the gurney toward the trauma unit.

"Can we get her into OR Two with Dr. Hastings?" Katie kept her eyes trained on Michael. This was a nightmare blossoming out of control.

"Nope. He's busy with an emergency appendectomy."

This little girl couldn't wait. If her kidney was bleeding out, she needed surgery immediately or she would die. Her eyes flicked from Michael to Josh.

"What about Dr. Hutchins?"

"They're all busy, Dr. McGann." Michael churned out the information, oblivious to the emotional storm brewing between Katie and Josh. "We've prepped OR Four for you. Do you need me to assist?"

Katie's eyes widened. She blinked, doing her utmost to wear her best poker face. All the other surgeons were busy. She'd have to do it—keep this child alive. She felt her hands go clammy as they clutched the side rails of the gurney.

Her heart rate quickened and she knew if she looked into a mirror right now she would see her pupils were dilating.

"Are you up to doing a nephrectomy?" Josh's voice was low. Not accusatory—the tone *she* would have used for someone out of their depth. Safety was paramount, particularly with lawsuits swinging like an evil pendulum above their every move these days.

"Of course!" she bit back.

Josh accompanied her, uninvited, into the lift on the way to the surgical ward, dismissing Michael from gurney duty with a smile.

"It's a routine surgery. I did one last week."

But not on a child...a little girl. And not with you here.

Katie didn't dare meet his eyes. If she was going to keep it together to save this little girl's life, a shot of Josh's deep blue eyes was exactly what would have calmed her three years ago. That time had long passed. Even so, she could almost see her heart pumping beneath the scrubs she'd tugged on after Snow-Angel-Gate.

She couldn't help herself. As the doors slid closed and the pair of them were left alone with their tiny patient, she lifted her eyes to meet his. They said everything she had wanted to see in them when they'd lost their little girl.

I'm here for you. You can trust in me. Let me help you.

"Don't worry. I've got this." Katie ripped her eyes away from his. "You should go back down. If anything major happens in the ER—"

"If anything major happens in the ER," he interrupted, "they will page us. I'm staying with you."

"What are you saying, Josh?" Katie couldn't keep the disbelief out of her voice. "Are you saying I'm not up to this?"

"No," he began carefully. "I'm saying you've had a long day, a couple of shocks, and whether you like it or not, you need me by your side. I'll just stay for a minute or so—until you get going."

The elevator doors opened before Katie could reply. Which was just as well. Because what could she say other than *You're right*?

She had struggled over the past three years, doing operations that reminded her of her little girl and the life she might have had. Earlier on she'd deftly handed over any critical surgeries on young children to her colleagues. Just being responsible for the delicate life of a child had been too overwhelming—her own body had proved she didn't have what it took to care for one. But in the past year she'd taught herself to close down—to behave like the clinician she was.

But with Josh here…? Game-changer. She had to prove to him she was over it. Over *him*. That she had moved on from the loss of their child.

Elizabeth.

Elizabeth Rose West.

A beautiful name for their darling little girl, who was nothing more than a statistic now. One out of seventy mothers give birth to a stillborn baby in America every day. The volume of that annual loss was almost too much to bear. She'd never even bothered to check the statistics on failed marriages in the wake of such a loss. Just shut it all out and moved away.

Katie gritted her teeth and gave her head a quick shake. Cobwebs and history didn't belong in there now. This child's life depended upon clear, swift thinking.

The anesthetist met her at the OR door for a quick handover. "A necrotomy?" He tipped his head toward the little girl.

"'Fraid so." Katie tried to keep her tone bright.

"Well, you did a great job with the last one—no reason this should be any different."

"Thanks, Miles. I appreciate it."

"Well, if you'll both excuse me, I'll go in with the patient and get the anesthetics in order."

"Sure thing. Oh! This is Josh. He's—" *Er...my husband, and I still love him, and...*

"Dr. West." Josh jumped in to rescue her. Again. "Locum over the holiday period. I would shake hands, but—" He gestured at the gurney he was trying to navigate into the OR.

"Miles Brand. Good to meet you." He took over moving the gurney, along with a nurse who had materialized from the OR. "Let's get this girl inside and on the table, shall we?"

"I'm going to scrub in while she's prepped," Katie said needlessly after he'd left.

"I'll join you," Josh offered with a soft smile.

An encouraging one. One she should graciously accept. Because what was happening right now was ticking all the I'm-Not-Ready-For-This boxes she'd systematically arranged in her brain's no-go area.

"Thanks."

They pushed into the scrub room together, shoulders shifting against each other's as they had back in the day.

Josh allowed himself a millisecond of pleasure before he realigned his focus. Covert calming. It was his specialty.

"What's the layout here?"

"Near enough the same as Boston," Katie answered, pointing out the shelves that held surgical caps and masks.

Their eyes met as she tugged on a standard blue surgical cap.

"Where's the one I got you?" It had been covered in wildflowers. What she smelled of, he'd told her when she'd unwrapped it.

"In the wash."

Her eyes flicked away and he knew she was lying.

He tried not to notice her tying on her face mask in an

effort to hide the painful thickets of emotion she was stumbling through.

Never mind, sweetheart. I feel it, too.

Stepping up to the sink, they both let muscle memory take over. The warm, steady flow of water was the predominant sound in the room as he and Katie took a good five minutes to systematically wash and scrub, first their nails, then their hands, which they held above the level of their elbows to prevent dirty water from dripping onto them.

Josh hit the taps with his elbows when they'd both finished. Katie nodded at the stack of sterile hand towels—one for each arm.

"You sure you're good?" He handed her a towel.

"Medicine is the only thing I *am* sure of these days."

Two nurses pushed into the scrub room with gowns before he could reply. There was room for hope in her response. Room to believe he was right to have sought her out. His lips parted into a smile for which he received a quick, grim nod.

Fine. He felt he'd been thrown a buoy. He could work with a nod.

She could do this, Katie silently assured herself. She'd done it before, and she would do it again.

"Arm," instructed the surgical nurse.

Katie stuck her arm into the sterilized blue sleeve and made a one-eighty twist to fully secure the surgical gown around her, finding herself standing face-to-face with Josh while his gown was tied. He arched an inquisitive eyebrow.

Are you ready? it said.

She arched one back. Hadn't they been through this?

"Left hand, please, Dr. McGann."

She lifted it up and widened her eyes to a glare. Why didn't he stop *smiling*?

"And the right."

Katie raised her hand, holding her arm taut as the nurse tugged on the glove. The other nurse was clearly pleased she had won Josh in the surgeon crapshoot.

"Thank you, Marilyn. Merry Christmas to you."

"Merry Christmas to you, too, Dr. West." The nurse giggled.

Katie frowned. How on earth did he know *Marilyn*?

She had half a mind to step across the small room and lick Josh's gloved hands, rendering him unclean for the surgery.

Childish? Yes. Something the head of the ER should do right before surgery? Probably not.

There was a life to save—and she was going to be the doctor who saved it.

CHAPTER FIVE

"ARE YOU DOING it open or laparoscopically?" Josh kept his voice low and steady. Curious.

"Open."

Katie's eyes flicked to his as he skirted the periphery of the surgical team gathering in the OR.

"Unusual."

Not for his girl, but he knew she was always at her calmest when she talked systematically through her surgery.

Katie nodded. Blinked. His heart skipped a beat before she responded in a clear voice.

"Not in a trauma like this. Laparoscopically is better for routine."

She wasn't saying anything he didn't know, but with a team of people in the room, communicating with a nod or a look wasn't good enough. Everyone had to be on the same page or mistakes would be made.

"There is potentially a lot of other damage in here, and we're better off with a clear view of what we're dealing with."

"Rib removal?" one of the surgical nurses asked, indicating that she wanted to have the correct instruments to hand.

"Hopefully not, but one could've been broken on impact. We'll have to check."

Katie was grateful other members of the OR team were chiming in. She knew Josh's steady, careful breakdown of the steps in the guise of "reminding himself" was to keep her mind off the tiny body lying on the operating table. Josh could have done this surgery in his sleep. So could she. And he was just reminding her of what was true.

"A partial nephrectomy with so much damage could lead to the need for another surgery," Katie continued. "I don't want that for her. I won't know until I see the damage, but radical is the best option to keep things minimal for—"

"Casey," volunteered one of the nurses as the little girl's body was stabilized for Katie to make the first incision. "Casey Wilson's her name. The parents sent up her information when you were scrubbing in."

Perfect. A name. Just the way to keep it clinical.

Her grip tightened on the scalpel. "I'm preparing to make the incision."

"The bruising certainly indicates massive trauma."

"The EMTs said the snowplow hit her side of the car. She's lucky to have survived at all."

Katie shook away this new piece of information as she made an eight-inch cut from the front of the girl's soft belly to just below her small rib cage. Her mind began to take over, and her heart beat with a steadier cadence. A clock could have marked time with her breaths.

Massive trauma to one kidney. The other, thankfully, was untouched.

She switched instruments and began to cut and move muscle, tiny pieces of fat and the collection of tissue that held the kidney in place. It was steady, systematic work. A glance at the stats here. A minute cut and stitch there. Updates from the nurses. Eyes fastidiously avoiding the tiny little girl's head, just beyond the surgical drape. A vague awareness of Josh moving opposite her at the surgical table.

As she guided her hands through the surgery, it hit her how quickly she'd lapsed into deriving comfort from Josh's rock-solid presence across the table from her. From the moment before she'd stepped into the OR, when fear had threatened to compromise all that she worked so hard for, even the tiniest of tremors she had felt in her hands had left her. And something deep within her heart told her it was having the man she'd once believed to be the love of her life with her.

She flicked her eyes up to meet his. Blue, pure, unwavering. He nodded before returning his eyes to the operation. There was severe bruising along Casey's rib cage—no doubt from the seat belt—but the kidney seemed to have taken the bulk of the trauma. Katie worked her way around the tiny organ, taking particular care to properly clamp and seal the blood vessels before ultimately and successfully removing the kidney.

Textbook.

"You want me to close?" It was an offering, not a doubt about her ability.

Katie shook her head. "I'm good." She'd made it this far. She was going to see it through.

Again, muscle memory took over as she pulled the surgical area back together, minus the small kidney, with a series of immaculately executed stitches. She ran the nurses through the aftercare before allowing herself another glance across the operating table.

"See?"

Josh's blue eyes twinkled at her. Katie could tell from the crinkles round them he was smiling.

"You did it."

"You ready for Secret Santa?" Jorja, despite nearing the end of a sixteen-hour shift, seemed just as sprightly as she had when Josh had first met her.

Was she rechargeable?

"Sure thing."

"We're all meeting down at the central desk at midnight." Jorja's hand shot up to cover her mouth as she stifled a yawn.

Ah! She was human.

Josh kept a good arm's length between them as they walked down the corridor toward the ER. He didn't want any more misunderstandings under the mistletoe. He'd tried dating a couple of times after he'd decided the only way forward was moving on, but had never got past ordering a drink before faking a pager call. Cheap trick, but faking affection would have been worse.

But that didn't mean he couldn't be chatty.

"This was a long shift for you. A double?"

"No longer than yours."

She nodded her head in acknowledgment. "I do it every year." She continued when Josh raised his eyebrows. "So I can be with my family on Christmas Day."

"Oh, right! So you're a local?"

"Yup." She nodded, her voice swelling with pride. "Born and bred Copper Creeker. All six of my brothers and sisters, too."

"Six!" Josh couldn't keep the surprise out of his voice.

"Yup!" Jorja chirped again. "It means the turkey has to be absolutely ginormous—so my brothers have started deep-frying it outside to keep the oven clear for Mom."

"Sounds good."

Jorja brightened. "Want to come? You're welcome. Everyone brings a boyfriend or a girlfriend."

Josh widened the gap between them. "Oh, no. No, thanks. Not for me. I'm on shift. Thanks, though."

Jorja's smile faltered a bit. Josh scrubbed a hand through his hair. She was a nice enough girl, but… But he already had a girl. The girl of his dreams. And he was a little busy proving to her how indispensable he was.

"It was a lovely invitation—it's just…"

"Don't worry." She stopped to pick a piece of errant tinsel off the floor and wove it round and round her finger, turning it pale, then pink again…pale, then pink.

"I'm sorry, Jorja." Josh checked an instinct to reach out and give her shoulder a comforting squeeze.

"I saw how you looked at Dr. McGann when we were under the mistletoe."

This time Josh really *was* surprised. He didn't know he'd been that obvious.

"You two know each other from before, don't you?"

That was one way to put it.

"We met in medical school."

Jorja discarded the tinsel in a bin and gave a wistful sigh. "It's always the good ones who are taken!"

Responding to that might be awkward.

"Hey!" The young woman's features brightened again as she tugged her errant ponytail back into place. "Who'd you get for your Secret Santa?"

"Isn't that supposed to be secret?"

"Yeah—but wouldn't it be fun if you got Dr. McGann?"

Josh considered for a moment and then lifted an eyebrow to indicate that, yes, there just *might* be some fun there…

"Here!" She dug into her nurse's smock and pulled out a crisply folded bit of paper. "I got Dr. McGann. Who'd *you* get?"

"Didn't you get her a present already?" Josh fought the urge to seem too keen.

"Oh, I just snagged a plateful of my grandma's Christmas cookies. She makes an amazing selection. Snickerdoodles, gingerbread men, buckeyes, peppermint crunch—you name it, she makes it."

"She sounds like my Gramma Jam-Jam! Never met a Christmas cookie she didn't like."

Her passing had been like losing a limb. Another loss he'd had to deal with without Katie by his side. It struck him that this mission was about more than trust. He'd known the second Katie had laid eyes on him that she still loved him. What they had was chemical. No amount of spreadsheets or flowcharts or "stages of grief" steps were going to take the connection they had away.

But this little reunion had brought more questions than answers so far. He knew in his heart that she could trust him. But when he'd needed her most she'd upped and left. Could he trust her to stick by him if things got tough again?

"Dr. West?"

Josh could see Jorja was talking to him, but did he have a clue about what? Not one.

Jorja threw her hands up in the air. "Typical man! Concentration factor…nil! No wonder I can't get a boyfriend. I can't even get a male to *listen* to me, let alone like me."

She swatted his arm, bringing his focus back to her. Again. *Oops.*

"Sorry, Jorja—I didn't quite catch what you said."

"Yeah," she deadpanned. "I got *that*. I was asking who your Secret Santa was so we can trade. If you still want to."

"Well…it sounds like—" he dug his scrap of paper out of his lab coat pocket and read "—Dr. Michael Rainer is going to be one lucky guy…having a plate of your grandmother's cookies all to himself."

"Michael…" She said the intern's name as if she were tasting it and wasn't entirely sure what she thought of it. Then clearly a decision was made. "Michael." She said it again, this time looking as though she'd just enjoyed a delicious bite of peppermint candy.

Josh grinned. Michael might have to watch himself around the mistletoe. He threw an arm round the nurse's shoulders and gave her a quick squeeze. This Secret Santa swap could be just what he needed.

Katie nodded at the cleared ER board with a satisfied smile. It probably wouldn't last long—but even a few moments of clean board always lifted her heart.

"Someone looks happy. Did the surgery go well?"

Michael appeared at her side, giving her a little jump.

"Yes." Katie nodded, feeling the weight of the success lighten her heart. "Yes, it really did."

And it meant more than anyone will know.

Well. One person would know.

She heard Josh's laugh before she saw him—and the hit of response in her belly shifted the charge of success into something more electric. It didn't take a doctor to know it was pure unadulterated attraction. It was adrenaline from the surgery, she reasoned. It would pass.

"Right!" Katie went into efficiency mode. "We've got both shift groups together. Quick reminder: Secret Santa gifts go into lockers, please—not here in the reception area."

A nurse guiltily tucked the foil package she'd been edging onto the counter back into her pocket.

Katie gave her lower lip a guilty scrape with her teeth. She hated being a Scrooge, but this *was* a place of work.

"Good work on clearing the board after a pretty hectic run. A couple of patients are in Recovery after surgery, but there's no one unexpected in Intensive, thanks to you all."

A smattering of applause filled the area around the central desk. The staff looked tired, but triumphant. Shannon—her keenest intern—for once looked as if she'd had enough. Michael still looked doggedly studious, but she could see the fatigue in his eyes when he pulled off his glasses and gave them a rub. A few of the nurses were hiding yawns. Most of them, actually.

They'd all been through the wringer and Katie didn't feel any different.

Despite her best intentions, Katie locked her eyes with Josh's. She might not have made it through surgery without him by her side and he knew it. It made her feel vulnerable and protected at the same time. The look in his eyes made her breath catch in her throat. Pure, undiluted love.

Saying goodbye at the end of this shift was going to be harder than she'd thought.

Her eyes widened, still holding the pure blue magic of Josh's gaze. *She hadn't called the agency for a replacement!* And, realistically, was there going to be a locum tenens out there in the mountainscape of Copper Canyon— or anywhere in Idaho—willing to tear themselves away from whatever they'd planned to do with their family over the holidays?

When she and Josh had had the holidays off they'd been inseparable. In more ways than one.

She hunched her shoulders up and down. She was just going to have to suck it up. Getting a replacement for Josh at this juncture was about as likely as Santa Claus walking through the sliding doors.

"Where *is* he?"

A huge gust of wind and winter storm burst into the waiting room, along with a bearded man dressed in full Santa regalia with a rosy-cheeked Mrs. Claus following in his wake.

"Where's my son?" the bearded man roared again.

Temperatures often ran high in the ER, and it looked like Santa's temper was soaring.

"What's your son's name, sir?" Josh was by his side in an instant—with a mix of concerned doctor and *Watch yourself, Santa* in his tone and body language. Josh was tall, and he had the confident carriage of a rodeo cowboy. Santa, however, seemed immune to what had all but buckled her knees.

"Klausen. Check your list, Doc. Check it twice if you have to!"

If Katie hadn't been so taken aback by Mr. Klausen's arrival, she would have tittered at this similarity to a certain red-suited fellow who, by all accounts, should be pretty busy shooting down chimneys about now.

"Chris Klausen," the man bit out.

His tone was so sharp Katie choked on her giggles.

"I've seen the trailer in the parking lot. It's the busiest

night of the year and I *know* they've got Eustace in there. The nativity was a shambles!"

"Dad?" Maddie appeared round the corner, a bandage on her head, her arms wrapped protectively round her ribs and a slightly fearful look on her face. "Mom?"

Katie stepped toward Maddie—ready to intervene if things grew more heated.

"Maddie!" Mrs. Klausen rushed to her daughter's side. "What happened? We just got the call that there was an accident."

The tension eased from Katie's face as the anger obviously born of fear for their children turned into protective hugs and kisses.

"Where are your brothers?" Her father pushed her back to arm's length. "I'm going to wring their necks!"

Then again...

"Dr. McGann, I was the one who brought him up to—"

Katie waved Michael to silence. They didn't need to hear the gory details out here with a crowd gathering.

"Sir, perhaps you'd like to follow me?" The last thing the couple's son needed, still in Recovery from surgery, was his father dressed as Santa shouting at him.

"You all right?"

Josh's voice trickled along her spine as she felt him approach. He was doing it again. White Knighting it in the face of adversity. She was glad he couldn't see her face as she pressed her lips together. Hadn't she just proved she could hurdle her demons in the OR?

Not without Josh by her side.

"Would you like to come with me, Mr. and Mrs. Klausen?" Katie put her hand up in an *I got it* gesture to Josh and snapped a glare back at Jorja, who was busy choking down her own case of the giggles. Most likely born of nerves, but inappropriate all the same.

"What for? Show us where the boys are, Maddie, and we'll get on our way."

"I think it would be best if we had a chat before you saw your boys." Katie was solid now—shifting her gaze from one rosy-cheeked face to the other.

"Maddie…" Josh put a protective arm around the young girl's shoulders. "Why don't we see if we can track down some gingerbread?"

"All right," Mr. Klausen grumbled, his attention fully focused on Katie. "Let's hear how naughty they've been."

Katie led the way into one of the comfortably furnished family rooms the hospital had created for delivering tough news. She and Josh had been led to one like it after the postmortem on their little girl.

No discernible evidence to indicate a problem. Just one of those things.

The words had sat in her heart like an anvil. If there had been a reason, she could have *done* something. Fixed it. Not felt the living, breathing, growing terror that she had no control over what might happen if they tried again.

"So what've they done? How's Eustace?"

"Your donkey is fine, sir." Katie's eyebrows lifted in surprise at the parent's priorities—but you never knew a person's history. Never knew how someone would respond in times of extreme stress.

"One of our surgeons had to give him a few stitches—"

"He was *hurt*?" Mrs. Klausen's hands flew to her mouth in horror. "Eustace!" She exhaled into her cupped hands. "Eustace… We've had him longer than the boys! Our first baby."

Okay. Well, that explained that.

"Your son Chris has some pretty serious injuries. Maybe we should sit down so we can talk through them before I take you through to Recovery."

"Recovery?" Mr. Klausen's face was twisted in incomprehension. "What do you mean?"

"He's really been hurt?" Tears sprang to Mrs. Klausen's eyes.

"Yes." Katie shifted her tone. The Klausens would need a gentle touch now that the fog of displacement was beginning to clear. Rage, anger, even disbelief were common when the worst thing that could happen to someone actually happened. Particularly when it came out of the blue.

"Why don't we all take a seat and I'll talk you through the surgery Chris has had? Then we'll get you up to see him and Nick, who is with him, as soon as possible. No doubt seeing you both will be the perfect medicine."

She hoped no one could see the fingers she crossed in the depths of her lab coat.

Josh eased the locker open with yet another surreptitious over-the-shoulder check that he was alone. Subterfuge hadn't been his initial plan of attack, but it seemed alone time with Katie was going to be hard to come by, so he was going to have to find just the right pocket to tuck his wrapped present into.

He was hit by Katie's scent in an instant. She'd always smelled like fresh linen with a teasing of vanilla. He gave himself a moment to close his eyes and take a scented trip down memory lane.

A noise further down the corridor jarred him back into action. Winter coat or…? What was that? In the very back of her fastidiously tidy locker, behind the hanging lab coats and winter wear, was a grainy black-and-white printout. The image of their little girl hit him straight in the solar plexus. If kissing Katie on the roof had brought back everything good about their marriage, seeing the last fetal scan they'd had of their baby girl brought back the blackest.

"What are you doing?"

Josh whirled around at the sound of Katie's voice, the sheen of emotion blinding him for just an instant. His hand shot protectively to his hip. He'd turned too sharply. Abrupt turns always gave him a stabbing reminder of how far he'd pushed the envelope. Why Katie had asked him to leave. Why he was here.

To make a smart move. For once.

Katie's eyes flicked from his hip to his eyes. He saw the questions piling up in her deep brown eyes and the flicker of her decision not to ask.

"What are you doing in my locker, Josh?"

He heard the tiniest of wavers in her voice—but her body language told another story. Hands curled into fists on her hips. Mistrust laced through those dark eyes of hers. Her chin tilted slightly, as if daring him to confirm all her worst fears.

He'd gone too far. Just as she'd predicted.

"Even angry, you are the most beautiful woman I've ever seen."

She stepped back, shocked at his words. He was a bit, too, but he meant them. Her face still carried the broad features youth afforded. Full lips. A cute little gap between the two front teeth that had rebelled against the years of expensive orthodontics she'd once confessed to enduring. It made for a slightly crooked smile that lit the world up when she unleashed it. Something she wasn't even *close* to doing now, from the looks of things.

"Josh…" Her smooth forehead crinkled. "Are you all right?"

"I—uh…" He swung his gaze back to her locker, still holding the wrapped package in his hand. The pendulum of Tell or Don't Tell bashed the sides of his brain.

You were right. I should never have taken up motorcycle racing.

You were wrong—you always needed me.

He thrust the tiny package forward so it sat between them like a buffer against all that was going unsaid. "I know it was supposed to be a secret, but… Merry Christmas…"

A rush of emotion crossed her face, darkening her eyes so that they were near black.

"I didn't… I don't have anything for you."

"Well, it was the luck of the draw that I got your name in Secret Santa." He hoped the white lie wouldn't come back to haunt him. "It's not exactly as if you were expecting me to turn up in Copper Canyon, now, is it?" He laughed softly, hiding a swipe at his eyes with a scrub along his forehead and a finger-whoosh through his hair.

Her expression softened.

"Are you going to unclench that thing or do you just want me to guess?"

He released his grip and let the small box rest on his palm. His eyes narrowed a bit as he watched her reach out to take it. The paper was crumpled. Worn, even. He'd wrapped that thing up the day after she'd thrown it at him and told him she'd had enough. Waiting…waiting for the perfect moment.

He cleared his throat when her fingers gained purchase on the box, her skin lightly skimming across his. He couldn't even remember how many times he'd imagined this moment. Her response would trigger a chain of events that would either make or break him.

She withdrew the box from his hand. He felt the absence of its weight and her touch instantly. Maybe ignorance *was* bliss. As long as he didn't really know how Katie felt about him, he could believe there was hope. Believe he'd never have to put his signature to that ragged pile of papers he'd been dragging around in the same backpack as the little box she was now slowly unwrapping.

The dawning of recognition wasn't far off. He'd used the same box the rings had come in. Placed them—engagement and wedding—side by side. The rings they had bought with downright giddy smiles wreathing their faces and the last handful of notes and coins they had between them.

There were only two other times when he'd seen her smile as much. Their wedding day and the day they'd found out she was pregnant.

Katie's expression became unreadable. That hurt as much as no reaction. There had once been a time when he could have told anyone her mood before she'd walked into a room. They had been *that* connected. Genuine soulmates.

"Oh…" It came out as a sigh. "Josh…" Beads of tears weighted her lashes as she held the box open, her eyes fastened to what lay inside. "I can't do this. Not right now. I just can't do this."

She turned on her heel, all but knocking Michael off his feet as he entered the locker room.

"Everything all right?" Michael pulled off his glasses and gave his eyes a rub.

"Yeah, sure." *No.* "She probably just got paged or something."

"Mmm…"

Michael seemed to take his response at face value, which came as a relief. Fatigue hit him like a truck. Heavy and unforgiving.

"Say, Dr. West… Would you like to have a coffee or something later?"

"What? Tonight?"

"No, no. Just before you hit the road again."

"Like a debrief?"

Michael's forehead scrunched. "I guess…"

"Sure thing. Just grab me next time you're free."

He gave him a gentle back-slap as he pushed the door back into the corridor open, smarting at Michael's words. The icing on the cake! So much for his fairy-tale moment when Katie slipped her rings back on her finger and his life became whole again.

He fought the urge to punch the wall. *It* hadn't done anything wrong. *He* had. He'd made a complete hash of giving

Katie the rings and now Michael wanted an exit interview. Fan-freakin'-tastic.

His eyes shot up. *More mistletoe*. Merry Christmas, everyone!

CHAPTER SIX

"DR. MCGANN, WOULD you mind signing these...? Hey, are you all right?"

Jorja skidded to a halt, openly gawking at Katie. Her go-to neutral face obviously wasn't cooperating tonight.

"Of course," Katie answered briskly. "What can I do for you?"

"Before I go I just need your signature on these release forms for Mr. and Mrs. Wilson."

"The parents of the little girl? The one who had the nephrectomy?"

"Yes, that's the one. Luckily they just had a few cuts and bruises. Nothing serious. So they want to head up to the Pediatric recovery ward. Hey!" Jorja's face split into an impressed grin. "I heard you aced that baby!"

Katie's heart tightened at the choice of words, but she couldn't stop a shy smile in return. She *had* done well. And Josh had been right. She didn't need to be pinned down by her grief. Just needed to learn from it and move on. Eyes forward was a lot healthier than always looking over your shoulder at the past.

She scribbled her signature on the forms and told Jorja where the Wilsons would be able to find their little girl. They must be frantic to be with her. Hold her small little hands. Kiss those soft cheeks of hers.

Katie's fingers tightened round the ring box in her pocket.

"I'm just going for a quick power nap. Are you off for the night?"

"Yup—me and my five thousand relatives are meeting up at Midnight Mass. Spouses, girlfriends, boyfriends, uncles, aunts—you name it. And little ol' me. Late, as usual, and all on my lonesome!"

"There's plenty of time for that." Katie smiled and gave the nurse's arm a squeeze. She was pretty, vivacious, and would be a great catch for the right man. One with lots of energy. Heaven knew, her brothers were busier than an online dating agency trying to find her a beau, if all the staff-room gossip she'd caught was anything to go by. "You have a good time with your family, Jorja."

"You too, Dr. McGann." Jorja's eyes widened as her lips opened into a horrified O. "I mean—keep manning the ship like you always do! It's what you always do, isn't it? Meticulous Dr. McGann!"

Jorja's face contorted into an apologetic wince as she thudded her forehead with the heel of her hand.

"Stop while you're ahead?" Katie suggested.

"I think that's best." Jorja pulled Katie in for an unexpected hug with a whispered "Merry Christmas" before skip-running back down the hall to the main desk, her tinsel scarf trailing behind her like a glittery red boa.

Katie stood and watched her for a moment, slightly envious. Not of her youth—she was only a few years older—but of all that was yet to come for her.

She eased open the door to the residents' room, grateful to see the two beds were empty, and dropped onto one of them with a sigh of relief. Double shifts were never fun—but today had been particularly taxing. Physically and emotionally she'd been through the wringer. Seeing Josh…?

That alone was enough to send her into a tailspin. But on Christmas Eve… The night they'd lost their baby girl…

She twisted the small box round and round in her fingers until finally daring to open it again. The night she'd hurled her rings at him… Well…sensibly placed them on the counter—hurling things had never been her style… That night had been like ripping her own heart out.

She fumbled in her other pocket and pulled out her phone. Yes, it was super-late—but if she knew Alice, there would be no begrudging an after-hours call.

The phone rang a couple of times and Katie grinned, remembering the silly ringtones Alice had kept putting on her phone when she hadn't been looking.

"Hello, angel…" a sleepy Alice answered.

"Hi—sorry. I know it's late, but—"

"It's all right, darlin'. I'm just watching the dying embers of the fire. What's that little scamp done now?" Alice cut to the chase.

"He gave me back my rings."

Katie heard Alice rearrange her position on the sofa, or wherever she was. "What? For good?"

"Well, I presume so." She hadn't got that far yet.

"On bended knee? Or with a scowl in a *Here, let's have done with it* kind of way?"

"Well…" She'd been so annoyed at seeing him in her locker it hadn't even occurred to her that there might have been a plan. "There wasn't a bended knee—but there wasn't a scowl either."

"So," Alice said in her perfunctory Irish way. That meant any number of things, and in this case Katie was guessing it meant *What the hell are you going to do now?*

"I don't want to give them back." The words rushed out before she'd had a chance to edit them.

"In a good way? Or in a *Fine, you've done your business now let me get on with mine* kind of way?"

Katie laughed. She loved this woman. There were incredibly few people she'd let into her heart...well, okay, Alice and Josh were really it...and she'd missed speaking with her.

"I was sorry to cut you off earlier."

Alice didn't wait for Katie to explain herself.

"I know it's a hard day for you, and there was me prattling on about my daughter and all. It was thoughtless. What you both went through, losing Elizabeth like you did...I can't begin to imagine."

"It wasn't thoughtless." And Katie meant it. "It's...it's life. And other people have it."

"What? Are you saying to me you *don't* have your own life?"

Um...a little bit?

"No."

"My goodness. Is that Katie McGann all grown up now? Are you telling me you're done hiding away in your idyllic mountain village, pretending you're the only one to have ever gone through something awful?"

"Say it like it is, why don't you?" Katie muttered.

Alice let her stew for a moment.

She looked down at her hands and realized she'd been fiddling with her rings during the call and had unconsciously slipped them back into their rightful place. On her left hand's ring finger.

"Well?" Alice had never been known for her patience.

"I've not been hiding. I've been...thinking."

"Thinking about getting on with your life or thinking about hiding away there forever?"

"Thinking about letting go."

"Of what, exactly?"

Katie lifted her hand and eyed the rings in the half dark. "Fear?"

"That's a good way to start the New Year, love." Alice's voice was soft, but then it took an abrupt turn. "But don't go hurtling yourself off of a mountainside with a couple of fairy wings for support."

Katie laughed again.

"I will be sure to have on full reflective gear and the entire mountain rescue crew on standby if I ever do such a thing."

"That's my girl. Now, let me get some sleep and I'll speak to you soon, all right? I love you."

"I love you, too. Merry Christmas, Alice."

"And to you, angel. And pass on my love to the rascal, won't you?"

Katie nodded and said goodbye. She rolled onto her side, putting her left hand in front of her face, flicking the backs of the rings with her thumb again and again, even though she could see they were right there.

All the emotion she'd been choking back throughout the day abruptly came pouring out of her in barely contained wails of grief. If she was going to let go of fear, she was also going to have to let go of the sorrow that the fear had been protecting. Sorrow over the family she would never have. The child she had only held once. The husband she loved so dearly that the thought of losing him all but crippled her.

She was so consumed with heartache she barely registered the door opening and the arrival of a pair of male legs appearing by her side. She rocked and cried as a pair of familiar arms slipped around her, holding her, soothing her.

Josh.

Of course it was. He knew her better than anyone. Knew she would need him.

After all this time apart, he was finally there for her in the way she had longed for. Present. Still.

He slipped behind her on the bed and gently pulled her into his embrace so that she could curl up in a tight little ball, chin to knees, arms tangled through his, fingers pressing into his shoulder as if her life depended upon it.

There were no whispered placations. No *There, there* or *It'll be all right*. They might love one another, but how could he assure her about a future they would never have? Neither of them knew if anything would be all right...if they'd have the big family they both longed for. If they'd be together at all.

When at long last she was all cried out, Josh eased them down into a seamless spooned embrace. For a moment she thought to fight him. *How could she trust this? This deep, organic comfort she had longed for during those cavernously dark days?* The weight of her fatigue decided for her. She was so tired, and lying there in his arms...the one place she'd always found comfort...she began to feel the release of dreamless sleep overtake her.

It would be all right. Just this once.

It was Christmas.

Her body instinctively snuggled into his. She heard his breath catch as her own steadied. With his arm as a pillow, she became tuned in to his heartbeat, to that warm, spicy scent she would know until the end of time, to his strength. Her own body hummed with a growing heat. A sense of familiarity and comfort.

One night.

There'd be no harm in that. Right? Just one night before they said goodbye forever.

She felt his fingers stroke along her cheek, then slip down along her arm so that their fingers were intertwined. It was what she needed. To simply...*be*. Without hope or expectation. Just some peace. Some sleep. Some long-awaited comfort in her husband's arms.

Josh moved his hand along an upward curve. What the—? He waited another moment until his brain caught up with his hand. It wasn't a pillow he was caressing. It was his wife. And that sweet scent wasn't hospital antiseptic… It was the ever-mesmerizing Essence de Katie.

He nuzzled into her neck, instinctively tipping his chin to drop a kiss onto her shoulder. He stopped himself, then decided just to go for it. It was Christmas Day and Katie was asleep.

His lips sought and found a bit of exposed shoulder in the wide V-neck of her scrubs. Mmm…just as he'd remembered. Silk and honey.

Katie rolled over to face him, eyes still closed, an arm slipping round his waist. He couldn't tell if she was still asleep or not. When they had been together, the night had always found them tangled into one pretzel shape or another. Just so long as they were connected, everything had been all right.

A little sigh escaped her lips and he couldn't resist pressing his own lips to that beautiful mouth of hers.

She responded. Slowly, sleepily at first, but with growing intent as their legs began to tangle together in an organic need to meld into one.

He felt Katie's hand slip onto his hip and under his scrubs. Their kisses deepened. He couldn't believe how good it felt to feel her hands on his bare skin. Especially, he realized with a smile, when the cool silver of her wedding rings intermingled with the warmth of her fingertips.

Her fingers slid along his hip and up his spine, causing him to jerk back sharply when her fingers hit his scars. She didn't need to know about the accident. Not yet.

"Josh?"

Katie remained where she was but he could feel her heart rate escalating.

"Are those—?"

"It's nothing." *It had been huge.*

"It didn't feel like nothing." Katie's eyes blinked a couple of times before refocusing more acutely on him. He could almost see the wheels whirring in her mind to make sense of what she'd felt.

"Merry Christ— Oh, my gosh, I'm so sorry!"

Josh felt Katie shoot out of bed at the sound of Michael's voice and a blast of light. For a moment he couldn't understand why the intern looked so embarrassed. He was too busy trying to figure out how to explain to Katie what she'd discovered.

"I'll just—leave you to it, then… Uh…" Michael wasn't moving, so why on earth was he—?

Wow. Did twenty-eight-year-old men still blush?

"Merry Christmas, Michael. You're up with the lark."

Katie was tugging her scrubs top down along her hipline. Ah…the slow dawn of recognition began to hit him. No one knew they were married. No one knew Dr. McGann was Katie West. *His* Katie.

"Not really, Dr. McGann. It's nine o'clock."

"What?" Katie shot Josh a horrified look.

He just grinned. He hadn't slept until nine o'clock since… That wasn't a tricky one to figure out.

"My shift started at *seven*. Why didn't you page me?"

"Oh…" Michael began awkwardly. "Jorja said you looked really tired last night, so I left a note with the morning shift to let you sleep in."

Michael nervously shuffled his feet, still unable to connect his gaze to Katie or to Josh, who thought he might as well stand up and be counted.

"Right. I see…"

Katie didn't really seem to know what to do with the information. Or how to explain being discovered in the arms of a man she wasn't meant to know.

"Well, let's get going, shall we?"

"Merry Christmas, Michael," Josh contributed merrily. If he was going to fake it about having been critically injured, he might as well go the whole hog and rustle up some fake Yuletide jolliness.

"Uh… Merry Christmas…"

Katie steered Michael away from the room without a backward glance.

Josh huffed out a mirthless "Ho-ho-ho…" and plunked back down on the bed. *Merry Christmas, indeed.* It shouldn't have come as a surprise. Shouldn't hurt so much. A psychiatrist would have a field day with them. No fluid Seven Stages of Grief for the Wests! No, sir. Just a tangled mess of How-the-Hell-Did-We-End-Up-Like-This?

He scrubbed at his thickly stubbled jaw. It had been a long time since he'd thought of himself as a plural. They had both been bulldozed by shock. At least they'd done *that* by the book. He'd skipped the next few stages and gone straight to testing. Testing limits. Pushing boundaries. Trying his best to show Katie there was still so much life to be lived and all along only succeeding in pushing her away. Making her more fearful than he had ever thought she could be.

From everything he'd seen, she was still sitting pretty in the snowcapped Village of Denial. As long as she didn't see him, everything that had happened could be her own little secret, locked away wherever it was she locked things up.

His heart ached for her, and at the same time he wanted to roar with fury at how fruitless blocking out the past was.

Hmm…good one. Anger.

Okay. He'd probably hit that one a few times, too. Depression? Didn't really compute. He simply wasn't that kind of guy. There were too many good things in life to counterweight the sorrows. Otherwise—what was the point?

Bargaining?

Maybe that was what being here was. If he won Katie back then his life would feel complete again. Just like in these last few precious hours. The first time he'd held his wife in his arms for two years. The first solid sleep he was guessing either of them had had since the split. The first time he'd let himself really believe they might be together again.

If he didn't believe…?

Nah. He wasn't there yet. No point in accepting things you didn't know the answer to.

"Dr. West! Good of you to finally join us."

Katie was back to her crisp efficient self. Surprise, surprise.

"Granny dump in Four."

She handed him a file without a second look. *Wow. Talk about terse!* Even at her most efficient Katie was never rude. Her heart normally bled for the elderly people families dropped off in the ER on Christmas Day so they wouldn't have to look after them on the holiday. It happened a lot in the city. Had to be pretty rare out in these parts.

He watched her reorder a few files, the crease between his eyebrows deepening. Katie knew exactly how Josh felt about caring for the elderly, given he had been near enough raised by his grandmother, with his parents so busy on the farm. He clamped his teeth together to bite back a snarky comeback. He'd expected more from her. Maybe she *had* changed and he was the last one to see it. The last one to accept the truth. They were different people now.

He shook his head. This sat wrong. At the very least she should have opted to tell him the condition the so-called "dump" was for.

He glanced at the chart.

"Peripheral edema." The notes went on to say the patient was complaining of swollen ankles and feet. Could be anything. Ankle sprain, obesity, osteoarthritis—and so the list went on, all the way up to congestive heart failure. That would have to be one cold family to drop their grandmother off at the ER, without so much as grandchild in tow.

"And what have *you* got this fine Christmas morn?"

Josh asked Katie, thinking he'd make a stab at civility. It wasn't like they'd spent the night wrapped in each other's arms or anything.

"New bride having a panic attack." Her eyes flicked to his. "Trying to live up to unrealistic expectations."

He turned and went to Exam Four. She was obviously in a mood. He'd already opened up about his expectations. She'd felt his scars. Thought the worst. Maybe this was her way of saying all bets were off.

He stopped just before entering his cubicle and turned, catching a glimpse of Katie's hand as she went into the cubicle beside him.

Ha! He just resisted throwing a punch up into the air. She still wore the rings. Hadn't sent him to the scrap heap just yet.

A grin lit up his face. Maybe it *was* going to be a merry Christmas after all.

"Now, Mrs. Hitchins, is it? I'm Dr. West. I understand you're not feeling at your best?"

"I don't think this is working."

The young woman sitting on the exam table lowered the paper bag she'd been breathing into when Katie entered.

"Is she going to be all right? Is she having a heart attack?" asked the young man beside her, presumably her husband. His face was laced with anxiety.

Katie pulled her stethoscope from around her neck and gave the couple as reassuring a smile as she could muster.

"I understand you've got your in-laws visiting for the first time, Mrs. Davis?"

"My family. Yes." Her husband answered for her. "Emily had just put the roast in the oven and then my mother, who has *always* made our Christmas dinners in the past, started asking about what Emily's family ate for Christmas. The next thing I knew, she was hyperventilating, saying she could hardly see… My mother kept offering to take over in the kitchen, and that's when Emily really took a turn. Is she going to be all right?"

Katie took Emily's vitals while he spoke, gently encouraging the twenty-something newlywed to return the paper bag to her mouth, assuring her husband they would do everything they could to help his wife.

She could hear Josh merrily chatting away with the woman next door. He was obviously bringing out the best in her from the sounds of their joined laughter. She would have expected nothing less. He had a wonderful way with grandmothers. Everyone, really. *Why had she been so sharp with him?* He didn't deserve to be sniped at when all he'd done was show her kindness.

What were those scars all about?

She forced herself to tune back in to her patient's husband.

"I'm happy to call my mother and tell her to take over. My mother does a *perfect* Christmas dinner. Doesn't she, Ems?"

Emily's breathing suddenly accelerated, and her eyes dilated as they darted from her husband to Katie.

"Deep breaths, Emily. Keep the bag up. *Deep* breaths. Mr. Davis—do you mind if I have a moment with your wife alone?"

"Are you sure there's nothing—?"

"Absolutely. If you could just take a seat in the waiting room, I'll be with you in a few moments."

After her husband had dropped a nervous kiss on his wife's head and left the cubicle, Emily's breathing changed. Lost its harsh edge. Katie rubbed her hand along Emily's back as she might a small child and kept repeating her mantra.

"Breathe slowly. Deeply. Count to three…count to five… deep and slowly…"

It was what had got her through her first few attacks after she'd left Josh. Part of her had actually been shocked that she'd done it. It had been so out of character! She'd checked into a hotel when her car had all but run out of gas and had just sat at the end of the bed and shaken for who knew how long?

She gave her head a little shake. This wasn't about her. It was about Emily and a mother-in-law whose son seemed to have problems letting go of the apron strings.

"First holiday meal for the in-laws?" Katie asked gently, lowering herself into the seat beside the exam table and making a Christmas-tree doodle on the corner of the chart.

Emily just nodded. Tears springing to her eyes.

Katie tugged a tissue out of the packet she always had in her lab coat and handed it to her.

"Would it be safe to say this is the first time you've ever experienced these symptoms?"

Another nod and a sniffle. A tear skidding down her cheek.

Katie stood and patted the empty space on the examination table. "Mind if I join you?"

Emily shook her head and Katie scooched up onto the table, her feet crossed at the ankles.

"I remember making my first—my *only*—Christmas dinner for my in-laws. I was a wreck!" She laughed softly at the memory. "My husband's family loved their food and they were happy slaves to their long-established Christmas traditions. And, of course, there was Gramma Jam-Jam's unbelievably perfect cooking to contend with. What I *didn't* realize was that most families *don't* buy the entire meal in from a fancy grocery store and heat it up."

She laughed again before going on, pleased to see Emily's breathing was becoming more regular as she spoke.

"I mean, I obviously knew people made Christmas dinner—it was just that my family never had. And when I volunteered to cook for my husband's family, I didn't realize what I'd gotten into until they started sending me emails about how they liked three-peak dinner rolls, whatever they were, homemade cranberry sauce—but only if there was orange zest and no orange pulp—mashed potatoes—but made with a ricer, which made no sense at all. And lots of butter—salted."

She held up her fingers and added another memory. "A big enough turkey so that there'd be enough leftovers for sandwiches to see them through at least the next week. There I was, a grown woman, and I'd never so much as *peeled* a potato, let alone mashed one."

"At least they ate the same thing!" Emily cut in. "David's family don't eat a single thing my family does. Beef instead of turkey, because they feel the one at Thanksgiving is enough. Roasted potatoes instead of mashed. Which is just *wrong*." She reeled off a list of her family's specialties before giving Katie a wide-eyed look. "What's Christmas without turkey and stuffing?" She spread her hands out wide in a *what gives?* gesture. "I mean—I've never, *ever* had Christmas without turkey and stuffing! It's like a sign that this whole marriage was never meant to happen!"

"Hey," Katie soothed. "Marriage involves a whole lot of things we don't think about when we say our vows. But you can *do* this! Think about your guy. Maybe he's been pining for beef each Christmas he's spent with your family? Embrace the changes as learning opportunities. Doesn't mean they have to be *your* things."

She took both of her patient's hands in her own and gave a decisive nod. "How 'bout this? When your in-laws leave, why don't you make a turkey for New Year's? Just the two of you. Stuffing. Mashed potatoes. The whole nine yards."

Emily sniffled, swiping at her tears to reveal a hint of a smile, giving Katie a nod to continue. Not that she would have been able to stop her. She was on a roll now. Her own marriage might be in tatters, but she damn well wasn't going to let *this* pair of young lovers fall to bits over a piece of roast beef!

"Have your *own* traditions! My husband and I made ours. Pancakes on Tuesdays after a double shift. Grilled cheese sandwiches with pickles and tomato soup on Valentine's..."

Katie felt a flush of pleasure begin to color her cheeks at the memory of the goofy traditions they'd made up through the years, then sobered. She was at work here—not on a magical trip down memory lane.

"You know what, Emily? If your mother-in-law is so desperate to cook...let her! Have your husband drive you home via a restaurant and get a to-go bag filled to the brim with turkey sandwiches—then put your feet up and enjoy letting someone else cook dinner. I bet you've spent days making the house and everything just perfect?"

Emily nodded, the light shadows under her eyes offering the proof that Katie wasn't just making a stab in the dark. "I do feel pretty tired."

"Okay! Why not go home, play the sick card? Put your feet up and enjoy the day with your husband. Play a board game and enjoy the aromas wafting from the kitchen. And in a few days...when they're gone...pull out your apron and make exactly what you want—just for the two of you. It sounds to me like you know how to cook! That's more than *I* could ever do!"

"The grilled cheese sandwiches?" Emily grinned at her.

"Burned at the corners, gooey in the middle. My specialty." Katie smiled back, giving her patient's knee a knowing pat. Family life could be tough. And the holidays could make it tougher.

"Don't give yourself such a hard time, Dr. McGann."

Katie started when Josh poked his head into the exam area, with his own patient grinning up at him adoringly from her wheelchair.

"I have it on good authority that your husband thinks your cooking is fantastic."

He dropped her a wink and pushed Mrs. Hitchins away, leaving Katie at a loss for words.

"He's cute. If your husband is anything like *him*…" Emily gave a low whistle of appreciation.

Katie briskly jumped off the exam table. Her husband was *nothing* like the Josh who'd just strolled past as if they hadn't just spent the past two years apart. This guy seemed reliable, steady…*present*. Someone she could trust *not* to scale sheer cliff faces or zip wire across the Grand Canyon. *That* was the Josh she knew. This guy…? He might have some scars she didn't know anything about…but he was here for her exactly when she needed him and she hadn't even known it.

"So!" Katie picked up Emily's forms. "I'm going to make a note that you were suffering from mild hyperventilation. Effectively you had an in-laws-induced panic attack—but we won't put that down," she added conspiratorially. "It is not uncommon this time of year. If you like, you can tell your family it was exhaustion. But you know how to fix it now…right?"

"Step back, take a look at the big picture and remember I married the guy I love?"

Her words bull's-eyed Katie right in the heart.

She'd never done that. Taken a step back from it all. The grief. The sorrow. She'd never remembered to take in the big picture. She'd just pushed Josh away as hard as she could. Even put a mountain range between them!

Images of her heart soaring over the Rocky Mountains with a goofy pair of fairy wings pinged into her head.

For a smart woman, she was feeling like a first-class ding-a-ling.

How could you hide from what was alive in your heart? Especially if it was love? Had time finally given her the perspective to see the situation for what it had been? Awful, *awful* luck.

"Exactly." Katie forced a smile. "You married the guy

you love. Now, get out there and go hunt down some turkey sandwiches!"

Emily gave her a tight hug and all but bounded out of the cubicle, tugging on her jacket as she went to find her husband.

The unexpected flush of emotion at their encounter made Katie pause. *Whoo!* She needed a few extra seconds for private regrouping.

So...if Emily was The Patient of Christmas Past...

Had she been so blinkered about Josh's adrenaline-junkie ways that she'd forgotten to look at the big picture? To look at *him*? He had been grieving, too. Maybe his relentless drive to cheer her had been the same desperation *she'd* been feeling for him to weep with her. Sob his heart out as she'd done, hidden away in the back of her closet so no one could hear her mourn.

There just wasn't any way to prepare for a loss like that, let alone know how to react. Had *she* been the one to react poorly? To lose sight of what was important?

The weight of the realization nearly buckled her knees. *What had she done?*

The iron taste of blood in her mouth brought her back to the present. *Hey! Let's just add a self-inflicted bloody lip to the mix.* Precisely the Christmas look she'd been hoping to present to her patients. To Josh.

She needed a Christmas cookie.

Stat.

If she got to the staff room fast enough, there just might be a few left after Jorja's grandmother's annual Christmas bake-fest.

CHAPTER SEVEN

"SOMEONE'S GOT THE MUNCHIES!"

"Hi, Michael." Katie guiltily swiped some crumbs away from her lips as she swallowed down an unsuspecting gingerbread man's leg. His head and arms had already been snapped off and munched. "Sorry, I was just…"

Just trying to drown my sorrows by massacring a gingerbread cookie?

Not strictly what you wanted your boss to say.

"Don't worry. I've already eaten a dozen. Maybe more."

The unexpected hint of a wicked smile crossed his face and brought out one on her own. She had a soft spot for Michael. Hair always a tousled mess. Ink marks regularly dabbing his cheeks. He'd joined the internship later than most medical graduates, having taken a year out to work with a charity in South America. Methodical. Steady. He was a serious guy. Not to the point of being humorless, but it was nice to see a smile on his face.

"Lucky you—getting Jorja as your Secret Santa."

"Yes! Yes, it was most excellent. A real surprise. Incredibly generous."

And a really effusive thanks for a plate of cookies Jorja hadn't even baked herself.

Katie looked up from her cookie to give Michael a closer look and was surprised to see a hint of color pop onto his cheeks. Did he…? Could he really…? Bouncy, gregarious

Jorja? Who wore costumes on any given holiday? Well…
Katie had been all but surgically attached to her books at
university and Josh-the-Gregarious had certainly brought
her out of her shell. Maybe Jorja brought out the hidden
Romeo in Michael.

Katie felt her beeper buzz and tugged it off her scrubs
waistline.

911—suspected cardiac arrest.

Katie didn't bother to wait for Michael's response.

The patient was her father.

"Who does a woman need to call to get a cappuccino in
this hospital?"

Josh knew that voice. He knew it very well. And he
knew the bottle blonde coiffure that went along with it.

"Mrs. McGann?"

"Josheeee!"

Katie's immaculately turned out mother twirled around
on her heels with the style and panache of a nineteen-fifties
screen legend, holding her hands out in a wiggly fingered
show of delight before planting a big lipsticky kiss on his
cheek. Nothing had changed there, then.

"What are you doing here, Mrs. McGann?"

And…why don't you find it strange that I'm here?

"Oh, Josh…"

Sheree McGann placed a perfectly manicured hand on
Josh's forearm. She was as touchy-feely as her daughter
was reserved. No apples had fallen near *her* tree.

"It's Randall. He's gone and had a blasted angina attack
and he didn't have any of his squirty stuff left so we could
finish—you know—*business*."

She raised her eyebrows and smiled when he made the
connection.

"Josheeee…" She gave his arm a squeeze. "I would just
murder for a cappuccino. Any top tips from an insider?"

She dropped him a knowing wink, but before he had a chance to answer, Katie skidded to a halt alongside them. Perfect timing? Or damage control?

"Mom! Is everything all right? Where's Dad?" Katie shot him a wary glance while she waited for a response.

"Katie, darling! You didn't tell us Josh was back in town. *Naughty* girl. It does explain why you've turned down our invitation to stay at the condo whilst we're here. Now, what does a girl have to do to find a barista on Christmas morning?"

"I bet we can rustle something up for you, Sheree."

Katie's blood ran cold, then hot, then cold again.

This isn't happening! This isn't happening. No, no, no, no, no, no. No!

She squeezed her eyes tight shut. Then opened them.

For the love of all the Christmases past and present... please be gone!

She eased one eye open. Nope. They were both still there. Josh and her mother, nattering away like a day hadn't passed since they'd seen each other last. At Elizabeth's funeral. That was the last time they'd all been together. At least her parents had managed to make good on *that* promise.

"Oh, Josh!" Sheree gushed. "It is *so* good to see you again. I kept telling Katie to stop hiding you away in all of those specialist hospitals and to join us up here in the Canyon. What did she do to finally lure you to our little mountain retreat?"

"Mom!"

Katie blanked Josh's wide-eyed expression. So she hadn't strictly told her parents she and Josh were no longer together? So what? They'd never been close. On top of which, shouldn't her mother be behaving a bit more as if her husband was having a heart attack?

"Where's Dad?" She wheeled on Josh. "Are you—is *someone*—looking after my father? I just got a 911."

"That was me, dear. I wanted to get back home as soon as…"

Her mother's voice trailed off and she pulled back to view her daughter at arm's length.

"Oh, honey. Couldn't you have made a bit more of an effort?" Sheree tsked as she top-to-toe eyeballed Katie with obvious disdain at her choice of scrubs and trainers. "It's *Christmas*."

Katie crinkled her nose and shook off her mother's comment. Typical McGann reaction. Ignore the real problem and focus on something superficial.

Fine.

She obviously wasn't going to get any sense out of her mother, whose breath smelled as though she'd already hit the wet bar. Mimosas or martinis? She leaned in for a sniff. Mimosa. Her eyes flicked to the clock. Eleven-thirty.

Well. It *was* Christmas.

"Where's Dad? Is he okay?"

"Oh, honey. He didn't have a heart attack. He was just behaving like his usual greedy guts self—eating too much foie gras last night—and he's out of his whatchamacallit… Nitro-something-or-other."

"Nitroglycerin?" Katie crinkled her nose. "You didn't tell me Dad was on medication."

Katie's mother gave a tiny shrug and continued speaking as if Katie hadn't said a word. "Remember what a little piggy he is, Josheee? You know, we were both just talking about you, and I said to him—"

"Why don't we all go see him together? I think I overheard Dr. Vessey saying *she* was doing a preliminary check on an angina case in Two."

Josh smoothed over his mother-in-law's ruffled feathers with the promise of a shot of espresso somewhere in the near future in exchange for a few moments with her husband and daughter.

"Oh, your father won't like that. That's why we had the girl at the desk send out the 911. You know him—refused the wheelchair, staggered in like a drunken pirate, insisting on seeing his little girl. He won't be treated by anyone but you, Katie."

"But—" Katie's face was wreathed in confusion.

"You know your father, dear. You always were his favorite."

"I should think so, Mother. I *am* his only child," Katie ground out, looking a little less like a glowering twelve-year-old.

Josh's grin widened. He was enjoying every single second of this. Not the part about his father-in-law staggering into the ER bellowing to see his daughter before his heart gave out…but all of this complicated, messy family stuff? This was a side of the McGann family he'd never known existed. And on top of everything, Katie hadn't told them they weren't together anymore. It was like fifteen Christmases all rolled up into one!

Out of this world. Heart-thumpingly out of this world.

"Shall we?" Katie bit out, clearly displeased with the notion of the proposed family activity.

Josh tucked his mother-in-law's hand into the crook of his arm as Katie stomped off in the lead.

"Temper, temper!" Sheree stage-whispered.

Katie's shoulders stiffened, but they weren't rewarded with the glare Josh was fairly certain would be playing across Katie's face. She could have whipped round and stuck her tongue out at them for all he cared.

Deck the halls with Katie's white lies, tra-la-la-la-la, la-la-la-la!
She's not told her parents she left me, fa-la-la-la-la!
Merry Christmas to me!

Maybe that dream of running off into the sunset hand in hand with his wife hadn't been so silly after all. And…seeing as it was winter…sunset came early this time of year!

Katie unceremoniously yanked back the curtain to her father's cubicle, shooting Josh a *back off, pal* look as she did.

Then again…

"Hi, honey! Will you tell this kid to stop it with her tests, already? I told her my daughter and son-in-law would sort me out. I want Copper Canyon's best."

"I'm a fully qualified intern—" Shannon began, before her reluctant patient gave her a dismissive pat on the hand.

"They're here now, honey. Thanks for being so attentive. I'm sure you've got a great career ahead of you." He dropped her one of his aging soap star winks in lieu of a wave farewell.

Katie shot an apologetic look at Shannon, indicating that she could leave. She had this one. Josh received a similar look, but it was a bit more of a bug-eyed *Scram, pal!*

"Oh, don't go, son!" Her father held up a hand in protest. "Josh, Katie's mother and I have been asking ourselves why you and Katie haven't come up to the house yet. Heaven knows we've had no luck getting Katie up this season—as per normal. Where's she been hiding you anyway? It's been—has it been *years* since we've laid eyes on you? Sheree, honey—when was the last time we saw Josheee here?"

"Dad! Can you stop jabbering for a minute, please? I just want to listen to your heart."

Katie fastidiously avoided Josh's twinkling blue eyes, blowing a breath or two onto her stethoscope before positioning it over her father's heart.

Randall McGann's words were like music to Josh's ears. *They really don't know. Katie hasn't told them.*

He ran the words over and over in his mind like a healing mantra.

A few seconds of silence reigned before Katie's mother jumped in.

"Darling, I think your father just needs a refill of his medicine. This little incident started when we were in the middle of a…a *bedroom workout*." Mrs. McGann's voice slipped into a slinky-dinky tone appropriate for a perfume commercial and her husband gave a knowing chortle. "If you know what I mean."

"Gross." Katie shook away the mental image building in her head. "Mom. Just… Can we stick with the facts, please?"

"What, honey? Your father and I were having sex. You and Josheee still have sex, right? It's what loving couples do?"

"Mom!" Katie's eyes darted to Josh and then assumed a full glower on her mother. "Can we *please* just…?" Katie huffed out a sigh. "Dad. Can you tell me what sensations you experienced?"

"Well, your mother was in the middle of a new trick she read about in a magazine, and I was just on the brink of having a wonderful—"

"Whoa! Whoa! Still too much detail. Let's just stick with your heart. The pains in and around your heart."

"Well, I didn't have the shooting pain down the arm that says you're having a heart attack, if that's what you're after, honey."

"Dad!" Katie's exasperation was growing. "I need details. Did you experience shortness of breath? Sweating? Did you lose consciousness—?"

"Uh… Katie, would you like *me* to do the examination?" Josh only just managed to keep the corners of his mouth from twitching into a broad smile. "I think you might be a bit too close to the patient. Your questions are coming out a bit more Guantanamo than—"

"This is *hardly* an interrogation, Josh!" Katie bit back, fastidiously keeping her eyes glued to her stethoscope.

"And I am *perfectly* capable of assessing an angina attack, thank you very much!"

"*Honey!* Is that *any* way to speak to your husband on Christmas?"

"Mom, he's not—" Katie froze.

This could be interesting.

Josh quirked an eyebrow. Her parents, for once, were silent. What to do? Break some pretty painful news to Mr. and Mrs. McGann on Christmas Day or come to his wife's rescue? The wife he really wanted back in his arms.

He held up his hands in mock surrender.

"Confession time! I'm not really supposed to be here."

"Ooh, you old rascal." Randall threw a high five at him from his hospital bed. "Did you fly in special, just to make sure our Katie's Christmas was a bit more naughty than nice?"

"Dad!"

Katie could not have looked more horrified than she did now. Josh couldn't help but laugh. He might be having the best Christmas of his life, but he would put money on the fact this was very likely Katie's worst.

The smile dropped from his lips.

Second worst.

There would never be a Christmas more devastating than the one they'd had three years ago.

"Nope. Sorry. Nothing quite so thrilling. I just meant I'm on shift, and my boss here—" he nodded at Katie "—would probably like me to see some of the patients I hear building up in the waiting room. Lovely to see you both."

Katie exhaled a sigh of relief when Josh left the cubicle.

"Okay, Dad. Will you hush for a moment and let me get through this exam?"

"As long as you promise to bring Josh over for dinner. Tonight."

"I can't tonight—I'm on duty."

"On *Christmas*?"

"Mom! People don't have health problems just during office hours."

"Tone, Katie! Your mother's had a rough morning." Her father gently chastised her. "Tomorrow, then. Or how 'bout New Year's Eve? That'd be fun. See in the New Year together as a family."

Katie looked at him dubiously. Since when did her parents give a monkey's if they did *anything* as a family?

"Surely the hospital doesn't have you working round the clock?" Her mother added to the appeal.

If only she could!

Her father crossed his arms across his chest. "Sheree—get a yes out of our daughter and promise not to cook."

"Honey—we'll get delivery. I know an excellent Korean barbecue here in town. They do the most delicious ginseng pork—"

"New Year's Eve—fine! Okay? I will bring Josh and we will have dinner with you. Now, can you just *hush* for a minute so I can see how clogged up your arteries are?"

Her father, duly chastened, nodded his assent whilst making a *zip it* gesture on his lips.

Case. Closed.

"You can clear the mistletoe poisoning and the burned fingers from the board."

"Both of them?" Katie's eyes widened in surprise but she whooshed the eraser over the names on the whiteboard.

Josh couldn't tell if he'd startled her or if she was amazed he'd seen two patients to her one—albeit particular—patient.

"Yup. The mistletoe-berry-swallower had to revisit the berries, if you know what I mean."

"Induced vomiting with charcoal?" She gave a shiver at his grossed-out face.

"Not quite the lump of coal Santa had in mind—but, yes.

We ran an EKG, did some blood and urine tests and apart from discovering that the hallucinatory effects of mistletoe aren't just a myth, and seeing the magic of receiving fluids through an IV, I think he'll be okay. Michael's just signing him out."

"The little girl with the burned fingers?"

"Minor. But each and every finger. Her teenage cousins were having a contest to see how many votive candles they could put out in three seconds. She came first."

"Nothing like the holidays to bring out the best in a family!" Katie intoned, her eyes still solidly on the board.

"Speaking of which—is everything all right with your father?"

Josh thought he'd better test the waters before going in for the proverbial kill. Telling Katie how much he loved her. Inviting her to Paris. Asking her to renew their vows.

"If being blackmailed into having dinner at my parents' on New Year's Eve is your idea of 'all right,' then yes."

"That should be fun for you!"

"Well, you're coming too, so you can wipe that smug look off your face."

"Ah!" His heart gave a satisfying thump. She hadn't called a replacement.

"Is that a good 'Ah!' or a bad one?" She frowned.

His eyes did a quick dart down to her hand. Yup! The rings were still there. His eyes flicked back up to Katie's.

"Your mother's not cooking, is she?"

"No way!" Katie looked horrified at the thought. "I don't think Dad even lets her heat things up for him anymore. He had food poisoning three months ago, from something she insisted she'd had in the oven all day. Turned out she'd only had the lightbulb on, and had put on the grill at the last minute to sear it and cover up the mistake."

"Maisie's on Main?"

Josh had stopped at the local diner on his way to the hospital when he'd arrived in town. Damn good toasted cheese sandwiches. They'd even put in the dill pickles when asked.

"Nope. Korean. Mom's into 'Asian trilogy ingredients,' whatever those are."

"Aphrodisiacs, I'm guessing."

"Joshua…" Katie's voice was loaded with warning.

"Uh-oh!" He put on a mock dismayed face. "You only ever call me Joshua when I'm in trouble. What did I do?"

Katie maintained a neutral expression on her face, but the tone of her voice spoke volumes. "Don't. Even. Go. There."

"Which 'there'?" He tried to joke. "The embarrassing fact your parents are still heavily sexed up and you act more like a parent than they ever did? Or the very interesting news that you haven't told them you've been asking me for a divorce for the past two years?"

"Holy cow!"

Michael popped up from underneath the central reception desk, much to Katie's obvious horror.

"You two are *married*?"

"No!"

"Yes."

Katie's negative response was drowned out by Josh's emphatic affirmation.

"Not that we're telling anyone—are we, Katie?"

"Uh…" Michael's eyes shifted from one to the other, as if he were expecting one or both of them to sprout wings. Or horns. "I'll just leave you two to it, then…" And he promptly bolted from the desk toward the staff room.

"Now look what you've done!" Katie's expression was one of pure dismay.

"What *I've* done? Are you *kidding* me? All I've done is everything you've asked of me for the past three years, Katie."

Whoops. Not quite the love-heals-all-wounds tack he was hoping to take.

"Everything but one!" She furiously obliterated her father's name from the whiteboard.

Josh's heart plummeted to his guts, then rebounded with a fiery need to lay his cards on the table. Katie didn't need to know he'd almost died. Didn't need to know he was being offered the chance of a lifetime in Paris. Didn't need to know a single one of those things to know if she loved him. But she *did* need to know them if they were to go forward truthfully. With trust.

He steadied his breathing before he began speaking, but the moment the words came out, he knew he should have walked away. Thrown a snowball. Pulled her into his arms under some mistletoe and showed her the other side of his love. Something—*anything*—to temper the volcanic strength of rage and sorrow he felt at what had happened to them.

"Is that really what you want? You honestly want me to sign those papers? Or do you just like holding it over me so we can both pretend *I* was the one who pushed *you* away after Elizabeth died?"

Josh could have punched himself in the face when he saw the look on her face.

There had been no need to be cruel. It was just that it hurt so *bad*. A physical pain compounded tenfold when he saw the tears spring into Katie's eyes before she turned on her heel and strode away.

It was time. Every pore in his body was rebelling, but the decision he'd needed to make since his arrival had been made.

CHAPTER EIGHT

NOT EVEN A snow angel was going to help dilute the bad mood Katie was in. A good stomp around the corridors of the hospital might do her good. Instill a bit of calm now that… She checked her watch… Nope! Wasn't over yet.

She glanced out the window… A perfectly beautiful white Christmas. If this day would just hurry up and be over, the little gremlins of Christmases Past could just go back to where they came from! She checked her watch again, tapping the surface of the glass as if the hour hand would suddenly leap forward.

Nope! Time didn't really seem to be playing ball today. Not in the slightest.

She kicked her pace up a notch. Including stairwells, she could get in a good three-mile walk. All she needed was to keep her pager from…

Zzzzt! Zzzzzt!

…going off.

She turned her race-walk into a run toward the surgical recovery ward. Was it the little girl she'd operated on yesterday? Casey Wilson? She offered up silent prayers as she kicked up her pace. Of all the surgeries in her entire career that needed to come out golden… *Please, please, please…*

If she could just block out the fact that she might not have made it through Casey's surgery without the sandy-haired, blue-eyed boy she'd lost her heart to way back in the innocent days of her junior residency…

She swiped at the tears cascading down her cheeks. Try harder. Block harder. *Shut him down.*

She was going to have to. Lives depended upon her ability to focus and to block out the pain that would drive her wild if she let it surface. Block out the need to be held in her husband's arms and have him tell her everything would be okay when she knew it wouldn't be. Couldn't be.

Where had those scars come from?

Run. Work.

Run faster. Work harder.

She reached the recovery ward breathless, more from fear than exertion. Was Casey all right?

"Hey, Dr. McGann." One of the nurses looked up when Katie approached the desk. "Sorry to set off your pager like that. It's just the Wilsons. They wanted to thank you for everything you did for Casey, and no one down in Trauma knew where you were."

"Oh! Good. That's all right." Katie's heart was still thumping away as she registered the nurse's words. "Fine. Good. Um…"

She saw Casey's parents through the glass door of the recovery room their daughter was in. Faces soft with pride and affection. She felt a swell of pride and a stab of loss squeeze all the breath out of her.

She and Josh could have been those parents. That family. Would most likely have been home with their little girl right now instead of haunting the corridors of the hospital, sniping at each other.

She could see it so easily. The three of them gathered round their Christmas tree, decorated with a mix of pre-school decorations and generations of hand-me-down ornaments. A fire crackling away and all three of them sitting together in a sea of wrapping paper, gifts and laughter…

"Can you just let them know I stopped by, got their message, but had to dash? Apologies."

"They're just right—" The nurse looked at her strangely as she angled her pencil in the Wilsons' direction.

"Sorry." Katie faked getting another page. "Gotta dash! Give them my best." She threw the words over her shoulder but kept moving. Away from the memories. Away from the pain.

T-minus I don't think I can do this much longer.

Katie rattled through the days and hours on her fingers and clenched them into fists. Didn't matter.

Too many. That was how many more hours she had with Josh.

She swept past the patients' rooms, hoping to find somewhere else to burn off her excess energy before returning to the ER.

"Merry Christmas, Dr. McGann! Can we offer you some eggnog?" A familiar rosy-cheeked woman caught her by the elbow before she flew past another recovery room.

"Mrs. Klausen?" Her eyes widened at the scene playing out before her. "What's going on here?"

A small card table had been set up next to her son Chris's bed, and the other children—Maddie and Nick—were busy hanging up stockings along the curtain rail. Mr. Klausen was poised to start carving an enormous roast turkey.

"Well, we couldn't let Chris be here all alone on the big day, could we?" Mrs. Klausen asked.

Katie scanned the family, each sporting an atrociously jolly Christmas sweater, faces wreathed in smiles. The delicious scent of turkey floated toward her as Mr. Klausen began slicing the large bird. Gone were the recriminations. The threats to wring necks, revenge plans for Eustace's injuries. There were just faces glowing with happiness. An overall sense of contentment that only being together as a family could bring.

"Join us!"

"You shouldn't be all alone on Christmas Day!"

"Eustace sends his love!"

"Can we at least give you a sandwich?"

A sting of guilt at her brisk treatment of her own parents hit her. It deepened as she wove Josh into the equation. She'd all but built a physical wall around herself to distance her from the things—the people—she thought had hurt her most in the wake of Elizabeth's death. But if she came at it from a different angle…?

Her parents and Josh were warriors. Relentless, driven, undeterred warriors. Carrying wave after wave of love with them.

Flawed? Hell, yeah! But who wasn't? She doubted Santa would have a long enough scroll if she were to start cataloging the ways she might have dealt with her grief in better ways. Been a better daughter to parents who clearly weren't the picket-fence type of mom and dad.

A more loving wife.

"Dr. McGann?" Maddie broke into Katie's reverie. "Are you all right?"

"Yes," Katie responded after a moment. "You know… would you mind if I took that turkey sandwich to go?"

"Truce?"

Katie approached Josh, who was doing his best sit-like-a-Buddha on a gurney he'd wheeled into a quiet corner.

"Truce?"

She tried again, her voice sounding more uncertain the second time.

Josh only just stopped himself from making a snarky comment about not knowing they were at war. But if he stopped and counted just how many scars he'd taken on in the past three years—both figurative and literal—maybe they had been. Heaven knew Katie had been nursing her own wounds, and these past two days had done nothing but reopen them.

He shifted across when she turned and pressed her hands against the gurney to hop up alongside him.

"Want some?" Katie offered when she'd settled.

Josh warily eyed the sandwich she waggled within his eyeline. He wouldn't have blamed Katie if she had laced the thing with strychnine, the way he'd spoken to her last.

"A peace offering." Katie held out a triangle of sandwich on the flat of her palm. "C'mon." She nudged him with her knee. "Go halvesies with me. I'll take a bite first, to prove I didn't load it with mistletoe berry sauce!"

He grinned. *Mind reader.*

He angled his head to take a surreptitious look at her through narrowed eyes. When she'd plunked herself down beside him on the gurney, he'd figured minimal eye contact would be the best way to go, but now that she was here... sandwich in hand... She took a smile-sized chomp of the thick sandwich and made a satisfied *"Mmm..."* noise.

He exhaled slowly. No doubt about it. No matter the time, date, place...no matter how angry he was or wasn't... she still took his breath away. If this were the olden days, there would be a kiss on her cheek, a hand slipped round her shoulder or her waist, a cheeky tickle somewhere or other and laughter. By God. He missed the sound of her laugh.

"Truce."

He put out a hand and received half of the turkey sandwich in his palm.

"It's from Santa."

"Really?"

"Sort of," Katie continued, almost shyly. "Remember the Klausens?"

"The 'I'm going to wring their necks when I get my hands on them' Klausens?" Josh held back from taking his first bite.

"The very ones. They're feasting it up on the recovery ward. Mashed potatoes, sweet potatoes, turkey bigger than an emu, stuffing—the whole kit and caboodle!" Katie took another chomp and grinned before her tongue slipped out to swoop up an escaped bit of cranberry sauce.

If this were the olden days, he would have licked that off, then hung around for a bit more lip-lock. He shifted again. For another reason this time.

Sweet dancing reindeer, who made this girl so sexy?

He thought back to this morning's escapade with her parents and felt the corners of his lips twitch before giving in to a full-blown grin. They might be the most surreal parents he'd ever met—but they were a good-looking couple. A good-looking couple who'd created one spectacularly beautiful daughter. A daughter who clearly didn't keep her parents up to date with everything in her life.

"Any chance you want to talk me through why you haven't told your parents we're not—?"

"Nope," she cut in, as if she were dodging questions about ditching school for the afternoon. "Aren't you going to eat that?" Katie popped the rest of her sandwich into her mouth, her fingers automatically reaching toward his untouched triangle.

He took a huge bite, smiling as he chewed, eyes hooked on hers. This was nice. And in the best possible way nice. He slipped his fingers through hers, eyes glued to the snow falling outside the window they were parked across from, not wanting to break the spell. This was more than he had hoped for. Just a few moments to sit and eat a turkey sandwich on Christmas Day with his wife.

He felt a tiny little squeeze from her fingers to his, and out of the corner of his eye he saw Katie lean her head back against the wall and close her eyes, a soft smile playing across her lips. His thumb shifted along her ring finger. His grin widened. Yup. Still there.

He took another bite. It was a helluva sandwich.

"I'm on my pager if you need me. And you know Maisie's number is just on the—"

"Go!" Jorja insisted, her finger pointed firmly at the exit.

Katie obeyed.

The instant she turned the corner outside the ambulance bay, she felt her step become a little bit lighter. She tilted her head back and let a huge snowflake land and melt on her tongue.

It was the first time she'd stepped outside the hospital for four days, and the crisp air gave her an unexpected shot of energy. She needed a little reflection time in advance of New Year's Eve, and seeing as it had crept up on her all of a sudden, she was stealing an hour or two of alone time.

The truce she and Josh had been observing had given her some much-needed time to regroup. And the steady flow of patients had kept them both busy enough not to have to talk about things. Sometimes you needed that.

She stood still for a moment, not wanting to hear the crunching of her boots on the snow, and listened to the perfect wintry silence Copper Canyon did so well.

Maybe "silence" wasn't the best word to describe it. Perhaps…peaceful winter wonderland soundscape? Her eyes scanned the hillside—the trees and houses still twinkling away with all their holiday lights. The wind wasn't strong, but there was the occasional creak and shiver of the evergreens as they rocked back and forth with the soothing cadence of a cradle.

She resumed her journey toward Main Street. The call of one of Maisie's grilled cheese sandwiches had grown too loud to resist. There was only so much hospital canteen food a girl could take, and she wasn't technically due back on shift for a few hours now.

With everything that had happened over the past few days, Katie found herself looking at the picture-perfect town with fresh eyes. She'd always been a big-city girl. Moving out here two years ago had been less by design and more a matter of the most convenient way to put as much distance as possible between herself and Josh as she could.

Now that he was here, she realized how little of it she had actually *seen*. Her parents' condo. Maisie's. That was about it. It was all she had been able to handle. How her mother—who only came out here once or twice a year—knew about a Korean restaurant that did home delivery was beyond her. Had she lost all curiosity about the world around her? Or just needed things to be as straightforward as possible?

Probably the latter. It was as if grief had physically filled her up and rendered her incapable of living in a big city. Too frenetic. Too much to process when she could barely take on board what was happening in her own life. And now…? Now she was getting better. Able to take on a bit more razzle-dazzle in her day.

Ready for Josh?

She opened her arms wide, as if to ask the small town what it thought. *Was* she ready? *Could* she consider life with her husband again? Or was all of this just life's way of wrapping up their marriage in a gentler style?

Her feet picked up the pace, as if leading her to the answer. Within a few minutes she found herself outside Maisie's big picture window, trying to decide whether to laugh or cry. Sitting in her favorite booth was none other than Josh West. She could only see the back of his head. He looked bent in concentration over something. The menu? She doubted it. He walked into a diner and ordered one thing and one thing only.

Maybe that had changed.

She moved toward the door, then hesitated. Something about seeing Josh sitting there felt big. Momentous, even. Magic Eight Ball spooky.

Maybe just a quick walk round the block would help

her. If he was still there when she'd done a lap, she'd go in. If not…?

She'd cross that doorway when she came to it.

Josh couldn't believe he'd actually done it. Put his signature on the divorce papers. He'd wanted to see what it looked like. Having his name there in black and white. Well… Black typeface and blue ink from the pen he'd sweet-talked from the waitress. He wondered if she would have handed the thing over if she'd known what he was going to sign.

Just looking at the Petition for Divorce made him wish he hadn't ordered anything to eat. Hadn't pushed his curiosity so far.

Nausea welled deep within him and he sucked down the rest of his ice water to try and rinse the taste away. His head began to shake back and forth. It looked wrong. Both their names on those papers. It *was* wrong. The best place for these papers was in a shredder or on top of a roaring fire.

The past few days working alongside Katie had been good. Really good. But she had shied away from any heart-to-heart business. Which was fair enough, but he was beginning to feel the strain. Two more days and he needed to call the hospital in Paris with an answer.

"Can I fill you up there, hon?" The waitress reappeared with a jug of water and Josh guiltily stuffed the papers into the inner pocket of his coat. No need to make her complicit in his need to experience everything firsthand.

"Mind if I join you?"

"Katie!" Josh's eyes near enough popped out of his head as his wife appeared behind the comfortably proportioned waitress.

"I see you've found the best grilled cheese in town." She slipped into the booth after making a *may I?* gesture and receiving a mute nod of assent.

"There are other places that serve them?"

"Not with pickles." She smiled, then conceded. "Not really. I can't imagine a Korean grilled cheese sandwich."

"Kimchi and Swiss on rye?"

They laughed, then fell silent. Josh linked his eyes with his wife's, wishing he could dive into them and find all the answers he needed.

"Are you stalking me?"

Katie screwed up her face in consternation. "No...this just happens to be the only place to get a good sandwich at—" She glanced at her watch. "At seven-thirty at night on the thirtieth of December."

"So you weren't worried I'd left town without signing your papers?" The words came out bitterly. He took another deep swig of ice water, feeling a shot of iceberg zap straight to his temples as he did.

"Oh, Josh." Katie's voice grew heavy with sorrow. "Do we really have to do this?"

He suddenly felt fatigue fill him like cement.

Yeah. We really do.

"What?" He maintained eye contact. She wasn't going to dodge him now. "You mean talk about why you walked out on me two years ago and why the only contact I've had from you is through a lawyer. Hell, yeah, we've got to talk about it, Katie! That's what adults who love each other do."

Her breath caught, as if she were going to contest him, and a moment passed before a sad smile hinged her lips downward. "Not in my family."

"Well, I'm not your parents. I'm your husband. And the second you ran off to marry me in Niagara Falls I became your family. Doesn't that count for anything?"

"Of course it does—*did*—Josh. It's just..." She shook her head at him, her eyes pleading for him to stop pressing.

"Just *what*?" He stopped himself just short of pounding the table with his fist. If he was going to hand over those papers, he had to know why.

"I just thought it would be easier if I went back to the

way things were before I met you." Her shoulders slumped and she looked away.

Josh's body straightened with a lightning bolt of undiluted indignation. "What does *that* mean?"

"It means that before I met you I was used to having no one to rely on. I didn't *need* anyone to get by."

"Is this because your parents weren't around?" he asked, already knowing the answer as dawn began to break in his thick-as-a-coconut husk of a head.

"Weren't. Aren't. Never will be," she droned, her fingers methodically folding a napkin into an ever-diminishing square.

"Why on earth would you have thought that about *me*?"

"Because you weren't there!"

"Of course I was."

"'I'm going up to the slopes with the guys, Katiebird.'" She mimicked him. "'Off to the track for a few rounds of speed cycling.' 'Heading up to Maine for the switchbacks.' 'Want to jump on the back of my motorcy—?'"

"Okay, okay." He held up his hands. "I get it." And did he ever? Especially when she got to the motorcycle part.

"And I guess…" She trailed off, her eyes filling with tears as she began micro-squaring another napkin.

"Hey…" He reached across the booth and stroked her cheek with his fingers. "What did you guess?"

"I guess I was scared that if—"

Her voice faltered and Josh took hold of her hand, rubbing the back of it with his thumb. Seeing her like this was torture.

"What were you scared of?"

"Josh!" She tugged her fingers through her hair in despair. "For a doctor, you really are thick as two planks, sometimes. Didn't you *see* it? I was terrified to get pregnant again because if losing one child had pushed you that far away, what would happen if I lost another? Or lost *you* to one of your crazy escapades? I just couldn't bear the thought of losing you, so I made the decision that I thought was best for both of us."

The words flew out as if they were all attached to the other in a long string.

Josh couldn't even speak. It hadn't occurred to him for a New York second that Katie had let him down. If anything, he'd felt he'd let *her* down. He was the one person who had been able to draw her out of her shell, make her laugh like a hyena, smile so broadly movie stars would have envied her…

"You know what, Katiebird?" He drew his finger along her jawline and kept it there when their eyes met. "If brains were leather I wouldn't have enough to saddle a June bug."

He felt her chin quiver. Tears…or a snigger?

"I have no idea what that means." She lifted her tear-beaded lashes to meet his gaze.

"I'm saying I don't have the sense Mother Nature gave a goose!"

"Cute Southern colloquialisms aren't helping to make what you're trying to say any clearer, Joshua West." But Katie giggled as she spoke.

"So you think I'm cute, do you?" He jostled her knee with his under the table.

"Maybe a little bit," she eventually conceded.

"Oh, really? And just how big is this little bit of cuteness you are affording me?"

"Maybe this much?" She allowed a pinch of air to pass between her fingers before closing them tight.

"That's pretty cute, if you ask me. My mama said I grew up on the far end of the ugly stick. Never said which end was which, though…" He picked up Katie's hand and put her fingers in a slightly wider pose. "Now, I don't want to go tootin' my own horn, but wouldn't you say *this* much is a bit more accurate?"

Katie gave him a sidelong glance, then burst into hysterics. His laughter was soon intermingling with hers, and it was only when their guffaws began to die out that she realized the handful of other patrons in the restaurant had been caught up in their chortle-fest as well.

"What are we doing here, Katiebird?"

"Apart from ordering grilled cheese sandwiches?"

"Yes, Katie," he replied good-naturedly. "Apart from that."

"Tying up loose ends?"

He shook his head at the same moment as she made a face at her own suggestion. It didn't sit right.

"Clearing the air?" he offered.

"Getting our facts straight," she said with a definitive nod, as if the matter were settled.

"Hi, hon—the usual?" The waitress appeared by their table.

"Yes, please, Eileen." Katie smiled up at her.

"You know—we *do* have a Brie and cranberry special on for the holidays."

"No, thank you."

Katie and Josh recoiled and responded as one, much to Eileen's obvious amusement.

"Funny how the only two people I've ever met who like dill pickles in their cheese sandwiches are sitting together." She gave the pair a *go figure* shrug and turned back to the kitchen without waiting for an explanation.

Josh looked over at his wife, saw her cheeks a bit flushed with emotion. It wasn't peculiar at all... They were the only thing she'd known how to cook when they'd met, so they'd eaten them. A lot.

"Have you already eaten?"

He nodded that he had, but didn't move. "Have you ever known me to turn down a chance to steal some of your dinner?"

She grinned and shook her head. He would stick around. Show his wife he was a changed man.

"Well, then. Prepare to defend your pickles!"

* * *

"Dr. West—" Michael ran to the door to catch Josh before he went to warm up the pickup. "Are you still good to meet up for that coffee?"

"Absolutely." Josh nodded, yanking up the zip on his snowboarding jacket before he hit the automatic doors. "Is it something we can chat about here at the hospital?"

"Uh, well…" Michael sent an anxious look over his shoulder back to the main reception desk, where Jorja and a couple of the shift nurses were laughing at who knew what. "Maybe not?"

Ding! Girl trouble.

"Got it." Josh put out a hand to fist-bump but Michael just looked confused. He lowered his hand. "I'm out tonight—but maybe sometime tomorrow?"

"Yeah!" Michael's grin widened. "That'd be great. Thanks, Doc." Michael raised his hand, then turned it into a fist, making a sort of weird revolution-style gesture.

"Tomorrow," Josh said with a grin, taking a hit of cold as the double doors parted to let in a blast of icy air.

He'd need a few minutes to get the truck ready in this weather. Beautiful to look at. A monumental challenge if you weren't where you were supposed to be.

"Are you ready for this?" Katie hauled herself into the truck and slammed the door against the cold wind.

"As I'll ever be."

Katie gave Josh a sidelong glance as he turned down Ol' Bessie's radio.

"It was a whole lot busier today than I thought."

"New Year's Eve!" Josh singsonged. "All the ailments people didn't want to pay heed to on the big day and the day after—and the day after that—building into a mother lode of excess straight up to the point of no return."

"I know," Katie agreed rigorously. "No amount of 'all things in moderation' speeches seem to stop everyone from going overboard on the holidays, and this year was no different!" she finished indignantly. Then she thought a moment.

Except on one front.

It was the first time she'd worked her way through patient after patient, case after case, and come out the other end feeling a sense of being whole again. Complete. She didn't need to visit Neurology to know what was going on. The wounds she'd thought she'd stitched together hadn't been ripped open when her husband had arrived in Copper Canyon. They had never been fixed in the first place— just hidden away and stuffed in a faraway corner that was too hard to reach. Leaving Josh behind was never going to bring Elizabeth back. Or her old life.

Who knew having Josh here would be more healing than she ever could have imagined it to be?

She couldn't help running her hands along the dashboard. "Check out this old jalopy! Still keeping her pristine, I see."

"Yup. I keep waiting for some movie producer to pull me over and offer me a million dollars to put her in a film, but it still hasn't happened."

She gave a barely contained snort. Ol' Bessie was the one thing in Josh's life he took care of, keeping her immaculate. She shook her head. That wasn't fair. He'd always taken care of her. But after Elizabeth…?

Her rigid belief that he'd gone off the deep end had shifted in the past few days. Maybe pushing life to the extreme had been his way of grieving. His way of trying to help her see the light at the end of the tunnel. She swallowed away the sting of tears and ran her finger along the trim of the red leather bench seats.

"Remember what you said to me on our first date?"

"You can sit here, right next to me." His hand patted the bench seat. Josh needed no time to remember.

"We hadn't even shared a soda or anything together."

"A *soda*?" Josh guffawed. "We weren't *twelve*, Katie-bird."

She'd felt twelve. All nerves and jittering expectations of the unknown. But when he'd looked at her…

Mmm…things had started pinging inside of her that she'd never known existed. Sparks, tingles, heated shivers—the whole bag of clichéd responses—each and every one of them feeling utterly fresh and new.

So when they'd discovered they both had some time off, and he'd asked her if she wanted a day out in the countryside, she'd pulled together all her courage and said yes.

Josh had been everything she'd admired in a man and in a doctor. He'd been a year into his residency, having just blasted through his junior residency, and she'd been on the first stint of her rotational internship. He'd had confidence, an infectious laugh, a genuine connection with his patients…and a drawl from somewhere down South that had lit her up like a—she smiled—like the big ball in Times Square on New Year's Eve.

Josh barked a laugh into the cab—with a puff of breath that disappeared shortly after.

"What?"

"You barely even acknowledged me when I held open Ol' Bessie's cherry-red passenger door for you. Me being all gallant and gentlemanly, and your big brown eyes were fixed on the dash, the road, the crazy bright scarlet, orange and yellow blur of the leaves we were flashing past as we left Boston. I thought I might've woken up with the chicken pox or something and not noticed."

He glanced over to see Katie smile at the memory and he patted her leg.

"But three days later you didn't stop talking, did you?"

She shook her head no. It was true. And he was the only thing she'd had eyes for.

She looked across at his hands—one loosely resting on top of the steering wheel, the other holding on at three o'clock. He looked relaxed enough, but she could see his thoughts were about as busy as hers were. On her parents? On the rings she still hadn't managed to take off her finger?

She kept her eyes on his hands, wondering how much the past couple of years had truly changed him. She still hadn't worked up the courage to ask him about those scars. What if what he had been through made him someone she could no longer truly access? That was what it had felt like in that awful dark year. Why would he risk his own life again and again when they'd just lost their tiny precious baby?

Josh would argue that no one changed—they just became more of who they had always been, just a bit smarter about things.

She'd changed. She was sure of it.

Her head tipped against the cool of the window. If she was brave enough to ask, Josh would probably say she hadn't changed—she'd just reverted back to the introvert he'd pulled out of her cocoon that magical first year in Boston. Her butterfly year.

"Are you having an entire conversation in your head again?"

Katie couldn't help but give him a congratulatory laugh. "Got it in one!" Then she surprised herself by chasing it up with a wistful sigh. She'd forgotten the comforting side of having someone know her inside and out.

"Something like that. Remember when—" she started, then hesitated. Memory lane could be a rough road to travel. Especially this time of year.

"The apples?" He shot her a quick look, before refocusing on the road.

How did he do *that?*

"Yes…the apples. What was it—three or four bushels we took down to your grandmother's for canning?"

"I think it was more like five. You were on a high-speed race—dodging all of my clumsy attempts to catch you up in a sexy clinch—so I did the only thing I could!"

"Oh, yeah? And what was that?"

"I had to win you over with my apple-picking prowess!" He dropped her a quick wink, his eyes barely leaving the road as he did.

"Ha!" Katie barked out. "Don't be ridiculous. I didn't know you were trying to kiss me."

"Course you did, Katiebird." His voice was soft now. Gentle. "You were just scared of what would happen once I caught you."

She had been terrified. Her whole life she had always been in control. Of everything. It had been easier that way. Easier to understand why her parents had never been around. Easier to zone in on a high-stakes medical career, knowing she could harness her mind and shape her ability to learn into an aptitude to heal. If she let herself fall for Josh, it would be a whole different ball game. Whole different park. She'd known then that she would never be able to control her heart once she gave it to him. And from the increased hammering she was feeling in her chest, it still held true.

She narrowed her eyes and slid them over to the driver's side of the cab to take in Josh's profile. Her tummy did its usual trip to the acrobatics department. Gold medalists had nothing on her!

All of a sudden she hurt inside. Hurt so much she could actually put a name to it. *Regret.* She regretted making Josh decide between adrenaline fixes or her. Regretted packing her bags and hightailing it without even scribbling a note to explain. Leaving him to grieve on his own.

She twisted the rings on her finger. She still hadn't quite managed to put them back in their box. The rings she had accepted with a vow to love Josh until her very last breath.

"I don't think I've ever seen Gramma Jam-Jam look

more surprised than when we pulled into the drive." Josh's quiet voice and soft laughter broke into the silence filling the cab.

"What?" Katie exclaimed, tucking a foot under her leg on the bench seat as she turned to face him. "You told me she was expecting us."

"You believed me?"

"Of course I did!" Katie insisted. "People don't just *spontaneously* drive down the Eastern Seaboard to their grandmother's to can and preserve and…"

"Uh-huh?" Josh started nodding, the smile on his face growing. "It's coming to you now, isn't it?"

Little ding-ding-dings of recognition started going off in Katie's head, and her eyes widened as each detail began to slip into a new place. "She set me to peeling and coring all of those apples, saying she needed your signature on something down at the bank in town. It was a Sunday."

"Yes, it was. We couldn't believe you fell for it, what with you being a highfalutin valedictorian and all!"

"*You* were a valedictorian!" Katie protested, fingers digging into the leather seat as Josh took a right turn onto the small lane that brought them up the side of the mountain to her parents' place.

"Doesn't count as much when you're in a class of one hundred in a town that wasn't too much bigger." He reached across and gave her leg a squeeze. "Lucky for me you were too blinded by my good looks to pay any attention."

"Ha! As if!" Katie lied.

"Don't go playing coy with me, Katherine McGann."

He withdrew his hand and Katie immediately slipped her own over the spot on her thigh to keep the warmth in.

"Well…that might've been a little bit true. And when your grandmother assigned someone a task—you did it!"

"That is most definitely the truth! Gramma Jam-Jam was a tough taskmaster!" Josh's laugh ended with a sigh.

"I am really sorry to hear she's passed."

"Yeah…well…" Josh drove on for a while before filling the cab with a big laugh. "Lucky for me she had no problem with white lies if the intent behind them was loving."

"What do you mean?"

"Once you were peeling all those bushels of apples, she and I set off like wildcats, scraping the shelves clean of jars, pie tins and whatever else I needed to bribe my grandmother into helping me win your heart."

"She did that, sure enough."

"She did…?" Josh's voice deepened with emotion. "Or I did?"

"Both of you," Katie answered hastily. Then, "You did." It was the more honest answer. "Of course you did."

Her mobile phone jangled, breaking the weighted atmosphere in two.

"It's my mom. Sorry." She winced apologetically as she pressed the button. "Hi, Mom—what's up?"

Josh couldn't make out what Katie's mother was saying, which didn't much matter as everything rattling round his head was making a big enough racket.

Katie still loved him. His wife still loved him.

Was that enough to bring them back together or had time just been too cruel? Maybe knowing she loved him would be salve enough for him to carry on. Go forward. Let each of them get on with lives that could never be the same if they were together.

"You *forgot*?"

Katie's voice had careened up a few octaves.

"Mom, not even five days have passed since you asked us. How could you forget?"

She listened in silence, then gave a brusque "goodbye" before jabbing a finger at her phone to end the call.

"Typical."

"What?"

"My parents are out tonight."

"Better offer?"

"Something like that."

"Are they in town?"

"They're at someone else's condo in the complex. 'Too good an invitation to refuse.'" Katie expertly mimicked her mother's mid-Atlantic accent, then huffed out an exasperated sigh. "I don't know why I let it get to me. Why I didn't *expect* it! You'd think after thirty-one years of being dodged by my own parents I'd be used to it."

"Is that how you see it?"

"That's how it *is*! Whenever I really needed them to just *be* there—nothing else—there was always an excuse. Always something 'too good to miss' for them to go to."

Her words hit home. He wondered if things would have been different between them if he'd let Katie go through a phase of wallowing in dirty pajamas, with a sink full of dishes growing God knew what kind of mold. It had killed him to see her so low, and he'd all but turned into a parody of himself to try and cheer her up.

It was also pretty obvious that Katie had learned some less-than-awesome tricks from her parents. Leaving him on his own when he'd begun to run out of false cheer and had needed her most.

His shoulders sagged. She hadn't known. He'd had just as thick a veneer of protectiveness over his emotions as Katie had over her numbness. Grief had rendered them both loners. She hadn't been avoiding him for the past two years out of malice. It had been out of grief.

"They should've had to apply for a license," Katie grumbled.

"What kind of license?"

"A baby license."

"What do you mean?"

"You have to get a dog license, don't you?"

"Yes…"

"Well, there are countless people out there in the world who actually want children and don't get them—and my parents have a child and don't give a flying pig!"

Josh took his eyes off the road, reaching out to put a hand on Katie's leg.

When he felt the front wheels of the truck start to skid, he instantly regretted not giving the road his full attention. Black ice. He resisted putting his foot on the brake. Drove into the skid. Everything the rulebook said.

"Josh!"

He fought the urge to overcorrect. And still the truck slid. He reached out his arm to brace Katie against the crash. She had on her seat belt but she would always be his responsibility. And in the blink of an eye, that lightning flash loss of control ended in an abrupt thud and a jerk as the truck lodged itself into a roadside snowdrift.

"Are you all right?"

They spoke simultaneously.

"Yes. Are you?"

It happened again.

They both laughed, their breath huffing out into the cold cab of the truck in tiny clouds of confirmation that they had both made it. They were okay.

Before he thought better of it, Josh unbuckled himself and his wife, pulling Katie into his arms, holding her tighter than he ever had. He felt her arms come together round his waist, slipping up along his back and pulling him close. Despite the layers of winter clothes, he could have sworn he felt heat move between the two of them, tightening the bond of connection he had feared was severed.

"That was a bit scary." Katie's muffled voice came from the crook of his neck, where she had nestled.

"It was a bit, wasn't it?" He stroked his hand along her hair, giving in to the desire to weave his fingers through it, enjoying the sensation of silk against skin. "We're all right, Katiebird. We're all right now."

Talk about a loaded statement!

He tugged her in a bit closer, not having a clue *what* they were. Together? Apart? Wrapping things up for good or starting afresh?

Whichever way the wind blew, he would be forever grateful for having her in his arms right now. Feeling her nestle into him a bit more, not pushing him away, hearing their breathing steady a bit. The skid and the jolting snowdrift stop had been a shock. Not a horrible one. But one that needed this sort of quiet recovery time.

He was surprised to discover that his fingers had taken on a will of their own and had shifted beneath the pashmina Katie had tied loosely round her neck. They were slipping up and along her neck, just to the base of her hairline, massaging away any stress or worry. As his awareness of her response to his caresses grew, so did the depth of their breathing. They weren't in their own worlds any longer.

Katie felt Josh spread his fingers wide along her back, fluidly changing the movement into slow circular caresses. Each change of pressure quickened her pulse. The ache of desire overrode her need to intellectualize the moment. She tilted up her chin and after a microscopic hesitation her lips met his.

The explosion of sensation all but overwhelmed her. Heat, scent, taste… Everything was accentuated. Her heartbeat accelerated as the fulfillment from each kiss deepened. Josh's touch felt simultaneously familiar and forbidden. Familiar after the years of shared history. Forbidden because of the deep well of pleasure she felt at his touch. Pleasure she didn't feel she deserved.

As their lips touched and explored, Katie felt as though her body was going through a reawakening. Where she had felt exhausted and dark, she now felt charged and vibrant. Where she had felt deep, weighted sorrow, she now began to feel possibility and renewal. Where she had felt numb…she now felt love.

Her fingers pressed into her husband's shoulders as their breath intermingled in searching kiss after kiss. When it seemed as though time had all but stood still, she felt him pull back. She felt the loss of his embrace instantly and it struck her how time and again over their courtship and marriage Josh had been nothing short of her pillar of strength. Almost shyly, she looked up to meet his blue eyes.

"Look at us, steaming up the windows like a couple of high school kids." Josh's voice was light, but the mood in the truck was laden with meaning. Past, present, future… too much to think about. Too much to consider.

Katie suddenly began to feel claustrophobic in the cab. "We should probably see if we can get the truck out of the drift in case anyone else comes along this road." She pushed open the door, surprised to find it resisting.

"I think we're wedged up against the bank. Come on out my side. We'll have a look."

Josh was reaching across her as he spoke, flicking open the glove compartment, raking around by touch as there had never been a cab light in the old truck. She drew back in the seat, surprised at how Josh's touch suddenly had become something to avoid. Having his warm body all but wrapped around her just moments ago had been like accepting a vital life force, but now that her brain had taken a few moments to play catch-up, she was treating the poor man like he was toxic. It wasn't fair. To either of them.

He tugged a flashlight out of the glove box, clicking the beam off and on as he pulled back into the driver's seat. "Guess that's us in action."

His voice sounded unchanged. Had he not noticed her flinch at his touch, or was he choosing to ignore it—his modus operandi of The Dark Days.

"Can we just get out of here?" Katie knew she sounded

impatient, but she didn't have the wherewithal to edit herself. "I feel like a sitting target."

In more ways than one.

"Not a problem." He stepped aside as she clambered out of the truck—a bit less gracefully than she'd intended, but suddenly a deep breath of icy air was paramount. She let the sharpness of the cold hit her lungs hard—hold her static for a moment and then release her with a billow of breath.

"You all right?" Josh's voice was all concern, but his focus was on the front of the truck—the front half of which was soundly encased in the snowdrift, as if it had been put there before the winter had begun.

She mumbled an affirmative, working her hands round herself and giving her arms a rub as she looked around at the quiet lane, surprised at how much she could see without streetlights. It was snowing lightly. And it was peaceful. So incredibly quiet and *peaceful.*

In any other circumstances it would have been romantic. She silently chided herself. Less than a minute ago it had been romantic! Passionate, even. How could five days have changed how she saw the world? As she thought the words, she knew they were ridiculous. Ten minutes could have an impact. Even less and your life could change forever. For better...or for worse.

She heard Josh crunching through the snow around the truck. "What's the damage?"

"Doesn't seem to be too much wrong with the truck—but I doubt we're going to get out of here without a tow truck. Unless you feel like digging it out of this eight-foot snowbank?"

"Seriously?" *Okay.* Her voice really couldn't have gone more high-pitched than it just had. Dogs would be howling soon.

"Sorry, Katie." Josh shrugged. "This gingerbread truck has well and truly crumbled."

"I don't know how you do that." Katie shook her head.

"What?"

"Not go mental over Ol' Bessie being near enough to-taled."

"Accidents happen. Life goes on." He shrugged it off.

Cool Hand Josh! One of the many reasons why she had married him. Her very own cowboy—calm, cool, and kicking the back tires on his truck.

"Does that make it work faster?"

"Yes," he answered drily, giving the tire another kick just to prove to her that the total opposite was true.

Katie couldn't stop a burst of giggles from burbling forth. His eyes met hers—and the familiar deep punch of connection put her insides through another spin cycle.

Okay, girl—time to decide if we're playing hot or cold. Time to stop playing.

"What are you doing here, Josh?"

"I could ask you just about the same thing, Katiebird." He leaned against the back of the pickup, one leg crossed over the other—his body language as stress-free as if he were talking about a bowling league.

"I *live* here." Her emotional temperature shot up.

"No, you don't." He tilted his chin up in the classic guy move. "You hide out in your parents' chalet—where, I would put money on it, you haven't done a single thing other than unpack your clothes."

Guilty.

She clamped her lips tight. What *was* this? A standing-up psychoanalysis session?

"When anything approaching life comes to your door, you hide out in your work, just like you've always done."

"No, I don't!"

Wow. Good comeback. Someone has playground patter down to a fine art.

She threw in a glare for good measure.

"Look, Katie. I don't want to fight."

"*I* don't want to fight!" she shouted back. Hmm…

Maybe she did. And why not? They were stuck out here in the middle of nowhere, with nothing but a truck stuck in a mammoth snowdrift, and…and… Inspiration hit. She scooped up a handful of snow faster than she'd ever done, crunched it into a ball and threw it at him. It landed on his chest with a satisfying thud.

"Feel better?"

"A little."

She sniffed, thought for a moment about using her sleeve, then sniffed again. Usually she was the one who got to play the grown-up. What was up with this role-reversal thing?

Another little marker went up in her Things-That-Are-Different-About-Josh list.

"Should we get a tow truck out here?"

"I'll call. What road are we on again?" She hadn't been paying attention. She'd been too busy making doe eyes at the man she was meant to have hardened her heart to.

"You're going to laugh."

"I doubt it." Being petulant wasn't making much of an impact on her grinning husband.

"Guess."

"No."

"C'mon, Katie. What do you *think* the road's called?" He drew her name out all slow and Southern-style, as if he were skittering the vowels down the back of her sweater with a revitalizing handful of snow. Verbal retaliation for her juvenile attack?

"I don't know. Rudolph Place?"

"Christmas Lane."

"It is *not*!" she retorted, swiping at the air between them.

"Sure is." He looked at his phone screen, where she could see him increasing the size of their location on his map app. "And if my map-reading is still as good as it was in the Scouts…we've got Christmas Farm up ahead, about a mile. Unsurprisingly, they sell Christmas trees."

"You can tell that from a map?"

He turned the screen so she could see it. A little bubble ad had popped up over the satellite image, with "Christmas Tree Farm" on it and their opening hours.

Ah. So he wasn't all-knowing. Just *mostly* all-knowing.

An image of an admissions form pinged into her mind. "That's where the Klausens live! I thought they'd made that up."

"You doubted the rosy-cheeked and extremely jolly Mr. and Mrs. Klausen's good word?" Josh teased.

"Yes." She scrunched up her face. "But you always knew I was a Scrooge."

"I knew nothing of the kind, my little Katiebird."

She didn't say anything in return. Couldn't. He knew more about her than anyone in the world. He'd been the only one she had well and truly let in.

"Look—there's a chapel just a couple of hundred yards down the road. We can hang out there. Safer than here in the pitch-black. Have you called a tow truck?"

Katie shook her head and blew on her fingers. "Let me grab my bag. I've got an automobile emergency services card in there."

"Prepared for everything, aren't you, Katie?"

"What's that supposed to mean?" She wheeled on him, handbag swinging around and banging into her hip as she struck a defensive pose.

It wasn't her fault she had had to behave as a grown-up for most of her childhood, let alone after the death of their daughter, when Josh had rediscovered his inner teenager.

"Nothing," Josh replied, fatigue suddenly evident in his voice. "It didn't mean anything. Should we start walking to the chapel while you call them so we don't get cold?"

Katie rang the company, only just managing to keep the bite out of her voice when she discovered they were short-staffed and the wait would be a while. Everyone had bad days. She and Josh were no different. And compared to what they'd been through in the past, this was a doddle.

They crunched along the side of the road in silence, Josh holding no particular path with the beam of his flashlight. It illuminated an icicle-laden tree here. A slushy puddle there. A thickening of the snow in the air all around them. The silence of the snowy night began to close in on Katie. More accurately, the silence between *them*. Between her and the man she had thanked her lucky stars she'd met all those years ago.

Without warning she suddenly flung herself into a snow-drift and began moving her arms and legs as rapidly as she could. She needed a snow angel—and fast.

Josh had been so wrapped up in his own thoughts he'd walked on a few steps before realizing Katie was no longer by his side. When he turned round, he hooted with unchecked laughter. There was his proper-as-they-come wife, looking like a frenzied wild woman. This was going to be the least peaceful snow angel ever created. Snow Tasmanian devil?

Katie abruptly stopped swinging her arms and legs, her eyes locked on Josh so intently it felt like a make-or-break moment. He opened his mouth, then shut it again.

Katie's hand shot out. "Aren't you going to help me up?"

"Of course."

He reached out his arm and felt himself being yanked into the snowdrift. His boot slipped on a skid of snow Katie had smoothed into angel submission and he fell with a thud onto his bad hip.

Containing the howl of pain was impossible.

"Josh!" Katie pushed herself up, a horrified expression playing across her face. "Are you all right?" She began issuing instructions. "Lie back. Breathe steadily. Follow my finger."

He batted away her hand. "I'm fine." He was still hurting and just needed a minute.

"Josh!" Katie's voice broke as her fingers ran along his cheek. "I'm so sorry. I didn't mean to hurt you."

"You didn't."

Yes, she had. But not in the way she thought.

He could be mean right now. Cruel. Because that was what it had felt like when she'd left him. Just about the cruelest thing anyone had done. But he'd known Katie hadn't left to hurt him. She'd done it to save herself. Save herself from a man who'd seemed intent on self-destruction. And here was a sign of that self-destruction for her to bear witness to.

Terrific. Everything going according to the Great Win Back Katie Plan? That's one big fat tick.

He smoothed his hand along his hip and gave it a rub, made sure everything was still in place. Ditto for the knee.

"Help me up?"

"Of course." Katie scrambled to her knees, shifting a shoulder under his to help him up from the snow. "What happened there?"

"Just lost my—" He stopped himself. No more lies. "I had an accident."

He felt Katie tense beneath the weight of his arm, but she just mmm-hmm'd him and waited for him to continue as they both pushed upward.

He took his arm off her shoulders when they were standing and gave himself a little wriggle of a once-over. Head, shoulders, knees and toes all in working order. Haphazard as they were.

He tipped his head in the direction of the chapel. "Shall we get in the warm?"

"Do you need a hand?"

He couldn't tell if she was furious or concerned. Probably both.

He shook his head and they walked on in silence. Josh concentrated on working the kinks out of his hip as Katie visibly struggled with the thousands of questions that were no doubt playing through her mind. She'd begged him again and again not to get hurt. Told him that she didn't have the strength for it. And here he was—giving her evidence that her decision to leave because he was too hell-bent on pushing the envelope had been the right one.

"So…" Katie prompted, unable to wait anymore. "This accident. Was it a bad one?"

"Something like that," he admitted, ignoring her exasperated sigh. "I'll tell you everything you want to know. I just need to sit down for a minute, all right?"

The chapel came into view as they turned the corner. It was a pretty little thing. Clapboard, white as the snow, with a green trim, he thought, though it was difficult to tell in the dark. Twists of fairy lights had been spun round the two evergreens flanking the front door to the chapel, and there was enough snow on the steps to tell him no one had been inside for the past few hours. A large and intricate star was shining at the very top of the church. He would have laid money on it being visible near enough everywhere in the valley.

Katie stepped up onto the entryway first and gave a relieved smile when the door opened. "Thank goodness for small-town security systems."

"I don't know if Gramma Jam-Jam even had keys."

"She had neighbors. Same as keys. Were you…?" Katie hesitated.

He shook his head, knowing where the question was heading. "I wasn't with her. One of my biggest regrets."

A huge mistake not worth making again.

"I'm sorry," Katie said with genuine feeling. "I know how much you loved her."

"Yeah, well…I seem to be chalking up valuable lessons left, right and center these days."

They stood face-to-face, there in the quiet of the church, their eyes saying more to each other than they could ever say aloud. Love. Pain. Regret. Josh could have ticked them off one by one and kept going. He hadn't been joking. All he needed to do now was prove he had learned from those mistakes.

"Let's go light a couple of candles."

"What?"

"C'mon. Over here." He tipped his head toward the far corner. "Let's go light candles for Gramma and Elizabeth. We've never done that together."

Katie eyed the end of the church where the candle table stood, her head making the tiniest of shakes back and forth.

He wove his fingers through hers. "C'mon, darlin'. Isn't it time we sent our little girl some light—seeing as we're together? Sent her a blessing at Christmas?"

"I don't *want* to say goodbye!" Katie's words all but echoed through the small church.

Josh pulled her into his arms and held her tight. "It's not goodbye, Katie. I didn't say anything about goodbye." He pressed a soft kiss onto her forehead before holding her back at arm's length so he could look at her. "Think of it as her mother and father saying hello. Letting her know we'll always love her."

Katie began to nod her head. Slowly at first, and then in a pronounced yes. She would never, ever in her heart be able to bid her daughter farewell. But hello? She could say that again and again. And yet without Josh she hadn't been able to say anything to her daughter. It hadn't seemed possible. And now here he was—her big ol' country husband—making the hardest thing in the world one of the simplest and most beautiful.

Hand in hand they approached the small table. Josh lit a candle for his grandmother, and then both of them lit Elizabeth's. As the flame flickered and gained purchase, Katie felt an emotional weight shift from her chest—the light of the flame was offering her a lightness of spirit she wouldn't have believed possible.

The moment lengthened and absorbed them both in its glow. Katie tipped her head onto Josh's shoulder and felt his head lightly meet hers. They'd both lost their little girl. It was right that they were doing this together.

As they watched the candle flicker and flit alongside the one meant for the woman who would have been her great-grandmother, Katie could almost picture Gramma Jam-Jam up there in heaven—wherever *that* was—teaching Elizabeth how to make apple pie. As she swiped away a wash of tears, she was astonished to realize there was a soft smile on her lips.

Was this what it took? Being together with Josh again? Josh, who *still* hadn't told her why he had howled like an injured wolf when he fell into the snow.

"Right!" Katie clapped her hands together a bit too loudly. "Shall we take a pew? Hear all about this big bad accident of yours?"

Josh's heart squeezed tight as he heard her trying to lighten the atmosphere. He was surprised she wasn't a fuming ball of I-Told-You-So.

He wandered a few aisles down and chose a pew, patting the space next to him for Katie.

She sat down next to him, but kept her eyes on the front of the church, where garlands were still strung across the apse. A simply but beautifully decorated Christmas tree twinkled away in the half-light.

"It was a motorcycle accident."

Katie sucked in a sharp breath and tightened her jaw. If the light had been better, he would have seen if those were tears that had sprung to her eyes or if it was just the wintry light.

He reached across to take her hand, and though she didn't turn to meet his gaze, he was relieved to feel the soft squeeze of her fingers. He had to keep reminding himself…she cared. She loved him. She might not like him very much—especially right now—but she loved him. It was worth fighting for.

The words began to pour out. "It was meant to be a Saturday-morning ride. Just a few guys out for a run—before traffic built up."

"But…?"

"But it got competitive. The roads were tricky. In the mountains up north of Boston."

He saw Katie wince. She knew the ones. They'd used to take breaks up there whenever their hectic hospital schedules would allow. When she'd finally taken those first days of maternity leave.

"We were riding the switchbacks and a logging truck came down the center of both lanes. It was veer or—"

He didn't need to paint the full picture. She was an intelligent woman. Move or get mashed was what it had boiled down to. And he'd moved.

"No one else was hurt, so there was that to be thankful for, and one of the guys was an EMT—he made sure I kept my—"

"Kept your what?" Katie whipped round to face him, tears streaming down her cheeks.

He brushed them away with a thumb. "My left leg. It's good. He knew every trick in the book. I hit some dark moments during recovery, and going through airport security is a bit of a bells and whistles affair these days—but I'm all good, Katie. I'm here."

"How long were you in the hospital?"

Josh sucked in a breath as he did the mental arithmetic. "About seven months. Maybe eight."

"ICU?"

"For a lot of it."

"Internal damage?"

"Some."

Katie's fingers flew to her mouth. *Josh could have died.*

He could have died and she would have been none the wiser. She'd left no address, no clue as to where to find her. Strict instructions with Alice never to speak of him again. Nothing. For a moment she thought she was going to be sick.

"What happened when you got out?"

"I roomed with a few guys. Doctors. Long enough to know what an idiot I was to let you walk out the door."

"And your motorcycle?" She registered his words, but needed more facts.

"Hung up my helmet, sold the Jet Ski, my snowboard— you name it. I realized life was a bit more important than what I'd been calling living after you left." He laughed. "You'll love this."

Her eyes widened. What exactly would she love about her husband's traumatic motorcycle accident and harrowing recovery?

"I've taken up yoga."

He watched her take in this new slice of information then reshape her face into something a whole lot happier.

"You're going to *yoga class*?"

All right. It was a tone of pure disbelief. But he'd take that over a telling-off for the motorcycle crash any day of the week.

"Three times a week. Sometimes four!"

"In Boston?"

"No, Katie."

He cleared his throat. Spilling this piece of news was going to be almost as rough as telling her about his accident.

"What?" She poked him in the arm. *"What?"*

She poked him harder when his eyes started taking an unnecessary journey round the small church. It was clapboard. There were pews. And a Christmas tree. *C'mon, already!*

"I can tell when you're holding back information. Where have you been? What happened to our—the house?"

"I rented it out."

"What? Why?" She pulled her hand out of his, clasping her two hands together over her heart.

"Are you kidding me?" Now it was Josh's turn to look astonished. "Live there without you? Sit in those rooms knowing the chances of you walking back through the front door were nil to—?" He sought for a word that meant less than nil and threw his hands up in the air instead. "There was no chance of me staying there once you walked out that door, Katie. Absolutely none."

She suddenly missed her nickname. It had rankled when he'd first used it, but now...why wasn't he? *Wasn't she his Katiebird anymore?*

Her stomach churned and she could feel her hands shake even though she was pressing them tightly together.

Was he finishing things between them?

She blinked and stared, her body and mind not comprehending what exactly it was Josh was saying to her. She felt the backs of his fingers shift away a stray lock of hair, then give her cheek a gentle stroke, and she watched his lips as he continued to speak.

"My life was with you, Katiebird, and then you—you left. What else was I meant to do?"

Katie's eyes shifted back up to Josh's and she just stared at him, hands still clasped as if they were the only things holding her thumping heart inside her chest. *She had left him.* She'd thought of it as saving herself, but in doing so had she destroyed Josh? Her eyes took in his beautiful face, the strong shoulder line, the chest she'd used as a pillow more than once.

The pounding in her heart began to drown out what Josh was saying. She could see him speaking, but the words weren't computing.

Okay. Regroup.

Katie ripped through the index cards in her mind to make sense of things. Reorder what she had believed to be true. Reimagine the last two years.

It hit her—almost physically—that what had enabled her to run away was the knowledge that Josh would always be there. In her mind's eye she had vividly kept Josh on the porch of their sweet little house, with its tiny little porch and tinier backyard, where their daughter would be old enough to ride on a swing about now. How they would have got a swing into the backyard was beyond her, but if anyone in the world would go to any lengths to make his little girl happy, it was Josh.

Leaving had been self-preservation for her—but in saving herself had she destroyed Josh? She swallowed. This was going to be so much harder than she'd imagined.

"If you haven't been in Boston, where have you been?"

CHAPTER NINE

JOSH TOOK KATIE'S hand between both of his and tugged it over into his lap, forcing her to scooch in closer to him. Were they going to do this? They were going to *do* this. There would be a serious amount of beans spilled tonight.

They both felt her pager go off at the same time. Mutual looks of dismay passed between them as Katie pulled back and unearthed her pager from beneath the snow coat, the sweater and finally her tank top.

She took a glance at the small screen, then immediately dialed in to the ER. A few "Yup…yup…" then a rattling of satellite coordinates and a "Got it…" later, she stuffed the phone back into her bag.

"We've got to go." Her expression was pure business now.

"Tow truck should be here any minute."

She shook her head. "No. It will take too long and we have to go by helicopter anyhow. Did you notice an open field near where the truck hit? We're going to have to meet it there in five."

"Helicopter? We?" he repeated, as if he hadn't heard either of the words before.

"We are going on a helicopter to help a woman give birth on a gondola."

"A *gondola*? When did Copper Valley become Venice?"

Katie snapped her fingers before tugging up the zipper

on her winter coat. "Earth to Josh! The gondolas that go from the ski resort down to Main Street! Copper Canyon's ingenious way to transport its punters to and from the valley has broken and there is a woman in labor. You've got to help her."

"Me?" Now Josh was fully alert.

"Yes," Katie answered perfunctorily, turning toward the door. "I don't do deliveries. Not since…" She skipped over the explanation. "A tree hit the power lines and took out the power for the gondolas. They're trying to get a generator up there, but that could take hours—"

"Wait a minute," he interrupted. "How are you suggesting I get myself up to this gondola if it's dangling somewhere between Copper Peak and the Valley?"

"You'll get winched down."

"No." Josh shook his head. He wasn't being contrary. He just couldn't do it.

"They're short-staffed at the hospital, Josh. You've done a run in Maternity. You did more winchman training than anyone I can call. Who else do you suggest perform the obstetrics on this?"

"You." There wasn't even a hint of a waver in his voice. "You're stronger than I am."

"And with the metalwork in my hip and leg, I *don't* get winched into airborne gondolas. I'm not up to the gymnastics. *You* are."

"But—!" Katie didn't even know how to finish her protestation. Every rug she'd believed had been cushioning her feet just a few days ago was being ripped out from under her.

"But what, Katie?"

Josh had her full attention now. Medical emergencies were not something she was wishy-washy about, and something wasn't sitting right.

"I haven't been able to do a delivery since—"

There was no need for her to finish the sentence. They both knew what she was talking about.

"Right." He took her hand in his and headed for the door, already hearing the distant hum of the helicopter on approach. "Today's going to be the day that changes."

Ten minutes later Katie and Josh were watching the ground disappear beneath them as they hustled themselves into flight jumpsuits, secured their helmets and rapidly scanned the small body of the search and rescue helicopter the hospital shared with the emergency services. Bare-bones equipment and no spare staff. It was suck-it-up-and-get-on-with-it o'clock.

Katie had been in the helicopter loads of times over the past year—but tonight everything was blurring. Katie the control freak had...lost control.

"Dr. McGann, we're about four minutes out. How are your headsets working?"

"I can hear you," she confirmed to the young pilot. Jason. His name was Jason. She knew that. She knew *him*. All of this was familiar. Just not the part about going to help a woman give birth in a broken gondola, hanging who knew how many meters in the sky—?

"Dr. West?"

"I'm ready if you are."

Josh's words were meant for the pilot, but Katie could feel his eyes all but lasering through her.

"Jason, what's the word from the crew who are working on the gondola? No chance of getting them down the normal route?"

"'Fraid not, Doc. It's midway between the resort and the valley—right over the Canyon. So we're looking at maybe..." He paused to calculate. "We're looking at a one-thousand-foot drop."

"Three hundred meters...ish. Not too far." Josh's eyes twinkled, making the number seem less horrifying.

His face told a completely different story from the man who had given up speed thrills for yoga. *This* was the sort of rescue he was made for. During their residency he had all but wrestled his way to the roof every time there'd been a helicopter callout. Adrenaline junkie or not—he was the person she was going to have to put all her trust in today.

Tomorrow? There wasn't time to go there.

She let Josh's steadying voice trickle through her headphones and into her heart as he rattled out statistics and tips. It was obvious what he was doing and she wasn't going to stop him. He was pulling out his "Calm Down Katie" arsenal.

"Want to talk through scenarios?"

"A lot of this is dependent upon that door being open, Doc," Jason piped in.

"Isn't there an emergency release inside?" Katie's heart rate spiked again.

"Yes—but I'm not sure they would've figured it out. From the phone calls, they are sounding pretty stressed."

"How long has the mother been in labor?" Josh's voice cut through to the quick of the matter.

"They reckon she started about three, maybe four hours ago?"

"Dilation?" Katie only just stopped herself from cringing as she waited for the answer.

"Not a clue. We're both going into this dark, Dr. McGann. Speaking of which—there are night-vision goggles. You both should put them on."

"What about once we lower Dr. McGann down? How will they work in the snow?"

"Not good." Jason didn't mince his words. "There's a couple of head torches. Better bring those down to work in the gondola."

"Hang on!" interjected Katie. "Aren't we going to strap her into the stretcher and bring her straight up?"

"All depends upon what you find, my love."

Josh leaned forward, elbows on knees, bright blue eyes glued to hers, his fingers making a lay-them-on-me gesture. She complied, slipping her hands across his broad palms, but part of her wanted to do nothing more than retreat. Trust a man who had pushed life so far he'd nearly died?

His fingers wrapped round hers, heat shifting from his hands up into her body. And then the lightbulb pinged on with full wattage. She loved Josh. Heart and soul. The last few days had reawakened that knowledge in her beyond any reasonable doubt. But he was the same man who had tested her and tested her when she had been beyond fragile. Did loving him mean putting away her fears from the past and learning to trust again?

"If you look up to your right, you can see the gondola— Wait. I think there are two. That might be the reason for the accident."

Katie and Josh shifted in their seats, craning to see what Jason was describing.

"Is anyone talking to the couple?"

"Someone at the hospital, I think. Want me to patch you in?"

Katie nodded, before remembering she needed to confirm verbally. Josh had shifted across the helicopter floor and started organizing the winch clips.

"What are you doing?"

"Getting you clipped up and ready to go down." Josh dropped her a fortifying wink. "You've got this, my little multitasker. You can listen and clip up at the same time."

And so she did. As her fingers busied themselves with the spring-gated hooks that would secure her rescue kit and the stretcher, she tuned in to the voice of a man describing his wife's labor pains to— Who was that? Jorja? Jorja was on the other end of the line. Good. She was solid.

Katie listened, methodically tugging her straps into place, checking and double-checking the hooks and clips, until she heard the words "I can see something—but I don't think it's the baby's head. Is that all right?"

"It sounds to me as if your baby is in the breech position, Mr. Penton." Jorja confirmed Katie's suspicion.

"We're just about there, Dr. McGann. You ready to go?"

Her eyes met Josh's. Heaven knew what he saw in there. Eight years of shared history? Three years of pain? Whatever it was, it spoke to him deeply. A sheen of emotion misted his eyes for a millisecond, and then just as quickly he was back to business.

"I've got enough fuel to hold here for ten to fifteen. If you think you're going to be any longer, let me know ASAP—so I can get back and refuel."

"Right." Katie put on her medical tunnel vision. Fifteen minutes. Breech birth. In a gondola stuck over a canyon in the dead of winter. Piece of cake.

She looked down at the gondola they were hovering over—high enough not to rock it, low enough to see the door was being jacked open, inch by painstaking inch. She needed to get down there—and fast. If the wind hit and the gondola started to tip—

No. It wasn't worth thinking about.

"Let's do this." Katie nodded to Josh, who set the winch in motion.

Being lowered to the gondola was half-surreal, half-ultra-real. The cold bit at her cheeks, and when she would have expected her heart rate to career into the stratosphere…it slowed. Everything became a detail—as if she were in a film and watching her own life frame by frame. The silhouette of the mountain. The snowflakes. Her breath condensing on the lip of her winter jacket.

She could hear Jorja offering Mr. Penton reassurances while his wife roared at the hit of another contraction in the background.

It streamlined her focus. If ever there had been a time she needed to give herself a pep talk—this was it. This was what she knew. Medicine. She had this one. Never mind the fact she hadn't assisted in a birth in three years. She'd gone to medical school for over a quarter of her life. This was the stuff legendary dinner party stories were made of! The day Katie West delivered a baby in a gondola!

Josh's voice crackled through the headphones to say Katie was nearly there. A sudden urge overtook her to climb right back up that winching cable and crawl into his arms. Seek the comfort she'd so longed for. She didn't want to do this. Couldn't. *He* was going to have to. She'd just stretcher the poor woman up, they'd winch her quickly into the helicopter and Josh could deliver the baby. He'd always been brilliant with obstetrics. He could be brilliant tonight.

Another female bellow of strength and pain and the sound of impending motherhood filled her headphones.

She couldn't go back up. And yet…

She looked down.

Hmm…vast chasm courtesy of Mother Nature, or get into that gondola and conquer three years' worth of fears?

The winch cable continued lowering her, oblivious to the high-stakes tug-of-war occurring between her heart and her mind, bringing her to a smooth halt opposite the gondola door.

All she had to do was unclip herself and…

Katie lodged a booted foot in the small opening Mr. Penton had managed to cleave with his hands. Three years of fears it was.

"Everything all right in here?"

Nothing like starting off with a bit of small talk when you're hanging outside a gondola!

"Not exactly!" howled his wife from the floor, her hand on her husband's ankle. "Mike, honey, we need to get this baby out of me before I rip your leg off!"

The thirty-something husband threw Katie the pained expression she'd seen on many a father-to-be. Times ten.

He was still straining to hold the doors open the handful of inches he'd managed. Katie braced her knee against the opposite door and took hold of the exterior handle. She wasn't there yet.

"Mrs. Penton? My name is Dr. McGann. You can call me Katie if you like. Or anything else that suits. But I need to borrow your husband for a few more seconds. We need the door open wide to get me and my gear in. If you could scooch yourself as far away from the door as possible…"

Adrenaline took over. That and eight years of education and a residency that had made her one of the best.

She locked eyes with Mike. "Fast and strong. Let's get these doors open and your baby out. On three—I'm going to push with my foot and you push the opposite door. Okay?"

She counted. They pushed. And with an awkward swing of her kit and the stretcher, Katie got the equipment in— only to have the doors snap shut behind her with her cable still attached. The roar of blood in her ears threatened to overwhelm her. Spots flickered across her eyes. She had maybe six to ten inches of cable between her and the door. The gondola rocked and Katie felt herself tugged and slammed against the glass-fronted door.

Make that zero. And add a bloody nose to the mix.

"I'm going to guess that wasn't meant to happen." Mike's quiet voice was barely audible above his wife's deep pants.

"It's okay." *No, it's not!*

She flicked on her head torch. *Please, please, please let the winch clip be on this side of the door!*

"Get. It. *Out!*"

"Lisa, babe. It's going to be fine. Just push a little harder," Mike coached.

"No!" Katie wrenched her head around, swiping the blood from her face. "Don't push until we see what's going on—all right?"

"What would be *all right* is to be in a warm hospital bed—like *someone* promised me!"

"Well, how did I know they were going to take so long to make the molten chocolate cake *someone else* insisted upon ordering?"

"Whoa!" Katie interjected. "Time for everybody to take a deep breath."

Including me.

"Everything okay down there?"

Josh's voice gave her a shot of Dutch courage.

"In some ways. Others…not so good."

"But our baby's going to be all right, isn't he?" Mike sent her a pleading look as his wife repositioned herself in between contractions.

"I'm really sorry, Lisa, but this is going to take just a little bit longer than you'd like."

"Katie? What's wrong?" Josh obviously had his mind-reading button on high alert.

"Mike. I'm going to need you to pry the doors open again. They're trapping the cable that has me linked to the helicopter."

"What the—?" She tuned out the expletives coming from the pilot's microphone.

"Katie—you have got to get that door open. The winds are picking up and we can't hold her steady."

"Tell me something I *don't* know," she ground out, taking in the fact that her release hook was inches away—on the other side of the door.

"Get this baby *out of me*!"

Short-circuit and potentially kill everyone on the helicopter and the gondola…or get a grip. Those were the options.

"Katie, my love, you can do this."

Josh's voice, soft and steady, trickled through her headphones.

"I'm right here. I'm not going anywhere."

Her decision was made.

"Mike. Your job is to get these doors open again, and

I'm going to unclip myself the second you do." Her eyes hooked his. "It's vital we do this now. When I'm free I'm going to help your wife. If you need to use the stretcher to keep the doors pried apart—do it. If you need to rip one of these chairs out to keep them apart—do it. If I can't get to your wife I cannot help your baby. Do you understand?"

"Katie? Have him tie you to a chair before you do anything," Josh directed.

"Grab that rope. Tie me in and tie for yourself as well— *Ow!*" Her face hit the glass again.

"Katie?"

"Fine. I'm fine. Mike's on the case. Aren't you, Mike?"

"For the love of Pete! *Move*, honey!"

Lisa's voice snapped Mike out of his daze, instantly shifting him into a man of strength and action. Ropes were taken from Katie's kit and turned into lassos round the gondola's chairs.

"We've got maybe ten more minutes of fuel, Katie."

"On it. You should have the cable in less than a minute."

"How long do you think it's going to take to get her stretchered?"

"A few minutes."

"I need to push!"

"Don't push, Lisa. *Whoa!*" A rush of freezing air hit Katie's face as Mike yanked open the door, the movement nearly tugging her out of the gondola but for the rope holding her to a chair. She shot a grateful look up to the helicopter holding her husband.

"Just unclipping now, and then I'm going to have a look."

"You're clear?" The pilot hardly waited for the confirmation to leave her lips before peeling off a few hundred meters.

"Right. Lisa—mind if I take a look?" She received a nod as the poor woman tried to control her pain.

"What's it like, Katie? What are you seeing?"

Josh's voice took away the edge of postcrisis that was

beginning to creep in now that life-and-death decisions were off the book.

"We've got about eight more minutes of fuel, Katie."

"Can you see my baby?"

For her anyway.

Now that the focus was rightfully on Lisa, Katie could hear fear taking over the roars of the woman's bravura.

"Let's take a look. I can see his— It is a he, right?" Katie received a pair of nods from the parents.

Damn. A tiny baby's buttock was just visible at the birth canal. A breech birth. At the hospital? Not a problem. Whip her into the ER and give her a C-section. In a freezing-cold gondola, hanging above one of the nation's steepest canyons…

"He's not in the best of positions for a natural birth."

Thank heavens for understatement.

"But everything will be all right, won't it?"

Katie froze. They were the words that had played through her mind again and again when the doctors had first told her they were having trouble finding her daughter's heartbeat.

"Will Huckleberry be all right?"

Huckleberry?

"Don't promise them anything, Katie."

Josh's voice appeared in her head. It was hard to tell if it was real or if she'd summoned up what he might say if he were there.

"Just tell them you will do everything you can."

That's what the doctors had said to her and Josh.

Huckleberry?

Apprehension was replaced by a need to fight the giggles. Inappropriate! *You're a doctor—act like a doctor!*

"What position is she in, Katie?"

Josh was in her headset for real this time.

"We're going to do our best to turn this little guy round."

"That's my girl," Josh encouraged softly. "Are you all right getting the mother into the basket?"

"I need to push!"

Katie began raking through her medical supplies kit. "Fight it, Lisa. Fight it as hard as you can."

"Katie?" The pilot's voice came through as she was tugging on a pair of gloves. "I'm sorry—we're going to have to refuel. I don't think we're going to have enough time."

"I don't think I can hold off much longer..." came Lisa's strained voice.

"Are you kidding me?" Katie demanded.

"I thought you said you could help." Lisa's voice was little more than a whimper now.

"Sorry. I was talking to the pilot." Katie forced herself to speak calmly. "The helicopter needs to go back to Copper Canyon. It means we'll most likely be delivering your baby here and then getting everyone back to the hospital. Mike, can you grab those heat blankets and lay them out on the floor here? We need to get a clean area for Lisa. Keep everyone warm."

"Back as soon as we can. We'll switch to your cell phone if we lose contact," Josh assured Katie. "I love you, Katie-bird. You can do this."

She let Josh's words swirl around her heart as the rest of her body prepared for action. The amount of complications that could stack up against them weren't worth considering. There was only one good outcome here, and the growing fire in Katie's belly told her to start fighting for it.

"I'm going to massage your belly...see if we can shift the baby round."

"Huckleberry," prompted Lisa.

Katie managed a nod. Naming a baby before it came out was dangerous. Naming a baby something that gave your doctor the giggles...? *Awkward!*

"I'm not feeling much of a shift here." She racked her brain to try and remember as many variations as she could.

"I need something for the pain!" Lisa panted. "I had it all planned out. An epidural, some lovely music, soft cozy blankets."

"I've got the music right here, honey. On my phone."

"Why don't you put your playlist on and I'll get you something to see if we can relax the uterus."

Katie's mind went blank as she stared at her medical kit.

"Josh?" She felt like she was speaking to the universe.

"Yeah, babe. I'm here."

Her shoulders dropped an inch in relief. Josh still had her back.

"Talk me through."

"You don't know how to *do* this? I thought you said you were a doctor!"

Mike could not have looked more horrified. Lisa was too busy fighting the onset of another contraction to care.

"You *are* a doctor, and you *can* do this."

Josh's voice came through loud and clear. Katie repeated the words in her head as if she were on automatic pilot.

And Josh continued to speak—a blond-haired, blue-eyed angel in her ear—enabling her to respond, to act, to react. First they worked their way through the basics—blood pressure, heart rate of the baby and the mother, checks for bleeding.

"Do you have an IV of fentanyl in your kit?"

"Yes." Katie reached for the bag, then chose the vial instead. "I think we're going to have to get her on her hands and knees. The massage isn't shifting the baby's position."

"Good thinking."

Josh fell silent while Katie explained to Lisa about the injection of painkiller. It would decrease the likelihood of having to treat her newborn with naloxone for respiratory depression after delivery—but it would need to be given again if the pain increased.

"Right, Lisa, can we have you on your hands and knees, please?"

Mike helped his wife roll to her side and press herself up. "Good. Now, can you drop down onto your forearms?"

"Why?"

"It's going to elevate your hips above your heart. That's a great way to encourage your baby to shift position on his own."

"Huckleberry, you mean," Lisa pressed as she dropped to her forearms with a huff.

"Yes." It was all Katie could manage. Naming a baby before it was born was too much for her to take on board right now.

"Have a feel and check the heart rate again," Josh instructed after a few moments had passed.

"I think it's working!" Katie couldn't keep the joy from her voice.

"Great. Katie—I think we're going to land in a second. We'll be out of contact for a minute. But I will call you, and you can put me on speaker if you like."

"No, don't worry," Katie answered as the infant inside Lisa's womb turned into a little acrobat. "I think I've got this one."

She tugged off her helmet and poured her entire store of concentration into Lisa and her child. They were going to *do* this. And when they did she was going to turn her life around. Just because the helicopter needed to refuel it didn't mean Josh was leaving her. He'd made it more than clear over the past few days that he had come here for *her*. To see if what they had once shared was worth salvaging. A year ago she might not have been ready. Wouldn't have been able to see the possibility. Now…? Now she wanted that man back in her life, and she was hard-pressed to keep the smile of realization off her lips.

As the medicine began to take effect and the baby shifted position, Lisa called out that another contraction was on the way.

"Great. Good!" Katie responded confidently. "Mike,

do you want to rub your wife's back? Because I think it's time to push."

"Really?"

"Really."

There was a head full of red hair at the entrance to the delivery canal, and in just a few…

"C'mon—you can do it. *Push!*"

And there he was, landing in her hands as if it were any old day. Huckleberry Penton. He was beautiful. Ten fingers, ten toes, a mouth, two ears…as perfect a baby as a family could hope for.

"You've done it, Lisa," Katie said unnecessarily as she cleared away the mucus from the little boy's mouth and nose, making way for a hearty wail. "Turn around real careful now—he's still attached to your umbilical cord."

Katie swiftly gathered together a sterile drape and a heat blanket to swaddle Huckleberry before double-clamping and cutting the umbilical cord between the two clamps. It was cold in the gondola, and the last thing this little one needed was pneumonia.

She dried off his head, resisting the urge to give him a kiss, and handed him to his mother. She kept the swell of emotion she was experiencing at bay by focusing on the postnatal checklist. She gave Lisa a gentle uterine massage, leaving the rest of the umbilical cord in place and checking that the rest of the placenta did not need to be immediately delivered. It would be safer to do that in the hospital.

"Shall we get an IV into you? It'll help replace all those electrolytes you've been losing and make sure you don't dehydrate."

Tears sprang to her eyes when she lifted her gaze to the couple, saw both sets of eyes wide with wonder, delight. They hadn't heard her. The only thing they could see or hear was their newborn baby boy.

Katie was astonished to realize the tears trickling down her cheeks were happy ones. She was genuinely happy for them. Not that she'd wished anyone ill when she and Josh had lost Elizabeth…but it had been tough to see parents with a newborn. More than tough.

It came to her that this was what she'd been waiting for—the desire to try for another baby. Three years ago she wouldn't have dreamed of getting pregnant again. *Ever.* Two years—she'd become numb to the ache to be a mother. But being with these two—being with her husband…could she really have the strength to try again?

The lights in the gondola suddenly flickered into life and almost instantly a hum could be heard, accompanied by a slight jerk as the gondola slipped into action.

"Hold on for the ride!" Katie grinned, but the smile instantly slipped from her face when she saw the expressions on the Pentons' faces.

"Um… Dr. McGann…?" Mike began, making a little dabbing gesture with his hand around his nose area. "I think you might need a little cleanup."

Katie's hands flew to her face. Her nose! With everything that had happened she'd completely forgotten her blood-smeared face.

She grabbed for a packet of antibacterial wipes and gently swabbed at her lips and cheeks, happy to note that there was a big grin on her face it would be near impossible to wipe away.

CHAPTER TEN

"QUIT PACING."

"I'm not pacing," Josh retorted, feeling about ten to Jorja's twenty-five years as he did so.

He'd been ramped up for going back in the chopper to get Katie down from that blasted gondola, but when the generator had unexpectedly kicked into action they'd been told to stand down. Now he was ready to lay everything on the line. See if it was time to hand over the signed divorce papers and try to find a way to move on or—and here was where it got tricky—see if there were some way—*any* way—he could get the real life he wanted back with his wife.

So sitting down, standing still, anything stationary was not an option. Pacing like a caged beast was a bit more like it. He'd just do it in front of the patient board to make it look a bit more…functional.

"The ambulance should be here any minute," Jorja finally allowed.

"And she's in it?"

Jorja looked at him like he was crazy. "Of *course* the woman who just gave birth in a freakin' gondola on New Year's Eve is in it! What are you? Nuts?"

"I meant Dr. McGann."

"Oh," Jorja replied. Then visibly experienced a hit of understanding. *"Oh!"*

Josh narrowed his eyes. "You've spoken to Michael, haven't you?"

"I work with him—of course I've spoken to him." Her eyes flicked back to the files she had been ignoring.

"About Katie—Dr. McGann…" Josh tried to give her his I'm-Not-Messin' look, failing miserably, from the looks of things.

"Sorry, Dr. West. Nothing's secret for long in a small town. But your business is your business. If you want to spend New Year's Eve trying to convince Copper Canyon's most unavailable doctor to go out with Michael so that *he* can get fired for inappropriate behavior and *you* can get his job—be my guest." She folded her arms defensively across her chest. "And good luck tryin'," she added, quite obviously not meaning the last bit.

Ah. Wrong dog, wrong tree.

If he hadn't been so stressed he would have laughed. He'd have to remember to meet up with Michael for that coffee. He owed him for the red-herring behavior. *Hang on a second!*

"Jorja, are you sweet on Michael?"

"I have no idea what you're talking about," she replied primly, giving a stack of patient files a nice clack on the countertop as she did.

"Jorja and Michael, sitting on a—"

"Dr. West!" Jorja put on her most outraged face. "I'll have you know my brothers are all taller than you." She sized him up quickly, to make sure she'd been correct. "And stronger. I will *not* have my name tarnished in such a way."

"Shame…" Josh leaned against the counter, thoroughly enjoying himself now. "I think you two would make a cute couple."

"You do? I mean…" She quickly dropped her happy face and went for nonchalance. "That's interesting. I've never given it much thought."

"Why don't you ask him out for a coffee? The diner makes a mean cup."

The ambulance crew burst through the double doors, pushing a gurney with Lisa on it, holding her baby tightly in her arms, and her husband by her side, sending a mix of anxious and proud looks at anyone who was looking while the EMT crew hurriedly rattled off handover information to Michael, who had appeared alongside them from the ambulance bay.

Jorja gave her cheeks a quick pinch, even though they didn't need any extra pinking, and flew out from behind her desk with a chart to assist.

They all passed him in a whirlwind of activity, leaving the waiting room entirely empty of people save a weary-looking mother with a pile of knitting well under way as she waited for her skateboarding son to get his leg put in a cast after inventing a whole new style of ice-skating.

No Katie.

Josh looked round the waiting room to see if it would give him an answer.

No dice.

Just the clickety-clack of the mother's knitting needles and the low hum of a television ticking off the New Year's Eve celebrations around the world.

He took a few steps closer to see if... Was that...? *Huh.* Paris. He glanced at his watch. That would have been over hours ago. Ah—there was London. He'd clearly hit the replay... Yes, there was the Statue of Liberty...and cut to Times Square...

New York City was moments away from dropping the gong on the New Year. That gave him a paltry three hours. He'd promised himself he'd have this sorted by midnight. He didn't know if he was Prince Charming or Cinderella in this scenario—but whatever happened, he was going to cross everything he had in the hope that Katie was up for a bit of glass-slipper action.

* * *

Katie sank onto the bench in the locker room, relieved to have found the place empty. She'd left the EMTs and Michael to sort out the Pentons and had taken a fast-paced power walk round the hospital, sneaking in at the front door in the hopes of just a few more minutes to regroup before she saw anyone—*c'mon, be honest!*—before she saw Josh again.

If the past few days had been an emotional roller coaster, the last few hours had been… She looked up to the ceiling for some inspiration… *Seismic.* Everything she had held to be true over the past two years had been a fiction. A way of coping with the tremendous loss she and Josh had suffered. But ultimately she had been hiding. And not just from her husband. She'd been hiding from life.

Her right hand sought purchase on her ring finger. It surprised her how much relief she felt at finding the rings still there. Side by side. First one promise and then another. Promises she'd blamed Josh for breaking when maybe all along *she* had been the one who had let him down.

He had changed. She could see that now. But she still wasn't entirely sure what sort of future—if any—he was offering her. He'd said he had come here to Copper Canyon to find her, but to what end? Another chance? Another child?

She opened up her palms and imagined the weight of the newborn she'd just held in them. Tears welled. Could she do it? Maybe she had changed too much. Become too clinical. Or had her time away been more about healing than hiding? Josh's surprise appearance had definitely taught her one thing—there was always room for another way of seeing things.

She glanced at her watch. Three hours and counting. What would this New Year hold in store for her?

She slowly unwound the scarf Josh had twirled round her neck before she'd descended to the gondola, then pushed herself up and opened his locker. His winter coat was hanging on its hook. She folded the scarf and put it in his pocket—but when it was obvious the wool wrap wasn't going to fit, she tugged it out again. A few pieces of paper fell to the floor with the movement.

She knelt to pick them up, eyes widening, stomach churning as she took in the contents of the paperwork.

She shouldn't have looked.

A sour sensation rose from her belly as she absorbed the writing on the letter, the airplane ticket and—her hand flew to her mouth, hoping to stem the cry of despair—the divorce papers.

Signed.

Unsealed.

About to be delivered?

She felt herself going numb. How could she have been such an idiot? Josh was here to give her the signed divorce papers. Why else would he have a job offer and a ticket to France falling out of his pocket? The whole "making peace" thing had just been a ruse to make himself feel better.

Running away again suddenly seemed too exhausting. She pulled her feet up and curled into a tight ball on the bench, no longer interested if anyone saw her. Two years of holding it all together, pretending she was nothing more than a dedicated physician—no personal life, no history, just medicine. And now everything she'd sought to keep under control was unraveling from the inside out.

She lay on the bench, her cheek taking on the imprint of the wooden slats, and for once she just didn't care. Her body was too weighted with the pain of knowing that her life wasn't going to be about suppressing anymore. It was going to be about letting go. She lay perfectly still for she didn't know how long, just thinking. Because once she started to move it would be the start of an entirely new life.

One without the baby she'd had to say goodbye to sooner

than anyone should have to. One without the family she'd always dreamed she'd have. A life without Josh. Her sweet, kind, loving husband who had brought out a spark in her she'd never known she'd had.

A surge of energy charged through her, making a lightning-fast transformation into a burning hot poker in her heart. She felt branded. Marked with the painful searing of anger, sorrow and indignation. She'd been such an *idiot* for thinking Josh had changed. It was all she could do not to ball her hands up and try to knock some actual sense into her normally oh-so-logical head. She'd actually believed that he was here to try again—to start anew. To try to make that family they had both ached for. And…for the most tender of moments…she had believed she could do it.

A primal moaning roar left her throat as she pushed herself up and shook her head. Maybe she could shake out everything that she didn't want to carry into the future. Turn into a whirling dervish and spin everything away. A human centrifuge. It would be hard—and by heavens it would hurt—but she could clear her system of Josh West again. And this time for good.

She glanced at her watch, surprised to see how close to midnight it was.

She needed air. Light. Cold. Anything to remind her that she was vital. Alive. Just one tiny thing to show her that she would survive this.

Josh pushed the plug into the extension cord, not even daring to look for a moment. He knew this was a make-or-break moment. He shifted his chin along his shoulder until he could catch a glimpse of his handiwork. It was cold, but with the wind dying down, the stillness added a strange sensation of otherworldliness to the twinkling lights he'd laced into hearts and trees and stars, to the lengths of decorations he'd stolen from the nurses' lounge.

Perfect. Even if he was a caveman in the home-decor department, he'd done a pretty good job of gussying up Valley Hospital's roof. Now to rustle up something poetic to say about—

He whirled around at the sound of the roof door slamming open.

"Can't a girl get a *single* moment alone?" Katie looked little short of appalled to see him standing there. "What *is* all this?" she snapped.

"Oh, just a little decorating..." Josh started—not altogether certain his words were even being received by his wild-eyed wife.

"All I wanted to do was make a snow angel. One tiny little freakin' snow angel to prove that the world *is* nice, and good things *can* happen, and what do I get instead?"

She didn't wait for him to fill in the answer to what was obviously a rhetorical question.

"*You!* The one person I loved the most in the whole world, leaving me again. And just when I thought we were beginning to repair things."

"Wait! What?" Josh strode up to Katie, hands outstretched in a *What gives?* position. "What are you talking about, Katiebird?"

"Oh, don't Katiebird me." She all but spit at him.

Josh had never seen her so riled, and the force of her anger nearly pushed him back. *Nearly.* He ground his feet in and pressed himself up to his full height.

Tough. It was less than an hour to midnight and he was damned if he was going to hit the New Year without finding out if he had a future with his wife. Her face told him everything he'd feared—but he wasn't going to let go of this one without a fight.

He held his ground. "What exactly are you talking about?"

"I'm talking about the divorce papers."

He raised his eyebrows. "You mean the ones you've been sending me by special delivery for the past two years?"

"I mean the signed ones in your locker."

Her stance was defiant but he could see the hurt in her eyes. He wished he'd never put a pen to those damn things. It was the type of thing a trip to the stationery store could never fix. That type of ink was indelible.

His voice softened. This wasn't going remotely the way he'd hoped, but at least it was as painful for her as it had been for him to see his name on those pages. "I thought it was what you wanted."

"I did too," she said after a moment, her booted foot digging a sizable divot in the snow.

"And now?"

"Now it looks like what I think doesn't matter." A guilty frown tugged her lips downward at his raised eyebrows. "I found the job offer and the ticket to Paris. The one-way ticket."

"Oh, you did, did you?" Josh found himself needing to suppress the grin splitting his face in two.

"Yes. Or should I say *oui*?" Katie couldn't meet Josh's eyes but she kept on talking. "Looks like you've gone and done what I haven't been able to do."

"And what's that, then?"

Josh took a step closer.

Katie put her arm between them.

"You've been able to move on. Get past everything we've been through." She lifted her gaze to finally meet his, her tears only just resting on her lids. They'd spill any second now. She tipped her head back to buy herself a few more moments of dignity, if that was what you could call standing on the roof of your place of work and hollering at your husband—ex-husband—for doing exactly what you'd asked him to do.

"When you were busy rifling through my things—"

"I wasn't rifling. I was—" She stopped to search for a

less invidious word than "rifling," accidentally biting the inside of her cheek in the process.

"Uh-huh? What *were* you doing?"

The twinkle in Josh's eyes stirred something within her. She knew what it was, but it was embarrassing to admit it considering the turn of events.

Lust. She just wanted to rip his clothes off and have her wicked way with him.

Would that *ever* go away? She stared at him, her body itching to stomp her feet or jump up and down. Anything to stop the skittering of goose bumps working their way across her body. Wow, did she *ever* need to make a snow angel!

She shifted her eyes up to the heavens. How the heck was she going to carry on with her life when she still fancied the pants off her husband?

"Did you happen to see the ticket beneath the ticket?"

"Um…what was that?"

Best not to appear too keen to have gotten the wrong end of the stick.

"Katie McGann." Josh stepped forward and took both her hands in his. His blue eyes were like sunshine, and a halo of twinkly lights lit him up from behind.

Oh, no, no, no, no… This can't be goodbye. Is this really goodbye?

"I came back here to do one thing and one thing only."

She couldn't speak. The other side of her cheek was being chomped on. Hard enough to draw blood.

"I came back here," he said in his soft, beautiful drawl, "with the sole intent of seeing if you would consider becoming Katie West again."

She blinked a snowflake out of her eyelashes. The rest of her body was frozen in place.

"Katie?"

"Yes?" Her insides had started doing a June-bug dance.

Her outsides still weren't up to much more than providing a landing zone for the supersized snowflakes.

"I am presuming you heard what I just said."

A little furrow was beginning to form between the one pair of eyes that could light up a room. What made them so *bright*?

"Yes, I did," she managed to croak out.

"And are you planning on drawing out the torture, or are you going to tell me what you think of the idea?"

"What? About Paris? That job offer sounds pretty amazing. Groundbreaking surgical techniques? Champagne? I bet it's practically free over there. And the architecture! The Eiffel Tower versus Main Street and grilled cheese sandwiches?" She squawked out a mysterious sound that was meant to say *No-Brainer*, wondering why on earth she was trying to talk him out of staying when all she wanted was to tip back her head and scream *Yes! A thousand times yes!*

Josh rocked back on his heels and gave her comments some thought. Katie's stomach began to lurch as her heart plummeted.

Why had she opened her big mouth?

"A chance to work with the world's best prenatal surgeon? It's a once-in-a-lifetime offer," he admitted, before a near-wistful look added a glint to his eyes. "And I *do* love those baguettes. Especially when they're all crunchy on the outside and that gooey cheese they have is just dripping out over the edges."

"You've already *been* there?" Katie's dog-whistle voice sprang into the stratosphere, her game face all but disappearing as she spoke.

"How else do you think I got the offer?" He thumbed away another snowflake. "But then I got to thinking. Do I sign those damn divorce papers you've been sending me, move on—or do I try to win back my girl?"

Katie swiped at a couple of snowflakes that were tickling her nose, too heartbroken to speak. He'd signed the papers and he had a ticket to Paris. Why did he have to be so *nice* about it all? Where was the adrenaline junkie she'd hardened her heart to?

"All of which is a really long-winded way of saying—" he paused to run the backs of his fingers across her cheeks before tucking her hair behind her ears "—there are *two* tickets to Paris in my locker."

Her heart gave a particularly large thump.

"I'm guessing you didn't see the second one."

"That would be a fair guess." Her voice broke with relief. Josh wanted to be with her. He wanted to start again!

The questions began tumbling out in a torrent. Would this really be a new beginning or would they fall into old patterns? Had he really thought through where he wanted to be, what he wanted to do?

She sucked in a breath, closed her eyes and asked the one that scared her the most. "Do you want to try for another baby?"

She felt his breath upon her lips as he spoke. "More than anything in the world."

Their foreheads tipped together and her breath intertwined with his. "Even if it's the scariest thing in the whole wide world?"

"Even if it's the scariest thing in the universe." He pressed a soft kiss onto her lips. "And I promise to be by your side every step of the way."

"Here in Copper Canyon?"

"Wherever you like." He started pressing kisses onto each of her cheeks, her eyelids, the tip of her nose. "We *do* have two tickets to Paris if you'd like to go check it out."

Her eyes flicked open. A penny dropped. "Joshua West—you aren't chicken to go to Paris all on your lonesome, are you?"

"Ha!" A cloud of breath hid milliseconds of acknowledgment. "As if. But it would be much easier to go into the big new world of surgery with my brave and talented wife

by my side. If she's interested in giving up her job here at
Valley Hospital, that is, for one in Paris…"

"Oh…I don't know. The boss here is pretty hard-core."

Josh grinned broadly. "I hear she has a heart of gold."

He dipped his head to kiss his wife again. It was a kiss
filled with the deep satisfaction of a man who had found
his way in the world again. Katie returned each and every
one of his kisses with all her love. As they sought and answered each other's caresses, they pulled back for a second to grin when the church bell began to toll midnight.

Katie's heart felt full to bursting. Everything was going
to get better now—the healing had begun and the New Year
couldn't start at a better time or in a better place…right
here in her husband's arms.

EPILOGUE

"DID YOU GET to the bakery?"

"Hello to you, too, my little Katiebird." Josh paused to drop a kiss onto his wife's forehead. "And, *excusez-moi*, but I think what you were trying to say was did I get to *la patisserie*."

Katie couldn't help but laugh at her husband's exaggerated French accent. Tennessee meets Paris was an interesting combo. Not that *her* accent was all that hot. Just mastering the medical vocabulary had been enough of a challenge. But they had both impressed not only themselves but their new colleagues as well. Sure, they both might sound like yahoos from America—but nearly a year in Paris had changed everything.

"I thought I'd go for something different, seeing as it's the holiday season."

"And Emmy's birthday," Katie added, as if either of them needed reminding.

Together they turned to beam at their daughter, her face covered in spaghetti sauce after Katie's unsuccessful attempt to get some of her dinner inside the cheeky nine-month-old. With a head of jet-black curls and a pair of bright blue eyes, she was a reflection of the pair of them.

"So?" Katie prodded. "What'd you get?"

Josh pulled out a box from behind his back. A box that

wasn't nearly big enough for the kind of birthday cake she'd had in mind.

"What's that?"

"Not what you had in mind for our cherished daughter's birthday?"

She resisted sticking out her lower lip in a pout. *Just.* "Depends… Is this one of those 'good things come in small packages' deals?"

"In a way…" Josh held up the small box and waggled it in front of his wife's eyes. This was fun.

Who was he kidding? There hadn't been a moment in the past year when the smile had been wiped off his face. The world's longest honeymoon, he had billed it. And a move to Paris. His wife back by his side. A daughter to crow over whenever he wasn't learning about mind-blowing surgical techniques with his new mentor.

"Want to open it?" He held up the package when Katie snatched at it.

"You know I do—I need cake!"

"Need or want?" he teased.

"Both."

He handed the box over, watching with bated breath as Katie ripped it open with the glee of a five-year-old.

The myriad of expressions playing across her face as she took in the contents of the box only broadened his grin.

"This is a napkin from Rooney's…" Her big brown eyes met his.

"Best chocolate cake in Copper Canyon," they recited in unison.

"Um…" Katie looked up at him quizzically. "I hate to point out the obvious, but there isn't any cake *in* here, buster."

"What's below the napkin?"

"Oh, my gosh…" Katie's cheeks pinked as she lifted the tickets out of the box. "Are we *really*?"

"I think the first place our baby girl should make a snow angel is in Copper Canyon. Don't you?"

Katie rose up on her tiptoes and gave Josh an appreciatively lingering kiss.

"I couldn't agree more, my love. Christmas in Paris and New Year in Copper Canyon. Doesn't get much better than that, does it?"

"So long as I have the two of you, Katiebird, I have everything I need." He gave her another kiss and dropped a wink in their daughter's direction. "But some of Rooney's finest chocolate fudge for our daughter will be the icing on the cake."

* * * * *

ONCE UPON A CHRISTMAS NIGHT...

ANNIE CLAYDON

To Cassie and George, with much love.

CHAPTER ONE

GREG SHAW OPENED the door of the doctors' common room, not bothering to switch on the light, and slung himself into a chair. All he wanted was sleep. He could have done with a few days off in between returning from America and resuming his job, but what you wanted wasn't always what you got. A day to get over the jet lag, unpack and re-stock the larder hadn't been enough and he'd had to satisfy himself with doing none of those things with any degree of completeness.

He should go home. Catch some sleep before he was due back on shift again tomorrow. He tried to work up enough enthusiasm to propel himself into action by promising himself a hot shower and a cooked meal, but the relief of sitting here alone outweighed all of that at the moment. In the darkness, he was hardly aware of the fact that his eyes were closing.

'Is it always so hot in here?' Jessie Saunders picked her way down the steep concrete steps, which seemed to lead directly into a sauna.

'No idea. Apparently the quickest way through is via the boiler room.' Reena was having to shout now, to make herself heard over the din. 'Watch out for that handrail, it wobbles terribly.'

'So it's fair to assume that Health and Safety haven't been down here recently.'

'Probably not.' Reena shot her a grin and led the way through to the far door, which gave way to a cooler, quieter corridor. 'The hospital records should be through there.'

The records room, as the notice on the door grandly announced, turned out to be a long, low-ceilinged vault, filled with row upon row of shelves. Reena felt in the pocket of her coat and consulted a piece of paper. 'Right, so the early stuff's over there in the far corner.' She pulled a large, old-fashioned key from her pocket and indicated a heavy metal door.

'What's that? I didn't know we had dungeons in the basement.'

'It's an old walk-in safe. It's cool and dry so they keep the earlier documents in there. I had to promise Administration that we'd wedge the door open and keep the key with us at all times.'

'And they know we're down here this late?' There was no reason for the basement to feel any darker or spookier now than it would have done at lunchtime. Somehow it did.

'I said we were going to have a look after work. They might have thought that was five-thirty.' Reena unlocked the door, pulling it back with an effort and wedging it firmly.

Jess shrugged, pulling a couple of pairs of surgical gloves from her pocket. 'Gloves?'

'Definitely.'

The boxes of papers stacked inside might be caked with dust, but they were stored in some sort of order. The year 1813 was located and the boxes pulled out into the cramped space outside the door.

'Oh, you'll never guess who I saw coming out of the canteen today.' Reena was carefully sifting through the contents of the oldest storage box, trying not to disturb too much dust.

'No, I don't think I will.'

'Give it a go, at least. Great smile.'

'The tooth fairy?'

'Ha-ha. Think taller. Darker and not wearing a tutu.' Reena rolled her eyes when Jess gave her a blank look. 'Your ex-boss.'

'You mean…' It would be disingenuous to pretend that she didn't know who Reena meant. 'Greg? He's back?'

Breathing would be good right now, but Jess's lungs seemed to have temporarily forgotten how. She kept her eyes firmly fixed on the large ledger in front of her so they couldn't betray her shock.

'Yeah. Wherever he's been for the last eight months, he's been getting some sun. He's looking good.'

Greg always looked good. Jess wondered whether Reena had any more substantive information and how she was going to ask for it without sounding too interested. 'So how is he?'

'I didn't see him to speak to, he was moving too fast for that.' Reena tossed her head and laughed. 'You know Greg. He's a busy kind of guy.' She turned her attention back to the half empty storage box.

He was back. He'd probably had two or three girlfriends since Jess had seen him last and had almost certainly forgotten all about That Kiss. Just the way she should have done.

'This looks promising… Jess?'

'Uh?'

'I think this is exactly what we're looking for.'

'Yeah?' Jess straightened, shrugging off the brief scrap of memory, which seemed to have lodged itself right in the centre of her consciousness. 'Let's have a look.'

* * *

Greg drifted into what passed for wakefulness in time to hear the clock in the small courtyard outside the common-room window chiming out midnight. Silence fell, and he sat up straight, easing his shoulders to iron out a few of the kinks. There was a scraping outside in the corridor, a dull thud and... If he didn't know better he would have said that the clatter was the sound of chains.

Leave it out. After eight months, spent jetting around America and Australia, with some of the sunnier parts of Europe thrown in, London in early November seemed claustrophobic, full of shadows. But it was home. He'd longed to be back home, and now here he was. Feeling just as empty and unsure as he had for the last ten months.

Another clatter. If it wasn't a chain, it was something that sounded pretty much identical. Greg was suddenly awake, his eyes straining in the darkness, and then clamped shut as white light hit his retinas, burning the outline of a shadowy figure into his mind's eye.

'Greg!'

'What...? Jess?' He blinked against the light streaming in through the open door and slowly began to make her out. She had on the same red coat that she'd been wearing when he'd seen her last. His mouth went dry. When he'd seen her last...

When he'd seen her last he'd been kissing her. The length of chain, slung over her shoulder and trailing behind her on the floor, was new, and she hadn't been quite so grimy then either. The temptation to reach out and touch her, pretend she had a smudge on her cheek so that he could wipe it away, was almost irresistible.

She was staring at him as if she'd just seen a ghost. She swallowed hard and seemed to come to her senses. 'I heard you were back.'

'Yeah. Only just. I landed yesterday morning, and got a call at lunchtime, saying that they were short-staffed in A and E and could I start work today.' Guilt trickled down his spine. He probably should have called her. He'd thought about it often enough.

She nodded. No hint in her steady gaze that their kiss figured anywhere in her attitude towards him. 'Well, it's nice to see you back. Have you got…things…settled?'

'Not quite.' It was never going to be completely settled. 'For the time being.' The urge to explain himself was prickling at the back of Greg's neck, but he had no idea where to start. 'Jess…'

'Yes?'

'What's with the chains?'

She flushed prettily. Dragged the knitted beret off her head, leaving her honey-coloured hair impossibly rumpled. A little longer than it had been last Christmas, and the style suited her.

'Ah.' She started to unwind the length of chain from her neck. 'It's for the dressing up. For Christmas.' She indicated a stack of plastic crates in the corner.

'You're going to dress up in chains for Christmas?' Greg couldn't help smiling and she shot him a glare in return.

'No, of course not. Gerry is.' She finally managed to free herself from the chain, opening one of the crates and dumping it inside.

'Gerry's going to dress up in chains for Christmas?' Gerard Mortimer, the senior cardiac consultant. Greg was sure that there were plenty of things more incongruous in the world, but at the moment he couldn't bring any of them to mind. 'Starting when?'

This time her look was ferocious enough to have cut through cold steel. 'Some of us are dressing up as characters from Dickens's novels. Gerry's going to be Jacob Marley's ghost.'

There were no words to say. Greg began to wonder whether he wasn't dreaming after all. It wouldn't have been the first time that Jess had featured in his dreams, but he had to admit that the chains were a new development. Maybe fatigue was lending an edge to his imagination.

'Are you okay?' She was staring at him intently.

'Uh...?' On the off chance that he was dealing with reality and not a set of unconnected threads from his unconscious mind, he should give an answer of some sort. 'Yeah, fine. Jet lag. So who are you dressing up as?' It couldn't hurt to ask, and Greg found that he was suddenly and irrationally interested.

'I'm not dressing up. I'm organising everything.'

'So this Christmas won't be as chaotic as last...' He bit his tongue but it was too late. The cat had clawed its way out of the bag and ushered something that looked suspiciously like an elephant into the room.

'I don't know what you mean.'

She was blushing furiously, refusing to meet his gaze. She remembered. And from the look of things she was no more indifferent to it than he was. Greg could barely suppress his grin.

'I meant that...the weather will probably be better.'

'Yes. I expect so. Last year was quite unusual.' She was backing towards the door now. 'It's late. I'd better be getting home.'

'See you tomorrow?'

'Yes... Maybe.'

'I'll look forward to it.' The door banged behind her, and Greg settled back into his chair. Just another ten minutes, to settle his jumbled thoughts, then he'd go home.

Last Christmas...

The dream seized Greg with all the colour and immediacy of a memory, which had shadowed him for the last thirty years. The large, opulent room and the child, sitting on a thick, intricately patterned rug on the floor.

He was making something. Without having to look, Greg knew what it was. The Christmas card was for his father, the picture on the front a wishful representation of a family—father, mother and their five-year-old son— under a Christmas tree. It was almost painful to watch his younger self, so absorbed in this task, so careful with the picture and the wording inside the card, because Greg knew what was to come.

The lavishly wrapped presents from America had been no substitute for his father's arrival, but the child had believed all the excuses that Christmas. It had taken years of broken promises to finally squash Greg's faith and make him realise that the time his father gave so freely to the company and the people he worked with was doled out like a miser's shilling to his family.

'It's not your fault.' Greg breathed the words to his younger self, wondering if there was any way he could comfort the boy. Apparently not. His own memories still tasted of the bitterness of dreams that had never been smashed but had just dissolved under the weight of reality.

The boy was growing, though, almost before his eyes. Finding his way in the world. A first kiss on a sun-strewn hillside in Italy, where he had been holidaying with his mother's family. The letter to his father, telling him that he was going to medical school, which had gone unanswered. The party that his mother and stepfather had thrown for him before he'd left home. The hard work, the weary nights and the smile of a woman he'd saved. She'd been the first, and from then on he'd known that this was what he was supposed to do.

Greg was reeling from the vivid clarity of the thoughts and memories flashing in front of him. Faces, dreams. The soft touch of a woman's skin. Jess. She'd been the last, delicious taste of the life that he'd left behind. Maybe not a perfect life, there had been the usual mistakes, the usual disappointments, but it had been his and he had a singular affection for it.

Finally, the parade of images slowed. Stopped. It was last Christmas, in the dark, deserted courtyard outside the hospital, and Greg could see himself, talking to Jess. Although he couldn't hear what they were saying, he knew well enough. Knew what was coming, too, and he held his breath, afraid that in some way he might alter history and divert their path away from that sweet outcome.

She must have been as back-breakingly tired as he was, but she still shone. Still wore that red sparkly headband that had brought a little Christmas cheer into an A and E department that had been in a state of siege after a cold snap, accompanied by snow, had filled the waiting room, and a flu bug had thrown the holiday rota into chaos.

Greg saw himself grimace. They'd got to the goodbye. Jess had worked for him for two years, and was leaving soon, to take up a post in Cardiology. It was what she wanted to do and he was pleased for her but even now, ten months later, the sudden feeling of loss stabbed at him.

There it was... Greg watched as his former self leaned forward, a brief kiss on the cheek. Saw her flinch back in surprise as he went to kiss the other cheek, and knew that he'd whispered something about a single kiss not being enough, using his Italian heritage as an excuse for his own craving to feel her skin against his again.

More talk, their bodies seeming to grow closer by the

second, and then he'd caught her hand. Pressed her fingers against his lips, smiling when she didn't draw back. And then Greg had heedlessly trashed the first of the three rules he'd lived by up until that moment. He'd gone ahead and kissed her, despite the fact that Jess was still a member of his team for another week, and he always, whatever the circumstances, kept it strictly professional at work.

'Think you're in control of this, don't you?'

He murmured the warning and his former self took no heed of it. Jess would show him differently, any minute now. Greg watched as she pulled away for a moment and then kissed him back, her hand sliding over the stubble on his jaw and coming to rest on his neck, in the exact place that had suddenly and inexplicably seemed to control the whole of his body.

She'd torn his breath away, taken everything that he was and made it hers. What was the second rule again? Don't let your love life get out of control? That had dissolved in the wash of pleasure that had been engulfing him, without anything more than a slight pop. This had been uncharted territory. He'd known no more about Jess's personal life than she had about his, and if that wasn't out of control he didn't know what was.

It was Jess who had come to her senses. Down-to-earth, dependable Jess, who had always seemed so immune to his charm.

'This might not be such a good idea. We work together...'

She'd given him a way out, and he'd stubbornly refused to take it.

'Not for much longer.'

'I suppose I won't be seeing so much of you after next week. When I take up the post in Cardiology.'

There had been a gleam of mischief in her smile.

The third rule had flared and burned in the heat of her touch. Don't make promises you can't keep.

'You'll see me. I'll find you.'

He had kissed her one last time, just to let her know that he would. And she had clung to him, to let him know just what his welcome would be like when he did.

'Happy Christmas, Greg.'

'Happy Christmas, Jess.'

Greg's eyes opened and he found himself staring at the ceiling. He hadn't even looked for her, let alone found her. In the week between Christmas and the New Year the call had come, telling him that his father was gravely ill. Instead of going to Jess's goodbye drinks, Greg had been on the motorway, on his way to his father's house. Too late, he'd realised that he'd left no message to tell her why he couldn't be there.

Days had turned into weeks. Every moment that Greg hadn't been at work had been spent either on the road or at his father's bedside. He'd known that he was dying, but somehow it had seemed all wrong when the man who had capitulated to no one gave way to death. Then the will had been read, and Greg's world had been turned upside down. He'd packed his bags and gone to America to try and sort it all out, knowing that it was too late to seek her out.

Maybe she'd forgiven him. She certainly hadn't forgotten him. And maybe now he could do what he'd neglected to do before, and had been regretting for the last ten months. Get to know Jess. Find out whether that kiss had been just an aberration, something that had happened which had never been meant to be, or whether it might, just might have been the start of something.

CHAPTER TWO

GREG BREEZED INTO Cardiology as if it was the most natural thing in the world, and he was simply looking for something he'd misplaced.

'Ah! Just what I needed.' The coffee that he'd bought for Jess was whipped from his hand, and Gerry lifted the take-away cup to his lips.

Best brazen it out. 'Thought you might.' Greg leaned against the reception desk and opened his own coffee.

'So, welcome to Cardiology. And who might you be?' Gerry's Irish accent was always broader when he was smiling.

'Feeling neglected, are we?'

'Not me.' Gerry tipped the coffee cup towards him as if in a toast. 'I'm easily pleased, though. Maura wants to know when you'll be coming over for dinner.'

'Soon. I'm on lates at the moment. But I can pop in at the weekend, see the kids. I've something for them from America.' Something that his father's personal assistant had procured from the toy store. Greg hadn't needed to ask whether Pat had done the same each time his own birthday or Christmas had rolled around. The meticulously wrapped presents for Jamie and Emma bore the same careful folds that he'd examined and practised himself as a child, thinking that this, at least, would be something he'd learned from his father.

'....last time. By the time Jamie's old enough for that remote-controlled car you sent him, I'll have worn it out.' Gerry's voice filtered back into his consciousness.

'I thought you'd like it. And I've got something a bit more age appropriate this time.' Greg would rewrap the parcels himself. Then at least he'd know what was inside them. 'I had some help in choosing. My father's PA is great with things like that.' He'd always loved his presents and had no reason to suppose that Pat had lost her touch. As long as the kids were happy, did it really make so much of a difference?

'Yeah? How are things going over there? You weren't exactly communicative when we spoke last time.'

'I know. It's complicated.'

Gerry bared his teeth in a wry smile. 'What, there's a woman involved?'

'What makes you say that?'

'That's generally your definition of complicated.'

'Never make assumptions.' Greg wondered what kind of rumours had been circulating about his protracted absence. Went as far as hoping that Jess hadn't heard them and then decided not to go there. 'Is Jess around?'

'I think she's doing a ward round.' Gerry flipped an enquiring look at the receptionist, who nodded. 'She'll be back soon. Can I help?'

'Not unless you're in charge of the Christmas pageant.' Gerry wouldn't question the excuse. Jess wasn't 'his type'. It occurred to Greg that perhaps it was the women he usually dated who weren't his type.

'So she's got you involved with that, has she?'

'Not yet. I thought I might lend a hand, though. Anything that involves you in chains has got to be worth a look.'

Gerry chuckled. 'Yeah. Think I got lumbered there.' Something caught his eye and he gestured. 'Jess. You've got a new recruit.'

By the time Greg had turned, her initial reaction to his presence, if indeed there had been one, was under control. He'd never seen her in anything other than scrubs or jeans before, but today she wore a skirt and blouse under her crisp white coat. Hair tied back, showing off the curve of her neck, and, though it came as no particular surprise to Greg that Jess had legs, somehow he couldn't drag his eyes away from them.

'Don't eye my staff up, mate.' At least Gerry had the grace to lean in close so no one else could hear him. Greg shot him a warning look, and Gerry laughed, turning to the receptionist, who immediately gave him something else to do.

'You want to help with the pageant?' Jess's voice next to him was uncertain.

'Oh. Yeah, I thought if you wanted a hand...' He stopped. Suddenly it seemed crass to just breeze in, as if the last ten months hadn't happened.

'Yes. Always.' She twisted her mouth. 'Greg, I... It was such a surprise to see you last night, and I didn't...' She took a breath. 'I just wanted to say that I heard about your father. I'm very sorry. I should have made sure that I got the chance to say that before now.'

He stared at her. He'd left her hanging, without a word, and she was the one who seemed to feel she had something to explain. 'Thanks. And...I was the one who wasn't around, not you.'

'That's understandable.' Suddenly they weren't talking about his father any more. It was all about Greg and Jess.

And that kiss. No, not the kiss, that had been just fine. The promise he'd made and then broken.

'You think so?' Calling her, from his father's place or long distance from America, had seemed somehow indefinably wrong. Now he was back in London, it felt wrong that he hadn't.

She shrugged. 'I'll give you the benefit of the doubt.'

That was all he needed. 'Well, in that case, do you want to meet up? To talk about the pageant, I mean. I could buy you lunch perhaps.'

She pursed her lips. 'You might like to reconsider that. I can think of a lot of jobs in the time it takes to eat lunch. Maybe just a coffee.'

He wanted so badly to push her, not to take no for an answer. But he didn't have the right. Thinking about her for the whole of the last ten months didn't count as any form of contact, unless she happened to be psychic. 'Whatever suits you. Would you like me to call you?'

She nodded, pulling her phone out of her pocket. 'What's your number?'

She thumbed in the digits as he recited them and his mobile sounded, one ring from his back pocket. 'There, you've got mine now. If you want to risk lunch, I'll make a list of things we need help with.'

He grinned. Jess had come through for him yet again. This time he wouldn't let her down.

Are you free for lunch on Sunday?

Jess wasn't about to admit that those seven words were the ones that she'd been waiting for ever since she'd last seen Greg. She texted back with the minimum of information.

Yes.

Come over to mine. I'll make lunch. You can give me a rundown on what you want me to do.

'Don't tempt me…' She hissed the words between her teeth, but couldn't help smiling to herself. He might have left her hanging, and it might have hurt, but Jess wasn't quite sure what she would have done if he hadn't. If Greg had come knocking on her door, she might just have taken fright and pretended she wasn't home.

Sounds good. What time?

I'll pick you up at twelve.

No, that was one step too far for the moment.

Send me your address. I'll make my own way.

There was a pause, and then her phone beeped again. His address, along with an electronic smile. Nothing like his real smile. Good. It was far too early to start thinking about all the things his smile did to her.

The climb up to the top floor wasn't anywhere near long enough to make her feel dizzy, but then Greg answered the door. A blue shirt, open just far enough to show improbably smooth, olive skin and jeans that fitted him like a glove. Dark hair, and dark eyes, which were even more striking here than in the fluorescent glare of the hospital. Couldn't he give a girl a break?

'That smells fabulous. What is it?' When she followed him through to the large, sleek kitchen, the smell curled around her like a warm, comfortable blanket.

'One of my mother's secret recipes.' Greg had clearly

come to the same conclusion that Jess had. The easy humour they'd shared at work was the best way to forget that they were alone together in his flat. 'You know the score. If I tell you what's in there, I...'

'Yeah, I know. You have to shoot me.'

'Yep. Or challenge you to a duel.'

'You prefer hand-to-hand fighting?'

'Every time.' He surveyed the pans on the stove, gave one a stir and then turned his attention back to her. 'Don't you like to be able to look straight into the other man's eyes?'

'Of course. How else would I know exactly what he was thinking?'

He barked out a sudden laugh. 'Touché. So tell me all about this Christmas extravaganza of yours.'

It wasn't really hers and it wasn't much of an extravaganza, but it was something to talk about over their meal. Greg chuckled when she told him about the plan for carol singers, dressed up as characters from Dickens, and loved the idea for storytellers in the children's wards.

'That's a great idea. Aren't you going to go through to the general wards as well?'

'I don't know.' Jess shrugged. 'I didn't really think of doing that.'

'Adults love to be read to as well. There's evidence to suggest that it's beneficial for stroke patients. I imagine that a good storyteller could capture a lot of interest with the elderly as well.'

'Hmm. Yeah, worth thinking about.' She should have known that Greg would be able to add something to the value of the project.

'So what else?'

'As it's the hospital's two hundredth anniversary this year, we're going to do a small exhibition in the main foyer.

How things were then. There are loads of old documents in the basement, and I was thinking of making a model of the building.' He was giving her the same look that everyone gave her when she got to this bit. 'It's not as crazy as it sounds. It's going to be done properly, I'm not thinking of just gluing a couple of empty cereal packets together. It'll be 1:87 scale, like the model trains.'

'Trains?'

Jess rolled her eyes. 'What is it about men and model trains? Yes, trains if you like, the railway ran past the hospital then as well. Only I can't find anyone who's got any trains.'

'I'll give someone a ring. One of my father's associates in America. She has a talent for getting anything you can think of.'

'We don't have a budget…'

He swept her objections away with a wave of his hand. 'That's okay. No budget needed. Pat has a talent for that as well.'

Jess eyed him suspiciously, but he didn't look as if he was going to come up with any further explanations. And she wasn't in a position to look a gift horse in the mouth. 'Thanks. That would be great.' In for a penny… 'And the model?'

His lips twisted into a smile. 'Yeah, okay. I'll sort that out too.' He put his fork down onto his empty plate with a clatter. 'Anything else?'

'No, I think that's enough to keep you busy. Or…Pat, was it?'

He grinned. Perhaps she had been a little too transparent. 'Yeah, Pat. I've known her since I was five years old. She was going to retire this year but I convinced her to stay on for a little while, to help me sort out my father's estate.'

'Oh. Good idea.' Jess wasn't even going to admit to herself that she would have been jealous if Pat had turned out to be a leggy blonde. Or, more exactly, a leggy blonde in her twenties. 'Was it very complicated, then?'

'Yes.' The sudden flatness of his tone said that Greg had divulged as much as he was going to on the subject. 'Did you enjoy your food?'

'Very much. You have a great apartment, too.'

He looked around, as if he hadn't noticed. 'Glad you like it.'

What wasn't to like? Greg didn't live ostentatiously, but all his furniture matched and it screamed quality. And that was before you counted the large, top-floor living space, the tall windows and the amazing view.

'You moved in here recently?' This kind of apartment was far beyond the reach of a doctor's salary. He must have inherited the money from his father.

'No.' He laughed at her surprise. 'I had a trust fund. By the time it matured, it was enough for this place.'

Jess almost choked on the last mouthful from her plate. Greg obviously came from a very different background from hers. 'That sounds...useful.'

He leaned towards her. 'The last time I saw you look that disapproving was when Ray Harris ended up as a patient in his own ambulance.'

'That was my professional face.'

'No, it wasn't. You looked as sour as a bowl of lemons.' He was teasing her now.

'Well, it was a bit much. Ray was just trying to help—the guy didn't need to take a swing at him. How hard do you have to hit someone to break their cheekbone?'

'Hard. And you were a model of restraint. I couldn't have done better myself.' He chuckled.

'Of course you couldn't. I was there, remember? I saw what you did to that drinks machine.'

'It wasn't working. I pressed the button and got hot water all over my feet.'

'You didn't press it, you punched it.'

They were both laughing now. This was almost unbearable. The highs and lows, the humour, the camaraderie, all of it free of the framework of hospital rules and common sense, which had kept their relationship on a professional footing. There was nothing to protect her now.

'So what's so bad about having a trust fund, then?' He was still grinning.

Jess shrugged. 'Thought I was off the hook with that one.'

'You're not on any hook. I'm just interested.'

'I've just never known anyone with a trust fund. Does it make a difference? To the way you look at things, I mean.'

He threaded his fingers together. Long fingers. She already knew that Greg had a sensitive touch. 'I had to work just as hard as everyone else at med school. Lived in the same sorts of digs. It matured when I was thirty and by that time I'd already earned what I really wanted out of life. I imagine that was just as my father intended.'

'He sounds like an astute man.'

Something flickered in his eyes and then died. She was evidently not about to hear any of Greg's thoughts on his father. He rose and collected the empty plates from the table. 'Go and sit down. I'll make some coffee.'

'I'll help you with the dishes.' Jess made to get up.

'My guests don't do washing up.' He grinned at her protest. 'Neither do I. I'm just going to stack these in the dishwasher.'

Right. Of course he was. Jess shook her head at her own lack of sophistication and obediently descended the three steps that divided the dining area from the living space, sitting down on one of the butter-smooth, leather sofas.

He was back in ten minutes, along with a tray, laden with coffee and after-dinner sweets. 'This is nice. Really nice. Thank you.' He was more than just a good cook, he was a good host. Everything was in the right place, at the right time. And Jess was pretty sure that the music playing softly in the background had been chosen with her own favourite tracks in mind.

'Thank you.' He seemed about to ask something and then hesitated.

'I can only say no.' Jess might not have the sophistication that Greg had, but she could read between the lines.

'Nah. You won't do that.' He settled back in his seat, the soft leather easing with him.

'I might. You think you can just charm me into anything?' He probably could, but letting him know that would be a bad move right now.

He thought for a moment. 'No, I don't.' He let the compliment, if that's what it was, sink in. 'Unfortunately.'

'Why unfortunately?'

'Because some things are a lot easier when you have a friend around.'

All right. He'd got her now. After that, she couldn't say no. 'What things?'

'I've inherited a house from my father. I need to go up there next weekend as there are some things I need to sort out. I'd really appreciate some company.'

Jess pressed her burning cheek against the cool, brushed steel wall of the lift. So Greg had secrets. That was okay, everyone had one or two. His family had money. That wasn't exactly his fault. As a colleague, even as a friend, that wouldn't have mattered one way or the other.

He wasn't either of those any more, though. Not quite a lover yet, but Jess was becoming acutely aware that it would only take one touch. One kiss, and this time nothing would be able to stop them.

And if they didn't stop? If they went ahead? Greg would have the power to tip her well-ordered life on its head. Jess had no doubt whatsoever that he would, that was what Greg was like, he thought outside the box. The scariest thing about it was that this only made him even more irresistible.

She sighed. There was no guarantee that he wouldn't transform her world and then leave. If the hospital grapevine was anything to go by, that's exactly what he would do. But that didn't matter any more. However many reasons there were to have nothing more to do with Greg, she was going with him next weekend. That was all there was to it.

CHAPTER THREE

JESS'S WARDROBE WASN'T large, but it was focussed. Plain skirts and trousers and an assortment of matching blouses for work. A tailored suit for interviews, a few pairs of jeans, ranging from new to falling to pieces, and tops, ranging from very warm to very summery. A dress, bought for a summer wedding, which she'd worn only once. Nothing seemed suitable for a visit to the house that Greg had inherited from his father, which sounded large—no, sprawling—and far grander than anything she was used to.

Going out and buying something might have been an option, but she felt unequal to the task. New clothes would only serve to make her feel more uncomfortable anyway. Taking a little more care with her hair and make-up and choosing favourite pieces from her wardrobe would have to be enough.

'You look nice. I like your scarf.' He grinned as he took her coat and weekend bag, opening the passenger door of his car for her.

It was the one thing she'd allowed herself to buy. A pretty lilac scarf that went with her plain grey trousers and sweater and the black leather jacket that she normally kept for best. Greg was wearing jeans and a warm, slightly battered, leather jacket but he had a knack of making scruffy look stylish. Sexy too, but Jess was trying not to think too much about that.

'Do you want to put your jacket in the back? It's a long drive.' Greg had taken his own off and slung it on the back seat before getting into the car.

'Yes. Thanks.' She shrugged out of her jacket and he took it, draping it carefully over his.

'Right, then.' He twisted the key in the ignition. 'Let me know if you get cold and I'll turn the heat up.'

By the time they reached the suburbs she was feeling hot and cold by turn. When they hit the motorway, her stomach began to lurch. What was she doing? She'd been so brave, so thoughtless in agreeing to come away with him. He was so much more than a nice guy and a good doctor. He was sophisticated, drop-dead gorgeous and far more than a girl like her could handle. She was sure to make a fool of herself.

'You okay?'

'Hmm? Yes, fine.' Jess turned her head away from him, staring at the hard shoulder of the motorway.

'Sure?'

Cold perspiration began to form on the side of her brow. Suddenly she felt trapped, carried inexorably towards goodness only knew what. 'Um. Actually, I do feel a little sick.'

'Did you have breakfast this morning?'

She hadn't had time. She had been too busy fussing over her packing and her appearance and stressing about her trip with Greg. 'Not really...'

'There's motorway services a mile up ahead. We'll stop there.'

Just to swell the small fountain of misery that was bubbling up inside her chest, he helped her out of the car when they parked. And because standing made her head swim, she allowed him to. He kept hold of her until she was seated in the corner of the bleak, utilitarian cafeteria and then hurried to fetch toast and two cups of tea.

'Feeling better?' An awkward silence had only been rendered slightly more acceptable by having something to eat and drink.

'Yes. I'm fine, just one of those stupid things.'

He gave the throw-away line rather more consideration that it deserved. 'I could try acupressure.'

'Since when have you done acupressure?' Suddenly there was something to talk about. Something they shared. 'Don't tell me you've been getting into alternative medicine.'

He grinned. 'Don't tell me you've been getting into labels. There are lots of interesting techniques out there that bear quantitative investigation. When I was in the States, I met a guy who uses it to very good effect, in tandem with drug regimes.'

'So you were working as a doctor in America?'

'Just taking an interest.' He steered deftly around the question. 'Here, give me your arm.'

'What, so you can experiment on me? In a café at motorway services?'

'Well, I wouldn't do it on a patient.' She felt his fingers on her wrist, the thumb pressing firmly between the two bands of muscle that ran down the inside of her arm. 'What do you think?'

'Too many variables. I don't know whether we can come to a definite conclusion.' She was on steadier ground now. Jess ventured a smile.

He chuckled quietly. 'Do you think it matters which arm you do it on?' He'd clearly decided she felt better and had switched to ruminating on variations to his technique.

'I wouldn't know. Here, you want to have a go?' She held out her other arm.

'Hmm. Probably a bit late now.' He grasped her arm anyway and tried again. 'How's that?'

'Feels...okay.' Much, much better than okay. She was starting to tingle all over. Either he'd hit on a discovery that had eluded other medical practitioners for centuries or her body had decided that responding to his touch was a good idea. Great. A little warning might have been in order.

'Jess, we've known each other for long enough...'

'Worked together.' She corrected him quickly. Working together was one kind of knowing. This was another.

'I'm not your boss any more.' Something dark, like liquid promise, glowed in his eyes.

'I suppose that makes things less complicated.'

He grinned. 'Yep. But I won't pretend that I haven't worked alongside you for more hours at a stretch than either of our contracts allows for. I've seen you exhausted, cranky, messy...'

'Thanks a lot!'

'Fabulous, formidable...'

'Better.' They both smiled at the same moment.

'We've got past the point where we need to apologise for all our little foibles.'

'You mean you have foibles?' He did have a way of lifting her worries off her shoulders. Always had.

He shrugged. 'Well, when I said *our foibles* I was just trying to make you feel better about yours.'

'Oh, so you think you don't have foibles?' Jess wrinkled her nose at him. 'What about that famous charm of yours?'

'Doesn't seem to work on you.'

'Works on everyone else.'

'Can I help that?'

'Oh, yeah, you can help it. And the love 'em and leave 'em...'

'It keeps things simple. Anyway, I've changed. The last person I loved and left was...' He frowned, as if consulting his memory and not quite believing the answer he got back.

'Who?'

'You, actually.'

'Me! We didn't....'

He leaned across the table towards her. 'You don't need to. It only takes a touch.' He ran one finger down the back of her hand and Jess gulped, pulling her arm away.

'So what about my foibles, then?' Time to change the subject.

'Your what?' His gaze slid across her body, making her shiver.

'Foibles. Pay attention.'

'I am paying attention.' He pushed the teacups and the plate that stood between them on the table out of the way. 'Okay, so your eyes look as if they have flecks of gold in them. That's not contacts, is it?'

'Of course not.' She nudged her leg against his under the table. 'Foibles, I said.'

'I heard. Well, you're resourceful, talented, generally a force to be reckoned with. Only you don't much like being out of your comfort zone.'

Yes, okay, he might have a point. There were good reasons for her to feel that way. 'Maybe.'

He leaned forward, and Jess couldn't help but move towards him. She felt his lips brush her ear. 'It's a rather nice comfort zone, though.'

'Stop it.' She was feeling better now. As if the weekend wasn't so much of a trial to be got through. Jess almost wished that it was more than two days.

He drew back. From the look in his eyes there was no

question that the dialogue was still continuing somewhere in the back of his mind.

'Do you want to drive?'

'What for?'

'Sometimes driving can help if you're feeling a bit queasy.'

She stared at him. He knew just as well as she did that this was an excuse. That somehow, indefinably, she would feel a bit more in charge of her own destiny if she was in the driving seat. He was good. Good at putting her at her ease. Very, very good at making her want him.

'Okay. If you don't mind.'

He shrugged. 'Why would I mind?'

His car was a pleasure to drive. When she put her foot down on the motorway, it responded with a purr, rather than the laboured growl that her own car would have emitted. Greg pushed the passenger seat back so he could stretch his legs, and confined himself to giving directions. An hour later they turned into a long, gated drive and drew up outside the house.

'It's big.' Jess scanned the complex roof structure, which accommodated an elaborate arrangement of mock crenellations beneath it. There was even a circular tower, tacked onto one side of the building, with a set of battlements and a flagpole at its top.

He grinned. 'Yeah. Not the prettiest of places.'

'It's not meant to be. Victorian, right?'

'Yes, that's right.'

'Then the architecture's not about welcoming visitors, eh?'

He looked again. Leaned back to study the red-brick patterns over the windows and the heavy portico, as if this was the first time he'd seen the place. 'Never really thought about it. So what is it all about, then?'

'It's a statement. This house is all about the people who live here being different from the people who live down in the village. They wanted to impress with their power, not their good taste.'

He nodded. 'You think so?'

Yes, she knew so. The girl from a two-up, two-down felt confronted and challenged by this place and Jess imagined that was exactly how she was meant to feel. 'It's one way of looking at it.'

He nodded, obviously turning the idea over in his head. 'Well, come inside. It's a bit more homely there.'

Not so you'd notice. The large hallway was big enough to contain her whole flat, with height to spare, and the sweeping stone staircase continued the theme of a fortified castle. Leading up to a wide half-landing that was illuminated by a large, stained-glass window, the whole thing reminded her of a film set for a medieval saga.

'Here you are!'

A woman's voice sounded, and for a moment Jess couldn't work out which direction it had come from. Greg turned and made his way towards the back of the hallway.

'We stopped for breakfast.' He spared Jess the indignity of mentioning why. 'What are you doing here?'

A laugh. The first piece of warmth that Jess had met in this place. A figure emerged from the gloom, walking towards her. Mid-fifties, tall and slim. One of those women that made style look like a fortuitous accident.

'I popped in to turn the heating on and put some food in the fridge.' The woman ducked around Greg and made straight for Jess. 'You must be Greg's friend. I'm Rosa.'

'My mother.' Greg was grinning. 'Who never misses a chance to check out who I'm associating with.'

Rosa dismissed him with a casual movement of her fingers. 'Don't be so parochial, darling. Your friends might want to check *me* out.' She grasped Jess's hand, holding it in both of hers, and leaned in to kiss her. 'There. Both cheeks.'

'The Italian way.' Greg was leaning against the heavy stone balustrade which enclosed the stairs, his hands shoved into his pockets.

'Don't listen to my son. I hope you'll come over to my home for something to eat.'

'You live near here?' This was Greg's father's house. He'd said that his mother and father had divorced when he'd been a child, but she seemed very much at home here.

'Two miles in that direction.' Rosa flicked her fingers towards the dark recesses at the back of the hallway. 'You can walk across the fields, it's a nice day.'

Jess shot a questioning look at Greg. Perhaps this wasn't in his plan for the weekend.

'Have you made cannoli?' Greg was smiling at his mother.

'Of course.' Rosa turned to Jess. 'Did he think to tell you to bring any walking shoes?'

No, he hadn't. Jess wasn't sure how well her own shoes would stand up to a cross-country walk. 'Perhaps we can go by road.'

'If you want. Or I think there may be a pair of wellingtons in the cloakroom. If they're too big I'm sure that a couple of pairs of socks…'

'We'll manage.' Greg looked at his watch. 'When do you want us?'

His mother shrugged. 'Whenever you're hungry.'

'How does one o'clock suit you?'

'Perfect. Make it one-ish. Don't worry about being a little late.'

Greg rolled his eyes and kissed his mother, helped her into the waterproof coat that was slung on a low settle in one corner of the hallway and bade her goodbye. Alone again with him, the temperature in the cavernous, empty space seemed to drop a couple of degrees and Jess drew her jacket around her.

'Sorry, Jess. My mother wasn't really checking you out, she's not like that.'

'It was nice of her to come by, this place could do with warming up a bit. I didn't realise that your mother lived so close to your father.'

'My father wasn't here much.' Greg's mouth twitched downwards and he turned away, moving to the door at the back of the hallway where his mother had appeared from. 'He lived mostly in the States, but he came over here three or four times a year to take care of his business interests in Europe.'

'He kept this place empty, then, most of the time?' It was a huge house, even for a family. For one man, who was hardly ever there, it was ridiculous.

'He used to entertain a lot when he was here.' There was a trace of bitterness in Greg's voice.

'I suppose it was handy to see you as well.' Jess followed him into the large, well-equipped kitchen, which could have accommodated an army of caterers.

He raised an eyebrow. 'He was mostly working. Mum used to bring me over, and half the time we'd just make our own entertainment because my father was locked away in the study, on the phone.'

'But she still brought you.' A picture of Rosa, walking her young son across the fields so that he could see his father, floated into her head. How must she have felt when the boy was ignored?

'My mother was an eternal optimist where my father

was concerned. She always encouraged me to see him.'
He dumped the kettle down onto the range and lit the gas
underneath it.

In this house, he seemed surrounded by things he didn't
want to talk about. But he'd come here. He'd brought her
here. On some level he must be aware of that, and that the
seemingly complicated tangle of his relationship with his
father wasn't going to straighten itself out all on its own.

'So this is where you grew up?' She settled herself onto
one of a long row of kitchen stools.

'Yeah.'

'And you didn't see much of your father.'

'Nope. Not a lot.'

She'd hit a sore spot, but she kept pressing. Sometimes
you had to do that. 'But your parents were on good terms?'

He barked out a short laugh. 'Yeah. She loved him, and
in his way he loved her. They just had very different priorities. And it's not particularly easy to maintain a relationship with someone who only has about five uninterrupted
minutes a day to spend with you.'

'No. I imagine not.' Jess wondered whether Greg was
talking about his mother's relationship with his father or
his own. Probably a bit of both. 'Neither of them married
again?'

'Not straight away. But that doesn't mean they were
secretly yearning to get back together. My father had his
share of women friends. They loved the lifestyle for a
while and then realised that they'd always be playing second fiddle to his work. And my mother remarried when
I was fifteen. The local doctor. You'll meet Ted when we
go over there.' There was sudden warmth in his voice.

'So it was his footsteps you followed in.'

'Guess so. Mum made him wait, but he was always there

when I was a kid. He'd take us out somewhere every week-end, we used to have great adventures together.'

'But they never moved away from here?'

'Why should they? Ted's practice is down in the vil-lage. This is my mother's home much more than it ever was my father's.' He shrugged. 'Although he came back here at the end.'

'You mean he died here?'

Greg nodded. 'He hadn't told anyone that he had can-cer. But when he turned up here, two days after Christmas last year, it was obvious that he was ill. My mother called me, and I arranged for him to be seen by a specialist. My mother looked after him, right up until the end.'

'That was a nice thing to do.'

'Yeah. She's a nice person. I think somehow my father reckoned that he could correct some of the mistakes he'd made, but it was too late.' He poured the tea and set a cup in front of her on the marble worktop. 'Does that cover it?'

'I don't know. Does it?' Greg's secrets ran deeper than this. Nothing that he'd said explained the eight-month ab-sence after his father's death. Or the air of weariness that broke through whenever he talked about his father.

'Difficult to say. Would you like to see the house?'

'Why not?'

CHAPTER FOUR

THE HOUSE WAS full of large, chilly rooms that could have been light if it weren't for the heavy drapes at the windows and the dark wood panelling everywhere. Jess smiled politely and tried to see the best in it all.

'What's through here?' She pointed to the door at the end of the corridor that led from the top of the stairs. If she could find some corner of this house that she could genuinely own up to liking, she was determined to do so.

'It's the inside of the old turret. I used to play in there when I was a kid.' He strode forward, opening the door. 'No one's been in here for a while.'

The room was circular, with tall narrow windows that curved to a point at the top and a complex, many-angled ceiling above their heads. Dust sheets covered what looked like seating and occasional tables.

'This is great, Greg.' This time she could give unqualified praise.

'You like it? It's not very practical.'

'It's fun, though.'

'Yeah, it's definitely fun. I used to fight my way up and down those stairs quite regularly when I was a kid.' He nodded towards the stone stairway, which followed the curve of the wall down to the ground floor.

'Your very own medieval castle.' Complete with a few

ghosts from the past, if the memories flickering in Greg's eyes were anything to go by.

'Yeah.' He was looking around, seeing things she couldn't. 'We had a film crew here once. It was just a B movie and I don't think they set much store by historical accuracy but I loved it. I made my mother bring me here every day, just to watch.' He grinned proudly. 'I had a bit part.'

'Really? Who did you play?'

'A nameless, grubby urchin. Didn't get any lines, but I gave it my all.'

'I'm sure you did. So what's the film?'

'My mother has a copy. I dare say if you ask her, she'll let you savour every moment of my time on the silver screen in glorious slow-mo.' He went to turn but something stopped him. The ghosts weren't done with him yet, and he seemed caught, unable to move, his breath misting white in the chill of the air.

'Those memories are important.'

'They're...' He was making a visible effort to resist some beguiling force, but Jess couldn't tell what, and it was difficult to imagine what Greg could want that he didn't already have. His attention was suddenly focussed back onto her. 'It's cold in here. You're shivering.'

So do something about it. Hold me. Keep me warm. 'I should have packed a warmer sweater.'

'I have a few here.' He turned abruptly. 'Come and pick one out.'

His sweater didn't fit, but it was warm, and Jess could fold the cuffs so that her hands didn't disappear completely. And it smelled of him. Warm and sexy, and not really hers. She'd packed her best jeans, on the off chance she might need them, and Greg produced a pair of wellingtons along with a pair of thick woollen socks from the cloakroom.

'Are you sure it's okay for me to turn up at your mother's looking like this?'

'I think you look rather fetching. Red suits you.' Greg's smile would have made her feel fabulous, even if she'd been wearing rags. 'Anyway, you wouldn't want to make me feel underdressed, would you?'

The idea was faintly ludicrous. His jeans were a shade of something between indigo and black, which you generally didn't find on the high street. His sweater wasn't new, but it was soft, thick cashmere, like the one he'd lent her. Coupled with those dark good looks, he was quality from head to toe and would have fitted in anywhere.

He caught his car keys up from the hall table. 'I'll get your coat from the car.'

They tramped across the fields, keeping up a brisk pace against the cold. Jess was glad of the woollen scarf and gloves that Greg had produced from the cloakroom, which was beginning to take on the nature of a magician's cubby hole, from which it was possible to conjure up all manner of useful things that appeared to belong to no one in particular.

'That's where we're headed.' He pointed towards a house, standing on the outskirts of the village.

'It looks lovely.' Jess didn't have to search for something nice to say this time. The yellow-brick, rambling farmhouse was everything that Greg's father's house wasn't. Blending in with the trees and evergreen bushes that surrounded it, as if it had just grown there instead of having been brutally hewn from the countryside. 'This was your real home, then.'

'Yeah.' His pace seemed to quicken, the nearer they

got. As if he was leaving some burden behind. 'Where did you grow up?'

Jess smiled. 'Nowhere so grand.'

He twisted the corners of his mouth down. 'This isn't so very grand, is it?'

'It is quite grand. We didn't have our own medieval tower at home.'

'It's only mock-medieval—' He broke off, grinning. 'Yeah, I suppose the tower's not your average home extension. But stop changing the subject. I've already spilled the beans.'

Maybe he had. Maybe he'd just told her what he wanted her to know and kept the rest back. 'Not much to know. Just me and my mum. We had a little house in South London.'

He nodded. 'No brothers or sisters?'

'No. My father left before I was born.' Jess shrugged. 'I don't miss him. I can't, I didn't know him.'

'Can't you miss things that you didn't have?'

'I'm not sure there were any.' She answered too quickly. Maybe even a bit defensively.

He laughed. 'May I have your autograph?'

'Why?'

'I've never met anyone who's had everything they ever wanted before.'

Jess nudged her shoulder against his arm. 'Don't be dense, Greg. There's not much point in wanting things you're never going to have.'

'No. But sometimes you have to acknowledge them.'

'Because?'

'Because you can't start to work on what you need, unless you acknowledge what's missing.'

Maybe. She'd need to think about that. 'I guess I miss knowing about him. Silly things, like whether my eyes are the same colour as his. Whether there's anything in his medical history that I should be watching out for.'

He chuckled. 'Always good to know. Have you any idea where he is now?'

'In a manner of speaking. He was killed in a car accident fifteen years ago. Someone came to tell Mum.' Jess remembered that day well enough. The stranger who'd knocked on their door, and who her mother had taken into the kitchen to talk with privately. The silence in the house, and then the sudden resumption of normal life, as if her mother had made a conscious decision to put all of that behind her and never speak of it again.

Greg's pace slowed and he found her hand, tucking it under his arm. They fell into step together almost automatically. 'Did anyone ever say they were sorry? For that loss?'

'No. No one ever thought it was one.' It was what Jess had told herself, too.

'I'm sorry. For your loss.'

'Thank you.' She smiled up at him. He must have repeated that phrase any number of times in his career, but he always seemed to mean it. It came as a surprise to find how much it meant to her, too.

'Can I ask you a question, Greg?'

'Since when did you need permission for that?'

'How did you feel when your mother remarried? I mean...did you mind?'

'Mind? Well, Ted was practically living with us anyway. And we all went to Italy and had an enormous party, and I got to stay with my aunt, while they went off on honeymoon. I kissed a girl, broke my arm coming off my cousin's motorbike and generally had a whale of a time. My mother was horrified when she got back.'

'I bet she was. How old did you say you were?'

'Fifteen.'

'Hmm. My mother married when I was twenty.'

'And?'

'And her husband's a really nice man. He gives her the life she's always deserved and she's happy with him.'

'That's nice. And?'

He waited. Laid his gloved hand over hers, tucking it more firmly into the crook of his arm.

'I don't know if I should even say it. It sounds so stupid...'

'Oh, go on.' He chuckled. 'You can't leave me hanging now.'

Why not? He'd done the same to her. But if Jess gave a little, maybe he would. 'It was just a bit confusing. All my life she'd been telling me that we could manage on our own, that I didn't need a father and she didn't need a husband. Then all of a sudden she upped and got married.'

He chuckled. 'Must have been love.'

'Yeah. Suppose it must have been.' Jess wrinkled her nose.

'Did you look that disapproving when she broke the news?'

'No! Of course I didn't. I'm happy for her, of course I am. I just... When I was little I used to think that it would be me who would get a great job, find somewhere nice for us to live. That I'd be the one to make sure she was comfortable.' Jess forced a smile. 'I'm just being silly.'

He shrugged. 'Sounds reasonable enough to me. You know the trouble with people—families in particular, I've noticed—is that you have these great plans for them, how you're going to make everything right and so on, and then they just go out and do it all on their own. It's frustrating.'

Jess couldn't help laughing now. 'Is that a touch of megalomania I hear?'

'More than a touch, I imagine. Aren't all kids megalomaniacs? That's what growing up does to you, makes you realise that you can't control the world.'

'Oh, so you're saying that I need to grow up, are you?' Jess suspected that she probably did.

'Don't you dare. Stay as you are.' He grinned at her and quickened his pace. 'Only perhaps you could walk just a bit faster. We'll be late if we don't hurry.'

Being late didn't seem to figure much in Rosa's household. Dinner was cooking on the range, and Greg and Jess were both kissed and seated in the warm, bright kitchen. Ted arrived, kicking the mud from his boots at the back door, and Greg rose to meet him, their handshake giving way to a hug.

'I hear you're a doctor.' He accepted a glass of wine from his wife and sat down, next to Jess.

'Yes. I've been specialising in cardiology for the last year.'

Ted nodded. 'Interesting. I expect you're at the sharp end of things, working down in London.'

'The department's done some groundbreaking work in the last couple of years. I'm very junior, though.' Jess grinned. 'But I get to watch sometimes.'

Ted laughed. 'Best way to learn.'

'She's being modest,' Greg broke in. 'She's a rising star in the department.'

'A young woman with a bright future, then.' Ted was watching her thoughtfully and Jess felt herself flush.

The meal was served and eaten and Jess was forbidden from moving when it came to clearing the plates away. Rosa and Greg busied themselves with the washing up, leaving Jess to talk to Ted. 'Your practice must serve quite a big area. In comparison to London.'

'Yes. There are three of us, and we cover about sixty square miles. We keep busy.'

'It must be demanding. Not many of you to go around.'

'It has its moments.' Ted reached for the pot to pour himself a second cup of coffee, and the sharp note of a phone sounded.

'Oh!' Rosa made a splash in the washing-up water with her hand. 'Really?'

Ted smiled. 'Looks like it.' He reached for the phone.

'What?' Everyone but Jess seemed to know what the call was about before Ted had even answered the phone.

'Ted's an immediate care doctor. Means he's on call for any emergencies where ambulance personnel need support at the scene. That's his alert phone.' Greg had put the dish-cloth down and was waiting, watching Ted.

'Okay. Yes, tell them I've accepted the call.' Ted snapped the phone shut and looked at Greg. 'There's a pile-up on the motorway. Want to take a ride with me?'

Greg was already reaching for his jacket and grinned towards Jess. 'Are you coming?'

'If that's all right?' She shot a querying look at Ted.

'I never turn down a helping hand.' Ted turned to Rosa. 'Sorry, darling.'

'Go.' Rosa was clearly used to this kind of thing. 'Just come back again.'

Ted chuckled. If Rosa's return smile was anything to go by, they'd worked this one out a long time ago.

It was beginning to get dark, shadows reaching across the lanes in front of them, as if to smother what was left of the day. Ted joined the motorway and hit the siren, speeding towards the site of the accident.

'There, look.' Greg indicated a slew of stationary head-lights up ahead.

'I see it.' Ted guided the SUV into a space and got out.

Jess could see flashing blue lights approaching from the other direction, and hoped that it was an ambulance.

They moved as if choreographed. Ted was in the lead, the reflective panels on his jacket advertising his presence. Greg was half a step behind him, medical bag and torch in hand, stopping to listen to a man who had detached himself from the small crowd that had gathered around three vehicles, which the force of impact had locked together, like in some gruesome sci-fi movie.

'Okay, take me to her.' Greg turned, beckoning to Jess to follow him, and the man led them to an upturned car.

'She's under there.' Panic was welling in the man's voice as he pointed to the tangled wreckage. 'We couldn't get her out. It's her leg, it's trapped.'

'That's okay. We'll take care of her.' Greg stripped off his jacket and dropped it on the ground. 'Jess, will you see what other casualties we have?'

He didn't look around to catch her assent. He didn't need to. Jess jogged over towards Ted, pushing through the circle of people that surrounded him.

'What have you got?'

'Someone's trapped underneath a car there. Greg's going to see if he can reach her.'

'Okay. I've a couple here, but there's nothing major. You go and assist Greg.' Ted passed her his car keys. 'Take the green bag from the car over to him.'

'Thanks.' Jess took the keys and made for the car, pulling out the large holdall in the back, hoping it would contain whatever they needed. She could see Greg carefully manoeuvring himself under the wreckage, trying to reach the injured woman, and doubted that her leg was his immediate concern. He couldn't treat her here. All he needed to do was to keep her alive until she got to the hospital.

She jogged over to the car, dumping the bag on the

ground and calling out to Greg to let him know she was there. A slight nod of his head told her that he'd heard, and that was all he needed to know for the time being. She could see the woman now, her leg pinned under the collapsed steering column, apparently unconscious.

The side of a truck blocked the driver's door and Greg had crawled in via the passenger door, twisting his body around the buckled frame to examine the woman as best he could in the cramped space. Jess unzipped the bag and quickly looked through the contents, arranging what she might need to one side.

They worked as if they were one unit. They'd done this before, although not for a while now, but the passage of time hadn't dulled their edge. Greg worked quickly, Jess putting what he needed into his hand, almost before he had a chance to ask for it.

'I think she's waking up.' Jess saw the fingers of the woman's outstretched hand flutter then clench. 'Pain relief?' Jess got the words out two seconds before the woman started to scream.

'Yep.' Greg's head snapped back as a flailing hand caught him square in the face, and he struggled for a moment to control his patient. 'Okay. Okay. I'm a doctor. You're going to be okay. We're getting you something for the pain.' He held her tight. Not just to stop her from moving and injuring herself any further, but for comfort. The screams subsided and the woman whimpered in his arms.

He called out the dosage, and Jess slid carefully inside the car, gasping as the sharp smell of blood and sheared metal hit her. She could reach the woman's arm, and she cut the sleeve of her coat and searched for a vein. 'Okay... That's it...done.'

'Good. Now go.' His voice was suddenly harsh, an order

instead of a request, and Jess wriggled backwards out of the wreckage.

She wished he wouldn't do that. He was the senior doctor, and there was no need for two of them to run the risk of being inside the wreckage. All the same, it rankled somehow that she wasn't by his side. The firefighters had just arrived on the scene, and she was pushed aside so that the senior man could speak directly to Greg and assess the situation.

She heard Ted's voice behind her. 'The hardest decision is knowing when to step back.'

Jess composed her face into a smile and turned. 'I just do as I'm told.'

'Really?' A smile played around Ted's lips. 'I'd be disappointed if that turned out to be true.'

He pulled her to one side, as someone came through with props to shore up the unstable wreckage. She could hardly see Greg now, masked by twisted metal and concentrated activity.

Ted was still watching every move that the firefighters made. 'See, they're going to cut through there. It won't be long now, and Greg knows what he's doing.'

'Yes, he does. He's a great doctor.'

Ted nodded, with the air of a suspicion confirmed. 'Damn shame.'

'What?'

'If he decided to re-evaluate his priorities.'

'But he's only just back from…' Jess stared at Ted. His measured demeanour wasn't just for show, he'd said no more and no less than intended. What *was* going on with Greg?

She could find that out later. For now it was enough to watch as the fire crew began the task of carefully peeling back the layers of metal that imprisoned the woman. She had calmed as the morphine kicked in, and Jess could hear Greg talking to her in between the shouts and the sounds of machinery. She knew he'd be watching her like a hawk, checking her responses, her BP, her pulse. His job was to make sure that she was brought out of the wreckage alive, and his quiet, reassuring tones were all part of the fight that he was putting up to do so.

Greg had shielded her face with his hand, holding her as the final agonising manoeuvres removed the metal that was trapping her legs. And then, at last, she was out.

CHAPTER FIVE

TINA WAS FREE of the twisted wreckage. Her leg was badly broken and she had a few nasty cuts, but she was comfortable and on her way to hospital. Greg smiled to himself as he watched the blue lights disappearing over the brow of a hill. He couldn't ignore the buzz. The excitement of meeting a challenge. The feeling that he'd helped make the biggest difference of all to someone.

It was starting to sleet, and when he turned, Jess was standing behind him. Little shards of ice were beginning to stick to her hair, and one glistened on her eyelashes. The temptation to brush it away hit him hard and twisted remorselessly in his chest.

'Good job.'

She was smiling at him. Greg wondered whether it was her smile or her words that meant the most to him. Perhaps they were inseparable.

'This is what you were meant to do, Greg.'

He didn't want to get into that at the moment. He was tired and Jess was beginning to shiver. 'Is Ted ready to go?'

'Yes, he's in the car.' She gestured towards the SUV.

'Let's make tracks, then.'

Greg stayed long enough to see Ted tip himself into an armchair and then borrowed his mother's car keys to take

Jess home. She was wet, cold and dirty. Lovely beyond any accepted sense of the word.

'I think I need a shower.' She grinned at him, half-apologetically.

'Yeah. Me too.' Greg saw her flush slightly and elaborated quickly. 'Your room has an en suite bathroom.' Therefore his did too. Two geographically separate showers. 'I'll get the fire going in the living room and heat up some soup.'

'Sounds fabulous.' She gave him a smile and made for the stairs.

The house didn't do sunny at all. It didn't really do welcoming, and Greg was aware that although he'd stopped noticing that a long time ago, Jess hadn't failed to. What it did do tolerably well was long winter evenings, curled up in front of the fire. Greg lit the firelighters in the grate, and arranged a couple of easy chairs close enough to catch the heat when the blaze got going.

She took her time upstairs. Greg had showered, heated the soup and bought a tray through to the living room before some sixth sense alerted him of her presence behind him.

'What have you been doing up there?' He turned and almost dropped the mug of soup that he was holding. She looked like cotton candy. Pink cheeks and a thick, white towelling robe that she'd found in the bathroom, with pink pyjamas on underneath. Thick socks on her feet. Wet hair, combed back from her face. Greg nearly choked with desire.

'Is it okay to use this?' She tugged at the robe.

'Of course. That's what they're there for.' He didn't even know were they came from. They were just there, and the housekeeper who came in three times a week made sure that they were laundered and fresh in all the guest rooms. 'Come and sit down.'

'Thanks.' She sat, tucking her legs up beneath her. Greg handed her a mug of soup and she rewarded him with a smile of complete happiness.

He stoked the fire until flames began to crackle in the grate. Sat back down in his chair and allowed himself to watch her. Relaxed, curled up in an armchair, revelling in the heat of the fire.

'Can I ask you a question?' Her gaze was steady on his face and Greg almost flinched.

'Of course.'

'What did you feel? When you got that woman out of the car.'

That sounded like a trick question. 'You know what I felt.'

'Yes, I do. I just wanted to make sure that...' She paused, studying the flames. 'That you hadn't lost that feeling. Or reconsidered it. Anything like that.'

What had Ted been saying to her? Or perhaps his mother had dragged her off into a corner somewhere for one of those woman-to-woman chats. But Ted and his mother knew no more than Jess did. Perhaps he was just not as good at hiding it as he'd thought.

'It doesn't get old. You saw Ted, he's been a doctor for thirty years and he still gets a thrill out of what he does.'

'Good. That's good.' She was watching the fire as if it contained the answer to everything. As if she could see her dreams reflected in it, if she only looked hard enough. 'When you were away...'

'Not tonight, Jess. Please.'

'You don't know what I was about to say.'

'Whatever it is.' He leaned back in his chair, letting the warmth from the fire relax his knotted muscles. Just one evening off from the continual, nagging demands that had dogged him from one side of the Atlantic to the other. 'Can we talk about it another time?'

She didn't seem sorry to let it go for a while, shifting in her chair, snuggling and stretching like a cat. 'Okay. Another time.'

He put some music on. Sleepy background music, playing softly so that it didn't drown out their conversation. The talk drifted, sliding effortlessly from the plans for Christmas at the hospital to model making and then on to storytelling.

'This is just the place. An open fire, cold outside, not another soul for miles.' She grinned wickedly. 'It was a dark and stormy night...'

'And the electricity was off.'

'And the water.'

'Water? Does that matter?' She shrugged and he grinned at her. 'Okay, then the gas is off too.'

She snorted with laughter. 'That doesn't matter either. Ghosts don't mind gas.'

'How do you know?'

'They're ephemeral beings. They are probably some sort of gas themselves.'

'If you say so. The gas was on, then, and the candle-light flickered low around the people stranded in the middle of nowhere.'

'Whose car had broken down.'

'And then they realised that they'd both forgotten to re-charge their phones.'

'Yep. And the landline's down as well.'

'And the walk down to the next village is blocked by snow.'

'And they've forgotten their snow boots.' She was laughing now.

'Reasonable enough thing to do. So they're alone in the house, quite unaware that something's lurking.'

'And they put some music on…'

'I thought the electricity was out.'

She grinned. 'He's very resourceful, he's managed to fix it. They put some music on to drown out the sound of the rain on the windows and the bumps and creaks in the house.'

'Yeah. Only it's snowing, not raining.'

'Snow doesn't make a noise on the windows.'

'Sleet, then.'

'Okay, sleet.' She nodded, the way she always did when she considered something sorted. In the firelight she was almost unbearably beautiful. 'They turn the music up loud, because they're out in the country now and don't have to worry about disturbing the neighbours.'

'Like this.' Greg leaned over, sweeping his finger across the shiny surface of his mp3 player, choosing a slow dance track and cranking up the volume.

'Just like that.' Her fingers started to follow the beat, moving gently on the arm of her chair. Almost a caress.

'And they dance.' The story was taking a volatile turn, but Greg didn't care. It was just a story. Something to ward off the darkness.

She hesitated. 'She's not really dressed for dancing.'

'But it doesn't matter, because she's exquisitely beautiful in the firelight.' Greg got to his feet. Took her hand and in response to his gentle tug she was on her feet. In his arms.

It was just the way it had been before. Jess could ward off all manner of bad spirits and all of his fears for the future. There was no past, no future, just the present. He led their slow dance, circling her in front of the fire.

'Nice.' The music has finished but they were still dancing, bodies pressed together. No friction, just moving in perfect synchronisation. 'This is nice, Greg.'

'Just nice?'

'Lovely.' She rested her head on his chest and he caught the clean scent of her hair. 'Scary.'

'Stick with me. You said I was very resourceful.'

She laughed quietly, snuggling closer to him. She wanted this as much as he did. A break from reality, where they could just follow their own instincts. Right now his instinct was to kiss her.

She didn't stop him. Let him press his lips against her cheek, taste the warmth of her skin. When he ran one thumb over her lips, she shivered slightly against him. And when he kissed her mouth she gave a sigh, as if she'd been holding her breath, waiting for this.

'What are we doing, Greg?'

'Dancing.' He brushed his lips against her cheek. 'Kissing.'

'Is it a good idea?'

'Yeah. It's a very good idea. Last Christmas...it wasn't just a mistake that's better off forgotten.'

'It was a long time ago.'

'It was just yesterday. Nothing's changed.' Everything had changed, but Greg could find his way back. Pretend that tonight was a loop in time, and they could simply pick up where they'd left off.

'You sure about that?'

'I'm not very sure about a lot of things at the moment.' He took her hand and laid it over his heart. 'This, I'm sure of.'

'Yeah.' She managed a watery smile. 'Tachycardia. You might think about making an appointment with Gerry.'

'I'd rather you dealt with it.' He laid his hand over hers,

sliding it inside his shirt, feeling his skin react to the heat of her touch. Electricity buzzed in the air around them.

Her hands slid to his neck and then up, to cup his face. 'Does this mean…?' She shrugged. 'I don't even know what it means.'

He laid a finger to her lips. 'It means just you and me, for tonight. Every moment until the sun rises. Everything else will wait.'

'Yes. I think it will.' She pulled his head down towards her, and kissed him. Drew back slightly, confident that if she gave him one taste, he'd take a second.

One hand moved to the tie of her bathrobe and he caught her wrist. 'I'll do it.' He'd fantasised about undressing her for too many months to miss it now.

'Hmm. Not exactly silk and lace.'

He laughed against her lips. 'Warmer. Nicer.'

'You're such a charmer, Greg.' That friendly, one-quarter mocking tone that she used whenever he tried to dress things up with pretty words. Jess was about the only woman he knew who talked about his charm, the rest of them just lapped it up and fell victim to it.

'So it's not working?'

'It's working.' She planted a kiss on his lips and charm suddenly felt as if it was a private joke, just between the two of them. Something that made her smile but didn't touch the honest, down-to-earth fire that he wanted more than anything else that he could think of.

Actions now. He was trembling like a teenager, afraid of not doing this right. It was crazy. He knew how to please a woman. But, then, Jess wasn't just any woman.

Carefully, he tugged at the knot at her waist, fumbling with it. It came loose and he slipped the bathrobe down her shoulders, tightening his grip when it reached her elbows and pulling her against him. She gasped with delight.

'Do you think I'm going to put up a struggle?'

He almost let go, shocked at the strength of his urgency, and then she kissed him again. Arms pinioned at her sides, almost helpless, and loving every moment of his desire for her.

'Are you going to, then?'

'Oh, yeah. Every time.' She slipped free of the bathrobe and it fell at her feet. 'You?'

'I think I might.' He'd lose. Greg knew that he couldn't resist her and that he couldn't protect himself with well-worn phrases or practised caresses. This was uncharted territory, and, dammit, it he just couldn't keep himself away from it.

He unbuttoned her pyjama top, finding that there was another layer underneath. Good. A pretty, lace trimmed vest, which somehow managed to combine the practical with the erotic.

'My turn.' She undid the buttons of his shirt, her tongue pressed between her lips in concentration. Pulled it away from his shoulders and tossed it away. The soft pressure of her fingers on his shoulders overwhelmed him, and Greg fell to one knee on the hearthrug in front of her.

'Now you.' His hands on her hips held her steady, and he nodded towards the vest.

'Don't you want to do it?'

'I want to watch.'

She pulled it off, shaking her head slightly to free herself. Breathing fast, but steadily, as if she was trying to pace herself. His hands put an end to that and she gasped then cried out.

He explored the smooth skin of her arms, the lush curves of her breasts. Ran his finger down her spine, to the sensitive knot of nerves in the small of her back, and she shivered, sagging forward against his shoulder. Greg pulled at the waistband of her pyjama bottoms, and slid them down, pulling her socks off, one by one, in a slow, tender striptease.

She pulled him to his feet, her gaze fixed on his face. Greg felt her fingers on his belt buckle, gently working it loose. Held in the luminous fire of her gaze, he felt rather than saw her undo the top button on his jeans.

'Sit down.' Greg let her back him towards an armchair, and almost collapsed into it. He wanted this. Wanted to offer his body to her in all its frailty, and let her break him and put him back together again.

She was down on her knees, completely naked, unlacing his shoes. Carefully slipping them off, as firelight flickered across her skin, bathing it in warmth and texture. He'd never seen anything so beautiful before in his life.

'Jess.' He leaned forward to kiss her. The time was right. Pulling the heavy throw from the sofa onto the floor in front of the fire, he laid her down on it. She was pulling at the fastenings of his jeans now, and he batted her hands away. 'Not yet, honey. This is all for you.'

Who wouldn't be beguiled by those words? Before he lifted her up, carrying her swiftly up the wide staircase, he'd already made good on their promise, right there in the flickering shadows of the hearth. Caresses that had made every part of her body react.

Soft, whispered words, kisses that had made her shiver in the heat of anticipation. When his slow, steady assault on her senses had proved too much, tearing the last of her inhibitions away, he'd held her tight in his arms, as if he'd known that she'd needed some protection from the fierce power of her own desire for him.

His bedroom was in darkness, and she wasn't there to admire the furniture anyway. The sudden chill of the sheets when he laid her down was just another sensation, another pleasure to nerve endings that were fast becoming unable to register anything else.

'Greg. I need...'

'I know what you need.' It wasn't just a hollow piece of male swagger. He did know what she needed. And somehow she knew just what he needed, too.

'Some light.' Before she'd said it, he had already been reaching for the switch by the bed, and a couple of lamps glowed into life.

'It's cold in here.' He curled his body around hers, wrapping her in his warmth.

'I need to breathe.' Her need for him was so urgent that she'd almost forgotten how.

He settled her beneath him, holding her tight. In one slow, smooth movement he was inside her, and Jess cried out. Sucked in a lungful of air and gasped it back out again as he moved.

'I need you to do that again.'

Greg had slept for a just a few blissful, unbroken hours before he woke, but it felt like more. Quietly, carefully, so as not to disturb Jess, he got out of bed and slipped on his jeans and a sweater.

As he passed through the hallway, the clock downstairs chimed midnight. Jess had just shaken his world, along with rocking, rolling and turning it upside down. Greg made for the one place in this house where he'd always been able to be alone and to think clearly.

This Christmas...

He was in love. The realisation hit Greg like a hammer, almost flattening him. But as he drifted gently forward in time, a week, then two, he rather got to like the idea. When Christmas came, his one thought was how he could make it special for Jess.

Did his father's company have a private jet at its disposal? Greg was sure that it probably did. He could take Jess somewhere sunny for Christmas, an island that was secluded enough for them to make love on the beach, without any fear of being discovered.

Greg reconsidered for a moment. Was that really so practical? Maybe not up till now but, then, he'd never had Pat's unending resourcefulness at his disposal. If anyone could locate a deserted tropical island for Christmas, Pat could.

For the purposes of reorientation he ran through the part about making love on the beach again. Then once more, with a set of subtle but enormously rewarding amendments. He could almost taste the salt on her warm skin.

He could afford to give Jess everything. She didn't need to work, she could do whatever she pleased. She could travel with him, and a little charity work would appease her need to help others.

Was he serious? The thought of Jess giving up her career in favour of sipping cocktails and doing a little charity work was about as likely as... Well, it was impossible. There had to be something else.

There was something else. He would have to dump the company he'd inherited from his father and had been struggling to save for the last eight months, but it was surprising how good the prospect felt. That would leave him with nothing to worry about other than how tall a Christmas tree the ceilings of his apartment would allow, and nowhere else to spend his time other than with Jess. Presents in the morning, a visit to the hospital to see how the carol singers were doing, and then on to his mother's for one of those late lunches that she did with such aplomb.

He'd so hoped...

Greg put up a struggle before he reluctantly let go of the fantasy and it disappeared back into his subconscious. This wasn't the time for hopes. Dreams either, although if this wasn't one then Greg wasn't sure what he should call it. Did he really think that he was going to be able to watch Shaw Industries go down, just because he had somewhere else to be? Would Jess ever respect him for abandoning the people who had worked for his father and now worked for him? People who had families to support, workers who were close to retirement and would struggle to find another job.

He had to face facts. His father, the ultimate autocrat, had structured the company to fail without him, or his son, to provide strong leadership. Like it or not, he was the only one left now. He was going to have to find a way to balance it all, something for the company, something for Jess, and whatever was left over for himself. He couldn't think about the chances against that working. All he could do was make a lunge for the slim thread of hope that it might.

CHAPTER SIX

JESS WOKE UP alone. The clock registered ten minutes past midnight, and she stretched her limbs and turned over to go back to sleep.

When had that happened? This inability to sleep without Greg beside her? She turned over again, burrowing deep into the duvet, and then gave up.

He wasn't downstairs in the living room, and Jess skittered over to the fireside, still warm from the glowing embers in the grate. Pulling on her dressing gown and socks, which still lay discarded on the floor, she made for the kitchen.

Not there either. It was as if Greg had vanished completely, sucked back into the vortex of the real world. She wasn't quite ready for that. Just a little more time in this no-man's land, where the unthinkable might just come true.

She padded back upstairs, wondering whether she should put her head around all the bedroom doors. Then a line of light under the door at the end of the corridor, which led to the tower room, changed her mind.

The grandfather clock in the hallway started to go through the truncated chimes that heralded the quarter-hour. Jess twisted the handle of the door, opening it quietly. Greg hadn't bothered to strip the dust sheet off the chair, and sat on it with his back to her, seemingly staring out of the window at the moon as it hung silently in the sky.

'Greg?' Her breath streamed white in the cold air. 'It's freezing in here.'

If she'd crashed two trays together next to his head, he probably wouldn't have jumped any further. He twisted round, a look of blank shock on his face.

'What's the matter? You look as if you've seen a ghost.' Jess regretted the words immediately. You generally said that kind of thing to people who clearly hadn't seen a ghost. For one moment she wasn't quite sure whether she hadn't hit the nail squarely on the head.

He recovered himself, reaching for her, and she let him pull her down onto his lap. 'You feel solid enough.'

'You're checking?'

'Best to be sure.' He kissed her, taking his time, and something stirred inside her. Something that had already had its fill and ought to be fast asleep now.

'What are you doing in here?'

He shrugged. 'I couldn't sleep, so I thought I'd get up for half an hour, rather than disturb you. I must have dozed off.'

'I woke up and you weren't there.'

His lip curled slightly, in obvious gratification. 'Couldn't sleep without me?'

'You think it's a good thing that you have a soporific effect on me?'

His eyes taunted her. 'You think there was any danger of you going to sleep one minute before I let you?'

She planted a kiss on the end of her finger and transferred it to his forehead. 'In other words, I'm like putty in your hands?'

He slipped his hand inside her gown, trailing his cool

fingers across the warm skin of her leg, and she shivered with delight. 'Looks as if you are.'

'Come back to bed.'

He grinned. 'Yes, ma'am. Whatever you say.'

As soon as he had her back in his bedroom he stripped her naked, his own clothes slung on top of hers on the arm-chair in the corner of the room. The bed was still warm, and Jess curled up beside him.

'Mmm. That's better.'

'Much.' His hand wandered across her ribcage. 'Jess, what are you doing for Christmas?'

She smiled into his shoulder. Christmas with Greg would be wonderful. 'I'm staying in London. There's a lot to do at the hospital.'

'Won't that all be organised by then? You deserve some time off.'

'I'll have time off. But I can't ask people to give up their time over Christmas without being there myself.' That didn't seem to be what Greg wanted to hear. 'Why?'

'Nothing. I just wondered.' He rolled her over onto her back, kissing her, lingering over her lips until he'd taken his fill. 'Maybe I can persuade you differently.'

'Not like that, you can't.'

'Oh, really? Is that a challenge?'

'No. Would you want to be able to change my mind when you know I'm doing something worthwhile?'

He didn't answer. The Greg she knew wouldn't have had to. As she gave herself up to his caress, the final, fleeting thought in Jess's head was that she hoped this was the Greg that she was sleeping with.

It was barely light when she opened her eyes. She was warm, almost blissfully relaxed, and alone again.

Where was Greg now? She clambered out of bed and

opened the door, craning her head around it, half expecting to see the door at the end of the hallway open.

Greg's voice sounded, quiet and muffled from downstairs. A pause, and then he spoke again. He was talking to someone.

She felt like a spy. As if she was snooping around his house, trying to catch him doing something he clearly didn't want her to know about. But he'd deflected the conversation too many times, left too much unanswered. He was hiding something. Jess moved noiselessly along the hallway, pausing at the top of the great stairway and leaning over the stone balustrade.

'The new controls do involve extra work, though, Ed. Everyone deserves to be paid for the hours they put in.'

Another pause.

'Ed, that's the end of it. I've reviewed all the options, and that's the fairest for everyone... No, that's final.' Greg's voice was firm, decisive. No surprise there. But the note of irritable bad temper didn't sound like him. Jess tried to turn away but she couldn't and instead she sank to the floor, as if the rough, stone buttresses could shield her from what she was hearing.

'No, I realise that, Ed. I'll prepare something for the board, so that they all know exactly where this directive is coming from. When's the meeting? Ten on Tuesday. That's nine o' clock Monday night our time, isn't it? Right. I'll get back to you before then.'

Eleven hours' time difference. That was the other side of the world. America was eight hours at most, wasn't it? And yet this sounded like business talk, certainly nothing to do with the hospital. Jess heard a clatter as a telephone handset was put back into its cradle and she sprang to her feet, racing up the hallway towards the guest room where her overnight bag still sat on the undisturbed bed. In less than a minute she was in the shower, the door firmly locked behind her.

So what on earth was he supposed to do? Greg took his feelings out on the loaf of bread that he was cutting for toast, and had to throw the resulting slice into the bin. He had a chance to make a difference here. The hours weren't exactly regular, but neither were they at the hospital. He had hoped that Jess might understand.

He'd been aware that she was there, even before he'd put the phone down, and had heard her blundering along the hallway. Greg couldn't deny that his exaggerated sense of his own innocence had something to do with the fact that he also felt guilty as hell.

There was only so long that he could resent Jess, though. And with the scent of her still on his skin, the feel of her echoing through his memory, *only so long* wasn't very long at all. She walked into the kitchen, showered and dressed, and Greg was lost again.

'Hey, there. You're up early.' He bent to kiss her but the immediate fit that had moulded them together last night was lost now, and his lips brushed her cheek instead of her mouth.

'So are you. I woke up and you weren't there.'

'I had something to do.'

Her look, half hurt and half suspicious, made his mind up for him. He could break his rule, just once. He'd let her ask him about the business and then she wouldn't need to wonder again.

He waited until she had coffee and toast in front of her, and sat down next to her at the breakfast bar. 'There's something I want to talk to you about.'

She turned her gaze on him, thoughtful and shot through

with golden tenderness. She'd done that last night, when the honesty had got too much to bear, soothing him, letting him know that it was all right.

'I wanted to talk to you about what I've been doing for the last eight months.'

She couldn't disguise her reaction and she didn't try. 'I have been wondering. I'm glad you want to talk about it.'

'You might like to wait until you've heard what it is.'

'Whatever it is, it can hardly be as fantastical as the hospital gossip.'

'There was gossip?' Of course there had been gossip. It was one of the oddities of life that in an institution devoted to the sick, you only had to sneeze and someone remarked on it.

She smiled. 'What do you think? Opinion was split between you having a secret twin that you'd gone to find and you having inherited countless millions. There was some talk of a treasure map, but that one didn't run for too long. I think Gerry suggested it as a polite way of shutting everyone up and it backfired on him.'

'No one said anything.'

'Everyone's forgotten about it now.' She smiled at him. 'I'm afraid you only get fifteen minutes of fame. Then no one remembers your name.'

He laughed. She made everything so easy. That was part of what had made her such an invaluable part of his team. No expectations, no prejudices. Just find out what the situation is and deal with it.

'So what was it really, then?' She was gently prodding him in the right direction.

'Well, there's no lost twin. No treasure map.' He almost regretted the absence of both. In fact, a treasure map might have been an adventure. 'The countless millions are a bit closer to the mark, although I believe my accountant knows how many there are.'

She was frowning. 'But, it's obvious that your father was wealthy—this is a big house. Is there a problem with that?'

'No, Jess.' She wasn't understanding him. 'My father was a *very* rich man.' He put as much emphasis as he could on the 'very'. 'Houses on three continents. A multi-million-pound business that I'm only just coming to grips with how to run. A racehorse.'

'A racehorse!' This was all taking time to sink in, and the rest was beyond her grasp at the moment. 'What's its name?'

'I have no idea. I don't really want to know, I might start getting attached to it.'

'Three continents?' She was getting there.

'Yeah. One in Australia, two in America, one in Rome and one here. The one in Rome's really nice.'

She was shrinking back from him, as if he'd just admitted to being an imposter from outer space who'd taken over his own body.

'I could take you there for a holiday, over Christmas maybe. I think you'd love it.'

She swallowed hard. 'But it's the business, isn't it? That's what the problem is.'

She might be feeling acutely flabbergasted, but you could never accuse Jess of not being able to size up a situation.

'Yes, exactly. My father and I weren't particularly close and he wasn't best pleased when I decided to go to medical school. It would have been nice to have a few personal things of his, but I'd always counted on him leaving his business interests to someone involved with the business.'

'But you're his son!' It made Greg smile to hear her assert his filial rights. 'You're his only child?'

He nodded. 'Yeah, no long-lost siblings. Or if there are, they're keeping quiet and I can't say I blame them. It's down to me to sort everything out.'

Jess stared at him. Most people would have been over-joyed to hear of such an inheritance. Most women would already be planning the trip to Rome. Somehow she didn't seem to be quite on board with that. 'But isn't that what you were doing when you were away?'

'I've made a start.' He took a sip of his espresso. 'The board of directors is split over practically every issue you can name. My father chose people who were ambitious and who would think out of the box. He was the ultimate authority who kept it all under control, and that worked well when he was alive. Now it's tearing itself apart at the seams.'

'And…you mean you're still running it?'

'Not the day-to-day stuff. But, yes, I'm running it. I don't have much choice; there are thousands of people de-pending on it for their livelihoods.'

'Couldn't you sell it?'

'Yes. But it needs to be sold as a going concern.' In truth, Greg hadn't even considered selling up. 'And it was so important to my father…'

'That's the thing, isn't it? It was the most important thing in his life and now he's given it to you. And if you give it up, it's like having to give him up all over again.' She spoke quietly, no trace of accusation in her voice. All the same, the words were like shards of broken glass, slic-ing at his heart.

'That's as may be.'

'Greg, tell me that you're not thinking of leaving again.'

'I don't want to leave you, Jess, that's not what all this is about.'

'Not me. The hospital. Your job.'

'I seem to have two jobs at the moment. I'm not sure how long I can sustain that.'

She just stared at him. Nothing could have hurt Greg

more than her complete, speechless incomprehension. 'Jess, you have to understand.'

'I don't, Greg.' She brushed tears from her eyes. 'But that doesn't mean I won't support you.'

That was something, at least. Perhaps when she'd thought about it a bit, or when she saw the house in Rome? The prospect was remote, but it was a possibility. 'There is something I need some help with.'

She nodded, looking at him solemnly.

'My father left a notebook. I didn't see it when I was here visiting him, but my mother said he showed it to her and told her that it was for me. I can't find it.'

'And you think that it's here somewhere?'

'That's what I'm hoping.'

She straightened, as if at last this was something that she could get to grips with. 'I'll help you look.'

The idea was outrageous. Unthinkable. Greg was far too good a doctor to just give it all up. He loved it too much. He'd never needed to say it, it was clear by the light in his eyes when he brought someone back from the edge. The child had a right to his father's time. The man had a right to pursue his own destiny. It seemed that Greg's father was going to take both of those rights from him.

She wanted to fight for him, but she didn't know how, so she turned her energies to the journal. Leather bound, Greg said, about the size of a paperback book. When he took her into the large library, shelves reaching up to the grand, moulded plaster ceiling, that started to look like finding a needle in a haystack.

'Okay. So why don't you sort the papers that you need to take from here, and I'll look through the books?' She surveyed the task in front of her and swallowed hard.

'You and whose superpowers, Jess?'

'How hard can it be?' She pulled the sleeves of her sweater up to her elbows and found herself suddenly crushed against his chest. 'What's this for?'

'For being too pig-headed to know when to give up.'

'They're only books.' A lot of them. Many leather-bound. Jess wondered what it would be like to have had access to a library like this. No wonder Greg seemed to know so much about so many things.

'And they don't frighten you, eh?' He was hugging her tight. Not the fevered embrace of a lover, just a man who seemed to need some warmth at the moment.

Nothing frightened Jess quite as much as the idea that Greg was thinking about tearing his life to shreds. 'We could narrow it down a bit. If your father was ill, he probably couldn't make it up to the top shelves.' She eyed the tall library steps.

'He could have asked someone to climb up there for him. We had carers here pretty much all the time. And there are the staff in the house, although my mother's given pretty much all of them the third degree and no one seems to have seen the book.'

'Hmm. Suppose I stand on top of the steps and you wheel them along so I don't have to keep running up and down to move them? Would that work?'

'Yeah, it'll work.' He grinned at her. 'You'll have to hang on.'

'Done this before, have you?'

'All the time, when I was a kid.'

'Well, then, you can show me how. Now, let go of me and let's get started.'

CHAPTER SEVEN

THEY WERE OFF the motorway and heading back into London. They'd searched for hours in every place they could think of and hadn't found the notebook. So Greg had loaded two plastic crates of papers into the boot of his car, taken Jess for lunch at the local pub and, in what was fast becoming a private joke between them, given her the car keys.

Jess's phone rang and Greg picked it up from the dashboard. 'It's Gerry.'

'Answer it.' She flashed a grin at him. 'If Gerry's calling me on a Sunday afternoon, it's probably not just for a chat.'

'And I'm answering your phone why?'

'It's my phone. I can ask anyone I like to answer it.' Jess wondered whether Greg would take up the challenge. He could quite easily pretend to press '*reject*' instead of '*answer*' by mistake, and let Jess pull over and call Gerry back.

He grinned, and turned his attention to the phone. 'Gerry? Yes, it's me. No, you can't speak to her, she's driving at the moment. We're not in her car, we're in mine.' He winked at her and held the phone away from his ear. Jess kept her eyes on the road but she could hear a stream of indistinct words from the other end of the line.

'What, you called to tell me this?'

'What's he saying?'

'Nothing of interest. I don't know where he gets the idea that I'm over-particular about my car. What did you call for, Gerry?' He listened intently and then grinned. 'He says there's an emergency heart bypass coming in shortly. If you want to sit in...'

'Yes!' Jess had been waiting for this chance for weeks. 'Tell him yes. If we swing past my place so I can pick up my car...'

'We'll be half an hour. Yes, see you then. Cheers, mate.' He cut the call. 'No point in making a detour all the way over to yours. We'll go straight there.'

'Sure?' Greg answering Gerry's call was one thing, but arriving together at the hospital on a Sunday afternoon looked an awful lot like a public admission that something was going on between them. And Greg had always been so careful to keep his love life well away from his work.

'You're ashamed to be seen with me?' He was grinning.

Hardly. 'I might want to keep you under wraps.' The thought occurred to Jess that she might be happier if he wanted to keep her under wraps. As if his job at the hospital was still a long-term proposition.

'Do you?'

'No.' She didn't care what anyone said, she was proud to be seen with Greg. And if he didn't mind being seen with her...

He nodded, seemingly pleased with what he heard. 'Next left, then. We don't want to get caught in traffic.'

Greg had found himself a cup of coffee and ensconced himself in the back row of the operating theatre viewing gallery. A couple of students sat ready to take notes and Greg ignored their covert glances. Right now they probably reckoned that another few years and they could stop climbing that steep learning curve and relax. He wasn't going to disenchant them.

Jess looked delicious. Scrubbed clean, covered from head to toe in shapeless, sterile theatre garb and concentrating hard on what Gerry was saying to her. He could only see her brow and her eyes, and somehow that was just as enchanting as being able to see everything. Like concentrating on one small part of a magnificent painting, admiring the virtues of a detail to enhance one's appreciation of the whole.

He leaned back in his chair, stretching his legs as much as was possible in the confined space. It would be a while before they were finished, but that was okay. It would be a chance to brush up on his knowledge of a speciality other than his own, and he could watch her. At the moment, a couple of hours where he had a cast-iron excuse to do nothing else except sit and watch Jess seemed like heaven.

He was sprawled on one of the chairs outside the cardiac department when she finally emerged. She looked tired, but her face was one broad sweep of a smile.

'Greg! What are you doing here still?' A trace of guilt intruded on the exhilaration in her eyes. 'I thought you'd gone home.'

'Nothing much to do there.' If you didn't count the boxes of paperwork in his boot. 'I thought I'd stay and watch. You did a good job.' Gerry had given her plenty of opportunity to assist and Jess had come through with flying colours. More than once Greg had seen Gerry's brief nod of approval at her deft, careful work.

'It was really good of Gerry to give me the opportunity.' She looked up at him, her eyes clouded. One of those looks that let Greg know that there was an awful lot of activity going on in her thoughts but gave him no clue about what it was. 'I think I owe you an apology.'

'Do you? What have you done?'

'This morning. I heard you downstairs on the phone.'

'I know.' He stuffed his hands into his jeans pockets. 'I heard you upstairs on the landing.'

'I was cross with you.'

'Yeah, I know that too.' Jess wasn't particularly good at concealing her feelings. He'd never thought that was a bad thing, and his introduction to the business world over the last eight months had only raised that quality in his estimation.

'I should have been a bit more understanding. The way you've been about me wanting to work this afternoon.'

That was the whole thing, in a nutshell. He resented getting out of bed at five in the morning just to settle a dispute between grown men who were only interested in scrambling to gain a bit more territory. Jess had considered this afternoon an opportunity.

'Don't you think this afternoon was worth it?'

'Yes, of course. I'm just saying...'

A pause and a slight grimace that made Greg wonder just how much of this she really believed.

'I'm saying that you've respected what I do. I should do the same and respect what you choose to do.'

Choose was stretching it a bit. The only thing that he had chosen to be was a doctor. And he was still unmoved by any definition of the word 'emergency' that didn't include some pressing threat to life or limb. If Jess thought that the Sunday working she'd done was more important than his, he was inclined to agree with her.

This was a genuine effort to meet him halfway, though. 'Thanks. I appreciate it, Jess. Your support...' Support was probably stretching it a bit as well, he could tell from the look in her eyes. But she nodded.

'I'll take you home.' He pulled the car keys from his pocket.

She hardly hesitated. 'Mmm. Thanks.' She fell into step beside him.

Greg closed his fingers around the car keys, smiling to himself. It was reassuring to be back in the driving seat.

You couldn't really call going out with Greg going out. When their shifts allowed, Jess would go to his flat in the evening and Greg would order some food in from a list of restaurants that seemed to be more than willing to make an exception to the normal insistence on actually turning up and eating on their premises when the name of Greg's father's company was mentioned. Jess could never bring herself to think of it as Greg's company. It was an unknown behemoth that he never talked about but which he seemed to be endlessly thinking about.

When he wasn't eating, he was answering emails. And when he wasn't answering emails, he was apologising for being about to. The long hours between eating and sleeping she spent alone, with just the TV for company. Was this what people meant when they talked about the beginning of the end?

'Can I help you?' Jess had decided to make a change. She'd brought some groceries in for dinner, and cooked for him then stacked the dishwasher while he sat at the kitchen table, staring at his laptop.

'What?'

'Can I help you? I'm a lot faster on a keyboard than you are so you could dictate your emails and I'll type.'

He tore his gaze from the screen for a moment. 'No, honey. Why don't you go and relax in the other room? I won't be long.'

She'd heard that one before, and each time he repeated it, it got just that bit harder to take. 'I'd rather be with you.'

'I have to work.'

'I know. I don't care what I do, I just want to be with you.' The words sounded a bit too much like something a whining girlfriend might say and Jess recoiled from them. 'I might find it interesting.'

He sighed. 'I doubt it. Trust me, it's not riveting stuff.'

That was the worst of it. She could have borne it if Greg was ignoring her in favour of something that was important to him, that he enjoyed. But this was, somehow, the ultimate insult.

Jess turned away, pressing her lips together. She should be supportive. She *wanted* to be supportive. But it was difficult when she had no idea where she stood with Greg.

'Can't I just have a minute? There's something I want to ask you.'

'Of course.' A couple of keystrokes saved whatever it was that he was doing, and he closed the lid of his laptop. 'I'm all yours.'

He wasn't, but the look on his face made Jess's world suddenly tilt. The worries, the nagging doubts, the questions about whether Greg really wanted to spend time with her or not all slid to the back of her consciousness and were replaced by that smile. The one that seemed to tell her everything she needed to know.

'I know you're busy, Greg. Why don't you let me do the model of the hospital? Or I can find someone else to do it. I was talking to Ash the other day and he said he'd help.'

'Ash?' He raised one eyebrow. 'The young guy in Orthopaedics?'

'He's the same age as me. And he's just split up with his girlfriend so he's got a bit of time on his hands.' Jess tailed off as Greg's brow darkened. That was just crazy.

Ash was good looking, fun to have around and could no more measure up to Greg than any other man she'd ever met. 'What?'

'Nothing.' He scrubbed his hand across his face. 'I suppose you're right. But…'

'But what?' Jess wasn't going to let him go back to work now. There was already too much that was being left unsaid between them.

'I promised you that I'd do it.' A quirk of a smile and suddenly he was back with her, his dark eyes seeming to see nothing else. 'I might start getting jealous if you and Ash disappear off together to build my model.'

'Jealous? Are you?' What the hell was she doing? She hated mind games and had no time for jealousy, particularly when it wasn't warranted. But suddenly Greg seemed to have started taking notice of her, and she was desperate for even these crumbs of his attention.

He saw through her in a moment. 'You think I don't have it in me to be jealous?'

'Just testing.' She broke off as he leaned over, his lips finding hers. Gentle hands, propelling her to her feet and then backwards. He perched her on the counter top, sliding his hips between her knees.

'Getting any answers?' One hand cupped her cheek and Jess struggled for control then gave up as pleasure oozed across her skin.

'Yeah.'

'What are they?' He pulled her tight against his body and she gasped. Nuzzling at her neck, he whispered into her ear, 'What are they, Jess?'

She was trembling. She wanted to tell Greg that the only thing she wanted was a little more of his time, his attention, but that seemed like a recipe for disaster. Her mother had always told her that you never begged a man for more of anything and she'd never questioned that. Suddenly it occurred to Jess that she might be about to beg, and she wondered whether her mother had done the same with her father.

'The only answer I have is that I must be getting a little crazy. I'm not going to play any more games with you just to get your attention. I'd rather just walk out of here now.'

He was suddenly still. 'You have my attention.'

Not for long, though. She felt as if she was on a ship, pitching in a storm. Sliding helplessly between doubt and love as the deck tilted back and forth beneath her. 'Do I?'

He stepped back, planting his hands on the counter top to either side of her, eyes clouded with frustration. 'What do you want from me, Jess?'

Frankly she had no idea. She wanted more than her father had given her mother. That was about as far as Jess had ever really considered the matter. 'This is not how I thought we'd be, Greg.'

'I can't do anything about that right now.' He turned away from her abruptly, leaving Jess to push herself down from her perch on the counter top.

'You always have a choice, Greg.'

'Yeah? What choice do I have? You don't seem to understand, Jess.'

The world tilted again and this time Jess was slammed hard against a wall of anger. 'Trying to understand is all I've been doing for the last few weeks. If you're too busy for me then you should just say so and stop stringing me along.'

He rounded on her. 'Oh, so I'm stringing you along now, am I? You don't think much of me, do you?'

'I'm not saying that's what you mean to do.'

He gave a short bark of a laugh. 'Well, that makes me feel so much better. I might be callous, but that's okay because I'm so knuckle-headed that I'm not aware of what I'm doing.' He marched over to the kitchen cupboard, seeming to need to do something. Flipping it open, he banged two cups down onto the counter.

'That's not what I said. If you want to think that about yourself, be my guest. But don't you dare put those words into my mouth.'

He didn't turn. He seemed to have switched into auto-pilot, reaching up for the coffee and measuring the last of the packet into the machine, spilling some as he did so. Jess huffed with frustration. 'Can't you at least look at me? We had coffee ten minutes ago.'

He slung the empty coffee packet into the sink, along with the measuring spoon. When he turned, his gaze was cold, proud, but there was something hot-blooded about it that made Jess shiver.

'I never chose to have anything to do with Shaw Industries, but I've been given that responsibility, and I can't walk away from it. That's all it is. This is not about you and me.'

'But it affects you and me.' That was about as close as Jess's pride would allow her to get to asking him for more.

'I'm not going to make any promises I can't keep, Jess. I have no idea how long this is all going to take. I wish things were different, but they're not.'

'You can't just allow it to take you over, Greg. At some point you're going to have to decide where your own priorities lie.'

He let out a short, sharp breath. A gesture of helplessness that told Jess he was out of ideas on this one. This seemed to be tearing him up inside. More precisely, *she* seemed to be tearing him up...

'Perhaps we should take a break. Just a couple of weeks to figure things out.'

He stared at her. Clearly Jess wasn't the only one who was having trouble believing that she was saying this. But they both needed a little space, to sort their own issues out, before they ripped each other to bits.

'A break. You mean we should call it a day?'

'No. I mean a break. A couple of weeks to take the pressure off. Work things out.' Right now, looking at him, it was impossible to credit that *'goodbye'* should feature anywhere in this. Ever.

Her heart was yelling at him to say no. To turn his back on the seemingly hundreds of people who waited for him in a not so orderly queue, out there in cyberspace. If he offered to take the night off, just this once, she'd say yes in a heartbeat.

'Perhaps you're right.' She felt his hand on her arm. So nearly enough to make her stay and yet so far from what she needed right now. 'I'll take you home.'

He really hadn't been paying attention. 'I've got my car with me tonight. I brought some shopping in, remember?' Jess wondered whether he'd get around to restocking the fridge after she was gone. Probably not. At least he had enough in there to last for a while, though.

'Yeah, of course. I'm sorry about all this, Jess.' He scraped his hand across his face and she almost relented. But if she did that, they'd only be having this same argument again soon.

'Don't be. We're just taking some time off, eh?' So why did this seem so final? Perhaps because there was no way back for Jess now, unless he gave a little. And she wasn't sure that he'd do that.

He walked with her to the lift and they rode down to the car park in silence. Greg watched her to her car gave her a wave and turned back into the lift. It appeared he wasn't going to watch her go. Jess waited, gripping the steering-wheel, her gaze fixed on him as he jabbed the call button for the lift. He wasn't going to look back. She started the engine and drove out of the car park, revving the engine into rather more of a roar than was strictly necessary. His mind was probably already on the problems that waited for him upstairs and he hadn't even heard her go either.

Greg kept his finger on the lift button, ignoring the insistent 'ding' that accompanied the twitch of the doors as the machine hinted to him ever so gently that there were probably people waiting on other floors and they should get going now. He heard her car slow as she approached the ramp up to street level and turned when he was sure that she could no longer see him in her rear-view mirror.

He didn't blame her for what she'd done. It would have taken considerably less neglect on Jess's part before Greg would have considered himself hard done by and left. There was nothing to say either in his own defence or in terms of promises for the future. He'd heard enough promises from his father to know just how much damage a broken one could cause. But things would change. She'd see.

CHAPTER EIGHT

JESS HAD BEEN trying very hard not to miss Greg for almost two weeks. It had been a stupid argument, she'd said things she hadn't really meant, and she guessed that he had too. But the main stumbling block remained. Was she just the latest in a long string of girlfriends that Greg had loved then lost interest in? If so, she couldn't bring herself to tell him that this one still loved him.

She had other things to think about, though. Like getting through the day, doing her job the best she could and smiling as if nothing had happened. Ignoring the nagging thought that her body's monthly rhythm had missed a beat. It was nothing. She'd been working hard, sleeping badly and not eating properly, that was all.

Today had been a busy day, but she'd kept on top of things and it seemed that she'd be leaving work on time tonight. And then, at five-thirty on the dot, the department secretary paged her.

'What have you got for me, Bev?' By the time she got down to the office she'd convinced herself that she didn't really want to go home after all.

'Some people were looking for you. I asked them to go to the waiting room.'

'Who? I didn't have a clinic today.'

Beverly shook her head. 'No, I think they might know you. One of them is a doctor.'

'Who is he?'

'No idea. But he's got that doctor's look about him.' Beverly tapped the side of her nose. 'Interested instead of nervous. They're in the waiting room.'

The waiting room was deserted, apart from a couple sitting in one corner. Something like foreboding prickled at the back of Jess's neck.

'Rosa. Ted.' She sat down in the chair opposite them. 'How nice to see you both.' What were they doing here?

Rosa smiled. That self-possessed, gracious smile that somehow managed to be genuine as well. 'It's good to see you too, Jess.' She looked around the waiting room. 'This is very nice.'

'Yes, they renovated the whole department a couple of years ago. Much brighter than it used to be.' Jess flipped a querying glance towards Ted.

'We were looking for Greg. You haven't seen him, have you?' Ted got straight to the point and Jess heaved a sigh of relief. For a moment there she'd thought that Greg might have told them about the things she'd said and they were here to remonstrate with her.

'Isn't he down in A and E? I haven't spoken to him today.' Okay, so not for two weeks. But there was something the matter, and suddenly that was of no consequence. It didn't matter if she hadn't spoken to him for two years, she'd still be there for him.

'No, we went there first.' Rosa shrugged, letting go with just a hint of well-manicured exasperation.

'And we didn't hang around because they were busy.' Ted had clearly guided his wife up here before she'd got in the way. 'Rosa's tried his mobile and his home phone.'

'He doesn't answer. His mobile's switched off,' Rosa finished for him.

Greg never switched his mobile off. The prickle at the back of Jess's neck got worse and she tried to shrug it off. 'He should be here. But he has another mobile. He uses it for work. His other work, I mean.' She wasn't sure quite what to call it.

Rosa nodded, pursing her lips. 'Shaw Industries.'

'Yes. But I don't know the number.' Jess hadn't wanted to know it. She'd tried staring at the sleek, black handset a number of times in the hope that it might dissolve into thin air, but that hadn't worked either.

Ted's relaxed, even-handedness broke in. 'We were wondering whether you could find out where he is for us. They looked very busy in A and E and we didn't want to interrupt them.' Rosa nodded, thin-lipped.

'Yes, of course.' Jess could get the information easily from the receptionist. 'He's probably on his break or something. Wait here, I'll find out for you.'

Jess hurried down to A and E, taking in the canteen on the way. Greg wasn't there either. But the receptionist knew exactly where he was. Jess walked back up to the cardiology waiting room, feeling a little sick.

'Rosa, I'm sorry, but he's not here. He's got a few days off this week.' And next week. She'd wanted Greg to cut back on work, but it had never occurred to her that he might choose Shaw Industries over his work here at the hospital.

Rosa rolled her eyes and made a gesture that defied translation but implied an immediate understanding of the situation. 'I'll find him.' She looked at her watch and pulled her mobile out of her bag, scrolling through the contacts list.

Ted took the phone from her hand. 'Not here, darling.'

He stood, waiting for Rosa to follow him. 'We're sorry to have bothered you, Jess.'

'It's no trouble.' Jess wasn't going to let them walk out on her now. 'I'll take you down to the canteen. You can get a cup of tea and make your call there.'

Ted asked whether there was anywhere else that Jess needed to be, and then insisted she join them. Rosa was on the phone almost as soon as she sat down.

'Pat? It's Rosa. How are you?' Rosa smiled into the phone. 'Really? You must give us a call when you arrive and come over for dinner. That would be perfect. I wondered whether you've heard from Greg today?'

Jess smiled. The ladylike version of taking Pat by the throat, shaking her and demanding to know where he was.

'Is he? No, that's all right, thank you, it's not important. I'll catch up with him.' Rosa's smile drained rapidly from her face as she cut the call. 'He's at the London office. A board meeting. He won't be finished until late if I know anything about these things.'

Jess took a sip of her tea to steady her. 'I'm sorry, I didn't know. I haven't seen Greg for a couple of weeks. Things have been…um…difficult.'

Ted came to the rescue again. 'That's a shame. We were thinking, hoping, that he'd not been in touch because he was spending time with you.'

'No. He's been working.' Jess chanced a look at Rosa and saw only understanding in her face.

Ted leaned back in his chair, smiling at his wife. 'Well, I suppose we should go and do that Christmas shopping, then. No point in wasting a journey.'

'But…' Rosa puffed out a breath. 'I suppose so.' She pulled a flat package, wrapped in brown paper, out of her handbag. 'Unless this fits through his letter-box.'

Ted scratched his nose. 'I doubt it.'

Jess stared at the package. 'The book. You've found his father's book.' Greg had said his mother had been searching diligently for it, and she must have found it.

'Yes. You'll never guess where it was.' She paused and Jess shook her head. 'It was in the tower. There's a big old chest in there, full of goodness knows what, and it had been slipped inside there.'

'And his father put it in there for him to find.'

'Yes.' Rosa twitched the corners of her mouth down. 'Although how much good it's going to be...'

'Greg's father had a secondary brain tumour. Quite a large one.' There was only compassion in Ted's face.

'Which might have affected his language functions.' Jess could imagine Greg's disappointment if the book was unintelligible.

Ted nodded. 'It seems that it did. Damn shame. We thought it would be better to deliver it personally under the circumstances.'

Rosa nodded. 'Silly really. I should have called first.'

'If you had, he wouldn't have answered. And we'd have come anyway.' Ted brushed away the wasted journey as if it was nothing. 'Jess, would it be inappropriate of us to ask whether you'll be seeing Greg in the next few days? If not, we can give him a call tomorrow evening and he can come up and collect the book on Sunday.'

She might not be going out with Greg any more but she could still be a friend to him. She knew how much he'd wanted to find the book and she couldn't bear the thought of him waiting and worrying about what it contained.

'I can take the book. I'll give him a call tomorrow morning, and if he's at home I'll pop it round in my lunch hour.'

'We don't want to put you to any trouble.' Rosa's eyes flashed with gratitude.

'You're not. I'll take good care of it. I know how important it is.'

'That's kind of you, Jess, thank you.' Ted took the parcel from his wife and handed it over to Jess.

'This was his last chance, wasn't it?'

Rosa nodded. 'Yes. He didn't say so, but I think he was hoping that his father might have written some of the things he never said to him.' She grimaced. 'He didn't. I never really thought he would. John was always too involved with his work.'

Like father, like son. Jess hoped not, for Greg's sake.

'So…' Ted drank the last dregs of his tea. 'Jess, have you finished for the day?'

'Pretty much. I just have to check in and make sure there's nothing else for me and then I'll be going home.'

'That's perfect. I'll have another cup of this gorgeous hospital tea and we'll take you for dinner. If you're free, that is?'

Of course she was free. And she couldn't deny that she wanted some company tonight. 'Or we could do a bit of shopping first? The shops are all open late for Christmas.' She glanced at Rosa, who brightened visibly. Jess had imagined that shopping would cheer her up a little.

Ted rolled his eyes, chuckling. 'Thought I was going to get out of that. Okay, we'll shop and then we'll eat.'

CHAPTER NINE

JESS HAD CALLED. She'd managed to talk Gerry into giving her a long lunch hour and she'd be here in…Greg looked at his watch…about ten minutes.

He scanned the living room. His cleaning lady had been in yesterday and everything was neat and in its place. His laptop was hidden away in the TV cabinet, and he'd bundled everything that had anything to do with Shaw Industries into plastic crates, stacked them in the store cupboard in the hall and locked the door.

He began to pace the full length of the hallway, looking at his watch as he did so. She had to come. If she didn't, he'd do what he'd originally planned, go and find her and tell her that things would be different from now on.

The intercom buzzed and he jerked round so quickly that he almost pulled a muscle in his back. He forgot all about waiting for a few seconds, to make out that he hadn't been waiting in the hallway for her, and punched the button to release the entrance doors downstairs.

A pause and then a quiet knock on the door.

'Hey.' Suddenly the last two weeks seemed like nothing. She was here, her face glowing as if it was Christmas Day. This *was* Christmas Day, as far as Greg was concerned. 'Come in.'

He remembered to stand back from the doorway and

she smiled at him—he'd so missed that smile—and walked past him into the hallway. He'd missed her scent too, to the point that it seemed to haunt him, clinging to pillows and sheets, even though they were fresh on the bed.

'What have I done to deserve this?' He wondered if he should kiss her and decided it was taking too much for granted.

'I have something for you. I have to warn you that it's probably going to be a disappointment.' She handed him a flat brown paper parcel.

That was okay, she was here, and that was all that really mattered. 'What is it?'

'It's your father's book. Rosa found it. She and Ted were at the hospital yesterday but you weren't around and they came up to Cardiology.'

Greg stared at the package. Suddenly he didn't want to open it. 'And they gave it to you?'

'Yes. I said I'd bring it to you. We did some shopping and had dinner.'

He'd been missing her like the feeling was going out of fashion, and she'd been swanning around going shopping with his mother? Fury tore at Greg's chest and he turned on his heel, marching into the sitting room and slinging the parcel down onto the coffee table.

He heard her behind him. 'What? What's wrong now?'

'Nothing…nothing. I'm sorry, Jess, yesterday was a long day. Thanks for bringing this round.' He turned, smiling as best he could. She'd be off now, as that was all she'd come for.

'Aren't you going to open it?' She stared pointedly at the package.

'No. I'll do that later. I've some things to do. You'll be wanting to get back as well.' He moved to usher her back towards the doorway but she evaded him.

'I've taken a long lunch hour. I told you that.' She took
her coat off and sat down on the sofa, plumping her handbag defiantly onto the floor.

'You've done what you came to do.' He couldn't help
the anger in his voice.

'Think so?' She jutted her chin at him and he almost
melted. Almost.

'You've delivered the book. Is there anything else?'

'Yes.' She sprang to her feet and marched over to him.
'Just this.'

She raised her arm and for a moment Greg thought she
might be about to slap him. He stood his ground, reck-
oning that he probably didn't deserve much better from
her, and felt her hand on the back of his neck, pulling him
roughly towards her.

She kissed him. Wild and warm and angry. Deep, passionate and finally tender. Just as he began to reach for
her, she was gone, picking up her coat and huffing in an-
noyance as she tried to thread her hand through one of the
tangled sleeves.

Oh, no, she didn't. If she thought she was going to
leave now... Greg covered the floor between them in three
strides and caught her by the arm. She spun round and he
pinned her against him. 'What was that for?'

She turned her face up towards him, defiance blazing in
her eyes. 'You can tell me to go now, and I'll go. But I'm
not leaving without letting you know how I feel.'

'I don't want you to go, Jess.'

He backed her against the sofa, almost collapsing on
top of her as she lost her balance and fell onto the cush-
ions. This time he kissed her. Anger and passion again,
melting together into an explosive cocktail. She moved beneath him, a little cry escaping her lips, and her sweetness
almost overwhelmed him. How he'd missed her.

That heavy-lidded, golden look almost destroyed him. He murmured her name, and she seemed to melt into him, as if there was no such thing as him or her, only them.

'I missed you, Jess.'

She hesitated. Silently he willed her to say it. 'I missed you too.'

Triumph shimmered through him, teasing every nerve ending. He should let her up now, but somehow he couldn't. Not until she kissed him again.

She didn't make him wait. Her kiss still had a trace of defiance, a dash of anger, but this time it was assured. The way he wanted her to feel with him.

'One more thing.'

'What's that?' She was smiling now.

He leaned in until his lips were almost touching her ear. 'Do you have a right to my attention?'

Her beautiful eyes clouded in doubt. He hated that he'd been a part of creating that doubt. 'Do you, Jess?'

'Yes? I do?'

He felt himself smile inside. 'Right answer. Only you could be more definite about it…'

'Could I?'

'Yes. It's the truth, and I need you to know it.'

She thought for a moment. 'Let me up, Greg.'

Damn! She wasn't going to say it. Greg shifted, sitting up, and she followed, sitting close, smiling when he put his arm around her.

'I have a right to expect your attention.' She whispered the words into his ear.

He chuckled. 'Was that so difficult?'

She rocked her head from side to side, as if weighing it up. 'Surprisingly easy.'

He wondered how long she had before she had to go back to work. Actually, it didn't matter. He'd say what he had to say if he had to follow her back, and gabble it into her ear in the lift up to Cardiology. 'If I sounded a bit gruff...over you going shopping with my mother...'

She made a face. 'Somewhere between noticeable disapproval and overt censure. Just to let you know, we didn't talk about you, or us.'

That only made things worse. Greg swallowed his disappointment. 'Rub it in, why don't you? Just when I was coming to terms with feeling left out.'

'Ah. Well then, we did talk about you a bit. Only I can't tell you about that, because Rosa was buying Christmas presents. Anyway, don't you hate shopping?' She smiled up at him, that beguiling, mischievous look flickering in her eyes. Jess had a way of making everything seem right.

'Well, Ted and I might have made a few faces at each other.' Even so, he liked the thought of watching Jess and his mother, discussing their purchases, deciding for and then against, laughing together at the brightly lit counters, ablaze with Christmas decorations. He could have carried her bags, shepherded her through the crowds in the shops and on the pavements.

'There you are, then. Anyway, shopping's a pretty cutthroat business at this time of the year.'

'Jess?'

'Yes?'

'Come back to me.'

'I... We...' There was only one answer that Jess could give to that. There had only ever been one answer where Greg was concerned. If she didn't give it immediately, it was only because she wanted so badly to do it right this time. 'Do you really think this is the right thing, Greg?'

His chest rose and fell in a short, explosive laugh. 'As a friend, I'd tell you that waiting around for any guy is bad news. That you deserve a lot better than someone who's fighting to keep his head above water and can't always give you the attention you deserve.'

'Yeah. And?'

'As a lover, I'll say that I'm a pretty miserable excuse for a suitor. That sometimes I get distracted, and I feel guilty about that and lash out at you, instead of doing what I should and telling you that I'm sorry. But you always have my heart, I promise you that.'

'You'd better make up your mind which you are, then.' Choose right. She was willing him to choose right.

'Are you free tomorrow?' Warmth filtered back into his tone.

'Yes. What about you? There's a whole twenty-four hours for Shaw Industries to come up with something that's more important.'

'I'll be there. I promise.'

'It's a date, then.' It was almost impossible to keep from smiling when his voice caressed her like this. Liquid caramel. Jess tried to think of something else but the only alternative she could come up with at the moment was melted chocolate.

'What time shall I pick you up? Is five o'clock too early?'

'No, that'll be great. I've got to pop into the hospital, take a look in the library to see if they've got any of the books we need for the storytellers, so perhaps I could do that first and then come straight over to you?'

'Why don't I meet you there? At about three o'clock. I could give you a hand.'

Pure, unadulterated happiness crashed over her, like a wave. Bubbling around her and then pulling her under. 'I'd really like that.'

He smiled. That slow, delicious smile that just kept on giving. 'When do you have to be back at work?'

'About thirty-five minutes. I have to go soon.'

'If I drove you back, it'd only take ten minutes.' He wound his arms around her waist, pulling her close again.

'I can stay if you want some company. I'll make a cup of coffee and you can take a quick look at the book.' She gestured towards the package on the table.

He shook his head. 'That can wait. I, on the other hand, have already waited long enough. I just want to hold you for a little while longer.' He kissed her and every nerve ending flared abruptly into life. Suddenly there was nothing else in the world that she needed to do as much as kiss him back.

'I'm sorry, Greg. I shouldn't have—'

He laid his finger across her lips. 'Hey. None of that. We are what we are. Everyone has issues. But we can work through them. We've just got to keep talking.'

'And?'

'When we've finished with the talking, we could try a little loving.'

'Just a little?'

He chuckled. 'Not if I have any say in the matter.'

CHAPTER TEN

THE HOSPITAL LIBRARY wasn't large, but it did have as many bookshelves as could be squeezed into such a limited space, and they were all full. Greg found Jess in there, poring over a list and consulting the shelves.

'Hey, there. Any luck?'

She shrugged. 'Not sure yet. None of this is any particular order. People just take books out and put them back anywhere.' She paused, grinning, and pulled a volume from a pile on the floor. 'Ooh, look! There's a good start.'

A Christmas Carol.' Greg took the book from her and flipped the pages. 'You know, I don't think I've ever actually read this. I've seen films, of course.'

'Then you should take it home. Might get you into the spirit of things.' She smiled at him, and Greg's world tipped slightly. He could almost see himself taking time out to actually do some reading.

He put the book aside for later. 'I've got something for you. A surprise.'

Her eyes flipped to his empty hands and then to his face. 'A surprise? What is it?'

'Well, if I walked in here holding it, it wouldn't be a surprise, would it? Anyway, first things first.'

Her ability to anticipate what he wanted was almost uncanny. She was in his arms almost before he'd had a chance to reach for her. Her kiss told him that everything his senses had been yearning for was right there. Not yet, though. He wasn't going to blow it by forgetting to say any of the things he'd left unspoken up till now.

'You look lovely.' She was dressed simply, dark trousers and a red sweater. A complicated twist of beads around her neck that weren't quite her style but looked great. 'You smell gorgeous. Did you dress up for me?'

She flushed awkwardly then met his gaze. 'Yes, I did.'

'I appreciate that.' He kissed her again. That physical language that meant more than words sometimes.

She nodded, eyes glistening. 'So where's my surprise?' She dug him in the ribs. 'Come on.'

He chuckled, breaking away from her and fetching the box that he'd left in the hallway, setting it down on the small library table. She gave him a questioning look then tore off the packing tape with which he'd resealed the box and pulled out layers of bubble wrap.

'Greg! It's...' She peered into the box. 'Look at the roof and the little chimneys.'

He reached inside and carefully drew the model out. 'You like it?'

'It's beautiful. Look, there's even grass in the courtyard and a little gatehouse and railings.' She was entranced, trying to take in all the features of the tiny representation of the hospital at once. 'What did you do?'

'I didn't make it myself, if that's what you mean. There's a company that Shaw Industries uses that make models of some of our larger engineering installations. I passed the job on to them and tipped the wink to Ash that he wouldn't need to do anything. Do you mind?'

'If you think I'm going to quibble about how you got your contribution to the pageant done...' she shrugged

'...I've been begging for things for months now. I'm not picky about where they come from.'

'Good. So, can I expect a—?'

She went to kiss him before he could even ask. Greg backed her against a free-standing bookcase, which wobbled precariously, so he changed direction, steering her against one of the wall cabinets. Holding back from her, letting their lips just touch.

It was all that was needed to start the long, slow burn that would build through the rest of the afternoon and most of the evening, until they had a chance to quench it. That might take most of the night.

He kissed her again, this time a little deeper. Or maybe it was Jess who did that. One of the things he loved about making love with her was that he was never really sure who was doing what for whom. Everything just flowed, one caress into another, without thought or artifice, pleasuring both of them in equal measure.

'We'd better be getting on, then.' He had no intention of leaving her satisfied. Not yet. Not for a long time.

'Yeah. There's a lot to do.' Her hand nudged the top of his leg and he shuddered. The trouble with Jess was that she could play this game so much better than he could.

He gave up and reached for the list, keeping one arm coiled around her shoulders. 'You know, I reckon most of these books are in the library at my father's house.' He still couldn't quite bring himself to call it his own. 'Can you do with some extra copies?'

'Yes. I need to get as many as possible. I've got a lot of volunteers for the storytelling.'

'So why don't you send the list to my mother and she'll sort them out and box them up? I'll be up there some time before Christmas and I can pick them up.'

'Would she mind? I'll make sure I get them back to you.'

Greg laughed. 'No, she'll be very happy about that. She called me last night and asked me whether I was considering being a total ass and ignoring you for much longer.'

'What did you tell her?'

'I told her I'm not considering that.'

She gave a small nod. 'Are we going to be okay, Greg?' The way she looked at him, in almost agonised belief that he could make everything all right, wrenched his heart.

'We're working on it, honey. Together.'

'Yes.' That seemed to be enough for her, and she took refuge in his arms, pressing her cheek against his chest. She trusted him. He would do all he could not to let her down.

He kissed her lightly on the lips. 'So, as we're here to work, what do you want me to do?'

She laughed. Soft, sweet laughter, like an angel caressing his senses. 'Sort out some of these books for me.'

The restaurant he took her to was only ten minutes' walk from the hospital, along a little cobbled alleyway by the river. Jess hadn't even known it was there, and guessed that it didn't need to advertise itself too much. A small foyer, where they were stripped of their coats, and up a flight of stairs into an understated but noticeably classy eating area. Waiters, who appeared and disappeared as if they'd just walked out of the walls, and a no-frills menu that clearly underplayed some very haute cuisine.

The first course came and was cleared away, waiters melting in and out of the space around their table like wraiths who knew exactly when to appear and when to tactfully disappear. Jess had asked about Greg's father's book, expecting him to shrug it off, keep his feelings close to his chest, but instead he sent one of the waiters downstairs to fetch it from his coat.

'Can I look?' Jess was unsure just how much he wanted to share.

He nodded. 'Yes. I'd like you to, if you don't mind.'

It was the first time he'd let her see anything to do with his father or Shaw Industries. Jess's hand shook as she flipped through the pages, full of closely written paragraphs and complex diagrams. This wasn't what she had expected. 'He's written something.'

'Yeah. Look a little closer.'

At first glance the text almost looked as if it should make sense. But when Jess scanned the pages more closely, she saw that Greg meant. Disjointed phrases, flashes, impressions that dangled the promise of some kind of meaning, but at the same time fell short of conveying anything. A chart that must have meant something but had no labels.

'I'm sorry, Greg. I know how much you wanted this to be something.'

He shrugged. 'I shouldn't have got my hopes up. He couldn't communicate with me when he was alive and he sure as hell can't do it now.'

Anger flashed across his face. Good. That was good. She'd rather see Greg rage at this than just coldly accept it.

'Isn't there anything in here that makes any sense?' She turned the pages slowly, looking for something, anything, that might be an intelligible message.

'Not to me. He shook his head. 'Maybe he didn't know what it meant either.'

'At least he tried.'

A short bark of a laugh. 'You always think the best of people.'

'Is that such a bad thing?'

He scrubbed his hand across his eyes. 'Not at all. Just saying.'

Jess's eye lit on a phrase. 'Look.' She laid the book on

the table, facing him. 'See what it says there? "Son is here."
That's on the previous page, too. He knew you were there
for him and that obviously meant something.'

'Yeah. Although he couldn't remember my name.'

Enough of this. 'You know better than that, Greg.' She
sought his gaze and held it. Perhaps she was expecting too
much. 'It's natural that you should feel that way as his son.
As a doctor, it's my place to tell you that he might not have
been able to vocalise his feelings but they were still there.'

'You're right. I know. I just can't feel that way at the
moment.'

'You will, in time. The tumour was obviously affecting
the language centres of his brain. It may be that someone
with specific expertise in this area would be able to help.'

'Do you think there's any point?'

'I don't know. I just think that you can't give up on him
now.' Jess might mistrust John Shaw's intentions but she
loved Greg. If she had to deal with the father to help the
son, she'd do it.

He nodded. 'I just wish he'd been able to give me a few
ideas about the right thing to do next.'

'Maybe he trusted you. He might have reckoned that
you'd make the right decisions all on your own.'

Greg stared at her. 'I...I don't think...' He shrugged,
summoning up a smile. 'I don't think that's something that
ever occurred to me.'

'Maybe you should give it some thought.'

'Maybe.' Greg closed the book and threw his napkin
over it, as if that was an end to it and even looking at the
volume was hard for him. 'Ah. Here's our pudding.'

One of the waiters appeared out of thin air, where he
seemed to have been hovering, waiting for them to finish talking. Laying their plates in front of them, he disappeared again.

'Where do they go?' Jess leaned across the table conspiratorially.

Greg laughed. 'It's all done with trapdoors and pulleys. Do you like it here?'

'Yeah, I do, actually.' If he'd told her about this place before they'd come, she'd have turned it down out of hand. But now that she was here it wasn't so bad. She felt relaxed, comfortable and the food was wonderful. She probed her chocolate pudding with her spoon. 'This looks lovely.'

'Yeah. Wish I'd gone for it.' He reached out towards her plate and Jess rapped his spoon with hers.

'Don't you dare. Anyway, the lemon meringue looks nice too.'

He took a mouthful. 'Yes. It's very good. So we'll come back here some time?'

They were grinning at each other across the table. 'Yes. Only next week we go to Aldo's.' Diners lined up at trestle tables, waiters who tapped their feet and stared at the ceiling if you didn't order quickly enough, and a good, filling meal.

'Okay. I like Aldo's.' He nodded and left her to tuck into the best chocolate pudding she'd ever tasted.

She woke up in his arms. Jess took a moment to appreciate the novelty of not having to wonder where Greg was, and then stretched a little, just to test whether he was awake or not. His hand wandered sleepily to her stomach and stayed there.

Last night had been perfect. Enough to drive every one of her misgivings from her head, along with every other worry. Taking his hand in hers and pulling it close to her heart, she drifted back to sleep.

When she woke again something was wrong. The room

was swimming and almost before her eyes were open properly she was on her feet and running for the bathroom.

'Are you okay, Jess?'

The vomiting was sudden and violent, but at least it passed as quickly as it had come, and by the time Greg made the bathroom, she was already rinsing her mouth.

'Yeah.' She was still shivering, cold sweat on her brow, and Greg wrapped her in his dressing gown, guiding her back to the bed.

'Here, lie down for a minute.' He propped the pillows up and she relaxed back into them, wishing that they'd swallow her up. Not quite the awakening she'd been planning on treating him to.

'Can I get you something? A glass of water?'

'No. Thanks, I'm okay.' She shrugged. 'Don't know what happened there.' Though she was beginning to fathom it out and she tried to ignore the conclusion that was staring her in the face.

Greg's face was clouded in thought. Apparently he too was beginning to fathom it out. 'How late are you?'

'What? Who says...?'

'How late?' His voice was firm, almost as if he was talking to a difficult patient.

'Don't be like this, Greg.' He couldn't know. She didn't even know so how could he possibly know?

'Okay, then. You can clear this up in a second. All you have to do is tell me that I'm imagining things.'

'You're...' She couldn't. Or, if he was, then it looked as if he was imagining the same things that she was. The things that she'd, put down to stress and the missed meals and sleepless nights of the last two weeks.

'Jess, stop this. You refused any wine last night, you're sick this morning. What's going on?'

'Nothing. Nothing. I just didn't want the wine. It smelled a bit off.'

'It was fine.'

'Maybe it's just a stomach bug.'

'How late?'

'Two weeks. And a couple of days.'

'How many days?' His voice was gentle, but Jess didn't dare look up into his face.

'Four.'

'Is that usual for you?'

'No, I'm… You can usually set your watch by my monthly cycle.'

'I'm assuming you haven't done a test?'

'No. I thought I was just a bit run down.'

'This isn't like you, Jess.' He wrapped his arms around her, letting out a long sigh. 'A test would only take five minutes and then we'd know.'

'Yes. Then we'd know.' What if she didn't want to know just yet? She might just want to hang onto the possibility that she was right, without having to actually face any of the hard questions that was going to pose. But now that Greg was involved, it changed everything. 'I'll stop on my way home and get a test kit from the chemist.'

'Jess.' He let out a huff of exasperation. 'Okay, this is what we're going to do. I'll pop out now to the all-night chemist and get a test kit. Then we'll get it done, and… well, we can work out what comes next when we know what the result is.'

Somewhere, deep inside, she was glad. Glad that Greg had forced the issue. That he'd been stronger than she was, and that he'd cared enough to be gentle, too. 'Yes. All right.'

He reached for her, grasping her by the shoulders and looking straight into her face. A pulse beat at the side of his brow. He wasn't as calm as he sounded. 'It'll be okay, Jess. We'll work this out together.'

She gulped back the tears. He was sticking by her, this far at least. Or perhaps he was just taking control. She preferred the former.

'Okay?' He wasn't going anywhere until she gave him a 'yes'.

'Yes. Okay.'

CHAPTER ELEVEN

GREG IGNORED THE smile from the woman behind the counter at the chemist. She probably had him down as a guy who couldn't wait to become a father. In truth, if he'd had the first idea about how to be a father he might have had a clue about what he wanted. Currently he had neither.

Jess was sitting up in his bed when he got back, toying with one of the dry crackers he'd got for her, his dressing gown wrapped tightly around her. He laid the paper bag down next to her and she hesitated, then snatched it up and made for the bathroom. He heard the door close and then the click of the lock.

Ten minutes and not a sound had come from the other side of the bathroom door. Jess supposed that she should go out and face him. Not yet.

Not yet.

She stood up from her perch on the side of the bath. She didn't feel any different. Looked in the mirror. She didn't look any different either.

'It's all right. It's going to be all right.' She whispered the words to her own reflection, and received a smile in response. It was going to be all right.

Her hand wandered to her stomach. Still flat, no signs yet. 'Hey, baby.' Her first words to her unborn child. 'Your mother loves you. Everything's going to be just fine.' It didn't seem odd to be talking like this. In the last ten minutes her world had turned upside down, split apart at the seams, and she'd fallen hopelessly and irrevocably in love with the scrap of life inside her.

Would her baby—their baby, she supposed—be like him? Would some accident of genetics mean that it grew into an olive-skinned, dark-eyed charmer? Strong and tall, owing nothing to its mother? She rubbed her stomach, letting the thought percolate for a while. She liked it rather better than she was ready to admit.

What would Greg say? Would he wonder if she'd somehow meant this to happen? He was a rich man, and most women would jump at the chance to snare him. Slowly but surely everything began to unravel. All the promises they'd made in the last few days. Then they'd had the luxury of being able to live with uncertainty. Things were different now.

'He can keep his money.' She mouthed the words at the mirror, in case he was outside, listening. 'We can do without it.'

A tap sounded at the door. 'Jess?'

She jumped guiltily and whirled round. Another tap, louder this time. 'Jess? Are you waiting for me to break the door down?'

She couldn't help smiling. A part of her wanted him to do just that. Pull her into his arms and protect her from all the monsters that were out there in the dark. Take her to live in his gilded castle, where he'd make her his queen and love her always.

She gulped in a breath. 'Yes. I mean no. Don't do that, I'll be out in a minute.'

She pulled the bath robe tighter around her, knotting

the tie firmly and took a deep breath. Unlocking the door, she stepped out into the bedroom.

He was perched on edge of the bed, his legs stretched out in front of him. He looked so... He looked like the man she'd always wanted. Jess's courage failed her.

'You're pregnant.'

She supposed that he could hardly fail to come to that conclusion from the amount of time she'd spent in the bathroom. Jess nodded her head.

'Hey. It's all right Jess. We're in this together and we're going to deal with this. I think we both need you to say it, though.'

The stress lines were back on his face. This was no walk in the park for him either.

'I'm pregnant. Seven weeks.'

He nodded. 'How do you feel?'

Jess swallowed hard. 'Fine. About the same as I did half an hour ago.' Apart from the fact that everything had changed.

His gaze had never left her face. 'Seven weeks. I guess its heart will just have started beating by now.'

'Yes. And its head is forming. Little bumps for its arms and legs.' Jess almost choked.

'Hey, there.' He was on his feet, holding her tight, before she even realised that she was shaking. 'I told you, we're in this together. I can provide whatever you need.' The words sounded hollow, almost like a business deal.

'I can look after myself.' However much it cost her, however alone she felt, she couldn't use this as an excuse to bind him to her.

'I know. I'll just tag along, then, while you're looking after yourself.' He smoothed a strand of hair out of her eyes. 'I can be your second-in-command. Hold your hair while you're being sick.'

'You will not.' She dug him in the ribs and heard his sharp intake of breath. 'I can hold my own hair, thank you very much. You can do the mopping up.'

He chuckled. 'That's the spirit. Look, let's give ourselves some time to let this sink in. What do you say I make some breakfast? Unless you *are* feeling sick again.'

She was feeling sick and terrified, exhilarated and somehow serene. 'No. I'm fine. And, yes, breakfast would be great.'

'Good.' He was halfway to the bedroom door and he stopped. 'Jess. You don't have to say anything, right now. But when you know…when you know what you're going to do…'

'I'm keeping my baby.' That was the one thing she was stone-cold certain about.

He nodded. 'Thank you.' He turned, as if he didn't want to show her what was on his face. Closed the bedroom door behind him, leaving her alone again.

Greg wiped the tears away. He was completely unprepared for this. When she'd said she was pregnant, all he'd wanted to do was to hold her. And although he had been torn by almost every emotion he could think of, when Jess had pulled herself up to her full height, faced him and with more than a trace of defiance in her eyes, had told him that she was going to keep her child—his child—his heart had almost burst with relief.

He would make things right. He could learn how to be a father. He could afford to give Jess and his child everything they might need or want. That he could promise right now. As to the rest—he was unclear about the scope and detail of that, but it was early days. He'd work it out as he went along.

His finger tapped on the kitchen counter as he waited

for the kettle to boil. Two beats for every one of his own heart, a little more maybe. He could almost feel that tiny heartbeat, racing away, powering the prodigious growth of a seven-week embryo.

He prepared breakfast, and was gratified to see that Jess ate all of hers. They took a walk in the park, talking about anything and everything. Everything but the thing that was so palpably on both their minds. Then lunch and he waited, with only a trace of impatience, for her to settle herself down to watch a film so that he could open his laptop and spend a couple of hours answering his emails.

Four hours later he found her asleep on the sofa, the DVD looping through the opening credits.

'Jess…Jess, honey, wake up.'

She opened her eyes, and smiled at him. Stretched, yawned behind her hand and then sat up. 'What's the time?'

'Nearly five. How are you doing?'

'Fine. You?'

'I'm good.' He sat down next to her on the sofa. Maybe he should have checked up on her, thought to cover her up while she slept. But the flat was warm and it seemed that all she needed right now was to get some rest. And what he needed to do was to take care of business. Make sure that he could provide for her.

She nodded. 'I suppose I should be getting back home.'

'Stay a while. Unless there's something you need to do.'

'No. There's nothing.' She shrugged. 'Well, nothing that can't wait. Today's been…'

'Yeah. Nothing much else matters, today, eh?'

'No.' Her gaze flipped to his laptop, closed now on the coffee table, where he'd dumped it when he'd come in here to find her. Then back to his face. 'Greg, I've been thinking.'

'Yeah? Not dreaming?'

She grinned. 'That as well. But before I fell asleep, I was thinking.'

Her cheeks were still flushed from sleep, her brown and gold eyes reflecting the light. Greg laid his finger against her lips, feeling the echoes from that one soft touch reverberate across his skin. 'Tell you what, why don't we have something to eat, and then I'll take you home. Let's make a time to talk next week, when we've both collected our thoughts.'

She twisted her mouth wryly. 'You mean you're making a plan.'

'Aren't you?'

She shrugged. 'Do I need a plan?'

'I think so. And you should take your time over it, decide what you really want.'

'That's easy. I want to have this child, look after it and love it the best I can. That's the only plan I need, isn't it?'

Perhaps it was. Perhaps he wasn't going to get a say in what happened from now on. 'I was thinking more about a plan for how I can help you do that.'

A flash of defiance. This wasn't going to be a walk in the park but, then, Greg hadn't expected it would be. 'Yes. Yeah, I'm sorry.'

'Don't be. However you feel is okay. Just don't stop talking to me, Jess.'

'No, I won't.'

'Good. That's all I ask.' Greg had a feeling that this was going to be much more complex, more daunting that he could imagine right now. He'd deal with the emotional side of it, he had to. For the time being he'd do his best to help her with the practical things.

He'd started to pace now. It was what he generally did when he had something to think through, but Jess wished he'd stop for a minute and come and hold her.

'I think you should speak to Gerry. He'll be able to give you the support you need work-wise.'

'I will. It's a bit awkward.'

'He's not an ogre, you know.'

'I know. But he's not just my boss, he's your best friend. I need to think carefully about what I'm going to say to him.'

'You're pregnant. You're not going to be working any more double shifts. What more is there to say?'

Jess couldn't look at him. She appreciated what he'd done today, supportive without being pushy, never once questioning that the child was his or that he shared a responsibility towards it. But he was unnerving her. All this sudden talk about shared decisions, practicalities. Her first, unthinking reaction was that she was going to be doing this all by herself.

'He knows about you and me. He's sure to put two and two together.'

'Just tell him, then. It's my child.' His Italian ancestry broke through his English reserve, his shoulders straightening and his proud head held high. For a moment Jess thought he was going to challenge her to a duel. 'You tell Gerry or I will. In fact, I've got a better idea, I'll meet you tomorrow and we'll go and tell him together.'

'We will not.' She wasn't going to put herself in that position. Taking each one of them on separately was challenging enough. Both at the same time was obvious insanity. 'I'll speak to Gerry.'

'If that's what you want.' A flash of that luminous, slightly wicked smile. 'I imagine he'll call me out for playing above my league.'

Jess snorted with laughter. Greg had a habit of taking the world and abruptly turning it upside down, making her feel that anything was possible. He didn't have a league, he was one of a kind.

'Right. Please tell me you weren't born that charming. I've suddenly got an interest in your genetic traits.'

'I wouldn't worry. I expect your genes are all dominant.'

She wrinkled her nose at him. 'I'll go and see Gerry tomorrow morning.'

'And I'll meet you at lunchtime.'

'Yeah. Only I might be a bit late.'

He sighed, as if he was dealing with a recalcitrant teenager. 'Not too late. You need to take your breaks.'

'Have it your own way.' His stubborn insistence on her welfare might be irritating, but she couldn't help liking it a little. 'And talking about food, I thought you promised me something to eat.'

'How does pasta e fagioli sound?'

'Just right. How do you make yours?'

He grinned. 'Nah. If I tell you…'

'I know. You'll have to shoot me, or challenge me to a duel.'

He nodded. 'And as I'm not going to follow through on either, I'm just going to have to keep my mouth shut.'

CHAPTER TWELVE

GREG HAD BEEN up since six, even though he wasn't due on shift until this afternoon. Partly because there was no point lying in bed when he couldn't sleep. And partly because tussling with the non-stop drip-drip-drip of emails into his inbox was about the only thing that made any sense at the moment.

His mobile rang and he punched the answer button irritably, without even looking to see who was calling. 'Yeah?'

'Good morning to you, too.' Gerry's voice sounded down the line, and Greg considered hanging up on him. Who knew whether Jess had seen him yet or what she'd said?

'What is it, Gerry?'

'First of all, try not to sound so grumpy when you answer your phone, it puts people off. Second, I hear congratulations are in order.'

'Thanks.'

Gerry paused, just in case Greg wanted to volunteer any more information. He didn't. He was in the middle of reading a report, and his eyes were still flipping back and forth across the words on the screen in front of him, although not much was registering.

'Greg!'

He'd lost the thread of the report's argument now anyway. Greg sighed and snapped his laptop shut. 'Yeah. Sorry, Gerry. I was in the middle of something there.'

Gerry snorted. 'Get used to it, mate. Babies are world champions for interrupting things.'

That was as may be. Gerry seemed to thrive on the loving, noisy chaos that seemed to erupt at his house at the unlikeliest of times. 'I can handle it.'

'I'm sure you can, and I wish you the very best of luck with it. Maura and I are always on hand for any parenting tips, though. Or you could borrow Jamie if you wanted a bit of practice. Actually, you can borrow him until he's eighteen if you feel that's of any help.'

'Keeping you up nights, is he?' Greg wondered whether he'd have the chance to roll out of bed and stumble to the nursery to hold his own child.

'Ah, not so bad.' Gerry chuckled. 'And even if this is as worry-free as both of you seem to be making out, I've still got a bottle of the good stuff in the cupboard if you decide you've got the time to pop in.'

'Thanks, mate. There was something I wanted to talk to you about, actually.' Greg knew he probably shouldn't be doing this but he did it anyway. 'Did Jess mention anything about her shifts to you? She looked pretty tired yesterday and if she's been working double shifts...'

Gerry laughed. 'Fussing already, eh? Pregnancy isn't an illness, you know.'

'I know.' Did it really sound as if he was fussing? 'Look, Gerry, I know I shouldn't ask, but I'd take it as a personal favour.'

'I don't do personal favours. All my staff get treated the same, and I'll be reviewing Jess's shifts with her this afternoon, just as I would with anyone else in her situation. Anyway, this is something you should be talking to Jess about, not me.'

'Yeah, I know.' Easier said than done. Greg looked at his watch and groaned. 'Listen, thanks for calling, but I've got to get going. Catch up with you later?'

'Sooner would be better.' Gerry's chuckle sounded in Greg's ear and then he cut the call.

Even though they'd made no solid plans to meet up, Greg had made sure that he caught up with Jess every day this week. Sometimes for a meal break, sometimes just for ten minutes snatched from a busy shift. He didn't need to, but Jess couldn't deny that she appreciated it, or that she looked forward to seeing him.

She hadn't seen him yet today, Fridays were always busy. That meant he would be looking for her, wouldn't it? That he would notice she was gone. Jess closed her eyes, wondering if that would make the darkness around her seem any less menacing, and pulled her cardigan around her. He would come. He'd find her.

Greg's phone rang and he ignored it. Gerry was going to have to wait, he had to concentrate on composing a particularly tricky email, and he only had fifteen more minutes left before his meal break was finished.

'There you are.'

Gerry's voice broke his train as he entered the room and Greg rolled his eyes. What did a man have to do to get some time to himself around here?

'What are you doing here?'

'Trying to get a bit of peace. I've got to get back to the London office before the end of today.' Greg sighed and snapped his laptop closed. It was about time he got back to work now anyway. This would have to wait until he got ten minutes for a coffee break.

'Have you seen Jess?'

'No. Why?' He supposed that Gerry had noticed that he was hanging around Cardiology rather more than usual and had divined that he'd been keeping an eye on her.

'Because she should have been back from her lunch break nearly an hour ago. Jess is never late.'

Suddenly the demands of the first and the second job shot into insignificance. 'Well, where is she? Didn't she say where she was going?'

'It's not my practice to get my team to tell me where they are for every waking moment.' Gerry's voice was calm, but Greg could hear the note of concern. 'Otherwise I'd have cottoned on to you a lot earlier than I did.'

'Yeah, right. Thanks for that, Gerry.' He had to think. Ignore the other things that constantly seemed to be crowding in on him and concentrate. 'Has she taken her coat?'

'No. She must be here somewhere, but I've paged her and called her mobile and she's not answering. Her sandwiches are still in the fridge.'

'Hmm. She wouldn't have gone far without them.' His groundless, lingering fear that Jess would simply not turn up for work one day, that she'd disappear along with his child, was looking less and less like an explanation for this. No one did a runner at lunchtime, leaving their coat and sandwiches behind. 'Do you think she's gone somewhere to put her feet up and fallen asleep?'

'I've checked all the common rooms and overnight accommodation. And the canteen. She's not down in A and E and she isn't in the admin offices. I had Beverly look in all of the ladies' lavatories and I've put a call out to all departments for her.' Gerry shrugged. 'I don't know where else to look.'

The knot in Greg's stomach was twisting tighter and tighter, as each possibility was ticked off an ever-diminishing list. 'Perhaps she's been kidnapped.'

'Leave off. This is a hospital, not a gangster movie.'

True enough. But Greg could—would—pay any sum to keep her safe. He wondered vaguely what safeguards his father had put into place on that score, and decided to shelve the matter until he got a chance to talk to Pat.

'Yeah. I just can't think. You don't suppose it's something to do with this history project she's doing on the hospital?'

'Maybe. She had a load of old photographs and was taking new ones for a "then and now" the other day.'

'Yeah, but she'd take her coat for that, wouldn't she?' Greg hoped with every fibre of his body that none of those old photographs had taken her into disused parts of the building. 'What about the basement? That's where the records are kept, right? She told me that there was an old safe down there…' For a brief moment Greg and Gerry stared at each other. Then Greg was on his feet and running for the stairs.

He almost stumbled on the steps down to the boiler room, and made the records room breathing hard. Pulling the door open, he called for her.

Nothing. In the far corner he could see a large metal door and he ran down the narrow corridor between the stacked boxes, dislodging one and letting it spill unheeded onto the floor behind him.

'Jess!' He tried to open the door and then beat on it with his fist. 'Jess are you in there?'

'Greg!' She sounded about a million miles away, but he could hear her.

'Are you all right?'

'Yes, I'm all right. Just locked in.'

'Sit tight, baby. I'll get you out of there.' Greg looked around for something that he could force the door with and saw nothing. In any case, he doubted whether the heavy security bolts would respond to a man's strength.

'Don't call me baby!' Her voice was faint, but he could hear the outrage in it and Greg smiled. It sounded as if she was holding it together in there. 'There's an air brick over the door. Can you see it?'

'Yes, hold on.' Greg fetched a set of steps, which leant against the wall, and climbed up, clearing the cobwebs from around the brick. 'Can you hear me better?'

'Yes. It's dark in here, Greg, the light's broken.' There was a plaintive note to her voice now.

'Just hang on. I'll send upstairs for the key.'

'The key's in here, with me, and there isn't another one. The door slammed shut behind me, and there isn't a key-hole on this side of the lock.'

Greg cursed under his breath. 'Okay. Can you reach the air brick? Don't try climbing on anything in the dark.'

There was a short pause, and the tips of her fingers appeared against one of the lower ventilation holes. 'Just about. But the key's too big to get it through.'

'That's all right. I can break a bigger hole out.' The old brick was crumbling, and it looked as if a well-placed shove would knock it out. 'Can you get back a bit? Be careful.' If she fell, and couldn't reach back up to the brick again, they'd be back where they started.

'Right.' He heard the sounds of her moving warily across the darkened room and then her voice again, fainter this time. 'Okay.'

'I'll be one minute.' Greg remembered he'd seen a selection of old tools abandoned in the corner of the boiler room. 'Then, when I give the word, I want you to cover your face.'

The brick was tougher than it looked. His first blow merely sent chips spinning back in his face, and Greg had to deliver two more before it gave and the chisel punched through to the other side. He called to Jess, and a minute later the key was slid through the hole and into his possession. Then she was in his arms.

'It's okay.' She was shaking, but Greg couldn't tell whether it was from the cold or from shock. His hand found hers. 'Are you all right? You're freezing.'

She nodded against his chest. 'I'm fine. Just a bit cold.' She seemed to be trying to burrow into his arms, and Greg held her tight, willing his own body heat to radiate into her.

'How long have you been down here?'

'I'm not sure. Since the beginning of my meal break.'

'That's almost two hours.' He rubbed her shoulders and back, trying to warm her, and she smiled up at him.

'That's better. I'm sorry.'

'What happened?'

'I came down here to get one last pile of documents for scanning. I wedged the door and put the key in my pocket.' She turned the edges of her mouth down. 'Fat lot of good that was. The admin staff made us promise to keep the key on us at all times, but neglected to mention that it was no good if we got locked in.'

Greg glanced down at the door wedge. 'Someone should have thrown that away years ago. It's not enough to hold a heavy door. Look, it's gone straight over the top of it.'

She didn't even glance downwards. 'Thanks. But it was my own stupid fault. I should have looked for myself.'

He wrapped his arms around her shoulders, settling her against him. That was where she was supposed to be. The place her body seemed to fit exactly. 'Accidents usually happen when we're not looking. That's the thing about them.' He ran his hand down her back, rubbing in the smooth, circular motion that he knew would calm her. 'Sure you're okay?'

'I'm fine.' She answered the question that he hadn't dared to ask. 'The baby's fine, too. She's used to the dark.'

'She?'

'Yeah. She told me.'

He chuckled. 'Must be right, then.' This was nice. For the first time in months everything seemed as it should be. The cold dread that had pushed every other worry out of his head had now given way to thankfulness that he'd found her, and it seemed to suffuse his whole body.

He dipped his head and planted a kiss on her brow. It really was the only thing that a man could do in the circumstances. She tipped her face upwards so he could reach her lips. It was impossible to do anything other than kiss her again.

She was always soft, always sweet. There was always that touch of fire that made his body react, as if his cells held the memory of her touch, craving it again. There was always more, too, and this time the sheer happiness of something averted curved her lips into a smile against his.

'Thanks, Greg. For coming for me.'

He'd been too busy to even notice that she had been missing. 'It was Gerry who told me you were gone.'

'You found me, though.'

She gave him too much credit. He could tell her so, or he could resolve to do better in future and move on. 'I'd better give him a call. Let him know that you're okay.'

She nodded. 'There's no phone reception in here. You have to go outside, into the corridor.'

He let her go, long enough for her to lock the secure room door again and gather up the pile of documents she'd come for. Greg considered confiscating the key so that she wouldn't be able to come down here again without him and decided that would be construed as over-protective.

The corridor outside, leading to the boiler room, was

a welcome few degrees warmer and he stopped, leaning against the wall and pulling her against him between his outstretched legs. Pulling out his phone and dialling Gerry, he curled his other arm around her waist.

'Gerry, panic over. I've found her.' He regretted the word '*panic*' as soon as the tips of her ears started to redden. 'I'm getting on to Maintenance—that door really isn't safe. It slammed shut even though Jess wedged it open.'

She looked up at him, a brief thrill of gratitude in her eyes. Greg imagined that she'd been sitting down here wondering whether she'd get a hard time for allowing herself to get locked in down.

'But she's okay?'

Thank you, Gerry. If he wasn't allowed to fuss, then perhaps he'd leave Gerry to do it for him. 'She says so.'

Gerry went for the bait. *'Well bring her up here. I want to make sure.'*

'Right.' He snapped the phone shut and grinned at Jess. 'Gerry wants you up in Cardiology.'

'I know. I've got things to do.'

'He wants to make sure you're all right.'

'I'm fine. I said so.'

'Hypothermia?' He pulled her closer to him.

'Somehow I don't think so. It wasn't that cold in there.'

'Shock?' Greg amended that to cover any possibility of imminent deterioration. 'Delayed shock. Delayed hypothermia perhaps. You've laddered your tights, so I imagine you've probably grazed your knee as well if I look a little closer.'

'Are you by any chance fishing for a diagnosis, Doctor? Because I have to tell you that making things up isn't going to work.' The glint in her eyes told Greg that she had his number. Fooling her was infinitely more difficult than fooling himself.

There was only one honest answer. He kissed her. He was going to have to do better, keep a closer eye on her. Unobtrusively, of course, or she'd call him out on it. He'd think of a way, though.

Jess wasn't used to being looked after. She wasn't used to the feeling of wanting to be looked after either. Greg had delivered her up to Cardiology, where Gerry had taken over as guardian-in-chief and had insisted that she sit for a while and relax, while he saw the patients who were waiting for her. Then, at six o'clock, Greg had appeared again, and despite all her protests he'd guided her into a waiting taxi and taken her home.

'Don't you have something to do tonight?' He'd hung around until she'd given in and asked him up for a cup of tea.

'No.'

'Liar.' The quick dip of his gaze had betrayed the truth.

He shrugged. 'Okay, you got me. But if you want some company... It won't do anyone any harm to wait on a decision from me for twenty-four hours.'

'Let them stew, you mean.' She grinned at him. Maybe keeping Greg occupied tonight wasn't such a bad thing. Every time she'd seen him this week he'd been disentangling himself from one set of responsibilities so that he could shoulder another.

'Yeah. I have a life too.'

'Glad to hear it.' And she needed him here. No, scrap that, she wanted him here. Needing him felt as if she was betraying her unborn child. She'd made a promise that she would look after it and no one, not even Greg, was going to put that into jeopardy by eating away at her independence now.

He looked around at her sitting room. 'This is nice. Cosy.'

'Small, you mean?'

'No. If I'd meant small, I would have said small.' He flopped down on the sofa. 'It could be bigger, though. Ever thought of expanding?'

Jess rolled her eyes. 'In which direction? There are flats above and below me and to either side. Guess I could build out over the pavement, but the planning authority might have something to say about that...'

He held his hands up. 'Okay. But if the people around you ever want to sell up...'

'They don't.'

'They might. Depends how much you offer them.' He had a look of exaggerated innocence on his face.

'Don't even think about it, Greg. There's plenty of room here for me.' She knew exactly what he was driving at. 'And the baby. For the time being, anyway.'

He nodded. 'Yeah. But you don't need to... What I mean is that you do have a choice, Jess. You can live wherever you want to. You could come and live with me.'

As invitations to move in went, this one was distinctly underwhelming. 'You want an answer to that?'

'Of course I do.'

A meal, a little candlelight and some kind of declaration of love would have been nice. He might just as well have emailed her. Or got the irreplaceable Pat to do it for him. 'I'll get us some tea, shall I?' It looked as if that talk that she'd rehearsed in front of the mirror and then with variations while she'd been trapped in the dark today was just about to be enacted for real.

CHAPTER THIRTEEN

She pulled the coffee table back to give him room to stretch his legs, and put a cup of herbal tea in front of him, sitting down at the far end of the sofa. Honey for sweetness. Biscuits, in case the need for calories threatened to make either of them cranky. Soothing lighting and a couple of candles in the fireplace, just in case Greg decided that their future together was a matter of romance, not business.

'So. You said you'd been thinking.' His eyes were dark, unreadable in the flickering light.

'I have. You want to hear it?'

'Always, Jess.'

Promising start. Now the difficult part. The only way that she could do this was to try to divorce herself from the heady feelings of love and the terrifying dread of loss that came with all of her dealings with Greg. 'This baby… You…' She took a deep breath. 'This is your child. I know that we took precautions…'

'Precautions fail, Jess. I never doubted for one minute that the child is mine.'

'Not even a minute?' They'd always used condoms. Sometimes a little hurried, their minds always on other things, but they'd been careful. Jess had thought they were being responsible.

'No. I won't say that I didn't think about it, but…' he

waved away any doubts that he may have had, as if they were nothing '…I trust you. There's no percentage failure rate on that.'

Warmth swelled in her chest, and Jess found herself smiling. 'Thank you. That's a really nice thing to say.' This was going better than she'd dared hope.

'So what else?' He leaned back on the sofa, as if he had all the time in the world. So different from usual. The way he might have been all the time if no one had thought to create Shaw Industries, or laptops, or email accounts.

She was trembling. The only way she knew how to do this was to pitch straight in. 'You have a right to a relationship with your child and I won't deny you that.'

'Okay.' A hint of suspicion crept across his face. 'Were you thinking about trying?'

'No!' She'd lost her way already in the maze of possibilities and emotions. 'Of course not. I didn't mean that at all. That's what I want too. I'm just trying to say that I won't ask anything from you that you don't want to give.'

'Understood.' He was obviously suspending judgement until he had the full story.

'And for Rosa and Ted, too. If they want an involvement… I mean, they have a right to a loving relationship with their grandchild. I'll do all I can to make sure that happens.' Jess could think about how she was going to accomplish that later.

He seemed to loosen up a little. 'Thanks. I think I can speak for them both in saying that they'll really welcome that. And that they'll really appreciate the fact that you thought to suggest it.'

'Well, those family recipes are too good to waste.' She grinned at him, trying to lighten the mood a bit.

Greg chuckled. 'Consider that done.'

'That's great.' They were getting somewhere.

'And how do you feel about me, then?'

His face was grave again. He'd picked up on the one thing that Jess couldn't make sense of, and asked the one question that she couldn't answer. Her imagination seemed only to stretch to two at a time. She and Greg. She and the baby. Three was a difficult and unmanageable number.

'How do *you* feel?'

He turned his dark gaze on her. As soft as silk and as demanding as any woman could ever want. 'I'll answer, even if you won't. This is my child too, and I want to be a proper father. I have the resources to give our child everything.'

What was that feeling of panic doing, quivering in her stomach? Wasn't that what every mother wanted to hear? 'I don't need your money, Greg. I've always provided for myself and nothing's changed. When I said that I'd welcome your involvement, I meant some of your time. Your love.' Maybe she'd gone a bit too far there. 'For the baby, I mean.'

'Not for you?' His eyes dared her to say yes.

'It's not me we're talking about here.'

He let out a sharp laugh of disbelief. 'What happened to being honest about how we feel, Jess? Are you going to tell me that you're sleeping with me but that you don't expect me to care about you? It's all just for kicks, is it?'

She couldn't break that faith. The trust that showed in his eyes and that she felt in her heart when he made love to her. 'You know it's more than that, Greg.' Of course he did. She could see it in his face right now. 'Although I don't discount the kicks. They're pretty good, too.'

'You've got a point. Why don't you come over here?'

'No. We're supposed to be talking.'

'You can talk from over here.' He was grinning now. Talking was about the last thing on his mind.

'I'll lose my thread.'

He gave a mock sigh. 'Yeah, me, too.' A pause, and then he hit her with it. 'Jess, I think we should think about getting married.'

'What?' She was already shrinking away from him when she realised that probably wasn't the thing any man wanted to see when he'd just proposed to a woman. If this could be construed as a proposal. 'Greg, you don't have to do that. '

'I want to.'

At this moment he probably did. He wanted to provide for his child. She should have expected this. Greg could be stubbornly honourable at times. But it was all far too risky. She'd known that there was always the possibility that things might not work out between the two of them, that his work schedule might swallow him up again, but she couldn't take that risk for her child. Marrying him now could just trap them both in a life of waiting for him.

She took a deep breath. 'I know you do. And I appreciate it, Greg, more than I can say. But I really don't think this is the best way forward.'

'Jess, this isn't just a business agreement.'

'I know, but my answer's still the same. It wouldn't be fair on you or me or our child. Let's find another way, eh?' She smiled at him. Tried to jolt him out of the rose-coloured, impractical world that he seemed to have steeped himself in.

An echo of the man she loved flitted across his features. The man who took what he wanted and gave so much in return. Then it died.

'Okay. We'll find another way.' His smile was carefully constructed. Proper in every way. 'I'll have to put you on notice that I won't be letting you turn all my offers down so easily, though. And I expect you to talk to me, Jess. You know that I can afford to give you whatever you want.'

Fair enough. There was something. 'I'll be having my first scan at sixteen weeks.' She hardly dared ask. Money was so easy for him to give but this might cost him far more.

'I'll be there. Just tell me when and where.'

'Thanks. I appreciate it.'

He reached out for her and she slid along the sofa towards him. The contact made her shiver both with warmth and foreboding. 'Don't say that. I want to see him just as much as you do.'

'Him?'

'Yeah. You reckon it's a girl and I think it's a boy. We could make a wager if you like.'

The look on his face told her that this was one bet she didn't want to have to pay up on. 'What kind of wager?'

'If I'm right then I get to keep you in my bed for a whole weekend. Somewhere nice. Paris maybe.'

'And if I'm right?' Jess was almost tempted. Who was she trying to kid? The temptation was pretty much unbearable.

'You get to keep me in yours for a whole weekend. Somewhere else nice. Rome perhaps. You'd like the house in Rome.'

She narrowed her eyes. 'Couldn't we just keep it simple? I bet you a fiver it's a girl.'

He sighed. 'I thought you weren't after my cash. Okay, a fiver it is. Or we could push the boat out and go for a tenner. You're missing out on a great opportunity, though. You really would love the house in Rome.'

'So you keep saying. Maybe another time.'

'I'll keep you to that.' His finger found her wrist, caressing the soft skin at the base of her palm. 'And what about tonight? Can I stay?'

'I'm...I'm tired, Greg.'

'I know. I just want to hold you.'

She wanted that too. Even if it did seem somehow disloyal to her baby.

He leaned forward, until his lips almost touched hers. 'We could keep it simple. Do whatever comes naturally.'

Jess gave up the unequal struggle. They'd covered enough ground tonight. Tomorrow was soon enough to tackle the rest.

Greg was like an addict. He said he'd give it up, had actually managed to give it up for days on end when sufficiently threatened, but he always went back to it. When deprived of his laptop for more than a few hours he began to get jittery.

There was no end to it. Taking Friday evening and Saturday off had only piled on the pressure. The following week he seemed busier still and correspondingly more distant.

'Rosa called me last night.' Jess had cooked their evening meal and was stacking the dishwasher.

'Hmm?' Greg didn't look up from his laptop.

'She said that she and Ted were leaving for Ecuador next week. They wanted to know if I'd like to go along.' Rosa had offered her congratulations and tremulously wondered whether it was too early to ask if anyone else was buying her a pram. And if the answer to both questions was no, whether she might be allowed to take her out shopping for one.

'Hmm.'

'I said yes, that would be lovely.'

'Good.'

'She seemed pleased.' Rosa had been delighted.

Greg looked up and focussed in Jess's direction. 'Good.'

'You think it's a good idea, then?'

He looked at her, suspicion flickering in his eyes. 'Am I missing something?'

Jess got to her feet. 'Yeah. You're missing something. Do you want a cup of tea?'

He nodded. 'Love one. You're such a star, Jess.'

'Jess, are you free? I've got a friend of yours down here.'

Greg's voice on the phone sounded relaxed, as if he was smiling.

He was still smiling when she got to A and E. 'What's up?'

He jerked his head towards one of the cubicles. 'Thomas Judd. You know him?'

Jess couldn't place the name. Greg grinned. 'Ten years old, fair hair and a very cheeky smile. When I examined him I found he has a pacemaker and he said that he'd had it replaced about six months ago.'

'Ah, yes, Tommy. Is he all right?'

Greg nodded. 'Yep. Involved in a car accident. Minor cuts and bruises and I've had the technician down to give him a pacemaker check to make sure that none of the wires were dislodged by the impact.'

'Where is he?' Jess scanned the cubicles. 'I'd like to go and see him.'

Greg caught her arm. 'His mother's here too. She's pretty knocked about but she'll be all right.'

Jess nodded. Her first road accident in A and E had reduced her to tears, until Greg had taken her to one side, explained that this was one of those cases that looked a great deal worse than it was and had sent her back in to clean and stitch the cuts on the man's face.

'She doesn't want Tommy to see her?'

'No. His father's on the way. '

'I'll go and sit with him. I've got time, I'm just about

to take my lunch break.' A warning frown clouded Greg's brow and Jess ignored it.

He opened his mouth and then thought better of it. Greg knew as well as Jess did that if he objected to her working through her lunch break he wouldn't have a leg to stand on. 'Okay. Just for half an hour.'

Tommy wriggled free of the nurse who was cleaning his cuts and hugged Jess when he saw her. 'I'm very glad you're here.' He enunciated the words as if he were a spymaster, about to send Jess out on an important mission.

'Well, I'm glad to be here. What's up, Tommy?' The boy was unusually uncooperative, batting away the nurse who was trying to tend to him. He'd already seen far too much of the inside of a hospital in his short life, and this level of treatment was something that he usually took in his stride.

'Get off me!' Tommy was clearly having nothing more to do with the nurse who was gently trying to tend to him. She winked at Jess and backed off.

'All right.' Jess sat down by the bed. 'You can tell me what's the matter and then I'll finish with those cuts. Deal?'

'Deal. Only I want you to do something first.'

'What's that?'

'Go and look after my mum.' Tears sprang to Tommy's eyes. The kid who was so brave, hardly ever cried. Jess choked back the lump that had suddenly formed in her throat.

'Tommy, she's got another doctor looking after her. He's much better than—'

'I want you!' Tommy thumped the bed. 'You have to go!'

'What's all this?' Jess hadn't been aware that Greg had entered the cubicle, and when his voice rang out behind her, it made her jump.

'I want Jess to see my mum. She's the best doctor in the hospital.' Tommy explained the situation slowly to Greg, just in case he was having trouble comprehending.

'Tommy, I'm not—'

'Good idea.' Greg cut her short. 'But first Jess needs to see you, so she can tell your mum that you're all right. And that you're doing what you're told.' Greg folded his arms, a sign that he wasn't having any nonsense. 'All right, chief?'

Tommy nodded wordlessly.

'So when Jess gets back she'll expect to see that cut on your forehead with a dressing on it. Which means that you need to keep still for Erica while she does it for you.' Kindness had been vying with firmness from the very start, and Greg was clearly having trouble maintaining his authoritarian stance in the face of Tommy's blue eyes. 'I'll bring you something to drink when I get back. What would you like? Some juice?'

'It doesn't matter. Just water.' Tommy was interested in one thing only, and everything else was unimportant.

'All right. But first of all I'll take Jess to see your mum.'

Greg closed the cubicle door behind them. 'Bright kid. Knows how to work the system.'

'He ought to, he's had enough practice.' Jess shrugged. 'He's not usually this awkward, though.'

Greg chuckled. 'I'd do exactly the same in his place. If one of my family was sick or injured, I'd do whatever I had to do to get them the best treatment I could.'

'Is it okay if I pop in to see his mother?'

'What, you were thinking of going back in there and trying to pretend you'd seen his mother when you hadn't?' Greg gave a snort of laughter. 'Good luck with that one.'

It looked as if Tommy's mother had broken her jaw. Major swelling, contusions and bruising. No wonder no one had thought it a good idea to let Tommy in to see her.

Jess smiled at the nurse tending her, and the nurse took the opportunity of someone else being there to slip out for five minutes.

Gemma was lying on her side so that blood and saliva could drain from her mouth, and recognition flared in her eyes as soon as Jess sat down next to the bed. 'I'm one of Tommy's doctors from Cardiology. I've just seen him and he's fine and being well looked after, but he's worried about you. So I promised him I'd come to see you and find out how you were doing.'

Gemma's gaze never left Jess's face, and Jess took hold of her hand.

'Don't try to talk, Gemma. Give me one squeeze for yes and two for no. Do you want your phone?'

One squeeze. Jess hadn't really needed to ask. She'd seen Tommy's face when he'd got the messages from his mother, telling him that she was there for him. Jess reached for Gemma's bag and found her phone, fumbling with it for a moment before she found what looked like the correct application, and held the screen up in front of Gemma.

A smile for Tommy, drawn with his mother's finger. A bit shakier than the ones that he used to receive when he was in hospital but that didn't matter.

'Here, you send it.' Jess saved the image into a text and found Tommy's name on the contacts list. His mother stabbed her finger on the 'send' button, and the time bar flashed up then indicated that the message had been sent.

'There. He'll be getting that right about now. I'm going to go back tell him to look on his phone.' Just in case the nursing staff had found Tommy's phone and managed to persuade him to switch it off.

Gemma's hand found hers and squeezed it.

'Hang on in there, Gemma. Your husband will be here soon.' For the life of her Jess couldn't remember Gemma's husband's name, but Gemma was bound to know who she meant.

Another squeeze.

'Is there anything else I can get you?'

Gemma's finger pointed towards Jess and then her thumb jerked towards the door.

'You want me out of here and go to see Tommy?'

Gemma patted her hand then squeezed it once.

'Okay. I'll come back and see you again. In the meantime, just hang in there. I've spoken to the doctor who's looking after you and you're going to be okay.'

Gemma's eyes filled with tears and Jess dabbed at them with a tissue. Her thumb jerked again, towards the door.

'Okay, I'm going.' Jess's eyes misted with tears. She knew that Gemma would rather be with strangers if it meant that Tommy had a friend with him. She would do the same for her own child. Suddenly she wanted more than almost anything to go and find Greg, to tell him.

A quick thumb's-up from Gemma and Jess turned and made for the door, scanning the space outside for Greg. A rattle from the bed behind her made her turn. Gemma's arm was flailing back and forth in a repeating arc, banging against the bed rail.

'Greg. In here,' she called to him, and out of the corner of her eye she saw him turn. She didn't need to question whether he'd come or not, and she ducked back inside the cubicle.

Gemma's eyelids were fluttering and she was groaning. Jess hurried over to her, checking quickly that her breathing was unobstructed.

She felt, rather than saw, Greg enter the cubicle. 'She's having a seizure.'

'Okay.' Greg was at Gemma's side, steadying her gently

so that a sudden movement wouldn't pitch her off the bed. 'How long?'

'Thirty seconds. A minute tops.'

The motion of Gemma's hand began to slow. 'Good. She's coming out of it now.' He bent over her. 'Okay, Gemma. You're all right. Try to relax.'

Gemma was slowly coming back. Greg was there, and however much it pained her to leave, Jess had somewhere else to be. 'Do you need me any more?'

'No, I think we're good.' Greg was smiling at Gemma, his hand reassuringly on her shoulder. 'Could you ask Steve to come in here, though? And if you see the husband when he arrives, find out if there's any history of seizures…'

He looked up from Gemma for a moment and their eyes connected. Just for a moment, but that was all it needed. After weeks of feeling that Greg was slipping away from her, that even when he was right there with her he was somewhere else, suddenly he was here. They were together.

'Anything else?'

'Go and check on Tommy.' He was grinning.

'Yeah.'

'Get me a cup of tea?'

'Sorry didn't quite catch that one.' She heard his exclamation of mock dismay as she turned on her heel and didn't need to look back to know that he was smiling.

CHAPTER FOURTEEN

IT WAS COLD up here. Jess wrapped her hands around her mug of tea.

'This is…' Greg shrugged. 'I don't really know how to describe it.'

'No, me neither.'

'Let's have a look at that photograph again.'

She handed him the scanned copy of the photograph that she'd found, and Greg studied it. 'So this window, here…' he ran his finger across the image '…is that one over there. And if I stand here… Yes, this is where the photo was taken from.'

Jess went to stand beside him. 'I think you're right.'

He looked around him. 'So this was a ward once. Right up here in the attic.'

She nodded. 'Yep. They used it for cholera patients during one of the outbreaks in London.' Jess shivered. The whitewashed walls, now lined with store cupboards, must have seen their share of suffering.

'Do you know the date of this photo?'

'Yes, it was written on the back—1851.'

Greg was deep in thought. 'Before Lister's procedures were adopted.' He shook his head. 'These doctors didn't even know that they needed to wash their hands. All they could do for infectious disease was put the patients up here. It must have been terrifying.'

'They did the best they could.' Jess looked for the hundredth time at the faces of the doctors and nurses, posing for the camera in well-ordered lines. 'We wouldn't be here now if it wasn't for them.'

'No.' Greg sat down on a large, wooden crate, leaving space for Jess to come and sit next to him. His face was drawn into a mask of regret, and he seemed to need her close.

'I didn't think it would be this sad. I knew the facts and figures, how there were so many things then that couldn't be cured, but when I see the faces...'

'Yeah.' Greg put his arm around her shoulders. 'See that kid in the bed there? Look at his arm, it's so thin.'

'Mmm. He can't be much older than Tommy. How's Gemma, by the way?'

'She's okay. They've wired her jaw and are keeping her in under observation. There have been no more seizures, though, and the CAT scan didn't show any reason for concern.'

'Good. Is that where you were just now?' Greg had said that he'd meet her half an hour after the end of his shift.

'Yes. I met her husband up on the ward. Nice guy.'

'And how's Tommy?' Jess knew Greg. He wouldn't have left without finding that out as well.

'Good. Texting his mother smiles, the way that she did when he was in hospital.' He grinned. 'So you can cheer up.'

Jess laughed. 'Right. Consider me officially cheery. Do you have time for dinner tonight?'

'Yes. In fact, there's something I want to tell you.'

'What?'

'I'll tell you when we eat.'

Jess searched in her handbag and found a couple of fruit bars. 'Here.' She handed Greg one and stripped the other of its wrapper. 'We're eating now.'

He laughed. 'I bet none of your Christmas presents last until Christmas Day, do they?'

She shrugged. 'Some of them do. But tell me now.' Their time together was too precious to waste. Dinner was about the only opportunity they got to just talk about nothing. Be together, without the distractions that seemed to press relentlessly in on them.

'I've made a decision.'

That sounded serious. Maybe she should have waited. On the other hand, they were alone here. 'Yes? What decision?'

'I can't keep on doing two jobs like this. Something's got to go.'

Thank you. At last he'd come to his senses. The cutting back on his hours at the hospital hadn't worked, Greg was just as busy, just as tired as he'd been when he'd been working a full shift rota.

'I think you're right. You can't keep this up for much longer.'

He nodded. 'So I've decided to leave the hospital. Run Shaw Industries full time.'

She could almost hear the silence. Almost feel the seconds, painfully ticking by. She mustn't do all the things she wanted to do—rage at him, cry and beg him not to do this. Greg wouldn't listen. He was driven by the practical. She had to be calm. 'This... Are you sure, Greg?'

'Sure's a luxury that even I can't afford.'

There was some hope, then. 'Perhaps you should think about it a little more. Not do anything hasty.'

'I have to make a choice. You yourself said that I can't

go on like this. I'm not doing either of my jobs to the best of my ability.'

'But you love medicine. This is what you studied for. Everything you've worked for. You can't just give it up.'

'There are other doctors.'

'Not as good as you.'

He curled his arm around her shoulders. 'Thanks for the vote of confidence. But there *are* other doctors, and the hospital will fill the vacancy easily. I'm the only one who can keep Shaw Industries going.'

'They've managed without you all these years.' Jess hated that damned company. Wished it would crumble into dust.

'That was when my father was alive. Jess, he's left me this responsibility. I can't not shoulder it.'

Why not? There wasn't any point in asking him. It was his father's first and last gesture of confidence in Greg, and he could pass that up about as easily as he could wave a magic wand and cure all ills. He might be good, but he wasn't that good.

'I know it's not what you expected, Jess. But this is the way forward. I can provide for you and the child.'

'Don't use me as an excuse for doing this. If you needed to provide for us, you could do it on a doctor's salary. And you don't. I can provide for myself and the baby. We've been through all this already.' She glared at him.

A muscle at the side of his face twitched. 'I'm not. But it's a fact, Jess. Like it or not, I'm in a position to be able to provide for my family.'

And try stopping him. Greg's mind was obviously made up on this point, and arguing about it with him would get her nowhere.

'The baby needs your time, too.'

'And this doesn't facilitate that? I've just cut my work commitments in half.'

But it was the wrong half. Couldn't he see that?

'The baby needs you.' She couldn't explain it. She'd clung on to the hope that Greg could be a better father than his own had been. Wondered if maybe, over time, he could show her how being in a family with him might work. Now she was beginning to doubt it.

He sighed, pinching the bridge of his nose as if he had a headache. 'Jess, you're making this complicated. I'm not telling you where you ought to work or what you should do. Shaw Industries isn't just a faceless, evil conglomerate, you know.'

'I dare say it isn't.' Jess frowned. That was how it appeared to her, and she was going to need a fair bit of convincing to think any other way.

'Do you know what we do?'

'Engineering?' Something like that. Jess hadn't taken a great deal of notice.

'Yeah, design and engineering. It started out when my father invented a drill head—which doesn't sound very exciting, but it was ground-breaking in a number of different areas. The basic design has applications of all sorts, it's even used downstairs in the operating theatre here.' He looked at her steadily. 'It might not be as much of a medical breakthrough as Lister made, but every little helps.'

He had an answer for everything. Everything apart from what would happen to his soul if he was separated from the job he loved, the one he'd chosen, and started to trudge in the treacly footsteps of his father.

'Is this really what you want to do, Greg?'

'It's what I have to do. At some point you have to choose whether what you want is more important than where you can do the most good. It's not about being happy, it's about doing the right thing.'

It sounded like a life sentence. A life behind bars, for something he hadn't done. Jess could think of nothing more to say to him. She was going to have to wave him goodbye and think about baking a cake with a file in it. Trouble was, Greg didn't seem to want to escape.

'This'll be okay, Jess. We can make this work. Let me show you.'

'How are you going to do that?'

He slid his hands around her waist. 'This weekend. I'll pick you up at seven o' clock on Friday night. Bring a toothbrush.'

'Sounds interesting.' Greg was trying to charm her out of all her reservations. He wasn't doing a bad job of it either. 'Where are we going?'

'Do you need to know?'

'Yeah, I do.' However much Jess was tempted to plunge into the exciting unknown with Greg, it still frightened her. It should frighten her. She had responsibilities now, and the tried and tested was always going to be preferable to the heady gamble that Greg offered. 'I need to know where I'm going.'

He nodded. 'Okay. We're going to Rome.' He quieted her protests with a finger across her lips. 'You don't have to do anything, it's all arranged. I've got to go over there to see the new headquarters building on Saturday. I'm hoping we'll have Sunday to ourselves.'

'I don't know, Greg.' It sounded fabulous, but it wasn't exactly the kind of thing that Jess did. 'Italy for the weekend?'

'Is just the thing. We'll stay at the house in Rome. You'll love—'

'Yes, I know. I'll love the house in Rome.' She should

at least try to see his point of view, for everyone's sake. And seeing Rome with Greg didn't sound like too much of a hardship. 'I'll be able to make my own mind up about that at the weekend, won't I?'

Something ignited, deep in those dark brown eyes. He pulled her close, wrapping his arms around her shoulders. 'Good. Thanks, Jess. I know things haven't been great recently. I've been under a lot of pressure, and things have been complicated. Thanks for sticking by me.'

'Isn't that my line?' She snuggled into him. She never got tired of his scent.

He chuckled. 'Not really. You have all you need, Jess.'

It didn't actually feel as if she was anywhere different. Since the car had picked her up at her flat, Jess had been shepherded through two airports at top speed and with the minimum of fuss, having had a good meal and a nap on the plane. She wasn't sorry that she hadn't had to struggle with airport officials and taxi drivers, or get lost in a foreign city, or study each coin as she counted it out of her purse. Somehow, though, in the absence of these inconveniences the house in Rome might just as well have been in any city in Europe.

They arrived in darkness. No chance to stop and see where she was as Greg caught her arm and hurried her inside. As he opened the front door, the car they'd come in slid away into the darkness. Jess imagined it would be back tomorrow to take them wherever they wanted to go. Greg opened the front door and picked up their weekend bags, ushering her inside.

She'd been half expecting an Italian version of the Victorian monstrosity he'd taken her to on their last weekend away. Nothing could have been further from the truth. Warm, clean lines that drew you in, past the graceful curved staircase, towards a kitchen that was stylish but also comfortable and unmistakeably designed for home cooking. A sitting room that didn't just invite you to sit but demanded that you take your shoes off, make yourself at home and join in the conversation.

'Rosa chose this house, didn't she?' The house bore none of the hallmarks of Greg's father's taste and all of the characteristics of his mother's.

'Yes. Is it that obvious?'

'Yup.'

He looked around. 'Yes, I suppose it is. Mum came over and chose the house and decorated it for him about ten years ago.'

'So she never lived here?'

'No. When she comes home she goes to Milan to be with her family.' He caught Jess's look and laughed. 'I told you their relationship was complicated. They were always friends, even though they were divorced. In fact, I think their relationship worked better when they weren't married.'

'Fewer expectations?'

'Yeah, I guess so. He wasn't much good at being a father or a husband. Once you accepted that and stopped expecting him to be home for things like Christmas and birthdays, things got a great deal easier.'

Jess swallowed hard. All her fears encapsulated in one damning sentence. But Greg was different. Wasn't he?

'So do you like it?' When Jess didn't reply, he nudged her. 'The house. Do you like it?'

'It's beautiful. Stunning, actually.'

He nodded, clearly pleased. 'Thought you would. Want to see upstairs?' The curve of his mouth was enough to chase everything else away for the moment.

'Yes. Are you going to give me the in-depth tour?'

He flashed her an I-don't-know-what-you-mean look. 'Bathroom probably. Hallway...inevitably. Bedroom.'

'Just one?'

'Just the one that matters.'

'Which one's that?' She reached forward, running her finger up the buttons on his shirt until she got to the top one.

'The one that has a box on the bed. Gift-wrapped.'

'Gift-wrapped?'

'Yeah.' His hands slid to her hips, pulling her against him. 'I like a bit of gift-wrapping.'

The nightdress lay spilled on the carpet where he'd tossed it in a heap of lace and silk. Jess had never had anything so luxurious and had loved the way it had felt on her body. Loved even more the way it had felt when he'd slowly peeled it off. Since they'd found out about the pregnancy, their lovemaking had changed. It had become more tender and sensual. As if all the things that they couldn't say might be encapsulated in a caress. Jess sighed. There were quite a lot of things that they couldn't, or wouldn't, say at the moment.

He was still asleep, and when she shook him he growled and rolled over. Fair enough. How he managed to function on the amount of sleep he'd had in the last few weeks was a mystery to Jess anyway. She poked him in the ribs and he protested groggily.

'I'm getting up. Just going to have a look around. I won't go far. Be back in an hour.'

'Uh. Okay.'

'You stay here.' He didn't answer and Jess supposed he'd gone back to sleep. Just in case, she wrote him a note and propped it up on the nightstand.

The house wasn't the largest in the small square but it

was the prettiest. Not ostentatious but oozing quiet class. Jess put the key that Greg had left in the hallway into her pocket, and looped the strap of her handbag across her body.

It was cool, but not as cold as London, and Jess left her gloves in her coat pocket. She looked around to get her bearings and fix the position of the house in her mind before she started out. Five minutes took her out of the quiet, sleepy streets and onto the main road.

Suddenly she knew she wasn't in London. The sound of Italian, spoken in the street. Different smells, different sounds. A teeming city, so like her own and yet so different.

'Breakfast.' Jess grinned to herself. 'I'll go for breakfast.'

She found a café. It was too cold to sit on the pavement but there was a seat by the window, where she could watch the world go by. The waiter's English and her Italian were more than enough to get her what she wanted from the menu.

She'd been to Italy before, when she'd been a student. Had slept on the train, her head on her rucksack, and shared a small cottage with three friends, far enough from anywhere to be affordable. This might just as well be another country, it was so different.

'Ciao, bella.' A man sat down opposite her at her table and Jess looked around. There were plenty of free tables.

All the same, he seemed intent on conversation. Jess couldn't understand much of what he was saying but his general drift was pretty obvious. She wondered whether a polite but firm rebuff would be better delivered in her shaky Italian or in English.

'Scusi...' A young, fair-haired man, dressed in a dark jacket and jeans, was towering over them both. 'The lady's with me.' He smiled amiably at the man opposite Jess, who gave a shrug and left.

'Who are you?' Now this second man had sat down at her table. At least he spoke English, so it was going to be more straightforward to send him packing.

He'd already reached into his jacket and pulled out a wallet, opening it to display an ID. The photo was unmistakeably of him and the card bore the logo of Shaw Industries. 'Joe Callaghan, ma'am. Security.'

Jess scanned the card and raised her eyebrows. 'Senior Security Officer, no less.' She leaned across the table towards him and whispered, 'So Shaw Industries is interested in the security of this café? What is it? A drop point for industrial secrets?'

'Nothing so exciting. Our only interest in this place is that currently you happen to be sitting in it.' Joe seemed quite unflappable. So far, anyway.

'So if I go somewhere else...' There really wasn't any point in asking, she knew the answer to that one. 'Have you been following me all the way from London?'

'No, I work for the Italian branch of Shaw Industries. My wife worked for the British Embassy over here and when we started a family we decided to stay.'

Nice touch. 'Which might lead me to believe that you're a trustworthy kind of fellow?'

Joe laughed. 'It appears that Mr Shaw thought so.'

'Dr Shaw? Or his father?'

'The younger Mr Shaw. He doesn't use his title in the company.'

Jess swallowed. It felt like Greg's last betrayal of all that she'd thought he held dear. But that wasn't Joe's fault. 'So when did you start following me around?'

'You make it sound like surveillance. I'm just here for your safety. There's a big difference.' There was a hint of steel in Joe's easygoing smile. 'And I've been here since last night.'

The thought that Joe might have been in the house somewhere occurred to Jess and she reddened. Catch-me-if-you-can, naked in the hallway, suddenly didn't seem as good an idea as it had in the small hours of that morning. 'Where *did* you spend the night last night?'

'In the guest house.'

'The flat over the top of the garage? With the red door?' Which just happened to be completely self-contained.

'That's the one.'

'And what? You were just looking out of the window and saw me walking past. So you decided to follow…protect…me.'

Joe gave his slow, easy smile. 'No. The security system alerts us when anyone goes in or out of the main house. And it's not up to me to decide anything. My instructions are to look after you.'

'Your instructions from whom? Dr Shaw?' Shaw Industries might call him Mr but she wasn't Shaw Industries. 'Did he know you'd be looking after me?'

She must have betrayed her indignity. The nagging thought that Greg had let her wander off on her own a little too easily this morning. Joe smoothly went into maximum tact alert. 'I get my instructions from Mr Shaw's personal assistant.'

Pat again. Jess wrinkled her nose. 'What's she like? Pat?'

'I've never met her. She seems very nice on the phone.'

'I'm putting you in a difficult position, aren't I?'

Joe suppressed a smile. 'Nah. A different position maybe. My job is to blend in with the furniture, not make conversation.'

'But it won't make much difference if you have coffee with me?'

Humour flashed in his face. 'Yeah, it'll make a difference. I won't be wishing that you'd waited until I'd had breakfast before you left the house.'

'Operation Coffee it is, then.'

Joe rolled his eyes and motioned to the waiter. 'Just coffee will do fine.'

CHAPTER FIFTEEN

JESS OPENED THE front door, fully aware that Joe had paused and was waiting to see her safely inside. Greg was still in bed, but he stirred when she walked into the bedroom.

'Hey, there. Enjoy your stroll?'

'Yes.' She climbed onto the bed and sat astride his body. 'Guess what happened?'

'What?'

'I got saved by Joe from Security.'

A flash of uncertainty appeared in his dark eyes. 'Saved from what?'

'A man sat down at my table while I was having coffee. Spoke to me in Italian.'

'Oh. Really?'

Jess nodded gravely. 'Really. It was terrifying. Good thing that Joe was there to rush to my rescue.'

He was man enough to know when he was beaten. 'Fair enough. I dare say you could have dealt with that on your own.'

'I dare say I could.' Gripping his wrists, Jess leaned forward, pinning his arms against the pillows. He grinned, stretching beneath her and tipping her forward slightly.

'Joe's been teaching you a few moves, eh?'

'No, this one's all mine. And just for the record, Joe

was a model of tact. Didn't even admit that it was you who had me followed.'

'Protected.'

'Whatever. I doubt you could have done any better yourself.'

'Clearly not. Are you going to let me up?'

'Not until you tell me why you thought it was a good idea to have me tailed by your security team. And how long this has been going on for.'

'Joe was called in last night. There wasn't anyone up till then.'

Jess sat up straight, letting him go. 'What were you thinking, Greg? That I can't manage for myself outside London?'

'It's nothing to do with that, Jess. I know you can look after yourself, but I can't help it if I want to do that too.'

'You're being over-protective.'

He sat up, wrapping his arms around her, and she slid into his lap. 'Maybe I am but I don't care. I'd do anything to keep you and the baby safe, Jess. When you got locked in that vault and we couldn't find you...'

'Right. You're not going to let me forget that, are you?'

He sighed. 'Why should you? I can't.'

'You can't be with me every minute of the day, Greg.'

'I know. And I've got to get going soon.' He kissed her. 'So Joe will make sure you've got everything you need today.'

She was in Rome. There was so much to see, so much to do, and she wanted to do it with Greg. Wanted him to show her this beautiful city. Jess swallowed her disappointment. 'You have to go?'

'Yeah. Sorry, sweetheart, but I did tell you that this was a working visit.'

Yes, he'd told her. And Jess was beginning to understand that all the excuses she'd been making to herself were just that. Work came first. First, last and apparently most things in between.

'Mmm. When do you think you'll be back?' She hated the tone that crept into her voice every time she asked that question. Needy. Wheedling.

Greg rolled out of bed and padded towards the bathroom. 'I'm hoping to get this over quickly but I may be late. It depends.'

There wasn't much point in asking what it depended on. When Greg said that he might be late, there was no need to wait up. 'I'll go and do some sightseeing, then, and you can always call me if you finish early. Is it all right for me to ask Joe if he'll show me around?' She followed him into the bathroom, watching as he stepped into the shower.

'Of course.'

'He's not going to be busy with…whatever he does?'

Greg laughed, turning in the shower. 'Going where you go *is* what he does for the next couple of days. I'm sure he'll find it far more interesting to give you the grand tour than sit around all day.'

She'd hoped that Greg would find it more interesting to give her the grand tour than sitting around in a meeting all day. The thought seemed to stick in the back of her throat as the muscles there knotted into a lump and instinctively she swallowed.

'Oh, and, by the way, he has a company credit card.'

'Meaning?'

He laughed, leaning out of the shower to kiss her. A few drops of water fell onto her sweater and Jess brushed them away. 'Meaning that if you want to go shopping, he'll use it to pay the bill.'

* * *

'So how was your weekend?' Reena caught Jess on her way to the canteen on Monday morning.

'Great. I had a lovely time. I've got some grappa for you in my locker.' Courtesy of Shaw Industries. Joe had persisted in pulling out the company credit card at every opportunity, and finally she'd let him choose a couple of bottles for her to bring home with her.

'Fabulous. Thanks.' Reena took her arm and leaned a little closer. 'What I really want is the goss.'

'Sorry.' None that Reena needed to hear or that Jess wanted to tell her. If she didn't think about it, maybe it would go away.

'You just spent a weekend with Greg in one of the romance capitals of the world. Don't give me sorry. Give me something more substantial.'

Right. Well, she'd spent both days with Joe, after Greg had been unable to get away on Sunday either. They'd walked for miles and seen some of the sights, but that probably wasn't what Reena wanted to hear. And Jess wasn't about to go into details about her nights.

'We saw the Trevi fountain.' If she didn't elaborate on the *we* then that sounded just the kind of thing that Reena wanted to hear. It was actually just the kind of thing that Jess wanted to be able to say.

'Yeah? That's so-o-o romantic. Did you throw a coin in?'

'Of course I did. What do you take me for?'

Joe had told her to turn her back and throw the coin over her shoulder. And when Jess had been a little too eager and thrown too high, the coin had hit something, bounced back and skittered across the paving stones until Joe had trapped it under his foot. He'd said that hitting the water on her second try was enough to ensure her return to Rome, but Jess wasn't so sure about that.

'Sounds great.'

'It was. We had a lovely time.' Just not the one her heart had wanted. She'd rather have been locked in the sluice room for the weekend with Greg. The thought made her smile. They could save that till next weekend maybe.

'So how was yours?' Best change the subject now, while she'd merely given the wrong impression, rather than telling any actual lies.

'Oh, fine. Good, actually. I got a lot done. I've finished all of the costumes for the carol singers.'

'Yeah? That must have taken you a while.'

Reena shrugged. 'It wasn't as difficult as we'd thought. Is that all now?'

'Well, we've got the model, the costumes, the carol sheets and enough books for the storytellers.' Jess counted everything off on her fingers. 'I've printed out all the documents and photos to go with the model and sorted out the rota for the ward visits. So, not counting any last-minute emergencies, I think we're all done.'

'With two weeks to spare.' Reena thought for a moment. 'Is that making you as nervous as it does me?'

'Yes. Feels all wrong, doesn't it?'

'Mmm. We should do it all now, before anything has a chance to go pear-shaped. Anything can happen in between now and Christmas.'

Jess squeezed Reena's arm. 'Nothing's going to happen. We're just not used to being ready in such good time.'

'That was down to you. If you hadn't started planning all this in August, we'd be running around in ever-decreasing circles and ever-increasing panic.'

Jess grinned. At least someone seemed to notice what

she did. 'Hang tight. Nothing's going to happen between now and Christmas. You'll see.'

'Have you got some time tonight?'

Jess looked at him as if it was a trick question. 'Yes. Why? What's up?'

'Shaw Industries has just vaporised. I've got a spare evening.' Greg had meant it as a joke but was surprised to find that a part of him rather liked the idea. Jess obviously approved of it as well.

'In that case, is there anything particular you want to do?'

'Actually, there is. I'll meet you in the canteen after I finish my shift.'

They rode together through the dark streets, the windows of the taxi streaked with freezing rain.

'You like this, don't you?' She tipped her face up towards his.

'Like what?'

'Rushing me off somewhere without telling me where we're going or what we're doing.'

'I like surprising you.' The line felt like...it felt like just a line. Something to say to keep the peace and prompt a smile.

'You mean you like a fait accompli.' She grinned up at him. 'If you don't tell me where we're going then I don't have a chance to object.'

She had a point. 'You mean I'm afraid of what you might say?'

'Are you?'

'Terrified. You scare the living daylights out of me.'

She bumped her shoulder against his and laughed. Funny, that. The way he was in absolute earnest and yet it didn't even occur to Jess to believe him.

He made the taxi stop at the entrance to a mews so that he could walk with her on his arm, down the dark, deserted street. She could look around, get an idea of what the place was like.

'You like this?'

She shrugged, looking around her. 'Very nice.'

Maybe she'd like it a little better when she knew what they were doing there. Greg withdrew the estate agent's key from his pocket and located the front door that he wanted.

She was watching him gravely now. 'What's going on?'

'This property's for sale. I wanted you to take a look at it.'

'You're thinking of moving?'

Greg didn't reply. All he needed to do was to get her inside and then maybe she'd fall in love with the place, the way that the blurb on the property had promised.

The rooms were surprisingly large inside the mews cottage. Jess imagined that in the daytime they'd be light as well. The furniture had been cleared and the walls were painted white, as if to give prospective buyers a blank canvas for their own imaginations. It was an amazing place. She couldn't think why he would want to move when his current location seemed to fit his needs so well, but as he obviously did, this looked like a place where he could be happy.

'There's a good school just around the corner.'

'Bit of a long way from my place.' An alarm bell began to clatter quietly in the back of her head. Like next door's smoke detectors going off.

'I was thinking that this could be your place. If you wanted.'

If only. 'I don't know, Greg. We said we'd leave that

decision for a while. Not rush things, just because I'm pregnant.'

'I'm not moving. This place is just for you.'

Jess looked around. Swallowed hard. The house was lovely. More than enough space for her and her baby. A little walled garden at the back and shops just down the road. 'Greg it's lovely, but...'

'If you don't like this one, my estate agent tells me that there's plenty of choice.'

'I imagine there is. How much is this cottage on the market for?' Jess couldn't make a stab at an exact sum but she knew it must be a lot. Probably more than she wanted to hear.

He shrugged. 'I can afford it. The only thing that matters is whether you like it or not.'

Jess could feel tears. Dammit, she wasn't going to cry. Tears would only give Greg the impression that she was labouring under a surfeit of happiness and that really wasn't the case. 'It's a lovely thought, Greg, and I do appreciate it, really I do. But I'm happy where I am.'

'I know. But you could be happier here.' He looked around. 'Or if you weren't, at least you'd have a bit more room to be as happy as you were before.'

'I can't afford to run this place, Greg. This is a private mews, there must be some kind of charge for upkeep. And the shops...'

'What's wrong with the shops?'

'Well, they're great, but they're all speciality shops. The kind of place I go into once in a blue moon. They're far too expensive for me to use all the time.' Jess stopped. She knew she was sounding ungrateful. But these were the kinds of practicalities that she had to think about. Babies didn't come cheap, and she was going to have to watch her budget.

'I thought of that.' Greg sat down on a pretty little window seat that looked out onto the garden and pulled an envelope from the inside pocket of his jacket. 'Here.'

'What's this?' Jess almost didn't take it. She really didn't like the look of it.

'It's a formal offer. I want to support you and the baby, and I want that support to be legally yours. If anything happens to me, I don't want anyone to be able to take it away from you.'

'Greg.' If he had been trying to make her feel miserable and embarrassed, he couldn't have done a better job.

'Look, Jess, I heard what you said about being independent. I understand that you don't want our relationship to affect our child. This means that it doesn't. It gives you a place to live and an income, no strings attached. It's a good place to start from.'

'Greg, no.' This was all too much. He'd sprung it on her so quickly and she couldn't think straight.

'Just read it. It gives you a much better income than you have now and is index-linked. There's provision for school fees, a college fund and a small trust fund for our child. A place to live—here if you want or wherever else you choose.'

He could do this. He could buy her, and her child, so easily. 'And what about the things I said I really wanted, Greg? What about your time? Your love? A father to go to for advice when our child needs it? Are they itemised in here too?'

He shook his head slowly. 'You can't make those things part of a contract, Jess.'

'Right. Absolutely right.' She proffered the envelope back towards him and he didn't move to take it so she laid it on the window seat, next to where he was sitting.

'Jess, I know that I've been busy recently.' His face was

stony now. She was alone in the house with a complete stranger. 'But things will be different. Everything will settle down in time.'

That was another piece of advice that her mother had drummed into her. Never go into marriage thinking that you can change a man, because it won't happen. Her mother had learned that the hard way with her father. This wasn't marriage, it was a contract. One that would bind her, and her child, to him. 'I don't want this, Greg.'

'You mean you don't want me.'

How could he think that? 'I mean that I don't want my life, my child's life, to be spent waiting for you. However much you can provide in a material sense, if you can't be there, it means nothing.' Tears began to trickle down her face. She was being inflexible, she knew that. But clinging to what was familiar was all she knew how to do right now. It had been her mother and herself, just the two of them. She had the blueprint right there.

'Jess, you're being impractical. What's wrong with accepting an easier life?'

'That's it, though. It's not an easier life, or a better one.'

'And what is? Living in a flat that's too small, counting the pennies? If that makes you feel virtuous, fine. But I'm not going to let you limit my child's opportunities.' There was no anger in his voice. Just a flat assertiveness that was colder and crueller than any emotion.

'Not going to *let* me? Greg, listen to what you're saying, please. My flat is perfectly adequate for me and the baby. You can't make me move.'

'No?'

This was how he did business, then. Jess supposed that he'd learned this kind of attitude in the boardroom. He'd become used to getting whatever he wanted.

'Just try it.' She turned on her heel and made for the front door. Behind her she could hear his footsteps.

'Jess.' His hand appeared over her shoulder, holding the door shut. 'Look, I didn't mean that. But think about this. It's all very well to be independent, to be able to fend for yourself if you have to, but this is crazy. I have a right to give my child a decent place to live. You can't just throw that back at me and tell me that you're all right on your own.'

She turned to face him, her back pressed against the door. 'You're wrong, Greg. You think that spending money is going to absolve you of every other responsibility. Well, it doesn't. My child can't be bought. That's non-negotiable, and if you want me to sign something then you can put that in your contract.'

'Ah. So all of a sudden it's *your* child. I don't have to be a doctor to know that you didn't manage to conceive it all on your own.'

She'd had enough of this. She'd tried not to be angry and resentful, but these days rage seemed to be simmering beneath the surface most of the time. And now it had broken free, like some living, breathing being.

'You don't need to be a doctor at all, do you? You're determined to throw away your career for the sake of Shaw Industries. What else are you going to throw away? Me? Our child? You're not going to get that opportunity, Greg. I'm not going to let you tie me up with contracts and agreements so that I lose who I am. Because who I am is all I have to give to my child.'

'You think it's so easy.' He almost spat the words at her.

'No. I think it's hard. You're the one who's taking the easy way out, and that's your prerogative. But don't expect me to just fall into line and support you in it any more, because I can't. I don't want it for you, or for me, or for the baby. That's the end of it.'

They stared at each other. The lines had been drawn and there was no going back now. He was too like his father. She was too like her mother. It had never had the faintest chance of working, they'd just been beguiled by friendship and great sex.

'Let go of the door, Greg.'

'I'll take you home.'

'The door.'

'Okay, then, I'll call a taxi.'

'I can find my own way home. Let go of the door.' Jess had to get out of there. Couldn't bear to look at him and see everything that she'd lost. He looked the same, but inside he was so very different.

He let go of the door and she pulled it open, almost stumbling out of it. She didn't hear it close behind her, but she didn't hear his footsteps either. She was alone, all the way to the high street, and then every step of the way home.

CHAPTER SIXTEEN

HE HAD TO find some kind of viable solution to this. It was obvious that things weren't going to work between Jess and him, she'd flung everything he'd offered her right back in his face. They'd have to come to some sort of agreement, though, for the baby's sake.

'This is it, then, Jess.' He had been talking to her all evening as if she was there, trying to reason with her. He knew that she wasn't going to budge and neither was he. 'This is the end of it.'

He re-read the email he'd written to his solicitor. If he and Jess couldn't work things out between them, he'd pay for someone to advise and represent her, and it would be a matter for the lawyers to negotiate. It wasn't the way he'd wanted it, but it looked as if wanting and getting were two entirely different things these days.

The cursor hovered over the 'send' button. This was the only way forward. No regrets and no more conversations with her when there was nothing here but empty air.

'Goodbye, my love.'

He clicked 'send' and his laptop responded with a tone, signifying that his email was on its way. Greg flopped back onto the sofa. In the morning he'd wake up and realise that he'd done the right thing.

A Future Christmas...

It was like a waking dream. Greg's heart was still beating hard, as if he had fought his way out of some cloying danger, which he couldn't remember but which still clung to him, like a broken cobweb.

It was Christmas Eve. He was walking across the fields to his mother's house, the warm glow of the windows beckoning him home. Outside a horse-drawn carriage clattered past on its way into the village, and when Greg looked through the front window of Rosa's house it seemed perfectly natural to find a scene that looked like something from a Christmas card—a blazing fire, a Christmas tree and four figures dressed in Victorian costume.

Jess sat by the fire, talking to his mother. A little to one side Ted sat in a chair, watching a boy of about three play with a hoop and stick. Greg noticed, with some surprise, that Ted seemed to have acquired a set of side whiskers, along with his frock coat and starched collar.

He focussed on Jess's face. Pink cheeks in the firelight, small hands folded in her lap. A sudden jolt of longing transfixed him to the spot, leaving him helpless and begging for some release from this. He had no idea whether Jess would respond to him differently in her new guise, but he didn't care. Just to touch the elaborate folds of her dress. To hear the silk rustle as she moved.

This wasn't right. He was just dreaming. He'd read the slim volume that Jess had given him from the library, and this was the kind of thing that happened when fiction combined with fact in the unconscious mind. Greg had heard about cognitive dreaming, and wondered whether he could change things, make them a little more realistic.

With an effort of will the picture merged and morphed into something different. Jess, in front of the fire, dressed this time in jeans and a warm sweater. She looked tired, the way any mother of a young child would. But where was his child? Greg craned against the window to catch sight of him.

He wasn't there. For the first time Greg realised that he was freezing cold, his silk business suit doing nothing to keep out the snow and the biting wind. All the same, he had to try and find his son. Working his way around to the kitchen window, he peered in.

He was there, with his grandmother, helping to make mince pies. Covered in flour, he was laboriously fashioning pastry circles with a plastic cutter. Greg found himself grinning. The boy had something of himself about him, dark hair and olive skin. But his face was that of an angel. Jess's face. Large hazel eyes that seemed to effortlessly combine intelligence and mischief. The way he laid his work out so neatly, his tongue trapped between his lips in concentration. He was just like his mother.

Ted appeared at the back door, stamping the snow from his wellingtons and throwing off his coat. The boy ran to him and he swung him into the air. Then Jess, at the kitchen doorway, smiling, happy. Or at least that was the way it seemed. By some preternatural sense that the dream afforded him, Greg knew that the smile was just for show, and that the single tear she brushed from her cheek wasn't one of happiness.

Greg was starving, freezing, right outside the window, but no one seemed to notice. He tried to tap on the pane but his arms were suddenly heavy. Looking down, he saw wide metal cuffs, soldered tightly around his wrists. Chains binding him.

He had to get them to see him. Had to make them know that he was home at last. He knew that Jess would welcome him. He could sit by the fire with her and warm himself.

*Watch the light from the flames sparkle on the baubles
on the tree. He would give everything he had in exchange
for just five minutes, to hold her and his son and tell them
both that he loved them.*

*The need was so great that it felt like a living, breath-
ing thing. Greg made a lunge for the window, but found
himself dragged backwards. Something was pulling him,
back across the fields. However hard he tried to struggle,
however much he instructed his sleeping mind to change
the course of the dream, he couldn't. He fell, and felt the
frozen ground, sharp against his face. Rolling over, he
managed to get a glimpse of where he was being carried
to so inexorably.*

*The glittering, ice-cold, steel and glass of the City were
growing closer and closer. Looming over him, blocking
out everything else. Greg tried to look back towards the
old farmhouse, which currently housed everything that he
cared about. But he couldn't.*

*Twisting, fighting with his bonds, roaring with frustra-
tion, he started to fall.*

Greg landed on the polished wooden floor, banging his
head on the coffee table on the way down. There was something digging in his ribs and on closer inspection it turned
out to be his laptop. He cursed, disentangled himself from
the power cable and looked at the clock on the mantelpiece.

Five minutes past midnight. He still had work to do but
somehow he couldn't bring himself to be bothered tonight.
How long had he been asleep? It seemed like hours, but the
music CD he'd put on a while ago was still playing quietly
in the background. Greg stood up and stretched. Maybe
an early night would do him good. He was still half-asleep
anyway, caught in the world of that crystal-clear dream.
Tomorrow things would seem different.

CHAPTER SEVENTEEN

'Happy Christma-a-a-s!'

'Happy Christmas.' Jess smiled down at the little girl in the reindeer costume, trying to catch some of the child's excitement for herself.

'Ah, Jess. I've been looking for you.' Gerry caught his daughter's hand.

'Hi, Gerry. Are you all right?'

'I'm supposed to be a ghost, right?' He lowered his voice. 'I'm assuming that means deathly pale.'

'Well, the make-up's great. Just be careful you don't get carted off to A and E.'

'You think I overdid it, then?'

'Just a little. Do you think that people like to see their doctors looking worse than they feel?'

'In my experience most people don't notice. But perhaps I'd better go and wash some of it off. Will you keep an eye on Emma for me?'

'Yes, of course.' There wasn't much else to do. All of the volunteers had turned up and were getting on with their allotted tasks. Which was a shame, really. Something approaching a crisis might have taken Jess's mind off what seemed like a vast, empty void of today and tomorrow.

It was her own fault. She'd turned down every invitation for Christmas Eve and Christmas Day on the basis that she'd be somewhere else. Just as long as her friends and family didn't get together and realise that she hadn't been with any of them, she'd be okay.

'Unca Greg's going to be Father Christmas.'

'What's that, sweetie?'

'Father Christmas. With presents.' Emma was clearly shocked that Jess didn't know about Father Christmas.

'Ah, that Father Christmas. You mean the one who squeezes down your chimney every year to bring you presents?'

Emma nodded. 'Look, there he is.' She pointed over Jess's right shoulder

'But he's not here yet. He won't come until you put your stocking out tonight.'

'No.' Emma rolled her eyes. 'He's here.'

'Well, perhaps he's just taken the reindeer out for a bit of a run before their big night.'

Jess turned, her gaze following the line of Emma's pointing arm. Just as expected, Father Christmas wasn't standing behind her. But Greg was.

She let go of Emma's hood and the little girl flew into his arms. Greg hoisted her high and Emma squealed with laughter.

The only man she wanted. A laughing child in his arms. Here at the hospital, one of the 'Christmas Volunteer' badges pinned to his red sweater. Having to look at everything she'd lost, right there in front of her, was making Jess feel sick.

'Jess.'

Her name on his lips was all she wanted to hear, and everything she couldn't bear to. Jess scanned the corridor, praying that Gerry would return soon.

'Jess.' He tried again. This time his voice was quieter. More tender.

'Greg. Hello.' She focussed wildly on the volunteer's badge. 'You've come to help. Thanks.'

He grinned. 'It's an excuse.'

She imagined it was. This wasn't Greg's world any more and the only way that he would be here was if he had an ulterior motive. 'Even if it is, we'll put you to work. I'll take help wherever I can get it.' She felt herself redden. It had probably been the wrong thing to say to Greg on almost every level that she could think of.

He didn't take the advantage that she'd handed him on a plate. 'I wanted to see you, Jess.'

'I got the letter from your solicitor. I've done as he suggested and contacted one of the people on his list.'

'That's not what I'm here about.'

'There's nothing more to say.' She saw Gerry approaching out of the corner of her eye and Greg turned to follow the line of her gaze.

'Gerry. Mate, you look awful.' He grinned, handing Emma back to her father. 'Sure I can't…?'

'Don't you start.' Gerry shot him a baleful look and Emma squealed with happiness. 'Since neither of you seem to appreciate my ghastly visage, I'll take my daughter to see Father Christmas.'

'Unca Greg?' Emma beat on her father's shoulder excitedly.

'No, darling. We're going to see the real one.' Gerry glared at them both, took Emma's hand and walked away.

'He's going in the wrong direction.' Jess couldn't bear another moment of this. Not when Greg looked so much like the man that she had first kissed last Christmas and so little like the one he'd become in the intervening year.

'He'll work it out. Jess, wait, please.' He laid his hand on her arm.

'I can't, Greg.' If she stayed any longer she was going to start crying. She'd done enough of that in the last two weeks.

'You can.' He moved closer. Close enough for her to catch his scent. Indefinable, but it was his alone.

'This is all in the hands of the lawyers now. We're probably not even allowed to be talking to one another.'

'We can do as we please. And, anyway, I'm not sure that lawyers are the right way to go any more. I've changed my...agenda.'

'No.' If only he had. Her own heart wanted to believe that he had, but the tiny heart beating inside her? That was to be protected at any cost.

'I want you to come with me.'

'Where to?' Dammit, he'd hooked her in. She wasn't going to go with him so it didn't much matter.

'Just take the step. Come with me.'

'When I don't know where you're going?'

'Yep.'

'No, Greg. I can't.'

'It's Christmas Eve, Jess. Don't you believe in the magic?'

She sighed. 'What is this, a fairy story? You think that just because it's Christmas everything's going to turn out okay.' She turned, flicking her finger against one of the gold bells on the Christmas Tree. 'See? Nothing. It doesn't even ring.'

'Maybe you just can't hear it.'

Jess rolled her eyes. 'And maybe you're having aural hallucinations. Anyway, your timing's way out. It's not even Christmas Day yet.'

He raised one eyebrow. 'The first step is believing. If we believe...'

'I believe, Greg. But I believe in reality, not an idealised view of the world. Things don't just go away because you refuse to recognise them.'

'I meant if you believe that things can change then you can find a way to change them. If you don't come with me now, I will be back.'

Jess was under no illusions on that score. But she knew that whatever Greg's intentions were, he wasn't going to be able to keep them up for long. The company would drag him away. It would always drag him away, and no one could just click their fingers and make it disappear.

'That's up to you. Don't expect my answer to be any different.'

He nodded. 'Okay. See you, Jess.' He turned and walked away. Stood aside as someone negotiated a wheelchair through the wide doors into the reception area and then strode out into the square outside the hospital.

He'd given up so easily. Another trait that Jess didn't recognise. He'd be leaving after Christmas, and then he'd have other things on his mind. She couldn't compete with Shaw Industries, and she didn't have the energy to try.

She turned, blind to everything other than misery and the certain knowledge that she'd done the right thing. She cannoned into the Christmas tree and stumbled back again in a cloud of sparkly dust.

'Hey… Careful!' Gerry was on his way back through Reception, Emma perched on his shoulders. 'You okay?'

'Eh? Yes, of course.' Jess decided that Emma would probably be easier to fool than Gerry. 'Did you see Father Christmas, sweetie?'

'No. Daddy can't find him.'

'Really? Where do you think he is, then?'

'That way.' Emma pointed in the opposite direction from which they'd just come. 'But he was here.'

'Here? I didn't see him.'

Emma leaned forward and brushed her hand across Jess's hair. 'He made you sparkly.'

Gerry shrugged. 'You can't argue with that. Do you want to come and see if we can track the man down?'

'He's in the little sitting room next to the canteen. Follow the signs for the grotto.'

'A grotto! D'you hear that, Em? Shall we see if we can find it?'

Jess leaned over the basin in the ladies' room and tried to shake some of the sparkle out of her hair. She guessed it didn't matter too much, it was Christmas after all, but if she was going to go to any of the wards, it probably wasn't a good idea to go shedding bits from the Christmas tree everywhere.

Last Christmas everything had been so easy. It had been easy to believe in Greg, easy to work with him, easy to kiss him. He'd taken her on journeys that she'd thought were hopeless, defied the flat line on the monitor and kept working. The old Greg had taught her that you didn't stop while there was still some thread of life, some chance that a heart would start to beat again.

There was no chance. She had to be realistic. If she didn't let this go now, there would only be further pain and disappointment, which would drive yet another wedge between them. She couldn't risk that, for the sake of her child.

The look he had given her just now. That old, challenging look that defied the odds and had, on more than one occasion, saved someone. Jess's heart beat a little faster. In the mirror she could see her reflection, a hint of his defiance in her eyes. Then, hardly aware of having made a decision, she turned and ran for the door.

The courtyard outside the main entrance was full of people, but the one person she wanted to see wasn't there. She searched the faces desperately and then she saw him. Standing by a parked taxi, chatting to the driver.

'Greg!' She hollered at the top of her voice and began to run towards him. He turned on the instant and when he saw her he smiled.

'You haven't brought your coat.'

Jess realised that she was shivering in the crisp, morning air. 'No. I'll go back and get it.'

'No, you won't.' He took his leather jacket off and draped it around her shoulders. 'Get in.'

The driver already seemed to know where to go, cutting through back roads and emerging again onto the main streets, which were decked with lights and heaving with last-minute shoppers.

'Let me take that.' She still had her clipboard clutched to her chest and he tugged at it. She relinquished it with as much grace as she could manage and he slipped it into the carrier bag that lay next to him on the seat.

'It's not going to make any difference, Greg.'

'We'll see.'

'I'm coming because you asked me to. But things aren't going to change, you've made your decisions.'

He nodded. 'And you've made yours?'

'Yes. I've made mine.' Jess glanced at the sliding window between them and the driver and saw that it was firmly shut. They had some measure of privacy, probably up to about the level of a quiet sneeze. She'd keep her voice down.

'And that's not going to change. You won't consider moving out of your comfort zone.'

She opened her mouth to tell him that wasn't fair, and

then decided that it probably was. 'I'm out of my comfort zone now.'

He grinned. 'Yeah, me too. And that's exactly where we both need to be.'

CHAPTER EIGHTEEN

THE TAXI SPED across the river and turned up towards the City then bumped into a quiet cul-de-sac. They drew to a halt outside a three-storey building, separated from the road by railings and a neat portico over a solid, black-painted door.

Greg caught up his bag, got out of the taxi and paid the driver. Waited for Jess to follow and then took the steps up to the doorway in one stride, pulling the old-style bell handle.

Jess jumped when the door was opened almost immediately. No time to focus on the engraved brass plate at the side of the door. A young woman, who seemed to know Greg, stood to one side.

They might just as well have stepped back two hundred years. Polished dark wood doors, a huge, gilt mirror and a pair of high backed wooden chairs, next to a small Regency table with magazines displayed neatly on it. It was a waiting area, but clearly one that people didn't spend much time waiting around in. Just enough to phone upstairs, and for someone to hurry down to meet a valued client.

'Thanks, Sarah.' Greg gave her a smile. 'Is he in?'

'He's waiting for you in his office. Would you like to go straight up?' Sarah smiled at Greg and then Jess, the same well-regulated smile. 'Can I take your coat?'

'Thanks.' Jess handed Greg's coat to her.

'Shall I bring up some coffee?'

Greg nodded. 'That would be nice, thank you.' He reached into his bag and pulled out a parcel, which was obviously a well-wrapped bottle, proffering it to her. 'Happy Christmas.'

Sarah's veneer slipped a little and she blushed. 'That's very nice of you...'

'We won't keep you too long. I'm sure you've got better things to do today.'

'There's plenty of time. We always stay open until lunchtime on Christmas Eve.' Sarah disappeared with Greg's coat and left them alone to climb the long staircase, which curved up through the centre of the building. It was almost dizzying, drawing the eye upwards to the ever-decreasing circles above her head.

'I love this staircase.' He leaned close, as if that was some kind of secret. 'Apparently it's one of only a few in London that are quite this shape.'

'Yes. It's lovely.' Jess had given up now. No more questions, no more *let's get this over with*. It would all play out, and then Greg would go home and she'd go back to the hospital.

He chuckled, placing his hand lightly on her back and steering her across the first floor landing to an open door, where a middle aged man in impeccable pinstripes stood.

'Charles.'

'Greg.' The man extended his hand. 'How are you?'

'Well, thank you. I appreciate you being here today. Jess, this is Charles Hamlin. Of Hamlin, Grey and...'

'Hamlin.' Charles chuckled as if this was a very old joke that still somehow managed to tickle him. He held his hand out to her and she grasped it shakily. 'Dr Saunders. A pleasure to meet you.'

'Jess, please. Nice to meet you too.'

'Sit down, please.' He waved her towards one of two chairs that were set in front of a large slab of mahogany piled high with papers, strewn with various knick-knacks and lit by a reading lamp with a green shade.

Jess looked around at the book-lined office. Charles was a lawyer of some sort. Anger spurted through her veins and she almost turned and ran, back down the aristocratic staircase and into the street, where she might be able to breathe again. She felt Greg's hand again, light on her back. Stay. Please stay.

She should get out of there right now, but somehow she couldn't. Maybe it was because Greg seemed so different, so much like the man he'd once been. The man she'd follow into any darkness, through any unknown door, because she trusted him.

She drew herself up as straight as she could, pretended that she wasn't wearing jeans and a sweatshirt with sparkle all over it, and sat down. She crossed her legs tightly, and wished that Greg would give her back the clipboard so she could either shield herself or hit him with it, whichever turned out to be appropriate. At that moment Sarah appeared behind them with coffee, on what looked suspiciously like a silver tray. What *had* she got herself into?

Greg had placed another bottle-shaped parcel from his bag on Charles' desk, and he unwrapped it while Sarah was pouring the coffee. His smile turned into a beam of approbation as he examined the bottle. 'I say. Thank you, I shall enjoy that immensely.'

Greg grinned and Jess shot him a pleading look. If he didn't get down to business by the time she'd finished her coffee, and maybe one or two of those rather nice-looking biscuits, she was going to lose her nerve and she'd be out of there.

'I don't want to keep you. Perhaps we can start over coffee.' Greg seemed to sense that she was getting restive.

'Of course. Dr Saunders...Jess...I assume that Mr Shaw has explained why we're here this morning?'

'Actually, no. I'm in the dark at the moment.' She glanced at Greg, hoping he'd get the message.

Greg chuckled. 'That's my fault. Jess, Charles was not only my father's legal advisor for many years, he was also his friend.' He paused and Charles beamed across his desk at both of them. 'My father didn't discuss his business with me, or my mother, but Charles was one of his closest confidants. That's why I want you to hear this from him.'

'This is about your father?'

'It's about everyone. Trust me.' Greg waited for her nod and then settled back in his chair, gesturing to Charles that the floor was his now.

'John Shaw was an extraordinary man. He was bold, inventive and had an enormous, if slightly unconventional talent for business.' Charles spread his fingers in front of him on an empty area of the desk. 'I think that John would forgive me for saying that sometimes that talent didn't extend to his personal relationships. I knew him well, and liked him very much, but trying to gauge his personal feelings was often a very...shall we say...hit and miss affair.'

'You mean he could be distant.' There was no sense in beating about the bush. Jess had nothing to lose here, and it was beginning to look as if she had nothing to gain.

'Exactly. Which was why Greg needed my help.'

Jess pressed her lips together. If Greg wanted to fall in line with everything that his father wanted, that was up to him but she wouldn't endorse that.

'Don't you want to know why this has suddenly become an issue?' Greg was frowning at her now. Perhaps she should at least appear to show some interest.

'Um, yes. I was wondering that, but I didn't want to interrupt.'

Charles's gaze flipped quickly between her and Greg, perhaps wondering whether they were about to start squabbling between themselves. A moment of silence appeared to convince him that it was safe to go on.

'To cut a long story short, Greg has used a management model that his father explored but never implemented, which proposed a radical reorganisation of Shaw Industries. The power base of the company would no longer be one man but is vested in the board of a charitable trust. The company is run by the trust and the profits that would have normally gone to the CEO are used for charitable purposes.'

'And this was his father's plan all along?'

'No, it was just one of a number of feasibility studies. But, as in everything else, he was very thorough. This particular structure was designed along one of the principles of quality management.' Charles leaned forward slightly. 'No man is indispensable.'

Greg was indispensable to her. And this…the thought that he might not be to the company…was a glimmer of hope. 'In business terms, you mean.'

'Of course. I realise your own profession takes no heed of that aphorism.' Charles chuckled. 'In fact, I rather hope that every man is indispensable as soon as he enters your door.'

Charles was wandering again. This time it was almost charming. 'But Greg's father never did anything about those plans.'

'No. He gave me no reason, but he did ask me to store the papers safely.'

'And the plan would still work?'

'Absolutely. The paperwork was all drawn up and Greg

and I have been reviewing it exhaustively for the last week.' Charles's gaze flipped momentarily towards Greg.

'Yeah, exhaustively. And Charles has been advising me, exhaustively, about the personal financial suicide involved in making the changes that I've proposed.'

'Quite. But my duty is to facilitate.' Charles turned back to Jess, his expression softening. 'I imagine you're wondering why we're having this conversation here, instead of over a nice lunch and a glass of Chablis.'

'Um. Yes.' Jess hadn't been wondering that at all. She had been too busy wondering about everything else.

Charles laid a small bundle of documents in front of her. 'It will take some time to effect the change, but these documents will set the ball rolling, to some extent irreversibly. We agreed on them yesterday, and met again early this morning to proof the copies for signature. Greg wants to sign them now, but before he does so he has asked me to explain their implications to you.'

'I still don't understand.' Jess turned to Greg, not Charles. She wasn't interested in any finagling over the structure of Shaw Industries, she was interested in Greg's motivations. Whether he could make different decisions from those his father had.

He was grinning. 'The crux of it is, Jess, is that I want out. But I want the company to survive, because a lot of good people would lose their livelihoods without it. So I had to do the one thing that experience had taught me was only going to be a disappointment and try one last time to get to know my father.'

That she almost dared to understand. Hardly dared to believe. 'And...what? You deciphered the book he left you?'

He shook his head. 'No. But its existence made me re-alise something. My father gave the better part of his life to Shaw Industries, and he knew far better than I do how to keep it strong. If I wanted to leave the company able to survive on its own, I had to make my peace with the past and go looking for him.'

'And you found him?' Perhaps she shouldn't ask that question in front of Charles. Jess didn't care. It was far too important and she wanted to know now.

'Yeah. Inasmuch as I ever will. This is his basic plan, with a few tweaks that…' he grinned in Charles's direction and Charles ignored him '…sever my connection with the company completely. And with it my income from the company.'

'Which will, of course, affect both Greg's lifestyle and potentially that of any of his dependants.' Charles cut to the quick and softened the blow with a vague wave of his hand. 'But that's something that you should talk about privately. Will you excuse me?'

He was already halfway towards the door. 'Charles. Thank you.' Jess couldn't just let him go like that.

'It's my pleasure.'

'What do you think?'

Charles's gaze slid towards Greg again. Perhaps she shouldn't have asked. Greg was his client, not her.

A small nod from Greg seemed to assure him that an answer was in order. 'I think…' He seemed to be searching for the right words. 'I think that life affords us few opportunities of this nature. You should choose wisely.'

The door clicked shut behind him and for a moment Jess's gaze was caught in Greg's. Staring, just staring at each other, as if the next tick of the clock was too valuable to just squander.

'I'm glad you took the step, Jess. Thank you.'

'I couldn't do anything else. Is this really what you want to do, Greg? Sign away the company?'

'Don't you think it's a good idea?'

'I think it's the best idea you've ever had. You were meant to be a doctor.'

'Yeah, I know. I nearly made the worst decision of my life and let Shaw Industries eat me up just because I thought that it would finally bring me closer to my father. But even giving up the job I love wasn't enough to make me see.'

'What did make you see?' Jess was shaking. Please, please. Let it be what she wanted to hear.

'You and the baby. I can't give you up, Jess, not for anything. Certainly not for my father's company.'

It was as if someone had flung the windows open wide. Light and sound and happiness burst into the dark place that Jess had begun to feel that she was going to be living in for ever.

'I...' She swallowed. She had to be sure. However much it cost her, she couldn't just take her own happiness and leave the people who relied on Shaw Industries stranded. 'The company will be okay, though? In good hands?'

'Yes. My father's plan was a good one, and it included sizeable benefits for him. I get nothing—in fact, some of my own assets are being transferred to the company.' He grinned. 'I haven't much use for a racehorse. Or a private jet. And most of the houses will be sold, although I'm planning to keep the house in Rome.'

Jess grinned. 'That's a good choice. I do like the house in Rome.'

'I know, that's why I want to keep it. But, seriously, Jess, this is going to affect you as well as me. It means that I won't be able to give...'

She leaned forward and laid her finger across his lips. 'There's only one thing I want. And I'm making this request on behalf of me and our child.'

He smiled. Pure happiness seemed to radiate from him, warming the room. 'Anything.'

'We want you to be the man that you want to be, whatever that is. We want you to give us some of your time and some of your love.'

A sigh shook his chest. 'You and the baby have all my love. I may not be with you all the time but everything that I am is for you and our child.'

'That's more than enough.'

'Even if I work double shifts sometimes. If I come home tired and full of the weight of the day.'

'That's okay. You know it is.'

'I love you, Jess.'

'I love you too, Greg.'

For long moments they just smiled, the words echoing around them like a web of finely spun joy. Then she was on her feet. He moved at the same time, pulling her towards him and onto his lap, holding her tightly against his beating heart.

'How long is Charles going to be?' Jess was trying, without much success, to keep at least one strand of her attention on the door.

'We won't be interrupted. Charles makes an art out of discretion.'

'Well, you'd better kiss me, then. Quickly...'

He cut her short. Kissed her slowly, taking his time to savour it. 'I was wrong, Jess. I'm sorry.'

'I was wrong, too. And I'm sorry.'

He chuckled. 'You're going to fight me over it? I was wronger than you.'

She laughed, wrapping her arms around his neck. 'There's no such word as "*wronger*". We were both wrong. But we've got this chance now, and I'm not going to let it go.'

'I thought for a while that I'd left it too late. That you wouldn't come with me.'

'Yeah, so did I. But I was just kidding myself. There was no way I couldn't have come.'

He dropped a kiss onto her brow. 'No way I couldn't have asked you. Or kept on asking if you turned me down the first time.'

'I want to tell you something, Greg.' Jess pressed her lips together.

'Whatever it is, it doesn't matter.'

'No, it does. I'll say this now and then there's an end to it. We can leave it behind here.' She dug him gently in the ribs. 'I'm sure Charles knows what to do with any worn-out thoughts that people leave floating around in his office.'

He chuckled. 'No doubt he does. What do you want to say?'

Jess took a deep breath. 'I thought that I could do it all by myself, Greg. I'd told myself for so long that I didn't need my father, that I didn't care that he wasn't around, that I started believing it. I didn't want to feel that loss.'

'You feel it now?'

'Yeah. In a strange way I do. But you'll help me through that, won't you? You'll show me that there's a different way to make a family.'

'We'll face that together. We'll show each other, darling.' He hugged her tightly. 'I won't let you go, Jess. I'm not going to let you fall.'

'Mmm. I know. Feels good.' She took a moment to let the happiness seep a little further into her bones. Banishing the shadows. Freeing her from them. 'And you'll get to meet my mum and stepdad on Boxing Day. If you want to.'

'Of course I want to. Do you think they'll want to meet me?'

'My mum will love you. And I think you'll get on with

my stepdad too. They were going to help me move some furniture.'

'Right. Or I could do it for you and we could all sit down and have a nice meal. Get to know each other.'

'Or I could forget about moving the furniture and tell them I'm coming to live with you.'

He chuckled. 'That would be my first preference. Is there any particular reason why you want to move the furniture?'

'They want to help. I realised last week that I want them to help too.' She twined her fingers around his.

He chuckled. 'I'm sure you'll find something else for them to do. If you don't, I'll be sorting something out with your mother myself. But I'm glad you took that step.'

'Me too.'

'Will you take another?'

'I'm starting to get used to it. Why stop now?'

He kissed her. Warmly, tenderly and full of assurance now.

'Was that it?'

'No. I just did that because I wanted to. The step I want you to take is to sign these papers with me.'

'Me? Why me?'

'There's no legal requirement for you to sign them. But I want your name on there too. I want this to be something we do together.'

'Yes.' She could hardly wait to write her name under his. Help set him free.

'Then we'll go back to the hospital. Make sure that everyone's doing whatever it is they're supposed to be doing. Then I'll take you home and feed you.'

'You'll cook?' The thought of Greg's cooking was already making her stomach growl.

He chuckled. 'Yeah, I'll cook. And then...' He paused

just long enough for Jess to feel a shiver of expectation. 'And then I'll make love to you until you can't think straight, and you'll say yes to anything.'

'I can't think straight now.'

'Well, I'll make love to you anyway. That's the plan, and I'm going to stick to it.' His lips brushed her ear. 'When I slip that ring on your finger, I want it to be the only thing you're wearing.'

Jess couldn't answer. She didn't dare draw the inevitable conclusion and then be wrong. Perhaps it was some other ring.

'That okay with you?'

'Y-yes?' She gulped out the word.

His eyes reflected the concern on his face. 'Jess? I'm sorry, am I going too fast?'

She took a deep breath. 'No. I'm just not quite sure where you're going, that's all.'

'Ah. Okay, where was I?' He stopped to think for a moment. 'Yeah. Making love to you until you couldn't think straight.'

'Liking it so far.'

'Good. Then I hold you, tell you that I love you and ask you to marry me. And then you say...?'

'Yes?'

He smiled. 'That's exactly what you'll say. Then I'll put the ring on your finger.' He caught her left hand and brushed a kiss on her third finger. 'Seal the deal.'

She didn't need to answer. He saw it in her face. 'Two deals in one day.' The first gave Greg his life back. The second gave her everything she had ever wanted.

'I'll wait until midnight. At one minute past twelve on Christmas morning we'll have this Christmas and all the other Christmases yet to come to look forward to together.'

'I love you, Greg.' She hugged him tight. 'What made you do all this?'

'Don't laugh.'

'I won't.'

'It was a dream.' He shrugged. 'About the path I was on. How things would end up. Does that sound completely crazy?'

A small shiver began to travel downwards from the nape of her neck but dissipated in the warmth of his embrace. Jess wondered if his dream had been anything like the one she'd had, and dismissed the thought.

'Not really. Dreams are just our unconscious minds, telling us what we already know.'

He nodded. 'Then I guess it was just me. Telling myself what my life would be like if I let you go. And that I love you and our child more than anything.'

'That's all either of us needs to know.' She could let him go now. Now that she knew he wasn't going anywhere. And the sooner she did, the sooner he could sign the papers and they could be out of there. Jess slid off his lap and sat back in her own chair. 'By the way, have you got a turkey?'

'No. Have you?'

'I wasn't really banking on doing much celebrating.'

He sprang to his feet, suddenly full of energy, and strode towards the door, flinging it open and bellowing down the stairs. 'Charles…Charles, we need to sign the papers. And do you know where we can get a turkey? It's Christmas!'

* * * * *

CHRISTMAS WITH HER DAREDEVIL DOC

KATE HARDY

To Gerard, Chris and Chloe, who shared Iceland
with me and fell in love with it as much as I did.

PROLOGUE

HAYLEY DID A double take as her best friend hobbled into the hospital canteen on crutches, with a full-length walking cast up to her right knee.

'What happened, Dani?' she asked as Danielle heaved herself into the seat opposite hers and rested the crutches against the wall so they wouldn't be in the way of anyone else in the canteen. 'Did you break your ankle?'

'It's not quite that bad—it's a second and third meta-tarsal stress fracture,' Danielle said, grimacing.

Hayley frowned. They'd been out to their usual dance aerobics class, two nights ago, and Danielle had seemed fine then. 'When did it happen?'

'According to the orthopods, three or four weeks ago, because the fracture shows up on the X-ray and looks as if it's been trying to heal for some time—but the actual diagnosis was this morning.' Danielle sighed. 'I suppose my foot had been aching for a bit.'

And Dani, being Dani, had no doubt ignored it be-cause she was too busy. 'Why didn't you say something, the other night?' Hayley asked. 'We could've missed class to let you rest your foot.'

Danielle flapped a dismissive hand. 'It was fine.'

Hayley raised an eyebrow. 'Fine enough for you to be wearing a walking cast right now?'

Danielle sighed. 'OK, OK. I thought it wasn't anything major and resting it for a day or two would be enough to sort it out, but it felt a bit worse yesterday so I thought I'd better get it checked out. I was pretty sure my doctor was going to roll his eyes at me and say it was just because I still needed to get used to my new running shoes. Except he sent me for an X-ray instead. And apparently almost everyone with a metatarsal stress fracture says the same thing as I did—they don't remember doing anything different or they've just got new shoes.'

'Ouch. So how long are you going to have the cast?' Hayley asked.

'They said it'll take between one and three months to heal,' Danielle said. 'So it's crutches this week and then I have to wear the cast and rest my foot as much as possible.'

'Rest' wasn't in Danielle's vocabulary, Hayley knew. It would drive her best friend crazy to have to sit with her foot up.

'And they said if I don't rest it properly and for long enough, I'll risk making it worse and then I'll end up needing surgery to fix it—which will take even longer to heal, so obviously I'd rather avoid that.' Danielle pulled a face. 'Bang goes finishing my training for that charity run in October. I won't even be able to *walk* the course, let alone run it. I'll have to return all the sponsor money.'

And the run was close to Dani's heart because she was raising money to buy an MRI scanner for newborns on the maternity unit. 'Unless the organisers will let me run in your place,' Hayley said thoughtfully.

Danielle stared at her in surprise. 'I can't ask you to do that. You hate running.'

'Yes, but it's for a good cause. I can run it for you. Remember, we agreed, this is the Year of Saying Yes. We've both had a horrible year.' Hayley's own life had imploded just over a year ago, when Evan, her fiancé, had been killed while trying to rescue someone from an industrial fire; and Danielle's husband Leo had left her unexpectedly for someone else, nine months ago. They'd supported each other through the wreckage of their lives and, the previous month, when Danielle's decree nisi had come through and the anniversary of Evan's death had passed, they'd agreed that they'd spend the next year saying yes to every opportunity that came their way. The theory was, it would help them both to move on and live life to the full. Or, as Dani had put it, living well was the best revenge and she wasn't going to spend the rest of her life crying over someone who didn't love her any more.

'We agreed we'd make the most out of life and say yes to every opportunity,' Haley reminded her. 'So you have to say yes to me taking your place, and we'll talk the organisers into bending the rules slightly if they have to. They can't expect you to run with a broken foot—and surely it's better to have a substitute so the hospital can keep the sponsor money towards the scanner?'

'If you're really sure,' Danielle said, 'then thank you.' She bit her lip. 'But that's not the worst bit.' She dragged in a breath. 'I'm so sorry, but I'm not going to be able to go to Iceland with you next week. The orthopods tried to sign me off work. I said I can do a lot of my job sitting down—which I can, so don't argue,' she said, holding up one hand to stop Hayley protesting. 'They've agreed to let me have the walking cast, provided I agreed to rest my foot as much as possible. But they said that hiking round Iceland for a week is totally out of the question. And, with the kind of walks we were planning to do, there's no way you could push me round in a chair—not when there's loads of rough ground, volcanic sand, and a fair bit of clambering about on slippery boulders. It's just not doable.'

'Then we'll talk to the travel agent and reschedule,' Hayley said.

Danielle shook her head. 'You wanted to go in the summer so you'd get to see the midnight sun. If we reschedule, then it'll be another year before we can go away—and you really, really need a break. Especially as you're taking up your new job in a couple of weeks.'

Her promotion to senior registrar, which was bittersweet because Evan wasn't here to be pleased that her hard work had paid off. 'I'm fine,' Hayley said.

'This is supposed to be the Year of Saying Yes, remember,' Danielle said. 'We said we'd do it so we'd have fun instead of being miserable.'

'I'm not so sure it'll be much fun, going to Iceland on my own,' Hayley said.

'But you'll still get to see the whales and the geyser and the glacier—tick all those things off your bucket list. You need a break, Haze. Go and have a wonderful time. And I'll talk to the travel agent to sort everything out this end.'

'It's not fair that you're missing out,' Hayley said.

'We can plan something else when my foot's healed,' Danielle said. 'We could maybe go to Vienna in November for the Christmas markets. We can eat lots of gingerbread and drink the best hot chocolate in the world.'

'Maybe,' Hayley said.

'Definitely,' Danielle insisted. 'And you can send me a ton of photos from Iceland.' She smiled. 'If I were you, I'd stock up on the fun now—if you were serious about running that charity race for me, you'll be in strict training for the next two months.'

'Two and a half months, less my week in Iceland,' Hayley pointed out.

'The couch to 10K running programme is supposed to take about twelve weeks,' Danielle said thoughtfully, 'but you do dance aerobics twice a week, so you're not really starting from couch level.'

Hayley did dance aerobics simply because Dani had pushed her into it two weeks after Evan's funeral, making her leave her flat instead of hiding within the four walls and wishing that her fiancé had never, ever become a firefighter. And Hayley had to admit that the combination of the music and the movement *had* made her feel better, if only for a little while. For the same reason, she'd forced Dani to keep coming to the class with her after Leo had walked out on her.

'OK. You sort out the training programme and I'll do it.'

'You,' Danielle said, reaching over to squeeze her hand, 'are the best friend ever.'

'No, that would be you,' Hayley said. 'And you can sit still while I sort out some lunch for you. Even *you* can't juggle a tray and hot coffee with crutches.'

'Try me?' Danielle said.

'Behave,' Hayley ordered with a grin.

'Yes, ma'am. And you're right—I can't hold coffee with crutches,' Danielle admitted, and fished in her purse for some money. 'Thanks, Haze. Just grab the first sandwich you come to—I don't mind what it is.' She paused. 'So you promise me you won't cancel the trip?'

'It's the Year of Saying Yes,' Hayley said. 'So I'll go.' Even though a solo trip felt daunting, Hayley knew that her best friend was right. She did need a break. And maybe ticking some things off her bucket list would help her move on.

She'd always miss Evan, but she knew he wouldn't have wanted her to spend the rest of her life on her own. So she was going to say yes. And, in accordance with their agreement, she was going to date the next man who asked her out.

CHAPTER ONE

THE LAND OF the Midnight Sun. Hayley had been stunned by the sheer quality of the light from the moment she'd arrived at the airport; everything seemed brighter in Reykjavik.

Evan would've loved this, she thought with a pang. Especially the whale-watching trip she'd chosen to do this morning. Now the boat was out in the middle of the open sea, the temperature had dropped quite sharply, but the sun was bright and she leaned against the railing at the side of the boat, listening to the guide and trying to spot the tiny puffins with their bright orange beaks.

'There are lots of birds just above the water ahead of us, and that often indicates cetacean activity—they'll be picking up bits of fish the whales have left behind,' the guide said. And then, a couple of minutes later, she called, 'Spout at nine o'clock!'

Hayley could actually see the spout of warm, moist air blown up by the whale; to her amazement, it really was like you saw in TV documentaries. A perfect misty funnel.

'And here's our minke!' the guide said.

The ship drew to a standstill, and Hayley could see just the dark back of the whale, like a slight hump above the surface of the sea. And then a fin appeared, bright white against the sea and the sky, almost as if the whale was waving to them.

This was magical.

She took a few shots on her camera, hoping they'd come out. And then, to her sheer joy, the whale breached, its snout coming up out of the water and then its body performing a perfect arc, revealing its white belly before the whale splashed back into the sea.

She'd never seen anything so awe-inspiring. The whale's snout came up again, and then a fin; then she saw the divided end of the tail as the whale dived down again.

'I'm sure you could all see the flukes then—that's the whale's tail—and this usually indicates that the whale's diving more deeply,' the guide said. 'So we're going to move on.'

This was a truly humbling experience, Hayley thought; it made her feel glad to be alive.

But then, a few minutes later, the guide called, 'Do we have a doctor on board?'

Her heart skipped a beat. When a tour guide put out that kind of call, it could mean a true emergency, and right now they were almost an hour's sail away from Reykjavik. She had no idea how the emergency services worked here. Would they send out a helicopter to the ship, or would the tour guide have to cut the trip short and they'd have to sail straight back to the city?

She made her way to the guide's post. 'I'm Hayley Clark, a doctor from England. Can I help?'

'My husband's having an asthma attack,' an American woman said, looking anxious and wringing her hands. 'And we don't have his inhaler with us.'

Just as well she worked in the emergency department, Hayley thought. 'Can you put out a call to see if anyone has a reliever inhaler we could borrow, please?' she asked the guide. 'Even a preventer inhaler would help.'

'Will do,' the guide said.

She turned to the woman. 'Would you like to take me to your husband? My name's Hayley and I work in the emergency department of a London hospital.'

'I'm Lulu Adams and thank God you're on board,' the woman said, leading her towards the next deck down. 'I can't believe Milton's having an attack out here. Normally it's pollen and cat hair that sets him off.'

'Cold can set off asthma, too, and the air's quite cool out here,' Hayley said, 'so it's always a good idea to keep a reliever inhaler with you—even if you don't think you're going to come across your usual triggers. Does your husband take his preventer inhaler regularly?'

'He's a man. You can't tell him *anything*,' the woman said with a sigh.

So this was probably an attack that had been brewing for a while, Hayley thought, with a patient who didn't bother taking his preventer inhaler that often. Milton Adams's doctor definitely needed to talk to him about the importance of asthma control. She just hoped she could keep him stable until they managed to get some proper bronchodilator medication for him. 'Does he have any other medical conditions?' she asked.

'Just the asthma.'

Which was tricky enough to deal with, by the sound of things. 'OK. Thanks.'

Do we have a doctor on board?

There were maybe a couple of hundred other people on the boat. The chances were, Sam was the only doctor. Plus this would be a test. Had he done the right thing in accepting the job at a London hospital, or had his experience in Manchester soured his love affair with medicine to the point where he really didn't want to go back to it?

He made his way to the bridge to talk to the guide, and on the way he heard her ask if anyone had an asthma inhaler that another passenger could borrow.

'My name's Sam Price, and I'm an emergency doctor from England. It sounds as if you have a passenger who's having an asthma attack and doesn't have an inhaler. Can I help?' he asked.

'There's another doctor gone to see him already, if you want to join her,' the guide said. 'You'll see her on the deck below. She's wearing a yellow raincoat.'

'OK. Thanks. Has anyone come up with an inhaler?'

'Not yet, but I'm going to put another call out,' she said.

Asthma attacks could be tricky. If nothing else, Sam thought, he could help calm down whoever was with the patient, so the other doctor could get on with treating the patient. He headed down to the next deck, and saw a woman wearing a yellow raincoat. She was talking to a man who was clearly panicking and wheezing, and the woman with them was wringing her hands and looking equally panicky.

'Hello. I'm Sam Price, and I'm an emergency doctor,' he said as he joined them. 'Can I help?'

'Hayley Clark—also an emergency doctor, from London,' the woman in the yellow raincoat said.

He noticed how blue her eyes were—like an Icelandic summer sky—and her sun-streaked blonde hair was caught back at the nape of her neck, with soft tendrils framing a perfect oval face.

What the hell was he doing, noticing the colour of her eyes when there was a sick patient who needed their attention? Besides, even if he was looking for a relationship—which he wasn't, after Lynda—she was probably already spoken for. Cross with himself for getting distracted, he paid attention to what she was saying.

'This is Milton Adams and his wife Lulu,' Hayley continued. 'He doesn't have his reliever or preventer inhaler with him, and we think the cold air probably brought on his asthma attack. He doesn't have any other medical conditions.'

'The guide's putting out a second call to see if anyone on board has an inhaler with them,' Sam said. 'But even if there isn't anyone, we can help you, Mr Adams.'

The man continued to wheeze, fighting for air, clearly panicked by the tightness in his chest.

Really, they needed to get him away from the cold

air that had triggered the attack and into a warm place. But, given the state of his breathing right now and the fact that he was quite overweight, no way would Mr Adams be able to cope with the steep stairs to go back inside the ship. First, Sam thought, they needed to get Mr Adams stabilised so he was calm, and breathing more slowly. Anxiety released cortisol in the body, constricting the bronchial tubes even further, and panicking that you couldn't breathe caused a vicious circle: it tightened the chest muscles, which made it harder to breathe, which in turn made the patient panic more and then the chest muscles tightened even further.

'Mr Adams, can you sit up straight for us?' Sam asked. 'It'll help you breathe more easily, because bending over constricts your breathing.'

Milton Adams continued gasping, but to Sam's relief, he did as he was told.

'I'm going to loosen your tie and undo the button of your collar,' Hayley said, 'because that's also going to help you breathe more easily. Is that all right?'

The man nodded.

'I told him he ought to bring his inhaler. I *told* him,' Mrs Adams said, almost in tears.

Hayley reached over and squeezed her hand. 'Mrs Adams—can we call you Lulu?' At the woman's nod, she continued, 'I know how worried you are about your husband, but right now I really need you to do an important job for me and count. Can you do that for me?'

'Yes,' Mrs Adams said, her voice slightly quavery.

Brilliant management, Sam thought—she'd acknowledged the woman's fears and distracted her by making her feel useful. What Hayley had just said about counting told him that she'd intended to use the same method he would've used.

'Mr Adams—can we call you Milton?' At the man's nod, Sam continued, 'We want you to try to take some really long, deep breaths for us. I know right now it's scary, but I promise we can make you feel better. I want you to breathe in through your nose for a count of four and out through your mouth for a count of six. Can you do that for us?'

Mr Adams nodded, still fighting for breath.

'Can you count for us now, Lulu?' Hayley asked. 'Four in, then six out. Count with me for the first set so we can get the rhythm right together. One, two, three, four...'

Mrs Adams joined in with counting.

Sam took the older man's hand to reassure him. 'OK. Breathe in—now out.' Breathing to the counts would slow Milton's breathing down, making it easier for him.

'Purse your lips as you breathe out, Milton,' Hayley said. 'That helps to slow your breathing and keeps your airways open. That's it. Keep going. You're both doing really great.'

Mr Adams was still wheezing, but his colour was improving. 'Can you place one hand on your stomach, Milton, just below your ribcage?' Sam asked. 'Then, when you breathe in, focus on pulling down into your stomach. Use your stomach muscles to help you push out,' he said. 'It's called diaphragmatic breathing and it will really help you take deep, slow breaths.'

Eventually, Mr Adams's breathing pattern settled and he seemed noticeably calmer.

Sam caught Hayley's eye. 'Shall we all go downstairs, so we're away from the cold air?'

She nodded. 'And we can ask the crew if they'll sort out a bowl of hot water and lend us a towel.'

'Good call,' he said. They could make a tent with the towel and the bowl of hot water, and then Milton Adams could breathe in the moist air to help him recover.

Everyone else on board was on the upper decks by the railings, watching what sounded like a couple of whales playing in the water, so it made their passage down the stairs a bit easier—even if they were missing out on all the fun. They supported Milton Adams down the steep staircase to the inner deck, but he was wheezing badly again by the time they'd got him sitting down by a table.

'Could you get your husband a cup of coffee from the bar, please?' Hayley asked Mrs Adams.

'He doesn't like coffee,' Mrs Adams said. 'Or tea. Only hot chocolate.'

'Maybe make the coffee milky and sweet?' Hayley suggested. 'The chemical structure of coffee is similar to theophylline, which is in most asthma medications, so a hot cup of coffee can help with wheezing, shortness of breath and chest tightness. Plus the warmth of the liquid will help break up the phlegm and mucus, making breathing easier.'

'I'll drink the coffee,' Mr Adams wheezed.

'Great. Are you OK to sit with Milton while I sort out a towel and hot water?' Hayley asked Sam.

'Sure,' he said. 'What I'd like you to do, Milton, is to sit up straight for me again, and count the number of blue things in the room.'

'Blue things?' Mr Adams looked nonplussed.

'Blue things,' Sam confirmed. 'Count them, and keep breathing like we did upstairs. I'll count while you breathe. In for four, out for six.'

As he'd hoped, the small task of looking round the room for blue things distracted the older man enough to help calm him further, and by the time Mr Adams had drunk the coffee and Sam and Hayley had arranged the bowl of hot water and towel as a temporary recovery tent so he could breathe in warm, moist air, he was looking in a much better condition.

When the boat arrived back at the dock, they were met by an ambulance. The guide came to join them as Sam and Hayley explained the situation to the paramedics.

'Thank you both so much for all your help.' Mrs Adams bit her lip. 'And you missed most of the trip and the whales because of us. I feel so bad.'

'We can arrange a replacement trip at no charge,' the guide said. 'And I'd like to thank you both, too. We have trained first aiders among the crew, of course, but we really needed a doctor to help us in this case.'

'No problem,' Hayley said.

'Call into the office whenever suits you best,' the guide said, 'and we'll rearrange your trip.'

'I ought to give you something for helping us,' Mrs Adams said.

'There's really no need,' Sam said. 'It's what doctors are supposed to do—help people who need it.'

'Agreed. Though if you really want to give us something,' Hayley added, 'then I'd like you to promise you'll talk to your asthma specialist about what happened today, Milton, and that you'll take your preventer inhaler regularly—even if you don't think you need it, because taking it regularly is what helps to keep you well.'

Milton looked slightly shame-faced. 'I will.'

'Good.' Hayley patted his shoulder. 'Best of luck, and enjoy the rest of your holiday.'

'You, too.'

When the ambulance doors closed and the Adamses were taken to hospital, Sam looked at Hayley. 'Would you like to go for a coffee? Or do you need to get back to whoever you're travelling with?'

'I'm on my own,' she said. 'So a coffee would be lovely—unless you need to get back to your travelling companions?'

'I'm on my own, too,' he said. 'Do you want to re-book your whale-watching trip first?'

She wrinkled her nose. 'I saw one come up out of the water and dive back in. Expecting anything more's probably greedy. Though if you want to rebook yours…?'

He smiled. 'I'm greedy enough as it is. I go every week.'

'Every week?' She looked surprised. 'Do you work at a hospital here, then?'

'No. I'm kind of on sabbatical,' he said. 'My brother has a tour company out here, specialising in extreme trips—taking people walking on a glacier and that sort of thing. I've been helping him. But I go whale-watching every Monday afternoon. It's the most amazing experience.'

She nodded. 'It's something Dani and I always wanted to see.'

'Danny?' Well, of course someone as pretty as Hayley Clark would be spoken for.

'Danielle. My best friend,' she explained.

How ridiculous that he should feel pleased that Dani was her best friend, not a partner. He was in no position to even think about starting a relationship, not with his new job starting in a fortnight.

Yet something about Hayley Clark tempted him.

Which was weird, because he'd had tourists throwing themselves at him all summer and not one of them had interested him.

What was it about her?

'She fractured her second and third metatarsal last week, so the orthopods said she couldn't come,' Hayley continued.

He'd come across those kinds of fractures before. 'Your friend's a runner, then?'

Hayley nodded. 'She was training for a charity run. Obviously she can't do that now, so we talked the organisers into letting me run in her place.'

'You're a runner, too?'

She grimaced. 'No. Actually, I loathe running. But the only way to keep her sponsorship money is if I run for her.'

'That's good of you.'

'She's my best friend, and she's been through a lot. And doing that for her helps me feel less guilty about coming here while she's missing out.' Hayley wrinkled her nose. 'Though I'm pretty sure she could've done the whale-watching—and if we'd asked at the tourist place, they could've found us some wheelchair-accessible trips.'

'But you would both have missed out on a lot. Not all the paths around the waterfalls and the geysers are wheelchair-friendly,' he said, 'and some of the slopes would make it seriously tricky going downhill.'

'That's what Dani said.'

He should shut up right now. What he ought to do was to suggest a couple of reliable tour operators and let her find her own way round the island. But the pull he felt towards her was too strong, and he found himself asking, 'How long are you staying?'

'Until Friday.'

Shut up, shut up, shut up.

But his mouth wasn't listening to his common sense. 'Then why don't you rebook your whale trip for tomorrow morning?' he suggested. 'And if you like, I'll take you on a personalised tour.'

She blinked. 'But aren't you helping your brother?'

It was the perfect get-out. He knew he ought to take it. But his mouth was on a roll. 'He's had a couple of cancellations,' Sam said, 'so I wasn't doing much this week. I'm free if you'd like to come with me.'

Hayley could practically hear Dani yelling in her ear, 'Say yes! It's the Year of Saying Yes.'

But Sam Price was a total stranger.

Even if he was a doctor and they'd just worked together to help a patient.

And, with that dark hair brushed back from his face and soulful hazel eyes, he was also the most attractive man she'd met since Evan, the first who'd even made her look at him, which made her feel guilty. It was only just over a year since Evan had died. Was she rushing into this?

She ought to be cautious. She was in a country where she didn't speak the language; even though everyone in Iceland spoke perfect English, this still wasn't England. She was a three-and-a-half-hour flight away from home. The sensible thing to do would be to say no.

But this was the Year of Saying Yes.

And maybe putting caution aside was something she needed to do for once. To help her move on.

'Yes,' she said.

CHAPTER TWO

THEY REBOOKED THE whale-watching tour for the following morning, then headed to a café in the centre of the city.

'I love the ambience here,' Hayley said when they were settled at a table.

'Reykjavik lives up to your expectations, then?' Sam asked.

'Very much,' she said. 'I had a walk round yesterday evening when I got here. I really want to explore that amazing-looking church—I've never seen a spire like that, kind of spreading out like wings.'

'The Hallgrímskirkja,' he said. 'It's meant to resemble the volcanic basalt flows—and actually there are a couple of caves by one of the beaches that have columns looking very much like that.'

'That's amazing.'

'The inside of the church is actually very plain,' he said, 'as it's a Lutheran church—the simplicity is lovely, though. And the views from the tower are amazing.' He paused. 'We could go and take a look after we've had coffee, if you like.'

'I'd like that very much,' she said, 'if you have time.' She looked him straight in the eye. 'And if your partner won't mind.'

'No partner,' he said. Lynda had broken their engagement the week after he'd been suspended, and he hadn't been tempted to date anyone since. It was going to take him a while to trust again. And he wasn't actually dating Hayley, even if he did feel a strong pull of attraction towards her.

Though he needed to be clear that she wasn't involved with anyone, either. The lack of a ring on her left hand meant absolutely nothing, nowadays. 'I take it that it's the same for you?'

She nodded. 'No partner.'

This felt like another step towards dating. But it wasn't, he reminded himself. No commitments and no promises. They were just doing some sightseeing together, that was all.

She took a deep breath. 'I'm not looking for pity or anything like that, but I should probably tell you that he died just over a year ago.'

So she was still grieving?

If so, that made her safe, because it meant she wouldn't be looking for a proper relationship.

But to lose her partner... He judged her to be around his own age, early to mid thirties, so it must've been either an accident or a seriously aggressive form of cancer that had killed her partner; either way, she'd clearly been through a lot. 'I'm sorry,' he said. 'That must've been hard for you.'

She nodded. 'He was killed in an industrial accident.

I'm just glad I'd kissed him goodbye that morning and my last words to him were "I love you"—I think if our last words had been something awful said in the middle of a row, it would've been harder to deal with.'

'Yes.' And Sam knew that one from experience. The morning when his career had imploded, he'd had a fight with his fiancée on the way to work. Lynda had wanted him to give up his mountain rescue work in favour of something that would boost his career at the hospital. Something on a dull committee. He'd refused.

But he should have taken notice of the way she'd been behaving towards him, that last year. Then he would've expected Lynda's reaction to his suspension, a few days later, instead of being shocked to the core by it.

'So how long have you been in Reykjavik?' she asked.

'Since the end of March,' he said.

She raised her eyebrows. 'That's quite a career change, from working in emergency medicine to being a tour guide.'

'Yeah.' Sam knew he was lucky. His family had believed in him. His older brother Martin had dragged him out to Iceland, saying that the job was only temporary, but he really needed the help—and someone who had mountain rescue team experience was the perfect person to come and help with glacier walking tours.

Sam knew that Martin hadn't needed the help at all—he just hadn't wanted Sam to sit at home alone and brood about the situation. And Sam would be grateful for ever to his brother for giving him something else to concentrate on, without expecting him to talk about the situation or his feelings.

Hayley winced at his flat tone. 'Sorry, that was really intrusive—you don't owe me any explanations. Please forget I said anything.'

'It's OK. It was a mix of a rough patch at work and a messy break-up.' Short and to the point. Hayley didn't need to know his team had been suspended after a diabetic patient's death from a silent heart attack. He'd been sure that they'd followed all the right procedures during his admission and treatment, but the patient's family had needed someone to blame for a death that shouldn't have happened and they'd made a complaint. The hospital trust had been duty-bound to take the complaint seriously and launch an investigation.

A week later, Lynda had broken off their engagement, worried that the stain on his career would transfer to hers because she was his fiancée—according to her, everyone would still think there was no smoke without fire. How it had hurt to discover that the one person he'd expected to bat his corner for him, the way he would've done if their positions had been reversed, didn't actually believe in him. All Lynda had wanted was to buy him out of his share of their house and get his name off the mortgage.

'I took a sabbatical because I needed a bit of space to help me decide what to do next. Iceland's a good place to think.' And he'd come to realise that Lynda hadn't been right for him anyway. She'd wanted him to be something he wasn't—the sort who'd serve on committees and boards, moving away from medicine to admin. Sam had wanted to make a difference where it really mattered, saving lives and making his patients better rather than talking budgets and politics. So her breaking up with him had done him a favour, really.

'I think we all get rough patches at work,' Hayley said. 'Days when you lose people, or you know the system isn't going to get your patient the right help and you can't do anything about it.'

There was a hint of sadness in those blue, blue eyes, and he guessed she was thinking about her fiancé. But it was none of his business. He wasn't going to push her to talk.

'Though I'm sorry you had to deal with a break-up at the same time as a rough patch. That's a bit of a double whammy,' she said.

He lifted a shoulder in a half-shrug. 'If I'm being honest, we'd been heading for the rocks for a while. I'd been kind of deluding myself.' Knowing he was being a coward, but wanting to get back on safer ground and talk about something less emotionally daunting, he asked, 'So why did you come to Iceland?'

'I've always wanted to see the midnight sun,' Hayley said. 'And there were other things on my bucket list, like seeing the whales.'

'What else is on your list?'

'Seeing a geyser erupt,' she said promptly, 'and touching a glacier, and seeing the split between the continental plates. Oh, and I saw this video of people walking behind a waterfall—I'd really like to do that, too.'

'I can take you to do all that, as well as that beach with the cave that's a bit like the church columns.'

'Thank you. But it's your job, so obviously I'll pay you the going rate for a guide,' she said.

'No,' he said. 'Apart from my weekly self-indulgence of going to see the whales, I haven't really done anything just for fun. So if you don't mind me muscling in on your bucket list, and maybe making some suggestions of places I think you might enjoy, it'd be a holiday for me.'

She frowned. 'Surely you've already visited all those places with clients—I mean, aren't they on every tourist's wish list?'

'True, but seeing something through someone else's eyes keeps it fresh,' he said. 'Please don't offer to pay me.'

'At least let me pay for the petrol,' she protested. 'And buy you lunch.'

He really ought to shut up. But his mouth wasn't working to the same script as his head. 'As long as you'll let me buy you dinner tonight,' he found himself saying.

'I'd like that. Thank you.'

'It's a deal.' He reached across the table to shake her hand.

When Sam shook her hand, it sent goose-bumps over Hayley's skin.

This felt more like a date than agreeing to share some travel plans. Yet in a way it was a kind of blind date, because she knew hardly anything about him— just that he'd had some kind of career crisis and a bad break-up, so he was taking time out to decide what to do next with his life.

But, if she pushed him to talk about it, that would give him the right to ask her the same: and she didn't want to talk about Evan and how her life had sunk into a black hole after her fiancé's death.

She was just going to focus on the fun stuff. That was the reason she was in Iceland, after all. To help her move on. And if this was some kind of date—well, it wasn't serious, but maybe it was something that she needed. Something that perhaps they both needed.

After coffee, they went to see the church with its soaring ceilings and tall windows. Hayley loved the sheer simplicity of it, and the beauty of the simple crystal font. She enjoyed the tour of the city afterwards, with Sam pointing out the places of interest—the Town Hall, the Tjörnin lake behind it, which was a perfect mirror for the town hall and old buildings that lined it, the Parliament building and the striking black glass building of the Harpa concert hall. Sam knew lots of anecdotes and stories and entertained her thoroughly, though she wasn't entirely sure whether he was teasing her when he told her about the locals throwing yogurt at the Parliament building as part of a protest.

Before they stopped for dinner, he asked, 'Do you have any food allergies, or are you vegetarian?'

She smiled at him, liking the fact that he'd been thoughtful enough to ask. 'No and no. I'm very happy for you to recommend somewhere.'

He took her to a little bistro by the Old Harbour. 'They do some of the best fish in Iceland here,' he said. 'And I can guarantee it's freshly caught.'

The place was tiny and candle-lit; the interior walls

were all of polished wood, and Hayley noticed that there were vintage photographs of the area hanging on the walls. 'Would I be right in thinking that this used to be a fishing shed?' she asked.

'A lot of the buildings in this area are,' Sam explained. 'They've been renovated and painted different colours. Some are shops, some are cafés and restaurants, and there's an ice cream shop here that does an amazing array of flavours.'

The ambience was lovely—but the food was even better. On Sam's recommendation, she chose 'catch of the day', which turned out to be a seafood risotto topped with fresh cod.

'The food is amazing,' she said.

And the dessert was spectacular: a chocolate dome that, when she poured hot caramel sauce onto it, melted into a rich chocolate pudding.

Even better than the food was the company. Hayley couldn't remember the last time she'd been out to dinner with a man, and Sam was *nice*. He had an innate kindness that appealed to her; and he was easy on the eye, too, with short dark hair brushed back from his face, hazel eyes and a sensual mouth.

Not that she ought to be thinking about his mouth. Or kissing. Or wondering what his hands would feel like against her skin. It made her feel disloyal to Evan—even though she knew that Evan wouldn't have wanted her to be alone for ever.

They lingered over coffee, took a last stroll round the Old Harbour area, and then Sam walked her back to her hotel.

'I can hardly believe it's half-past eleven at night and it's still so light,' she said, marvelling. 'Back at home it would be dark by now.'

'With your hotel being this side of the bay,' he said, 'you're going to get amazing views of the sunset across the sea.'

Just what she'd hoped for.

Ahead of them was a steel sculpture of what looked like a Viking boat; it glowed gold in the light of the setting sun. And when Hayley looked back over her shoulder, the sky was ablaze with orange and gold and hot pink.

'The midnight sun,' she said softly. 'I've always wanted to see it. And it's as incredible as I thought it would be.'

When they reached her hotel he asked, 'Shall I meet you on the dock outside the ship at nine?'

'That sounds good. See you there,' she said.

He didn't attempt to kiss her, and Hayley was shocked to realise that she was faintly disappointed. And then she felt ashamed. They weren't dating and they hadn't even agreed to have a holiday fling. Sam Price was simply a kind stranger she'd met by chance, and he'd offered to keep her company in her travels. She really shouldn't be throwing herself at him. And wasn't he still getting over a bad break-up? The last thing he needed was someone mooning about over him. Maybe she should have made a polite excuse and stayed on her own after all. Tomorrow, after the whale-watching trip, she'd feign a headache.

'Goodnight,' she said, and headed for her room.

Her window overlooked the sea, so she took some last shots of the sunset and emailed them to Dani, along with an account of her day and the fact she was acting in accordance with their agreement about saying yes to opportunities. She woke in the middle of the night and was surprised to see it was still quite light; back in London at this time it would be dark. She woke again in time for the sunrise and was stunned to see how the sea turned into a shimmering mass of gold and silver.

After breakfast, she walked down to the old harbour to meet Sam for the whale-watching trip. This time, nobody on board needed a doctor's help. They saw a school of porpoises, and then two minke whales together. When the whales leaped out of the water in a perfect arc and she gasped with pleasure, it felt natural for Sam to slide his arm around her shoulders—and for her to slide her own arm around his waist.

Though at the same time it felt wrong. This was exactly what she would've done with Evan. And Sam wasn't Evan. 'Sorry,' she said, sliding her arm away from his waist. 'I think I got a bit…well, carried away with the emotion of seeing the whales.'

'Me, too,' Sam agreed, removing his arm from her shoulders. He looked just as shocked as she felt.

They were careful not to even let their hands touch accidentally until they were back on land. She should make up some excuse, Hayley thought, say she had a headache or something—though it would be a shame to miss out on the trip they'd planned.

Sam looked slightly awkward. 'Would you still like to come and see the waterfall and the geyser?'

He was clearly offering her a chance to back out, recognising that the moment he'd held her on the ship had been difficult for her. But she could see something in his eyes. Something that struck a chord with her. Loneliness maybe, even if it wasn't something either of them would admit to. And it would be good to have some company. 'If you'd still like to go,' she said carefully. After all, it must've been awkward for him, too.

'Let's go, then.' Sam drove her out to see the Gullfoss waterfall.

'The water looks almost golden,' she said in amazement when they'd made their way down the path to the double drop.

'That's how it gets its name—*"gullfoss"* means "golden falls",' he said. 'Partly it's because of the sediment in the water.'

As they drew nearer to the edge, Hayley slipped on a smooth piece of stone and Sam caught her arm, steadying her. His touch felt almost electric. And she could see in his expression that it was the same for him—instant attraction that neither of them had been expecting or looking for, and it seemed that neither of them quite knew what to do with it or how to react.

'Sorry,' she said.

'Uh-huh.' But he didn't move his hand away. He just looked at her, as if he was as surprised by the feelings as she was. And then he cleared his throat. 'They say if you don't like the weather in Iceland, wait five minutes—and look, the sun's just come out.'

She looked to where he gestured, and hanging over the waterfalls was a bright rainbow.

It was a natural phenomenon, she knew, caused by the sunlight and the spray from the waterfall. But in a weird kind of way it felt as if it was Evan telling her was it OK, that she was ready to move on and he approved.

She shook herself. 'Photo opportunity,' she said brightly, moving away just the tiniest bit so his arm fell naturally away from hers.

And how stupid that she missed it being there.

What was she, a recycled teenager?

She was just going to have to ignore it and be sensible. She smiled, and took a snap of the rainbow on her phone.

When she'd had her fill of the waterfall and the rainbow, Sam drove them out to the Geysìr area. 'The old Geysìr is the one that all geysers are named after,' he said. 'Apparently it used to be even bigger than the one in Yellowstone, but it's been dormant for years.'

'So I won't actually get to see a geyser going up?' she asked.

'Oh, you will.' He smiled. 'Strokkur erupts pretty much about every ten minutes. And if you have a slow-mo setting on your phone, I'd recommend that because then you'll really see how it works. The water at the top of the pool is cooler and acts as a kind of lid to the hot water below, so the pressure builds up and then you can see it boil over and the geyser erupts. Then it leaves a sinkhole and the water drains back in, and the cycle starts all over again.'

She could see a circle of people standing round what she assumed was the geyser, and then suddenly a massive plume of water shot into the air. 'Oh! That's amazing.'

'Let's go and get a better view,' he said, and walked with her to where everyone was standing.

As he'd suggested, she filmed it on slow-mo. 'Dani would've loved this,' she said wistfully. So would Evan, though she didn't say it.

Then, as they moved deeper into the fields, his fingers accidentally brushed against hers. Again, she felt that swoop of butterflies in her stomach; and when she caught his eye, she was pretty sure it was the same for him.

What were they going to do about it? Ignore it? Or see where it led them?

There wasn't any future in it. Couldn't be. After the end of this week they'd be in different countries, thousands of miles apart, and he'd said nothing about returning to England.

The sky had turned the deepest summery blue, and the scenery was amazing. There were little puffs of steam rising from underground pools, and a tiny pot that produced a bubbling spout a few centimetres tall. Sam seemed to be careful to keep a little distance between them when he showed her the site of the old Geysir, now just a pool with the occasional bubble to remind you that the water was extremely hot, and the twin pools of Blesi—one perfectly clear so you could see into the yawning cavern beneath it, and one that was the most amazing milky azure blue.

'The milky colour's from silicates in the water,' he said. 'That's the cool one—it's only about forty degrees Celsius.'

'Cool?' she asked.

'The other one's hotter,' he said.

'The milky blue pool: is that what the Blue Lagoon's like?' she asked.

'Pretty much. We can go there this evening, if you like—that's provided we can get a ticket, because evenings are pretty popular,' he added.

'I'd like that.' She smiled at him.

'Give me a second.' He made a quick phone call, and she noticed that he spoke in fluent Icelandic. 'OK. We're in luck—I've booked us in.'

'Thank you.'

They had dinner at a little village outside the city— lamb stew and rye bread, followed by blueberries and thick Icelandic yoghurt—and then stopped off firstly at her hotel so she could pick up her swimming things and then at his seafront apartment so he could pick up his.

'I can't remember the last time I felt this relaxed,' she said as they sat in the warm water of the lagoon, her face covered in a mask of white silica and an ice-cold smoothie in her hand.

'That's what this is meant to be about,' he said with a smile.

'This must be amazing in the winter—sitting in a hot pool under the stars.'

'And with the rocks all covered in snow,' he agreed. 'It's pretty.'

Their gazes met, and for a second she thought he was going to kiss her.

He didn't, but she could feel the anticipation brewing between them as he drove them back to the city and parked outside his apartment building. Every time they'd accidentally touched that day, she'd been so aware of him. And she didn't think she was alone in that reaction.

'Shall we walk along the harbour again to catch the sunset?' he asked.

'That'd be nice.'

At her hotel, he turned to face her. 'Goodnight, Hayley.'

'Goodnight. Thank you for such a lovely day.'

'My pleasure. Would you like to see the glacier, waterfalls and beaches tomorrow, if it looks as if it'll be dry?'

Spending more time with him? Part of her thought it was a good idea; part of her didn't. But she found herself agreeing.

'You'll need sturdy shoes,' he said.

'And a waterproof, just in case the weather changes?'

He smiled. 'Yes. Wear layers. And hiking trousers are better than jeans, if you have them—we're going to get wet by the waterfalls, plus they're better protection than denim against the wind.' And then the look in his dark eyes grew more intense. He lifted one hand and placed it gently against her cheek. In answer, she tipped her head back very slightly. And then he brushed his lips against hers—more asking than demanding. She slid her arms round his waist, and he kissed her again, his lips teasing hers until she opened her mouth and let him deepen the kiss.

Desire flooded through her, mixed with a dose of guilt. But this wasn't being unfaithful to Evan. He wouldn't have wanted her to spend her life alone and mourning him. He would've wanted her to keep seeing the joy in life and focus on the good stuff. Sam Price was the first man she'd wanted to kiss since she'd lost Evan. And this was meant to be the Year of Saying Yes. So she leaned into Sam, kissing him back.

When he finally broke the kiss, there was a dark slash of colour along his cheekbones and his mouth was reddened; she was pretty sure that she looked in the same state.

'Goodnight. I'll see you tomorrow,' he said. 'I'll meet you here at nine—if that's not too early?'

'That's perfect,' she said.

And she couldn't wait.

CHAPTER THREE

ON WEDNESDAY MORNING, Hayley walked out of her hotel at nine on the dot to see Sam walking towards her from his car.

'Perfect timing,' she said with a smile.

'Absolutely,' he agreed.

Hayley tingled right down to her toes. Crazy how this man made her feel like a teenager. It had been a long, long time since she'd felt butterflies in her stomach just at the sight of someone.

'Before we go,' she said carefully, 'I think we ought to talk about last night.'

He nodded. 'I'm sorry. I shouldn't have kissed you.'

This was the crunch moment. 'I'm not sorry,' she said, and watched his eyes darken. 'We're both single.'

'So are you saying…?'

That maybe, just maybe, a holiday romance would be good for both of them. No strings, no consequences, no promises. And no depth, so saying goodbye would be easy. 'You're getting over a bad break-up. I'm getting over my partner's death. We're both…a bit stuck where we are, I guess. Neither of us wants anything permanent right now.'

He seemed to be following her thought processes exactly. 'But a holiday romance might help us both move on,' he said.

She nodded. 'With an end date. I'm only here for a couple more days.' Neither of them would get hurt in such a short space of time.

'Just so you know, I don't do this with every woman I meet,' he said. 'You're the first woman I've kissed since Lynda and I split up.'

'You're the first man I've even noticed since Evan died,' she said softly. 'And I think my years in emergency medicine have made me a reasonable judge of character. I'd already worked out that you're not one of these men who have notches carved on their bedposts. You're one of the good guys.'

He inclined his head. 'Thank you. Though I wasn't fishing for compliments.'

'I didn't think you were.' She smiled. 'So where are we going today?'

'I think,' he said, 'given what you've just said, I'd like to start by kissing you hello.'

'Sounds good to me.'

He took a step forward, rested his hands on her shoulders, and brushed his mouth lightly against hers. The butterflies in her stomach started doing a stampede; then he slid his hands down her arms, wrapped them round her waist, and kissed her more thoroughly.

Her knees were weak by the time he broke the kiss.

'Good morning,' he said.

She smiled. 'It is now.'

He stole another kiss. 'We're going to start at Reynisfjara, to see the beach with black sand and the basalt columns,' he said. 'And then we'll go to see a glacier and your waterfall.'

'That sounds perfect,' she said.

Once he'd parked at Reynisfjara and they were out of the car, he looked at her and held out his hand. She took it with a smile, and they walked hand in hand onto the beach. The sand was black and slightly pebbly, in sharp contrast to the turquoise blue of the Atlantic, and Hayley stood watching the waves crash onto the shore.

'The sea's pretty calm right now,' Sam said, 'but in the winter the Atlantic rollers can get absolutely huge.'

She could just imagine the massive waves thundering in.

'And right at this point there's nothing but ocean between you and the Antarctic.'

She blinked. Was he teasing her? 'Seriously?'

'Seriously.' He led her over to the cave with the hexagonal basalt columns.

'It reminds of me of Giant's Causeway in Ireland,' she said. 'And it's definitely like the church in Reykjavik.'

Tourists were standing on the shorter columns, posing for photographs. 'When in Rome—or, rather, Reynisfjara,' he quipped, and helped her climb onto the columns so he could take a photo with her camera. The touch of his hands, even through the material of her T-shirt, sent a thrill right through her.

Once she'd climbed down again, he pointed out the

colony of puffins above; the tiny birds with their distinctive orange beaks moved incredibly fast, and Hayley had to admit defeat when she'd tried to take ten photographs of them and all had failed.

They walked hand in hand back to the car, then he drove them up a steep, winding track to the Dyrhólaey promontory, where they had a clear view of the rock with a 'door' in it that gave its name to the area. Sam stood with his arms wrapped round her waist. Up here where the wind was keen and the air was clear, she felt almost as if she were on top of the world.

'So what are those rocks jutting up over there?'

'Basalt stacks,' he said. 'The Reynisdrangar. Local legend says they were trolls who were trying to drag a ship from the sea onto land—but then the sun rose and the light turned them to stone.'

A land of legends, ice and fire.

A land that was going to start to heal her heart.

'Bucket list time,' he said. 'We're going to Solheimajökull—you can actually get up close to the glacier and touch it.'

When they parked, she could see a lake, and immediately behind it was the glacier.

'But it's dark grey,' she said. 'Aren't glaciers white or blue?'

'The grey's from sediment,' he said, 'and the white bits are snow and fresh ice.'

She peered up at the glacier. 'And are they people over there, walking on top of the glacier?'

He nodded. 'That's the kind of thing my brother Martin's company offers—though it's not safe to walk on a glacier without a guide who knows the area and can tell if there are sinkholes.'

'And you're qualified to do the guided walks?'

'Yes. I was part of the mountain rescue team when I worked in Manchester—we're not far from the Peak District or the Lakes. Actually, I was part of the team well before I qualified as a doctor, because I grew up in the Peak District. I'm also a qualified diver,' he said.

Mountain rescue and diving. Both of which were really dangerous. Both of which meant putting your life on the line. A chill went down Hayley's spine. It was just as well they'd agreed this would be only a holiday romance. She didn't want to be in another situation where she fell in love with someone who put himself in danger on a regular basis. She really couldn't bear to lose someone else the same way she'd lost Evan.

'Do you want to walk on the glacier?' he asked. 'I brought some kit with me, just in case.'

Under the rules of her agreement with Danielle, Hayley knew she ought to say yes. Instead, still thinking of the danger of his work on the mountain rescue team, she asked, 'Are you sure it's safe?'

He smiled. 'I know the area so, yes, it's safe. I wasn't sure of your shoe size, so I brought a few different pairs in case your hiking shoes weren't sturdy enough.' He glanced at her feet. 'Actually, if we do it, I'd really prefer you to wear the boots I brought with me. Not that there's anything wrong with your hiking boots,' he hastened to add, 'but ice walking needs a little bit extra.'

'If you're sure it's safe,' she said, 'then OK.' Walking on a glacier would be even better than touching one.

She put the shoes on and he fitted the crampons for her. 'These are to make it safer for you to walk on the ice,' he explained. He also gave her a helmet, ice axe and a walking pole. 'This will help to stabilise you and help you get a grip when you need to,' he said, 'as well as help you test the ice to make sure it's solid before you set foot on it.'

After a safety briefing, he showed her how to walk on the ice. 'You need to stamp down to get a good grip,' he said.

'I'm glad now that I didn't go for a run this morning before breakfast,' she said.

'As part of your training for the charity race, you mean?' He smiled. 'You'll definitely get a good work-out here. It won't do much for your speed, but it'll be good for stamina.'

They went along the path that led to the glacier, and then they were walking across the ice. Hayley could hear crunching sounds with every step. Part of her was terrified, part of her was thrilled and part of her was awed at the sheer beauty of the ice landscape. 'The way the snow lies on the dark ice, all rippled—it's a bit like the way a sandy beach looks when the tide goes out,' she said. 'I thought glaciers would be just white or blue, nothing like this. With all that dark veining going through it, in places it looks like marble.'

'The veining is caused by ash from previous erup-tions,' he said. 'I love the sheer wildness of the land-scape out here.'

It showed in his voice and his eyes. And he really looked in his element out here, strong and confident, knowing exactly what he was doing. He wouldn't have looked out of place in an ad in a glossy magazine, tall and muscular and utterly gorgeous.

Hayley gained in confidence as she walked beside him, until she felt one foot start to give way. 'Sam!'

He grabbed her immediately, and drew her over to a safer part of the ice. 'OK?' he asked.

'A bit shaky,' she admitted, 'but I'm not going to stop.'

'You're doing fine,' he said, and took her hand.

It took a while for her heart to slow down again after the near miss, but having him holding her hand gave her more confidence, to the point where she was happy to stop and take photographs again.

When they'd gone back over the ice sheet to the start of their walk, she returned the ice pick and walking pole, took off the crampons and changed back into her own hiking shoes.

'That,' she said, 'was amazing. Thank you.'

'My pleasure.'

They took a swift lunch break at a small café, and then he drove them to the waterfall she'd so wanted to see, Seljalandsfoss.

'It's a bit slippery in places,' Sam warned, 'and the path is actually a collection of boulders, so watch your step.'

'Hey. I just walked on ice. I can do this.'

Walking behind the curtain of water was magical. As she'd expected, there was a lot of spray; and the noise as the water shot down into the pool was almost deafening. Watching the world from behind a waterfall was like nothing she'd experienced before, and she loved it.

'This is incredible,' she said, squeezing Sam's hand.

He smiled, and kissed her lightly; she tingled all over. It was the most romantic place she'd ever been kissed, behind a wall of water.

Then he helped her up the steep boulders to the other side of the waterfall.

'Today's been amazing,' she said when they got back to the car. 'I mean, how many times do you walk on a black-sand beach, on a glacier, and behind a waterfall all in the same day?' Then she grimaced. 'Sorry. I sound like a tourist.'

'No, it's nice that you recognise how special this place is,' Sam said.

'Can I buy you dinner tonight?' she asked.

'I was thinking, maybe I could cook for you,' he suggested.

'That'd be nice, but can I at least contribute wine and a pudding?'

'No need,' he said. 'And actually it'll be nice to cook for someone else, as well.'

Hayley could understand that; sometimes it just didn't feel worth the effort, cooking for one. Nowadays she relied on supermarket ready meals or a bowl of cereal.

Back at his apartment, Sam said, 'I rented this place for the summer. There's not exactly a lot to show you round—the kitchen's here, the bathroom, the living room, and through there's my bedroom.'

'Small but perfect for city living,' she said. She wondered why he wasn't staying with his brother, but it felt too intrusive to ask. The flat was very neat and tidy, and looked more like a show flat than a home, though there were a couple of photographs held onto the fridge with magnets. When she took a closer look, the photographs were of Sam and another man who looked enough like him to be his older brother, both standing on the top of an ice ridge.

'That's Martin. My brother,' Sam confirmed when he saw her looking at the photographs.

'Is there anything I can do to help?' she asked.

'Nope.' He made coffee and handed her a mug. 'Go sit down and chill out. The best bit about this place is the view—you don't need TV or anything when you have that,' he said.

As he'd promised, the view from his living room across the bay to the mountains was stunning, and Hayley found herself absorbed in it until he came to tell her that dinner was ready.

She joined him in the kitchen, where he'd set the small pine table for two.

He'd made a simple prawn salad for starters. 'I'm afraid it's bottled sauce rather than home-made,' he said.

She smiled. 'That's fine. It still tastes good.'

'So are you a cook?' he asked.

Once. 'When I get time. I'm often guilty of buying ready meals at the supermarket,' she admitted, 'but I guess it goes with the territory of working in emergency medicine.'

The main course was simple grilled fish, with new

potatoes and asparagus—plus Hollandaise sauce, which he also admitted was ready-made.

'No need to apologise. I wouldn't have a clue how to start making it,' she said.

After dinner, he suggested going for a walk along the harbour to one of the coffee shops. Hayley thoroughly enjoyed walking there hand in hand with him, and watching the sun setting. When they walked back to his apartment, he slid his arm round her shoulders and hers fitted naturally round his waist. She felt closer to him than she'd ever been; and when he stopped to kiss her in the soft light that wasn't quite twilight, desire thrummed through her.

Outside his apartment building, he stopped and looked at her. 'I can drive you back to your hotel now— or maybe you'd like to stay tonight?'

Stay tonight.

Sam only had one bedroom, so Hayley knew what he was asking. Stay the night—and make love with him.

Part of her wanted to say yes. She'd enjoyed her day so much, everything from the sheer exhilaration of the ice walk through to the romantic stroll across the black sand beach. Yet he would be the first since Evan; part of her wondered, was she really ready for this or did she need more time?

'No strings,' he said, 'and if you say no, it's absolutely OK. We'll still go out exploring tomorrow.'

But it was the Year of Saying Yes.

And every time today they'd held hands or he'd put his arm round her or kissed her, she'd wanted more.

It was time to move on.

And Sam Price was the man who'd help her to do that. No strings. No commitments. Just these few days. A holiday fling with no complications for either of them.

'Yes,' she said.

'Is there anyone you need to call, to let them know where you are?' he asked.

'Maybe the hotel, as they're expecting me?'

'Sure,' he said.

She made the call quickly to explain she was staying with a friend for the night; and then she took his hand and drew it up to her lips. 'Ready,' she said.

Without comment, Sam took her hand and led her up to his flat.

Once inside, he kissed her, this time with more urgency than he'd kissed her by the waterfall. She slid her fingers under the edge of his long-sleeved top, and gently tugged upwards.

He took a step back and lifted his arms, letting her take it off completely.

She sucked in a breath as she took in the view: he was bare-chested, slightly dishevelled from where she'd just removed his top and utterly sexy. It made her want to touch him, especially because he had perfect musculature: well-toned arms, a broad chest and a six-pack leading down to a narrow waist. Sam had told her he'd worked with the mountain rescue team as well as in emergency medicine, and she could see he'd kept himself fit since he'd been in Iceland.

'So do I pass muster?' he asked lightly.

'Just about,' she teased.

'Good.'

'Not a gorilla,' she said with a smile, brushing the light sprinkling of hair across his chest, 'but also not looking as if you're so vain that you wax.'

'I had my back waxed, once.'

She waited, knowing there was more to this story: from what she'd learned about Sam so far this week, she knew he wasn't vain.

'It was to raise money for equipment for the mountain rescue team,' he admitted. 'I got people to sponsor me per strip. They paid me double if they wanted to take the strip off themselves.'

'Sounds painful. Having my eyebrows done is bad enough,' she said.

'It was for a good cause. Like you doing the running for your friend Dani.' He traced the curve of her eyebrows with the tip of his finger. 'You're beautiful.'

'So are you,' she said, and splayed her fingers across his chest.

'And you're wearing too much.'

'Do something about it,' she invited.

He peeled off her top, then traced the curve of her collarbones, making a shiver of pure desire run through her. Then he drew one finger slowly down her sternum until he reached the V between her breasts. 'Your turn,' he said, his voice husky.

Her hands shook slightly as she undid the button at the waistband of his hiking trousers, then took the tab of his zip and drew it down. She could feel the heat and hardness of his erection as she pulled the zip downwards, and it made her catch her breath. She pushed the material downwards, and let it pool around his ankles. He pulled off his hiking boots so he could step out of his trousers and she was amused to note that he removed his socks at the same time.

'My turn.' He did the same with her hiking trousers, teasing her by sliding his fingertips underneath the waistband and stroking her skin, and then finally undoing the zip and sliding them down. She copied what he'd done with his own hiking boots, and he smiled when he saw her socks. 'Pink and fluffy.'

'They're warm, and they stop my boots rubbing.'

He dropped to his knees before her and removed her socks. 'You have beautiful feet. Pretty toes.'

Her toenails were painted an in-your-face scarlet.

'I don't wear nail polish at work. This is my indulgence,' she said.

'And it's a nice one.' He rocked back on his haunches and looked at her. 'You're beautiful, Hayley. And I want you. More than I've wanted anyone in a while.'

'It's the same for me.' She dragged in a breath. 'But I'm not on the pill.'

'I have condoms,' he said. 'Not because I habitually seduce a girl in every group I take out—more like my big brother's idea of a flat warming present.' His mouth twitched. 'But he also got me a coffee machine, so I'm good.'

'Coffee and condoms.' She couldn't help smiling back. 'It's an interesting combination.'

'I can think of a more interesting combination.' He stood up, and brushed his mouth against hers. 'And a more comfortable place.' He took her hand, and led her to his bedroom.

It had the same clean lines as the other rooms in his flat, all pale wood and cream walls and slate-coloured linen.

And then she stopped thinking as he kissed her again, cupping her face and catching her lower lip between his. When he deepened the kiss, she tangled her fingers in his hair. He drew her closer, and unhooked her bra, then let her breasts spill into his hands.

'So beautiful,' he whispered.

She wasn't sure which of the two of them finished undressing the other, but at last they were naked. He pushed the duvet aside, then lifted her and laid her gently against the pillows. She tipped her head back, and he traced a necklace of kisses across her throat. She caught her breath, wanting more and pushing up towards him. He slid one hand between her thighs, teasing her with clever fingers as he stroked upwards; by the time he reached her sex, she was quivering.

But he hadn't finished. By any means. He shifted on the bed so he could stroke her skin with his hands and his mouth, until she was simmering like the volcanoes the island was built upon.

'Now?' he whispered.

'Now.'

He reached into the drawer of his bedside cabinet and retrieved a condom, then ripped open the foil packet.

'My turn,' she said, and rolled the condom on, taking it slowly. By the time she'd finished, his breathing had quickened.

And then at last he knelt between her thighs and eased his body into hers.

It felt good. Strange—his weight and the feel of his muscles weren't what she'd been used to, what she'd been missing—but good.

And when her climax hit unexpectedly, spilling through her, she held on to him very tightly, feeling the answering surge in his own body.

Once he'd dealt with the condom, he turned to her. 'Help yourself to anything you need in the bathroom—the towels are all fresh.'

'Thanks.' She enjoyed the shower; she was getting used to the slightly sulphurous smell of the hot water, and she still found it amazing that the water was heated purely by geothermal energy. Iceland really was the land of ice and fire.

When she came back to the bedroom, wrapped in a towel, he'd pulled on a pair of jeans, though he hadn't bothered putting on a shirt.

'I know your hotel's only just down the road,' he said, 'but would you like me to put your clothes through the washing machine?'

She hadn't thought that far ahead—about having to leave here tomorrow in the same clothes she'd been wearing all day, even if she was only going between here and her hotel to change. 'Actually, thanks, that'd be good. Then I won't have to stop in at the hotel in the morning to get clean clothes.'

'Here—put this on, or if you'd prefer to wear one of my shirts then help yourself to whatever you want in the wardrobe.' He handed her a soft, fluffy towelling robe, then gathered up her laundry and headed out to his kitchen.

Sam was strangely domesticated for someone who seemed so at home in the wild landscape. And she rather liked that.

She borrowed a T-shirt from his wardrobe so she had something to sleep in, and wrapped the robe round herself before following him to the kitchen. He poured her another glass of wine, and they curled up on his sofa and watched the final rays of the sunset. Then he gently led her back to bed and made love to her again.

And it was so, so good to feel another body curved around hers as she finally fell asleep.

The next morning, Sam woke Hayley with a kiss. 'What would you like for breakfast?' he asked. 'I have to admit to developing a waffle habit out here—Martin bought me a waffle iron and some maple syrup to go with the coffee machine.'

'I'd love waffles. Thank you.' She smiled. 'Can I do anything?'

'There's very little that needs doing so, no, it's fine. I've put your dry clothes in the bathroom, by the way.'

She appreciated his thoughtfulness. 'Thank you.'

By the time she'd showered and changed, she could smell waffles cooking. She thoroughly enjoyed them, and was amused that he'd also provided a dish of blueberries and a dish of Icelandic yogurt in a nod to healthy eating.

'So would you like to see the geological stuff today?' he asked.

'Yes, please. And I'd also like to take you out to dinner,' she said, 'as it's my last day.'

'Thank you—I accept.'

She insisted on doing the washing up while he had a shower; then he drove her to Thingvellir National Park.

'The name means "Parliament Meadows" and it's where the original parliament was located,' he explained.

They walked down through a path in a canyon whose walls were dark brown and it felt to Hayley like some kind of lunar landscape.

'So is this rock basalt?' she asked.

'Lava lobes,' he said. 'We're walking between two tectonic plates—this is where you can actually see the drift between the North American and Eurasian plates.'

'The place where the earth actually splits.' And where new land sprang up. 'Maybe this is a lesson for us,' she said. 'Even when something breaks and changes utterly, life still goes on—the land here grows and changes.' Just as they would grow and change from the wreckage of their old lives.

He looked at her. 'Maybe.'

Maybe, she thought, they were both starting to heal. And last night with Sam had shown her that she was ready to move on. To learn to love someone else. And she'd always be grateful to him for helping her get past the place where she'd been stuck.

After a day's exploring, they ate a final dinner in the city centre, then stopped for an ice cream in the Old Harbour area and walked back along the sea wall to her hotel, where they sat with their arms round each other and watched the final gold, orange and red of the setting sun.

'Thank you for making this week so good for me,' she said. There was a lump in her throat; right at that moment, she didn't want to leave. 'I have a ridiculously early flight tomorrow.' And she had a feeling that what she would miss most about Iceland was Sam. 'So I guess...' She swallowed hard. 'I guess this is goodbye.'

'I'm not very good at goodbyes,' he said.

'Me, neither.'

'So let's do it in Icelandic. *Bless*,' he said.

'*Bless*,' she repeated.

He kissed her lightly. 'Safe travels.'

'You, too.' She wasn't going to get clingy with him now. 'And thank you for everything.'

'Pleasure. Be happy, Hayley.'

'You, too.' She stroked his face.

He kissed her a last time, then turned and walked away.

Their paths would probably never cross again. Though she had a feeling that their holiday fling had done both of them some good.

And now it was time to get on with the rest of her life.

CHAPTER FOUR

'HE'S UTTERLY GORGEOUS—he reminds me of that American actor I like,' Danielle said, looking through the photographs on Hayley's laptop. 'I'm not surprised you fell for the guy.'

'I didn't fall for him,' Hayley protested.

Danielle scoffed. 'Of course not. That's why he's in half your photographs.'

'That's simply because he was there, showing me round the island. He was kind.'

'In those pictures, he doesn't look at you as if he was just being kind,' Danielle pointed out. 'And you don't look at him that way, either.'

Hayley felt the colour burst into her face.

Danielle laughed. 'Don't be embarrassed. I'm glad you kept up the spirit of the Year of Saying Yes. That trip did you a lot of good.'

'It was just one night,' Hayley muttered. 'Anyway, have *you* done anything on that front?' she asked, trying to deflect her best friend's attention.

'We're not talking about me. We're talking about

you. Besides, I haven't met anyone who's really caught my eye, whereas you have.'

'It was a holiday romance. A fling,' Hayley said. 'I enjoyed it while it lasted, but now it's over and I'm fine with that, too.'

'But it did you good. Now you can really start to move on. You know Evan wouldn't have wanted you to lock yourself away.'

'I know.'

'And it's the Year of Saying Yes.'

'Right now I've only got time for work and training,' Hayley pointed out.

'We'll see,' Danielle said.

On Monday morning, Sam cycled to Muswell Hill Hospital and walked into the emergency department, ready for his first shift in his new job. As he'd expected, there was some admin to sort out first, including getting his hospital identity badge; and then Michael Harcourt, the head of the department, took him round to introduce him to the other staff.

'Ah, Dr Clark—just the woman I wanted to see,' Michael boomed as a woman in a white coat came out of a cubicle. 'Hayley, meet your replacement, Samuel Price. Sam, Hayley's just been promoted to senior registrar and you've taken over from her. You'll be working together.'

Of all the places...

Sam hadn't told Hayley that he was about to start a new job in London, and she hadn't told him where she worked. London was a massive city with quite a few hospitals. What were the chances that they'd end up working together? The way her pupils expanded momentarily told him that she was just as shocked and surprised as he was.

This was going to make things awkward. They'd had a fling in Iceland, agreeing that it would be nothing more than that, and they'd said goodbye. What now? Would she want to see if their fling could be something more, something deeper? Or had he just been her transition person, the one who'd helped her to move on after her partner's death, so she wouldn't want to pick up where they'd left off?

The problem was, he didn't know what he wanted, either. He'd really liked the woman he'd started to get to know in Iceland. But then again he'd liked Lynda, too—and his ex-fiancée had let him down so badly. Could he even trust his judgement any more? Would he be making a huge mistake if he started seeing Hayley?

She recovered first, holding her hand out. 'Welcome to Muswell Hill Hospital, Dr Price.'

So she was going to pretend that they'd never met before? OK. That was probably the safest way and saved any awkward explanations. 'Thank you, Dr Clark,' he said, giving her a polite nod and shaking her hand.

'We usually work on first-name terms here,' she said. 'Everyone calls me Hayley.'

'And I'm Sam,' he said.

'I've got a patient coming in any second now with a suspected broken hip. Want to come in at the deep end?' she asked.

'The deep end suits me fine,' he said.

'Good, good. Just as it should be. I'll leave you in Hayley's more than capable hands,' Michael said, and clapped him on the shoulder. 'Look after the lad for me, Hayley, there's a good girl.'

'You know we always look after our own in the Emergency department, Mike,' Hayley said with a smile. 'Let's go and find our patient, Sam.'

When the head of department had gone, Hayley looked straight at Sam. 'We probably need to talk and clear the air—but now isn't the time.'

Yes, they definitely needed to clear the air and establish a few boundaries—the more so because he still felt that physical pull towards her. 'Right now the patients have to come first—but I agree, we need to talk.'

'Lunch?' she suggested.

'Works for me.'

They went to the ambulance bay to meet the paramedics for the handover.

'This is Mrs Ethel Baker,' Dev Kapoor, the lead paramedic, said.

'Hello, Mrs Baker—can we call you Ethel?' Hayley asked.

At the elderly woman's nod, she said, 'I'm Hayley Clark and this is Sam Price, and we're going to look after you—we just need to talk to Dev first, if you don't mind, so he can tell us all about what's happened to you and save you having to go all through it over again.'

'All right, love,' Ethel said, her voice sounding very soft and very weary.

Sam noticed that Hayley took the older woman's hand and held it while she listened to Dev giving them the handover information; he liked the fact that she clearly had compassion and realised that the elderly woman must be in some pain and feeling very scared about what had happened to her.

'Mrs Baker's seventy-eight and she lives on her own. She had a fall last night and couldn't get up again, and she didn't have a call aid button round her neck. Her carer found her this morning and called us.'

No doubt she was cold, stiff and dehydrated, as well as suffering from whatever had caused the fall, Sam thought.

'She can't stand or walk,' Dev said, 'and we suspect a broken hip.'

Which could cause problems with future mobility and independence, Sam knew. 'Is there any medication we need to know about?' he asked.

'We've brought it all with us,' Dev said, handing him a labelled bag. 'The main thing is her Parkinson's medication.'

'Thank you,' Sam said.

'We gave her gas and air for the pain in the ambulance, and when the carer rang the emergency services we advised her not to give Mrs Baker anything to eat or drink, just in case she needs to go into Theatre. So she hasn't eaten or drunk anything since last night,' Dev confirmed.

'And I'm really gasping for a cup of tea,' Ethel said. 'Can I have a cup of tea now?'

No, she couldn't—not when she might be going into Theatre within the hour.

'We'll make you comfortable as soon as we can,'

Hayley promised, 'though we will need to sort out some tests first.'

Between them, Hayley and Sam wheeled her to one of the cubicles so they could assess her, and all the while Hayley held Edith's hand. Sam remembered the feel of her skin against his, and had to shake himself. Until they'd talked and worked out how to deal with the situation, he needed to keep a lid on his feelings.

'Can I ask you, is this the first time you've had a fall, Ethel?' Hayley asked.

'No—sometimes I freeze or I trip over my own feet. It's just how the Parkinson's is. Sometimes I'm on and sometimes I'm off,' Ethel said. 'I know I should have had my call aid button with me, but I just forgot to put it on yesterday.'

'It's easily done,' Sam said. 'Did you hit your head at all when you fell, or can you remember if you blacked out?'

'No. I was just cross with myself at being such an old fool as to fall over.'

There was definitely nothing wrong with her mental state, Sam thought; it was pretty clear to him that she hadn't hit her head. 'Are you in pain now?' he asked.

She nodded. 'It really hurts here.' She pointed to her upper right thigh.

Dev's assessment of a broken hip was probably right, Sam thought, because Ethel's right leg looked slightly shorter and was turned outwards; together with her inability to stand or walk and the position of her pain, the symptoms pointed towards a fracture.

'We can give you some more pain relief,' he said.

Though the fact she'd broken her hip from a single fall worried him. Ethel was very slender, and it made him wonder. 'Has your doctor said anything to you about osteoporosis or brittle bones?'

She pulled a face and shook her head. 'Nothing like that,' she said.

'When you get older, especially if you're a woman,' Hayley said, 'your bones get less dense and develop a kind of honeycomb structure, which means they break more easily—it's called osteoporosis. Once we've got your hip sorted out, I'm going to ask the ward to refer you for a scan so we can see if your bones are thinner.'

'If the scan shows we're right,' Sam said, 'we can give you some tablets to help strengthen your bones, so then if you do fall again you're less likely to end up with a fracture. And we can give you some calcium and vitamin D supplements to help, too.' He paused. 'Can I ask, do you smoke or drink?'

Ethel looked slightly guilty. 'I don't drink much, just a port and lemon at the Legion on a Friday night with my mates. I've been trying to give up the ciggies—I just have the odd one or two. But don't tell my daughter. She thinks I stopped smoking five years ago. Though my old gran lived to a hundred and she smoked like a chimney,' she added, a spark of defiance in her voice.

Hayley smiled. 'So did my great-gran. But here's your reason to give up—smoking makes your bones thinner and that puts you at greater risk of breaking a bone the next time you fall.'

Sam liked the way that Hayley was sympathetic and

realistic at the same time. She was kind, but she didn't try to pretend that problems didn't exist.

'You won't tell my daughter about the ciggies?' Ethel asked.

'No, but do you know if anyone's contacted her to tell her you've been brought here?' Sam asked. 'If not, we can call her.'

'She's down in Brighton,' Ethel said. 'She works and she's got kids. I don't want to bother her.'

'If you were my mum,' Hayley said, 'I'd want to know straight away if you were taken to hospital.'

'I don't want to worry her,' Ethel again.

'We can tell her not to rush because you're going to be here for a while, if that makes you feel any better,' Sam said. 'But I agree with Hayley. I'd want to know if my mum was in hospital—and I'd be really upset if they didn't tell me.'

Ethel sighed. 'All right, then.'

Sam took her temperature and recorded it on the chart, then wrote her up for painkillers and a drip for the dehydration.

'We're pretty sure you've broken your hip,' Hayley said, 'but we need to send you for an X-ray to confirm the diagnosis.'

'If it's broken,' Ethel said, 'what happens then?'

'You'll need surgery,' Sam said. 'The surgeon might be able to use screws, rods and plates to fix it—or you might need a hip replacement.'

'So I won't be able to walk for ages?' she asked, looking worried.

'They'll have you on your feet again, the day after

the operation,' Hayley reassured her. 'But let's make you more comfortable and get that X-ray done first.'

'All right, love.'

While Ethel was being seen by the radiologists, Sam removed a bead from a toddler's nose and Hayley phoned Ethel's daughter, who promised to drive straight up to the hospital. The X-ray confirmed everything they'd feared, and Hayley rang the orthopaedic team to ask for a surgeon to come down to the emergency department.

'Let's go and break the news to Ethel,' Hayley said, and they went to sit by her bed in the cubicle.

'I'm afraid you've definitely broken your hip, Ethel,' Sam said. 'You've broken it inside the socket of your hip.' He took a pad from his pocket and drew a picture of the fracture to show her. 'Unfortunately this kind of break won't heal well, so you'll need a hip replacement.'

'But luckily everything's still where it should be, so it's not complicated enough to worry us,' Hayley added. 'One of the surgeons is coming down to see you.'

'So what happens now?' Ethel asked.

'You'll have the operation later today,' Sam said.

'It'll take a couple of hours,' Hayley added.

'Will they put me out first?' Ethel asked.

'Not necessarily. The surgeon will talk through the anaesthetic options with you,' Sam said.

'After the operation, you'll stay on the orthopaedic ward,' Hayley continued. 'They'll give you painkillers and a drip, pretty much as you have right now, and they'll start to get you back on your feet tomorrow. A physiotherapist will come and see you and teach you some exercises to help with your strength and mobility.'

Ethel frowned. 'So how long will I have to stay in hospital?'

'Until you're back on your feet and mobile again,' Sam said, 'though you might not be quite as mobile as you were before and you might need more help at home.'

Ethel shook her head. 'I don't want to go into one of them nursing homes.'

'Do you live in sheltered accommodation now?' Hayley asked.

'No, I live in the same house I went to the day I married my Brian,' Ethel said. 'Fifty-eight years, I've lived there. But I do have a carer come in every morning to get me up and every evening to help me get to bed. That's the bit I have trouble with.'

'You're going to need a little more support than just twice a day,' Sam said gently. 'I know you're not keen on the idea, but you might need to go to a nursing home for a few weeks after you leave hospital—just for respite care, until you're totally on your feet again and ready to go home.'

Ethel pursed her lips. 'I'm not going into one of those places. They just stick you in a room in front of a telly and talk to you like you're a toddler. I might be old, but I haven't lost my marbles yet.'

Hayley squeezed her hand. 'Nursing homes aren't all like that. Is there anyone in the family you could stay with? Your daughter, maybe?'

'I can't live with my daughter,' Ethel said. 'I love

her dearly, but we'd fight like cat and dog. Anyway, she doesn't have the room.'

'Maybe you could move closer to her, in sheltered accommodation,' Sam suggested, 'so you'd still have a lot of your independence but your daughter wouldn't be so worried about you because she'd know there was someone nearby if you needed help.'

Ethel didn't look convinced. 'I don't want to move.'

'We'll talk about it again after the surgeon's seen you,' Hayley said.

'I'm still not going in one of them nursing homes,' Ethel warned. 'They stink of boiled cabbage and pee.'

Hayley smiled. 'We can try and find you one that doesn't.'

'Hmm. Can I have that cup of tea now, please? I'm gasping.'

'Sorry, but you can't have a cup of tea until the surgeon's seen you,' Hayley said. 'You're going to have some form of anaesthetic, so it's not safe to have anything except water before the operation—and even water's banned for two hours before the operation. It's to make sure you're not sick during the operation and end up with something in your lungs.'

'Well, worse things happen at sea, as my old mum used to say,' Ethel said.

'I'll make you that tea myself after your op,' Sam said. 'And toast. I'm really good at toast.' He looked Hayley in the eye. 'And waffles.'

And he was gratified that she went very slightly pink. So she remembered, then? The question was whether she wanted to repeat it.

'We'll come and see you again as soon as the surgeon's available,' Hayley promised.

Between them, they saw an eight-year-old who'd been tripped over in the playground and ended up with a Colles' fracture of his wrist, a woman with what turned out to be an allergic reaction to her new eyelash extensions, and a man complaining of back pain after he'd overdone the gardening the previous day; and then it was time to see Ethel's daughter and the surgeon.

The surgeon sent Ethel for a DEXA scan, and meanwhile, Sam talked to Ethel's daughter about rehab options and how to get her mum the right support. The DEXA scan confirmed that Ethel had osteoporosis; and Sam accompanied Ethel and her daughter up to the orthopaedic ward to help settle them in.

When he got back down to the emergency department, Hayley tapped her watch. 'Quick lunch?'

And an overdue talk. 'Fine.'

She led him to the canteen, and they both selected a sandwich and coffee before finding a quiet table.

'Ethel's settled,' Sam said. 'I promised I'd go and see her at the end of my shift and make her that cup of tea.'

'Above and beyond, hmm?' Hayley asked.

'No. Just putting myself in the shoes of our patients and using a bit of empathy,' Sam said.

'I wasn't being snippy.'

'No.' The woman he'd met in Iceland had been warm and sweet. He'd liked her a lot. But that was when he'd thought she was only going to be a temporary part of her life. What now?

'I had no idea you were going to be our new registrar,' she said. 'You never said you were coming to London.'

Because he'd thought he'd never see her again. 'I had no idea I was taking your old job,' he countered.

She gave him a wry smile. 'Is this where we both do the bit from *Casablanca*, except it's hospitals rather than gin joints?'

'Pretty much,' he said.

'OK. Well, I'm not going to pussyfoot around it.' She lifted her chin. 'You and me—I hope we can be friends.'

'Friends,' he said. Which wasn't quite how either of them had seen things in Iceland. And the attraction was still there between them; a couple of times during their shift this morning, they'd accidentally brushed against each other, and he'd seen her pupils dilate slightly. Just as his own probably had, and his skin had tingled where it had touched hers. Had it been the same for her, too?

'Anything else would be too complicated,' she said. 'I've seen too many departmental relationships end in tears. And especially now, as you and I are working closely together.'

'And I've taken over your old role, so you're effectively my boss. Fair enough.' Hayley had made it very clear she wanted to shut down the connection they'd shared. Which was a shame, because the more Sam saw of her, the more he liked her. They'd slipped into an easy working relationship, as if they'd known each other for years and knew how each other thought. The kind of relationship he'd thought he had with Lynda—and he'd been very wrong indeed about that. So maybe Hayley was right and they'd be better to keep this strictly platonic, rather than try to build on what they'd shared in Iceland. Trying to find a safer subject, he asked, 'How's the running training going?'

She looked surprised and then pleased that he'd asked. 'OK, though obviously Dani's not able to go alongside me and pace me when we do the outdoor runs. She sends me off and sits on a bench in the park with a stopwatch going and listens to music while she waits for me to get back to her. But at the end of the day my finish time doesn't really matter. What matters is that I actually finish.'

Maybe this would be a way of getting some of the easiness back between them. 'I've only just moved here and don't know any good running routes,' he said, 'so if you want me to join you when you're training outside and act as your pacemaker, you'd be doing me a favour as well. It'd be a win for both of us.'

'I guess.' She looked thoughtful. 'Do you mind if I talk to Dani about it, first?'

'Sure. Make it clear I'm not thinking of muscling in on her training sessions. It's simply a way of helping us both out.'

'So you and me, we're good?' she checked.

'We're good.' And he was just going to have to ignore that attraction he felt towards her, because they weren't going to be anything other than friends.

'Great. So have you settled in London OK?'

'I'm getting there,' he said. 'My flat's near enough for me to cycle in to work, and the department seems nice.'

'They're a good bunch on our team,' she said. 'Everyone pulls their weight, and everyone gets on well together. Actually, there's a team night out on Friday—it's the monthly quiz night at the pub across the road. We always have a team and there's usually one from Paediatrics and another from Maternity. And the pub does the best chips in London. Why don't you come along, if you're not busy?'

'I might just do that.'

'Oh, and while I remember—the departmental Christmas meal is the first week of December,' she added.

'Christmas?' He raised an eyebrow. 'It's only August. Isn't it too early to be thinking about Christmas?'

'If you don't book a venue well in advance, nowhere's got any spaces left,' she said. 'Surely it's like that in Manchester, too?'

So she remembered where he used to work. 'I guess.'

'We also do a Secret Santa, where you draw someone's name and buy them a present—Jennie, the senior receptionist, is in charge of that and she takes the deposit and choices for the meal, so have a word with her.'

'Right. Thanks.'

'Great. That's that organised, then.' She glanced at her watch. 'I guess we'd better get back to the department.'

CHAPTER FIVE

ON TUESDAY, HAYLEY and Sam were both rostered onto Minors and didn't see much of each other all day. But Hayley caught him at the end of their shift. 'I've spoken to Dani. She says if you'd like to join us tomorrow, we're doing the training straight after work and then grabbing something for dinner from the café in the park—obviously sitting at one of the tables outside, because we'll be a bit sweaty and disgusting after our run.'

'Sounds good. Thank you,' Sam said.

Wednesday was just as busy, but again Hayley caught up with Sam at the end of their shift. She'd already changed into her running gear, and waited for him to change, too.

'So where are we running?' he asked.

'Alexandra Park,' she said. 'It's by Alexandra Palace, the old BBC television studios—part of it used to be a theatre, in Victorian times. And there are amazing views from the park across the whole of London.'

'Are we walking there?' he asked.

'No. We're getting a taxi,' she said, 'because of Dani's foot.' She waved to a shorter, dark-haired woman who was sitting on one of the benches in the hospital's main reception area, and whose foot was encased in a walking cast. Next to her, propped against the bench, were crutches.

'Danielle Owens, meet Sam Price,' Hayley said when they'd gone over to meet her.

Danielle and Sam shook hands. 'Nice to meet you,' Danielle said.

Sam wondered how much Hayley had told her. Then again, they were best friends, and he knew from his sister that women talked about that sort of thing.

'So you're going to help us with the running training?' Danielle asked.

'If you don't mind,' he said politely.

'I'm glad of the help. I can't exactly get a megaphone and shout at Haze from the middle of the park to pick up her pace,' Danielle said, glaring at her cast. 'I wish I hadn't had to ask her to do this in the first place.'

'You didn't ask. I offered. And even *you* can't run with a fractured second and third metatarsal,' Hayley said firmly.

'Oh, I could do it, all right,' Danielle said with a grin. 'It just wouldn't be sensible. And I want this thing off my foot as soon as possible, so I'm doing what I'm told.'

'For once,' Hayley teased.

They took a taxi to the park, and Danielle went through the training programme briefly with Sam.

'So we have about six weeks between now and race day,' Sam said. 'You're doing interval training indoors on a treadmill, and then the longer runs outside.'

'Because the interval training will help with the

pace, but running indoors is very different from running outdoors—and, as the actual race is outside, then Haze needs experience in running outdoors,' Danielle explained.

'Agreed. This looks like a really workable plan.'

'Great. I'll let you set the pace for the four-miler, then,' Danielle said with a smile. 'I'm going to get some coffee from the café and do the dreaded four-letter-word thing with my foot. See you both when you're done.'

Sam discovered that Hayley had been telling the truth: the park was pretty, full of people walking dogs and parents with small children. The Alexandra Palace sprawled behind the trees, a huge yellow-brick Victorian building with red-brick detailing and arched windows, a glass roof and a tall transmitter mast. When they ran past the palace itself, the views over London were stunning. He settled into a slower pace than he would normally have taken, bearing in mind that Hayley was still a relative novice to running.

A couple of times, his hand accidentally brushed against hers, and it sent a tingle through him. Did she feel it, too? But she'd made it clear that as far as she was concerned they were colleagues only, so it was pointless wondering. Besides, even though he liked her professionally, that was a whole different thing than trusting her with his heart. There was a huge difference between a no-strings fling and a real relationship.

They rejoined Danielle around forty-five minutes later.

'So how was it?' Danielle asked.

'Wonderful,' Hayley said without batting an eyelid.

'You hated it,' Danielle said with a sigh.

'I'd much rather do dance aerobics than running,' Hayley admitted. 'But this is for a really good cause—the MRI scanner for the newborns in your department.' She looked at Sam. 'And it was better running with someone else. Even though you obviously had to slow down for me and I feel a bit guilty about that.'

'Don't. Running's still running,' he said. 'I enjoyed it too.'

Danielle pushed a menu towards him. 'My shout,' she said.

'There's no nee—' he began, and she rolled her eyes.

'Yes, there is. I'm saying thank you for helping us out. Be gracious,' she said.

'I told you she was bossy,' Hayley said with a grin. 'Take advice from someone who's known her since the first day at university. It's quickest to just agree with her, because she always gets her way in the end.'

'Then thank you, Danielle.' Sam chose pasta, salad and a glass of mineral water; Danielle and Hayley chose the same.

'So how are you finding Muswell Hill, did you do a lot of running where you were before, and where exactly were you before?' Danielle asked after she'd ordered and paid.

He laughed. 'In order: OK, yes, Manchester.'

She looked pained. 'A man of few words? How very disappointing.'

'If you meant the hospital, you work there yourself so you know what it's like. If you meant the area, I haven't been here for long enough to really explore it,' he said.

'But what I've seen is pretty, and I like the park. It's about a twenty-minute walk from the hospital, isn't it?'

'Uphill all the way, so it's a good warm-up for a run,' Danielle said. 'What made you move to London from Manchester?'

That wasn't something he was ready to open up about, at least not yet. He'd given Hayley the very bare bones; given that she was effectively his senior, he probably ought to fill in some of the gaps reasonably soon. 'It was time for a change,' he said lightly.

'Fair comment,' Danielle said. 'Haze said you spent the whole summer in Iceland, working with your brother.'

'It was kind of a sabbatical,' he said.

'Doing stuff like glacier walking? And I've seen all the photographs, by the way.'

'Yes, glacier walking's part of it. I did tours for very small groups in a four-wheel drive car, so our clients got to see some of the sights off the beaten track as well as the tourist hotspots—all of which are actually worth seeing,' he added, 'as you'll know since you've seen the pictures.'

'Don't you need training to do glacier walking?' Danielle asked.

He nodded. 'I was part of the mountain rescue team when I was back in Manchester, so it was an extension of the training I'd done in climbing.'

'Rock and ice,' she said thoughtfully. 'Does that mean you're into extreme sports?'

He looked at her, intrigued. 'Does that mean you are, too?'

'Please don't encourage her,' Hayley said. 'Remember, she's in a walking cast.'

'I don't do extreme stuff,' Danielle said, looking wistful, 'but I really did want to touch a glacier—I'd hoped to persuade Haze into doing the walking tour on it while we were there. That and the whales were the two things I was really looking forward to most.'

'Go to Iceland next summer, when your foot's healed properly and it will cope with the demands of ice walking, which in my professional opinion won't be for at least two months after that cast comes off,' Sam said. 'I'll get Martin, my brother, to take you out on the glacier.'

'Thank you. I accept. I have to admit, I was hideously jealous with every picture Haze texted me.' She reached over to squeeze Hayley's hand. 'And that proves I was right to make her go. She needed a break.'

'Before I started my new job,' Hayley said swiftly.

Sam intercepted the glance between them and could guess what Dani had really meant: space to move on from her partner's death.

'Iceland's a good place for thinking,' he said. 'It's something to do with the quality of the light out there.'

'You're hardly going to do glacier walking in London,' Danielle said, 'so what do you plan to do here?'

'Actually, you can do ice climbing in London, which is the next best thing.' He'd looked it up and planned to book a slot on the ice wall for his next day off. 'And, as there isn't exactly a need for a mountain rescue team in London, I've signed up for the MERIT roster.'

MERIT—the Medical Emergency Response Incident Team—was a small team of doctors and nurses who could be called out to the site of an accident to see casualties who had life-threatening injuries but might be trapped for another hour or more, or to do triage at the scene of major incidents such as a bus crash or an industrial fire.

There was a shared glance between Hayley and Danielle that he didn't quite understand. Now didn't feel like the right time to ask for an explanation, so he added, 'But what I really want to try is rap jumping.'

Hayley blinked. 'I've never heard of it. What is it?'

'Like abseiling,' he said. 'Except you go forwards instead of backwards.'

'Hang on. You're telling me you stand at the top of a building and then you just jump off?' Danielle asked.

'A very tall building or a cliff,' he agreed. 'But you're belayed the whole time, and you have a brakeman who slows you down—so you don't just hit the ground from a hundred and eighty feet up and break most of your bones. It's a gentle landing. Let me show you.' He found a video on the internet and handed his phone to her. 'Here.'

Hayley and Danielle watched the video together, both looking more and more shocked as the seconds ticked by.

'That's *horrific*,' Hayley said. 'Why would anyone want to take such a risk of something going wrong and put themselves in danger like that?'

'The adrenaline rush,' he said. 'And there are plenty of safeguards. It's probably less of a risk than cycling to work in London, and I do that every day.'

'You obviously didn't deal with many cyclist casualties in Manchester,' Hayley said feelingly. 'My first week's placement in the emergency department put me off cycling in London for good.'

'Everything carries a risk,' he said.

'But some things are riskier than others. Some things are…' She grimaced and looked away. 'Oh, just ignore me. I'm ranting.'

Why would she be so antsy about people taking risks? She'd said her fiancé had been killed in an industrial accident. But those were so rare. Was there more to this than she'd told him? Had her fiancé taken some extra kind of risk? What kind of accident had it been? Not that he could ask any of this without being intrusive. He could hardly ask her best friend either. So he'd just have to wait until Hayley was prepared to confide in him.

He switched the conversation to a safer topic, and discovered during dinner that he really liked Hayley's best friend: there was absolutely no sexual chemistry between them, but he liked Danielle's energy and sense of humour a great deal.

And he didn't let himself think about the chemistry between himself and Hayley. The way his skin felt super-sensitive when it accidentally brushed against hers. The way his pulse rate speeded up when he caught her eye. The way he really, really wanted to kiss her again.

'Can we give you a lift home in our taxi?' Danielle asked. 'I say "our"—Haze and I live in neighbouring streets.'

'It's fine,' he said. 'It's a downhill walk from here to

the hospital, and anyway I need to collect my bike for tomorrow morning.'

'OK.' Danielle reached out to shake his hand, and then said, 'Oh, come here,' and gave him a hug. 'It was nice to meet you, Sam. And we'll see you for training on Friday.'

'We can't train on Friday night. We've got the pub quiz,' Hayley said.

'Sorry—I was so focused on the race that I forgot it was this Friday. And our department is so going to beat you this time. I've had the team mugging up on literature and art. We know our stuff.' Danielle turned to Sam. 'How about Saturday for training?'

'It'd have to be the morning,' he said. 'I'm working a late shift on Saturday.'

'That's fine by me. Shall we meet here at nine?' Danielle suggested.

'One condition,' he said, 'you let me buy pastries and coffee afterwards.'

'I love pastries and coffee,' she said, her face full of enthusiasm. 'You're on. See you Saturday.'

'See you Saturday.' He looked at Hayley. 'See you in the department tomorrow.'

And he tried not to mind that she didn't hug him, the way Danielle had.

'Right, madam. So when exactly were you going to tell me that your new registrar was the gorgeous guy from Iceland?' Danielle asked, once they were in the taxi and out of Sam's hearing. 'Come on. You must've known that I'd recognise him from the photographs.'

'Um… Sorry.'

'So what happens now? Do you carry on where you left off in Iceland?'

Hayley shook her head. 'We're colleagues.'

Danielle raised an eyebrow. 'And why is that a problem? Half the couples I know first met at work. And he's *lovely*. I don't just mean the way he looks. He's a really nice guy. Not my type, but absolutely yours.'

'He cycles to work. He likes extreme sports.' Hayley sucked in a breath. 'And now I know he's signed up for MERIT. You and I both know how dangerous it can be out there. No, there are way too many risks in his life for me.'

'You need a little risk in life to keep you moving,' Danielle said gently. 'Don't throw the baby out with the bath water.'

'I can't do it, Dani,' Hayley said. 'I can't take that risk. What if something goes wrong?'

'What if it doesn't?' Danielle countered. 'And you know as well as I do, between the Medical Incident Officer and whoever's in charge of the inner zone at an incident, the MERIT team is only allowed in if it's safe for them to be there. I think you should give him a chance.'

'I can't. Losing Evan was like having a black hole punched into the middle of my life. I can't go through that again.' She dragged in a breath. 'Yes, I like Sam. I more than like him. He's good to work with, he's great with the patients and whoever comes in with them, and he's… Well, you've met him.' Physically, he was just her type and she was finding it hard to resist him. Every time his hand had accidentally brushed against hers in the park, she'd been tempted to let her fingers catch his and hold on. She'd really had to hold herself back.

'I think he more than likes you, too,' Danielle said. 'The way he looks at you is pretty obvious.'

'We agreed to be just friends. It's too complicated for anything else. We work together.'

'There's nothing wrong with working with your partner.'

Hayley looked at her and narrowed her eyes. 'Danielle Owens, is there something you'd like to tell me?'

'No.' Danielle flapped a dismissive hand. 'I'm not seeing anyone—and anyway, we're not talking about me. This is about you and Sam. Just give the man a chance.'

'I can't,' Hayley said. 'I just can't take the risk.'

Though she thought about it all the next day. And the next.

She was definitely aware of Sam. Every time their hands accidentally touched at work, it made her tingle all over. And she kept catching herself looking at his mouth and remembering exactly how good that mouth had made her feel. Remembering what it had felt like to make love with him. Remembering what it had felt like to wake up in his arms.

But how could she let anything happen between them again, knowing that he would voluntarily put himself at risk? That he was more than prepared to step into a disaster zone to help, regardless of the risk to his own life? She'd been there before and she'd lost. Badly. How could she put herself back in that position?

'Hey,' Sam said, when they broke for lunch. 'The pub quiz this evening doesn't start until seven, right?'

'Right.'

'Do you want to go for a coffee first?'

She ought to say no. But somehow she found herself agreeing. And so they sat in a café a couple of doors down from the pub, drinking lattes and eating pastries.

'There's something I wanted to talk to you about,' he said. 'The reason why I spent the summer in Iceland. Why I nearly left medicine.'

'You don't need to explain anything. Apart from the fact that I have nothing to do with the decision on employing staff in the department, I already know you're perfectly competent,' she said. 'We worked together on that boat to help Milton Adams with his asthma attack, and I've worked with you for a week here. I've seen more than enough to know you're good at what you do.'

He inclined his head. 'Thank you. I appreciate that. But things tend to leak out, so I'd rather you heard this from me. I took a sabbatical because I was suspended.'

It was the last thing she'd expected. She stared at him. 'You were suspended? But… Why?' She didn't understand.

'We lost a patient. He came in saying he'd been feeling fluey for about a week—his GP had told him to rest, but he wasn't feeling any better and his wife had nagged him to get another appointment. He couldn't get an appointment with his GP, so he decided to come in to us to stop his wife having a go at him. He said he'd had a bit of indigestion, but nothing serious.' He frowned. 'Something didn't seem right to me, but I couldn't quite put my finger on it. Not until I asked him about his medical history and he told me he was diabetic.'

'He'd had a silent heart attack?' she asked. Diabetes could cause nerve damage, which made it less likely that the patient would feel any pains in the chest during a heart attack.

He nodded. 'I said I wanted to give him an ECG because that was the only way of checking if he'd had a silent heart attack, and if the ECG showed that was the case we'd start him on treatment immediately. We checked his sugar levels and they were off the scale. Halfway through the ECG he arrested again. Except we didn't manage to get him back.' He sighed. 'His family were distraught. I guess they couldn't accept that it had happened, and they were looking for someone to blame because that was the only way they could make sense of it. They made a negligence claim. Obviously the hospital had to investigate the case properly, so my team was suspended, pending enquiries.'

'Obviously they cleared you.' Or he wouldn't be working as a doctor now.

'Yes. I was the one who'd made the correct diagnosis and we'd followed protocol exactly. And all our paperwork was in good order, because that's how I was taught and what I expected from my juniors, too.' He grimaced. 'We did everything right. But it still didn't save our patient.'

'He'd already had at least one silent heart attack, from the sound of it,' she said. 'He could've had another one at any time—at home, on the way to the hospital or even in the waiting room. And, because he didn't get the usual pain signals, he didn't seek treatment in time and there was existing damage to his blood vessels and heart muscle, which meant his next heart attack was fatal. It wasn't your fault.'

Her reaction stunned him. It was what he'd expected from Lynda—real belief in him, instead of asking if he might have missed one little thing.

Hayley believed in him.

And she'd known him only for a few days—he and Lynda had been together for three years. If anyone should have doubts about him, surely it should be Hayley?

Something felt as if it had cracked inside him.

'I know you can't save everyone who comes into the emergency department,' he said. 'But this one really hit home. We all felt as if we'd failed. I resigned from the mountain rescue team. How could I go out to rescue people if I wasn't fit to practise medicine?'

'It was a formality,' she pointed out.

And if his own fiancée hadn't doubted him, maybe Sam would've felt that way, too. But the combination of the suspension and Lynda's lack of belief in him had knocked his belief in himself as a doctor.

'I wasn't the only one with doubts,' he said. 'One of my team has left medicine completely.'

'That's a shame.' She paused. 'And the timing was hard, too, being just after you broke up with your ex.'

This was his cue to tell her about Lynda. But the words stuck in his throat. In the end, he said, 'Martin realised that I was sitting at home brooding, going over and over what had happened and trying to work out what I could've done differently so I could've actually saved my patient. He dragged me out to Iceland on the grounds that he needed help with his business. He didn't actually need my help at all,' Sam admitted, 'but it was good to be kept too busy to think. And, as I said earlier, there's something about the light out there that makes it a good place to let things marinate in the back of your head. And it made me realise I didn't want to throw away thirteen years of training.' Five years of studying for his degree, two years of post-graduate foundation training, three years of core training and three years of higher specialty training, as well as the expertise he'd gained since then.

'I think,' she said, 'if medicine hadn't been your calling, then you would've ignored the tour guide on the boat when she asked if there was a doctor on board. Especially as she must've told you I was already helping.'

'An uncontrolled asthma attack can be pretty scary to witness,' he said. 'I thought I might be able to help you deal with whoever was accompanying the patient. And I guess it was a kind of test, to see if I'd done the right thing in accepting the job here.'

'You did,' she said. 'I don't know how good you're going to be where our quiz team is concerned, but you're definitely the right person for our team at the hospital.'

'Thank you. I wasn't fishing for compliments.'

'I know. I was just telling you straight, like Dani would.' She paused. 'This won't go any further than me, though I assume Mike knows.'

'It was in my application form—and I told him about it at the interview,' Sam said.

'If he'd had any doubts about you, he wouldn't have hired you,' she pointed out. 'And he did the right thing.'

'Thanks. I have to admit, I had my doubts when I applied.'

'That's understandable. I've never been suspended or investigated, but it must really knock your belief in yourself.'

'It did.' But what had really destroyed him was Lynda's lack of faith. The way she hadn't stood by him. The fact she'd broken their engagement because she'd thought he'd hold her back in her career.

'But from what I've seen you don't cut corners,' Hayley said. 'Your boss in Manchester must have told you that.'

He smiled. 'She did. I learnt a lot of Hindi swear words from her, the day she told me I was suspended.'

'I'm glad you didn't leave medicine,' she said. She lifted her coffee cup and clinked it against his. 'Here's to teamwork. Welcome to Muswell Hill. And also you'd better be good at general knowledge questions, because Dani will be unbearable if the Maternity team actually beats us in the quiz.'

He smiled then. 'Teamwork,' he echoed.

The emergency department team was victorious in the quiz, and Sam teased Danielle mercilessly about it the next morning when he met her and Hayley in the park for training. By the end of the next week, he felt completely part of the team and as if he'd worked at Muswell Hill Hospital for years instead of a fortnight.

But then he called in his next patient. 'Pauline Jacobs?'

She was middle-aged, overweight, and her face looked almost grey. 'I haven't been feeling well for the last few days,' she said. 'I know I shouldn't be bothering the emergency department, but I couldn't get an appointment with my doctor for another couple of weeks, and the pharmacist told me to come here.'

'You've done the right thing,' he reassured her. 'I'm Sam Price. May I call you Pauline?'

'Of course.'

'Tell me about your symptoms, Pauline,' he invited.

'I'm just so tired,' she said. 'I'd say I had the flu, but you don't get flu at the end of September, do you?'

He went cold.

No.

Not again.

'It's not common,' he said. 'So you're suffering from extreme tiredness and feeling fluey.'

'And I've been getting dizzy,' she said. 'Plus I'm out of breath just going up one set of stairs—by the time I've got to my desk on the second floor at work, I need a sit-down. I know I need to lose weight and I ought to go to the gym and get fit, but between teenagers and my job I don't get a second to myself. I haven't got time to do exercise.'

He was pretty sure he knew where this was going. 'Are you taking any medication?' he asked.

'Statins for my cholesterol, blood pressure tablets, and my diabetic tablets.'

'Have you been diagnosed diabetic for long?' he asked.

'Three years. I do watch what I eat, I really do, and I even turn down cake when people in my department bring them in for birthdays—but it's so difficult to lose weight.'

Especially when she was heading towards the menopause and had a battery of hormones to contend with as well. 'I think,' he said gently, 'you've had a heart attack.'

'But wouldn't I get chest pain?' Pauline asked, looking puzzled. 'When you see someone on the telly have a heart attack, they clutch their chest and everything. I've had a bit of indigestion, but that's my fault because I know garlic does that to me.'

'What I think's happened is something called a silent heart attack,' he said. 'And they're quite common— about a quarter of all heart attacks in the UK are silent. You're diabetic, so I take it your doctor talked to you about being careful about foot care?'

She nodded.

'That's because diabetes can cause nerve damage and the usual pain warning signals aren't transmitted,' he said. 'So the same reason you might not feel any problem with your feet is the same reason why you didn't feel any chest pain. I'm going to check your blood sugar levels and then give you an electrocardiogram— an ECG—which measures the electrical activity of your heart. It doesn't hurt,' he reassured her. 'I'll just stick some flat metal discs to your arms, legs and chest, and the wires will send all the information I need to the machine. Is that OK with you, Pauline?'

'Yes,' she said.

Pauline's blood sugar level was sky-high. He showed her the reading. 'You'd normally be after a reading of four to six.'

'But that's over twenty!' She bit her lip. 'I haven't been stuffing my face with cakes and sugar, honestly I haven't.'

'Stress and illness can make your blood sugar level rise,' he said. 'I'm going to give you some insulin to bring your blood sugar level down, and then we'll look at the ECG.'

The printout from the ECG showed him exactly what had happened. 'OK, Pauline. There's some good news, and some not so good news,' he said.

'Tell me the bad stuff first,' Pauline said with a grimace.

'You've had a silent heart attack,' he said. 'But the good news is that it's what we call an NSTEMI.'

'Which is?'

'A non-ST segment elevation myocardial infarction,' he said. 'What that means is that it's less serious than the other type. The supply of blood to your heart is only partially blocked, and that means a smaller section of your heart will be damaged. I'm going to admit you to the cardiac ward,' he said, 'and they'll give you some blood-thinning medication to make sure no clots develop and cause a more serious heart attack. They'll also do some blood tests to measure if a special protein called troponin shows in your blood—which I'm pretty sure it will, because those proteins go into your blood if there's any damage to your heart. They'll give you a special scan called an echocardiogram, which shows a picture of the inside of your heart so they can see which areas have been damaged and how it's affected the way your heart functions. And they'll also want to check if your arteries have narrowed slightly.'

'What happens if they have?' Pauline asked.

'They can give you something called an angioplasty. It's where they put a little tube called a balloon cath-eter into an artery in your groin or arm, which goes through your blood vessels and up to your heart, guided by X-ray. The tube goes into the narrowed section of the coronary artery, then they inflate a little balloon at the end of the tube to open the artery, and put a bit of flexible metal mesh called a stent into the artery to help keep it open.'

'And that fixes every—' She stopped mid-word.

One look told Sam what had just happened.

History was *not* going to repeat itself. He wasn't going to lose Pauline Jacobs to a silent heart attack. He wasn't going to lose another patient to a silent heart at-tack ever again.

'Crash team!' he yelled, and hit the button.

He moved the back of the bed so Pauline was lying flat, gave two rescue breaths, and started chest com-pressions. When he'd counted to thirty, he checked Pau-line's airway and gave two rescue breaths, then went back to chest compressions.

By the time he'd done the second set of thirty chest compressions, the team was in place, the defibrillator and pads were attached to Pauline's chest and Hayley pronounced, 'She's in VT.'

'We need to shock her,' he said. 'I'll keep doing the compressions until you're ready to defibrillate her.'

'Charging,' Hayley said.

He continued with the compressions.

'And clear,' Hayley said.

He moved his hands so she could give the shock, then went straight back into the rhythm of thirty compressions and two breaths.

'Still VT,' Hayley said. 'Charging again. And clear.'

The second shock made no difference. Neither did the third.

'We are *not* losing her. Keep going,' he said. 'Adrenaline and amiodarone.'

'Drawing them up now,' Darryl, one of the nurses, said.

Sam continued with the compressions while Hayley administered the medication.

'Darryl, can you take over compressions?' Hayley asked.

'No,' Sam said. 'I can keep going.'

'Sam,' she said, her tone gentle yet firm.

'No,' he said. 'I'm not losing her.'

'Which is why you're going to let Darryl take over the compressions and you can do the next shock. Your arms are tired. Darryl will be more effective.'

He knew she wasn't playing power games, just being sensible—and because he'd told her what had happened in Manchester, he also knew that she was well aware of how this was affecting him. She was right to make him back off a bit. If their positions had been reversed, he would've said exactly the same.

'OK. Sorry.'

'No problem.'

'Charging,' he said. 'And clear.'

This time, to his relief, the defibrillation worked and Pauline's heart went back into a normal rhythm. She was still unconscious, but at least her heart was beating again.

'All righty. Well done, team,' Hayley said. 'You know the drill—Sam, let's get her on oxygen and a twelve-lead ECG. Darryl, call the cardiac unit and get her admitted. And then, Sam, if you can go with her to the CCU and do the handover?'

'On it,' Sam said.

'Me, too,' Darryl added.

'Are you OK?' she asked Sam gently when Darryl had left the cubicle.

'I'm fine.' He wasn't, but he had no intention of admitting how much this had shaken him and brought all his doubts back.

She squeezed his shoulder. 'Come and find me if you need me, OK?'

'Thanks.'

Once he'd done the handover at the cardiac unit, Sam was back in the thick of things—a teenager with abdominal pain that turned out to be a navel piercing that had become infected, a runner who'd been caught in the eye by a branch and had a scratch across his cornea, and a toddler with febrile convulsions.

At the end of his shift, he went to check on Pauline, who was lying in bed but was conscious.

'Thank you,' she said when she saw him. 'I believe you saved my life.'

'Not just me—the rest of the team saved you, too,' he said. 'How are you feeling?'

'As if a tank rolled over me,' she admitted.

He grimaced. 'Sorry. I'm probably responsible for the bruises on your chest. I did the compressions and I might've been a bit too enthusiastic.'

'If you hadn't done them, I wouldn't be here now.' Her eyes filled with tears. 'And I thought it was just something stupid wrong with me and I should've just put up with it instead of coming to hospital.'

'I'm glad you came in and didn't leave it,' he said. 'You're in the right place.'

'They're going to do that thing with the balloon you were telling me about.'

He smiled. 'I'm impressed you remembered, considering you conked out in the middle of it. I know I can drone on a bit, but I don't normally make people unconscious.'

She laughed, then winced. 'That hurts.'

'Give it a little time,' he said. 'But I just wanted to see how you were doing.'

'I'm still here, thanks to you.'

'Good.' He hadn't been able to save his patient in Manchester from that silent heart attack, but he'd saved Pauline Jacobs. And that went some way to making things better. 'I'll let you get some rest.'

When he got back to the staffroom of the emergency

department, Hayley was leaning against his locker. 'Well, hey there. How are you doing?'

'I'm fine,' he lied. It felt as if someone had pulled a plug and he was almost drained right out. But he'd promised to help her with the running training. He and Dani had agreed that she'd do the indoor sessions with Hayley, and he'd take the outdoor ones; tonight, they were planning to run a full 10K round the park.

'Given the caseload you had today, I don't think you are,' she said. 'I know how I'd feel if I had to deal with a case that reminded me of my worst day ever, so I'm pulling rank. No running training tonight. I'm cooking you dinner. It's nothing fancy—just stir-fried chicken, vegetables and noodles—but it's fast and it's healthy.'

'I'm not hungry.'

'I don't care. I'm cooking and you're eating. And you can wheel your bike back to mine.'

'That's a bit bossy,' he said, narrowing his eyes at her. Lynda had been bossy like that, too.

'Yes, it is,' she admitted, surprising him. Lynda wouldn't have admitted to being bossy.

'But sometimes, when you've had a rough day, you need someone just to push you to put one foot after the other,' Hayley said softly.

'But you're meant to be training for the race.'

'I'll switch my training days round. It's fine. Come on.'

Sam didn't have enough left in him to protest. He just let her follow him out to the bicycle shed, unlocked his bicycle, and put one foot in front of the other to go back to her flat.

CHAPTER SIX

'LUCKILY I'M ON the ground floor so you won't have to haul your bike up two flights of stairs,' Hayley said, and ushered him inside.

Sam left his bike propped against the wall, blocking her narrow entrance hall, and followed her into the main part of her flat. It turned out to be about the same size as his apartment in Reykjavik, with a bathroom, a bedroom, a living room and a kitchen that had an area to eat in. All the walls were painted cream and the furniture was light-coloured, making the place seem bigger and airier than it actually was. There were framed photographs on the mantelpiece in the living room, a big bookcase stuffed with an eclectic mixture of medical texts and novels, and a mix of photographs and postcards attached with magnets to her fridge. Everything was neat and tidy—pretty much as she was at work, he thought.

'Can I do anything to help?' he asked.

'Yes, you can lay the table and sort out something for us to drink—there's wine in the fridge if you want some, or there's a jug of filtered water.' She smiled at him. 'London water isn't exactly nice, and filtering makes it taste a little bit better. Or there's a bottle of sparkling water in the cupboard, though obviously it won't be chilled.'

'Plain water's fine, thanks.'

'The cutlery's in the drawer next to the sink, and the crockery and glasses are in the cupboard above it,' she said.

'OK.' Strange how just the mechanical act of setting out cutlery and plates made him feel more normal. And he was pretty sure that Hayley knew that, which was why she'd given him the task in the first place.

She busied herself with the wok, and five minutes later they were both sitting at her kitchen table with a plate of food in front of them. He wasn't hungry, but it would be rude to just leave it, so he forced himself to eat.

Only when they'd finished and she'd made them both a mug of coffee did he look at her and ask the question that had been bugging him since he'd accompanied her home. 'You're not making me talk about it?'

'Nope.'

The question must've been written over his face, because she said gently, 'There's a time for pushing someone to talk, and there's a time for giving someone space until they're ready.'

That sounded like personal experience. No doubt to do with her fiancé's accident. And hadn't she said she knew how she'd feel if she had a case that was similar to the one in her worst day ever? But it would be way too intrusive to ask her what sort of case that'd be. Instead, he said, 'Thank you.'

'No problem. Now, your choice: would you like to listen to some music, or watch something really undemanding and fun on TV? Of course, if you really want to watch an in-depth documentary on the finer points of quantum physics,' she added with a smile, 'I'm sure we can find one.'

'I think I'll give the quantum physics a miss,' he said. 'But thank you. I really don't mind.' He probably ought to make his excuses and leave. But he really appreciated that she'd worked out what he really needed—what he hadn't quite worked out for himself: space to let things settle in his head, and a bit of company so he couldn't brood about it.

'In that case,' she said, 'it's my choice and you get to watch my favourite episode of *Friends*—the one where Monica puts a turkey on her head. And we're having my posh chocolate biscuits with this, but don't tell Dani because she'll nag me about proper nutrition during race training and she'll force me to eat one of those protein bar things that are full of dates and taste *weird*.'

'I promise,' he said. And he couldn't help smiling when she sang along with the theme tune to the show and did the little claps. 'You really love this, don't you?'

'It's my favourite show ever,' she said with a smile. 'Which is why I've got it in a box set, in case it ever goes off my streaming service. Dani says I'm like Joey—I think a sandwich makes everything better.'

He laughed. 'She might have a point.'

'But it *does*. Or posh chocolate biscuits.'

'I guess.' And it was surprising how much better he did feel, sitting next to her on her sofa with a mug of coffee and Viennese chocolate fingers.

They somehow ended up moving closer during the TV show, and it seemed natural to put his arm round her. She leaned into him, and he turned his head so he could kiss her hair. She turned his head to look at him, and her pupils were huge; it seemed that the attraction between them in Iceland hadn't gone away at all, for either of them.

When he looked at her mouth, he couldn't resist dipping his head and brushing his mouth against hers. His lips tingled at the contact, and he wanted more. This time, when he kissed her, she kissed him back, and a shaft of pure need lanced through him.

Except he wasn't being fair to her. When he finally broke the kiss, he whispered, 'I'm sorry. I shouldn't have done that. It's been a hell of a day.'

She rested one hand against his cheek. 'I know—but remember that you saved Pauline Jacobs, and it wasn't your fault that you lost your patient in Manchester. If you have a silent heart attack, you don't have a clue about the damage that's been done to your heart, and if someone else had treated that patient in Manchester they would've ended up with exactly the same result that you did. It wasn't your fault. As you said, the relatives were grieving and they needed someone to blame. You were exonerated.'

But at the end of the day his patient had died. He sighed. 'Pauline's going to be covered in bruises from the chest compressions.'

'But she's here to tell the tale. Thanks to you.'

'And to the rest of the team.'

'But mainly to you,' she said. 'Because you're the one who spotted it was a silent heart attack. You were partway through doing the assessments and sorting out her blood sugar when she crashed.'

'I guess.' He dragged in a breath. 'I ought to go.'

'You don't have to.'

He gave her a rueful smile. 'Oh, but I do. Because I'm having inappropriate thoughts—seriously inappropriate thoughts—about you. And I'm not going to use you to make me feel better, Hayley. You deserve more than that.'

In answer, she reached up to kiss him again.

The next thing he knew, they were lying full-length on her sofa. His hands were under her top and his own top was somewhere on the floor.

'Um,' he said. 'Sorry. This wasn't meant to happen.'

'I know.' She stroked his face. 'We're supposed to be just colleagues. Friends, maybe.' She took a deep breath. 'Except I remember Iceland.'

'So do I,' he said softly. 'So what are we going to do about it?'

'The sensible thing would be for you to leave right now and go home,' she said.

But the way she said it sounded as if she thought there was an alternative. 'Or?' he asked.

'Or,' she said, 'I have a washing machine. I could run your things through it.'

Just he'd done for her, the night she'd stayed at his flat in Iceland.

'Which would your preferred option be?' he asked carefully.

'Both options are complicated.'

He frowned. 'How?' Surely him going home would put an end to things?

'We have work tomorrow. If you stay and we arrive at the hospital together—especially with you walking next to me, pushing your bike—the hospital rumour mill will go into overdrive.'

'Fair point.' He paused. 'And if I don't stay?'

'Then, if I'm honest, I think we're going to be delaying the moment rather than avoiding it altogether.'

'So if it doesn't happen now, it's going to happen sometime?' he asked.

She nodded.

He knew she was right. He was finding it harder and harder to resist her. The more he got to know her, the more he wanted her. 'So,' he said, 'it might be less complicated if I stay.'

'Except I don't want gossip. And you know how I feel about relationships within a department—it's a bad idea.' She drew in a breath. 'So this has to stay just between you and me.'

Keeping their relationship secret. As if she had no faith in him. He felt sick. He'd been here before. Lynda hadn't had enough faith in him to stick by him when he'd been suspended. What was the point in starting another relationship that wasn't going to last the distance? One where Hayley didn't even want people to know they were seeing each other in the first place?

'And I don't mean this to be like some dirty little secret,' she said, as if picking up on his thoughts. 'I just don't like being the centre of everyone's conversation, with people suddenly shutting up and looking guilty when you walk into the room.'

The penny dropped. After her partner had been killed, people would have talked about her, worried about her—and she'd obviously hated it.

And then something else hit him. She'd said she didn't approve of relationships within a department. 'Did your partner work in the emergency department?' he asked.

'No. I think it would have been worse if he had. People meant well. But I hated everyone talking about me.' She blew out a breath. 'It just takes time, until you're ready to move on.'

Had their fling in Iceland helped her to move to the place where she was ready to start a new relationship? Or was she still stuck?

Sam only realised he'd spoken aloud when she said, 'Both. I want to move on. I know Evan wouldn't have wanted me to grieve for ever—just as, if it had been the other way round, I would have wanted him to find someone who loved him as much as I had.'

That, Sam thought, was the difference between Lynda and Hayley. Hayley had loved her partner for who he was. Lynda had loved the idea of what Sam could be: a mover, a shaker, CEO of a different hospital. Her career plan for both of them meant that, once he'd reached the top, he would've worked in partnership with her to develop a kind of super-hospital. Except that wasn't what Sam had wanted. He'd wanted to

follow in his grandfather's footsteps and be a doctor—
to spend his days with patients and feel that he'd been
able to make a real difference to their lives.

He hadn't talked to Hayley about what she wanted
from her career, but from working with her he was pretty
sure that she didn't want to work in the admin side. Like
him, she seemed to prefer treating her patients.

'So if we weren't working together, would you consider dating me?' he asked, wanting it out in the open.

'Yes. No. I don't know.' She raked a hand through
her hair. 'Do you want me to be honest?'

'Yes.'

'This is complicated,' she warned.

'Tell me anyway.'

'OK.' She took a deep breath. 'There's something
between us. There has been right from when I first
met you. I want to do something about it, but then I
feel guilty because of Evan. And then I feel stupid for
feeling guilty, because he wouldn't want that. And then
I feel ashamed of being such an idiot. And then I feel
scared about starting all over again.'

'I think,' he said, 'you're warm and kind and caring—and it's natural to feel guilty and awkward and
scared. How long were you and Evan together?'

'Two and a half years. You?'

'Three, so I know what you mean. It's starting all
over again, finding someone you're attracted to and
someone that you've got a lot in common with. And
you're always going to compare the new relationship
to the old, and wonder if you're doing the right thing.'

Or making the same mistake. Not that he was going to tell her that right now.

'And wondering if everyone's going to judge you and think it's too soon…'

'Does it matter what other people think?' he asked.

'I guess not.' She wrinkled her nose. 'As I said before, it's complicated.'

'That pretty much sums up life,' he said. 'You brought me here tonight to feed me and give me a hug. To offer me comfort after a rough day.' He paused. 'But I think you need comfort, too, right now. And maybe we can both help each other towards a better place.

'You mean, having sex to take our minds off things?'

'Yes and no.' He stroked her face. 'As you say, it's complicated.' He *liked* her: she was straightforward with their colleagues, compassionate and kind with their patients and their relatives, and outside work she was funny and clever and sweet. 'We want to see each other—and at the same time we're scared of starting something that might go wrong. A no-strings fling doesn't feel quite right, but are either of us really ready for a new relationship?'

'I don't have any answers,' she said. 'But can we keep it simple for now, until we work out what we want and where this is going? Keep it just between you and me?'

'Yes,' he said, and kissed her.

She stood up, taking his hand, and led him to her bedroom. Like the rest of the flat, it had light-coloured furniture and cream walls, and everything was neat and orderly. And he liked the framed print of a bluebell wood that hung over the bed. The whole place just radiated calmness, much like Hayley herself.

He was about to kiss her when he remembered something important. 'We can't do this. At least, not right now.'

She blinked. 'Why not?'

'I don't have any condoms.'

'I do.'

Which was odd, because he was pretty sure that Hayley Clark didn't take men to bed on a casual basis. Their fling in Iceland had been based on strong pull of attraction, something that was still bubbling below the surface.

But he let it go. Right now he really wanted to kiss her again. Make love with her. Lose himself in her and let her lose herself in him. And he had the strongest feeling that it was just the same for her.

She pulled the curtains and turned on the bedside light. He switched off the overhead light, leaving the room bathed in the warm light of the lamp, then pulled her into his arms and kissed her.

This felt so good, so right.

And when they'd made love and he'd dealt with the condom and she'd dealt with the laundry, it felt good to curve his body round hers, drawing her back against him. Back in his own flat, he would've been brooding over the events of the day. Here, with her, he felt as if he was starting to heal.

The next morning, Hayley woke just before her alarm, warm and comfortable.

Apart from that one night they'd spent together in

Iceland, this was the first time she'd woken in someone's arms for more than a year. Part of her still felt a bit disloyal to Evan, but part of her felt that it was so good not to be alone and to wake sharing the day with someone else.

She twisted round in his arms, and woke him with a kiss. 'Hey, sleepy. We're on early shift.'

He was wide awake almost instantly. 'How long does it take to get to the hospital from here?'

'We've both got time for a shower and breakfast,' she said. 'You have the first shower while I get your stuff out of the washer-dryer. There are clean towels in the airing cupboard.'

'Thank you. If you have an iron,' he said, 'I'd appreciate borrowing it to get the creases out of my shirt.'

She liked the fact that he hadn't immediately assumed that she'd iron his shirt for him, even though she wouldn't have minded doing it. 'No problem.'

'And I'll make breakfast while you shower,' he said.

'Thanks—that'd be good.'

By the time she'd finished sorting out the laundry, set up the ironing board and made some coffee, he'd appeared with a towel wrapped round his waist and his hair still damp from the shower. 'What would you like for breakfast?' he asked.

'There's bacon and ketchup in the fridge and bread in the cupboard,' she said. 'If that works for you?'

'It does. Leave it to me,' he said.

When she'd had her shower and dressed, she headed back to the kitchen.

'Perfect timing,' he said, and assembled a sandwich for her.

'Thanks.' Evan hadn't been able to cook at all; they'd joked that he could burn water and keep his whole crew busy if he actually tried to make breakfast.

But Evan had never seen the inside of this flat. Hayley had negotiated an early termination of the lease on the flat they'd shared together, unable to bear walking in the door and not seeing him there. This flat was much smaller, but it was handy for work and it suited her just fine.

This was her life now.

And she'd promised Dani that she'd live it to the full.

'Thank you for last night,' Sam said. 'You're right—I was reliving that case in Manchester, and I needed someone to push me out of it. To make me put one foot in front of the other, as you said.'

'No problem,' she said. She'd had people to do that for her after Evan had been killed—people who'd made her eat and get out of the flat and *function*. Though she had a feeling that there was something Sam hadn't told her. The man she'd been working with was bright and capable. Although anyone would have their confidence knocked by being suspended during an investigation, he'd known that he'd done all the right things for his patient and he'd been exonerated. Why hadn't his partner supported him through the investigation? Had she been related to the patient he'd lost, maybe, and blamed him for it? Or had they broken up just before the investigation and he'd maybe thought that he'd been distracted by the break-up and not asked the right questions of his patient, so he felt as if it was all his fault?

It wasn't something she could ask straight out: the

questions were harsh and obtrusive. And she couldn't quite work out how to frame them in a kinder or more tactful way.

Thankfully, he changed the subject. 'We need to re-schedule your race training. Dani's right, running out-side isn't the same as running inside. Are you free after work tonight, or are you training indoors with Dani?'

'It's meant to be a day off,' she said, 'so we'll swap it for yesterday. If you don't mind, that is.'

'No. We'll do a run in the park tonight.' He paused. 'Are you, um, free at the weekend? We could maybe do something.'

'I'd like that,' she said. It was going to be strange, dating again. But if she didn't let herself think about the dangerous things Sam liked to do in his free time— or the fact that he'd signed up to the MERIT roster— maybe she could do this. Maybe she could move on from the sadness of the past and find a new future with Sam.

When they'd finished their sandwiches, he insisted on washing up.

And then he paused. 'So I guess I'll see you at work? And then for the running training after.'

'OK. Be careful on the roads.'

'I will.' He kissed her lightly. 'See you on the ward.'

She bit her lip. 'And as far as work's concerned—'

'We're colleagues and starting to be just good friends,' he said. 'Got it.'

Which was what she wanted. But the hint of hurt in his eyes, quickly masked, made her feel guilty. It wasn't so much relationships in the department that bothered her—it was the gossip. Even when it was meant well.

Over the next couple of weeks, Sam and Hayley grew closer. He was careful to be strictly professional with her at work, and although he did the outdoor training runs with her when it was just the two of them, everyone knew it was under Dani's instructions and he was just helping out as a friend. When they went out on a date, it always seemed to be somewhere a little out-of-the-way, so they'd be less likely to bump into someone from work.

Though she refused flatly to go on the team night out he'd organised for the middle of October. 'You've got to be insane, Sam. Go-karting's risky enough by itself, but go-karting on *ice*?'

'They have special tyres,' he said. 'It's safe. I don't understand why you're worrying.'

'You're a thrill-seeker,' she said.

He frowned. 'I like extreme sports that make my heart beat a bit faster, yes. It makes me feel alive.'

'You're crazy,' she said.

He didn't understand why she was so antsy about it. She'd been fine about glacier walking; she'd enjoyed it, even.

And then a nasty thought hit him. He wanted things to work out between him and Hayley, but she was so critical about the things that he found fun—just as Lynda had been. Although Hayley wasn't Lynda, was he making a similar mistake? Was he subconsciously ignoring signs of trouble if he ignored her criticisms?

He pushed the thought away. He was being unfair. Hayley was one of the good guys.

'Come with us,' he said. 'Even if you don't want to do any of the actual driving, you can still have a drink and something to eat with us.'

'It's really, really not my thing,' she said. 'Have fun. But I'll be on duty so someone else on the team who actually wants to do it can go and join in.'

He couldn't argue with that. But it did make him wonder if there was something she wasn't telling him. Was it to do with her late fiancé? He needed to find a tactful way to ask.

The day of Sam's team outing, Hayley was working. Have fun, she texted him, even though she wished he'd picked something less dangerous to do. Then again, he could've suggested abseiling or the rap jumping he'd shown her on his phone, which would've been even worse.

Why, why, why did he have to be an adrenaline junkie?

And how was she ever going to silence her fears?

He hadn't been called out on the MERIT roster yet, but she knew it was only a matter of time. And if that call-out involved a fire...

'Stop it,' she told herself. 'Don't trouble trouble.' And she forced herself to concentrate on her patients.

Halfway through the afternoon, Sam walked into the department, looking slightly shamefaced, accompanied by Josh Willoughby, one of their newest junior doctors.

'Josh? What's happened?' she asked.

'I had a little bit of an accident,' Josh said, hanging his head. 'I, um, might have cracked a rib.'

'While you were go-karting *on ice*.' She gave Sam a pointed look.

'It was great fun, Hayley,' Josh said. 'Don't blame Sam. It's my own fault. I was showing off, going too fast, and I missed a corner.'

'Did you hit your head or anything?' She looked at Sam. 'Has he shown any signs of concussion?'

'I didn't hit my head; I just banged my ribs. I heard a crack and it hurts, which is why I think I broke it. But I definitely don't have flail chest,' Josh said. 'I can breathe just fine. A broken rib will heal itself within a month and all I need to do now is to take painkillers— if I don't get the pain under control properly I'll breathe too shallowly and I might end up with a chest infection.'

She couldn't help smiling at his earnestness. 'Did you learn that at uni or from us?'

'A bit of both,' Josh said with a smile. 'Sam's already checked me out and I know I'm fine.'

'But the fact Sam's brought you in makes me think there might be more to it than that,' Hayley said. She looked at Sam. 'Anything you'd like to tell me?'

'I didn't have a stethoscope handy and I want to be sure there isn't a pneumothorax,' Sam said. 'There's bruising already around the area where he hit the side of the go-kart, and it's tender. It hurts when he moves or breathes deeply. I know that's standard for a cracked rib, but I just want to be sure.'

After Manchester, she thought, it wasn't surprising that Sam was totally meticulous.

'Do you think you have any shortness of breath,' she asked Josh, 'or have you had any pain near the shoulder?'

'No,' Josh said.

'OK. I want to have a listen to your chest. Would you mind taking off your top?' she asked.

'Is that what it takes to get women to ask me to take my clothes off?' Josh asked. 'I have to break a rib?'

'I'm asking,' she said sweetly, 'exactly the same question a *male* doctor would ask you.'

'Spoilsport.' He took off his top, and she winced as she saw the bruising.

'That's nasty,' she said.

'And it'll get worse over the next few days,' Josh said cheerfully. 'I'm fine, Hayley. Really.'

'Hmm.' She examined him and Sam's diagnosis was spot on, though she wasn't entirely happy with Josh's breathing. 'X-ray for you,' she said.

'I really don't nee—' Josh began.

'Yes, you do,' she cut in gently. 'Humour me on this one.'

'But you've got all the clinical signs.'

'Sometimes,' she said, 'your intuition tells you that there's a problem—and at the advanced age of thirty-two I've learned to listen to my intuition.'

'She's right,' Sam said. 'Textbooks can't teach you about hunches; that comes with experience.'

'OK. X-ray it is,' Josh said.

Hayley could see immediately from the X-ray result on her computer screen that Josh had a slight tear in his lung, caused by his broken rib; air escaping from his lung was trapped between his lung and the wall of his chest. By the time he came back to the emergency department, Josh was slightly breathless.

'I was just running too fast to get you to sign me off,' he said.

'Nice try.' She showed him the X-ray on her screen. 'OK, Josh. Forget about my hunch. This is all textbook. If this X-ray belonged to one of your patients, what would you say?'

He sighed. 'There's a pneumothorax.'

'And what are we going to do about it?'

'Unless you have underlying lung disease,' Josh said, 'the tear in your lung will mend and the problem will resolve itself over a few days.'

'And if you're breathless?' Sam prompted. 'Which you are, right now?'

'Then you need to remove the air.' Josh wrinkled his nose. 'I know this is going to sound stupid, considering how many times I'm on the other end of a syringe, but I hate needles.'

Hayley smiled and patted his shoulder. 'You'll be fine, sweetie. You know the procedure, which is probably putting scary pictures in your head because today you're on the receiving end, but you also know I'll give you a local anaesthetic so it's not going to hurt. I can't let you walk out of here struggling to breathe when you've broken a rib and got a pneumothorax from go-karting on ice.' She gave Sam a sidelong look. 'Perfectly safe, indeed,' she mouthed.

'Sorry,' he mouthed back, looking guilty.

'OK, Josh. Sharp scratch,' she said, and administered

the anaesthetic. She inserted a thin tube through Josh's chest wall with the aid of a needle, then attached it to a large syringe with a three-way tap. 'That's the hard bit done,' she said.

Josh grimaced. 'I hate needles. But I guess you're not so bad at this.'

'Glad to hear it—though I'd also like to know if I need to brush up on anything, because I never want to hurt my patients unnecessarily. Not that I really want to use my team as test cases,' Hayley said with a smile. 'OK. I'm going to suck out some air into the syringe, release it through the three-way tap, and repeat until I'm sure that most of the air has gone. Happy?'

'Happy,' Josh said.

'And while you're there,' Sam added, 'we might as well test you on your knowledge of painkillers.'

Which was a brilliant way to distract the younger man, Hayley thought.

'What would you prescribe to someone with a broken rib?' Sam asked.

'Paracetamol or anti-inflammatories, and if it's moderate pain then you can alternate them two hours apart,' Josh said, 'or in really bad cases you need something stronger like codeine. And before I can prescribe anything at all I need to know if my patient's a smoker, or taking any anti-clotting medication, has high blood pressure or asthma, or any history of heart or kidney disease or stomach ulcers,' he said, ticking them off on his fingers.

'Or if they're pregnant, have a history of stroke, or

they're already taking aspirin,' Hayley added. 'That's all absolutely right, Josh. Does any of it apply to you?'

'No. Though I'd be really famous if I was pregnant,' Josh said thoughtfully.

Hayley laughed. 'You certainly would. OK. We're done. Is the pain mild or moderate?'

'Moderate,' Josh said.

'Take normal doses of paracetamol and ibuprofen. Alternate them two hours apart, just as you suggested,' she said. 'If the pain's worse tomorrow, come and talk to me about codeine. Are you on shift tomorrow?'

'Not until Tuesday,' Josh said.

'OK. Go home, take painkillers and rest,' she said. 'No heavy lifting. And I want to see you straight back here in which circumstances?'

'If I get a high temperature, chest pain, I'm coughing up loads of gunge or I'm really short of breath,' Josh said.

'Good. Make sure you do. Off you go,' she said. 'And next time you want to do something exciting, please don't listen to any suggestions from Dr I-Love-Taking-Stupid-Risks Price here.'

'I won't,' Josh said.

'I'll give you a lift home,' Sam said, 'once I've grovelled a bit to Dr I-Told-You-So Clark, here.'

'I'll be in the waiting room,' Josh said with a wary look, and disappeared out of the cubicle.

'Go on, then. Say it,' Sam said with a resigned expression on his face.

'I don't need to, because you already said it for me,' Hayley said. 'Poor Josh.'

'If it makes you feel any better, I feel really guilty,' Sam said.

'All this putting yourself at risk... It doesn't make sense, Sam. Why do you do it?'

'Why are you so anti anything with the slightest bit of risk?' he asked.

This was her cue to tell him the rest of it. The thing that held her back and scared her every day.

Because my fiancé used to risk his life every single day, and he died.

But here wasn't the right place to tell him. 'Can we have this discussion later?' she asked. 'I'm on duty and the waiting room's full.'

'All right. How about I cook us fresh pasta after your shift and we'll talk then?'

'That'd be good.' And by then hopefully the hard lump currently sitting just above her breastbone would dissolve into the right words.

'Your place or mine?' he asked.

'Yours,' she said.

'OK. I'll see you at half-past six.'

At half-past six on the dot, Hayley rang Sam's doorbell.

'Can I get you a glass of wine?' he asked.

She shook her head. 'But I'd kill for a mug of tea.'

'Go and put your feet up.' He made them both a mug of tea, and carried them through into the living room. She was sitting on the sofa, and she looked bone-deep weary. Miserable. As if something had been eating away at her.

And he had a pretty fair idea was it was, given that

she'd promised to talk to him about why she was so antsy about risk. 'I'm sorry about what happened to Josh, Hayley. The last thing I wanted was for anyone to get hurt.'

'It's the last thing anyone wants,' she said, 'but it still happens.' She left her mug of tea where he'd placed it on the coffee table. 'And it leaves your life utterly crumpled in its wake.'

'What happened to make you so scared of risk, Hayley?' he asked softly.

'Evan. My fiancé.' She dragged in a breath. 'He was a firefighter.'

And he'd been killed in an industrial accident.

Things started to become horribly clear. Sam had a nasty feeling that he knew exactly what she was about to tell him—that Evan had been trying to save someone from the industrial accident and had lost his life the process.

'Evan risked his life every single day,' Hayley said. 'He'd done all the training. He was good at his job. He'd never, ever do anything reckless or put any of his crew members at risk. But, that particular day, there was a fire at a local garage and workshop. Obviously with it being a workshop, there was flammable stuff everywhere—oil, chemicals, all sorts of things that could make the fire so much worse. A propane cylinder exploded, and the fire crew managed to get two more of the propane cylinders out before they went up. But then someone said the boss had had gone back in five minutes before to rescue his cat and her kittens from the office on the mezzanine floor, and nobody had seen him since. Evan thought the guy had probably keeled over from smoke inhalation, so he went in after him.' She shuddered. 'And the building collapsed when Evan was halfway up the stairs to the mezzanine floor.'

No wonder Evan hadn't survived, Sam thought.

'The last propane cylinder was right beneath where he was when the building collapsed, and it exploded. Evan was killed instantly.' She choked on a sob. 'At least, I hope it was instant. I hope he never knew what happened, that he never felt even the slightest bit of pain or knew what was happening to him.'

'I'm sure it was instant.' Sam held her close.

And now a lot of things were clearer to him. Why she was so panicky about risk. Evan had taken a risk, going into a dangerous situation to save someone from smoke inhalation, and it had gone tragically wrong.

'He was one of the good guys. Everyone loved him. Evan was the sort who'd do anything to help anyone.' She looked Sam straight in the eye. 'He was a lot like you. He put himself in danger to help others, just like you do. Except you do all the dangerous sports stuff as well. And I can't cope with that, Sam. You love it and I feel like the world's most miserable cow, holding you back from doing something you enjoy. It isn't fair of me. But it scares the hell out of me, Sam, and I'm so tired of being scared. Of worrying that I'm going to lose you, the way I lost Evan. And I just can't understand *why* you do it. Why you put yourself in danger all the time.'

He stroked her face. How could he make her understand that it didn't have to be that way? That not all risks meant there would be a tragedy?

'I've always liked extreme sports,' he said. 'I suppose it's the adrenaline rush—it makes me feel alive.' And he'd really needed that feeling after he'd been suspended, because it meant that he was feeling something other than as if he'd been sucked into the middle of a black hole. 'I used to go climbing with my dad and Martin right from when I was small, because we lived near the Peak District and Dad loved climbing. So did my granddad. I think it's in my blood. So when I was old enough, it just made sense for me to join the mountain rescue team. And I never once had a problem on the team when I was on a rescue, not even something little like a twisted ankle or a scratch or a bruise.'

'Don't you think of the risks when you go out?' she asked. Her voice was calm, but he could see the anguish in her eyes. 'That you could fall? That a cliff could crumble beneath you without any warning and you'd end up breaking your neck at the bottom?'

He wanted her to understand that he wasn't just being a thrill-seeker. 'I do,' he said, 'and that's why I'm careful to use the right safety procedures on a rescue, and why I only use companies that have good safety records for the leisure stuff. And, yes, I know Josh cracked a rib today at the go-karting, but...' He stopped.

'But?'

He winced. 'Now you've told me what happened to Evan, I don't know if I can say it to you.'

Her eyes widened. 'Try me.'

'I don't want to make you feel bad.'

'Say it anyway.'

'OK. But remember you asked me to tell you what was in my head.' He took a deep breath. 'Sometimes, no matter how well you plan something, accidents just happen and you can't second-guess them. That's why our department exists in the first place. Accidents happen.'

She just looked at him as if her heart was breaking.

He stroked her face. 'I'm sorry Evan died. But there are always risks in everything you do, Hayley. You might be crossing the road or walking in the middle of a park. You can't guarantee that you won't be hit by lightning, or that a branch from a tree won't give way unexpectedly and fall onto your head, or that someone's foot won't slip and hit the accelerator instead of the brakes and a car will crash into you.'

'But the chances of those kinds of things happening are so small. Whereas putting your life on the line over and over and over again,' she said, sounding anguished, 'whether it's at work or what you do for fun—it's not a matter of *if* something happens but *when*.'

'But if nobody goes to rescue people in an emergency,' he said, 'then people will die when they might have been saved.'

'I know.' She looked miserable. 'And I feel guilty about that too. I'm being selfish. But when I lost Evan it was as if I'd been sucked into a black hole. I don't want to be in that position again.'

'Would I be right in saying that Evan loved his job?' Sam asked softly.

She nodded. 'He'd always wanted to be a firefighter,

right from when he was small. He loved what he did. He was good at it—whether it was putting out a fire, or rescuing someone from a broken lift, or cutting a car open so the emergency services could get the casualty to safety, or talking to kids at school... He absolutely loved it.' A single tear leaked down her cheek. 'And he *died*, Sam. He was killed on duty.'

He wiped the tear away with the pad of his thumb. 'I'm so sorry that you went through this. And I wish there was something I could do or say to make it better. But I can't bring Evan back.'

'I know. And I just...' She swallowed hard. 'I'm sorry.'

'Don't be. I'm glad you're talking to me.' And what a hypocrite he was—he'd told her next to nothing about Lynda. 'At least now I understand why you're so wary about risk.'

'And you've signed up for the MERIT team.'

'Yes, though I'm sure you already know that the MERIT team are only allowed into an area if it's safe for them to treat patients. All the risks are monitored and kept under control as much as possible,' he said gently. But he also knew that it wouldn't be enough for her. Not now she'd lost Evan to his job. 'If you want me to withdraw my name from the team, then I will.'

She shook her head. 'I can't ask you to do that.'

'You're not asking. I'm offering,' he said.

'And you'll regret it. You'll start to feel that I'm holding you back and you'll resent it. In the end, it'll come between us,' she said.

Maybe she had a point. His mountain rescue work

had certainly come between him and Lynda. Then again, Lynda hadn't given him a decent reason to give it up. Only that she'd wanted him to join some tedious committee or other instead because it'd be more high-profile and look better on his CV. In Sam's view, that wasn't enough.

'Did you ever tell Evan how much his job worried you?' Sam asked.

'No. Because, actually, it didn't worry me. I used to be able to accept the risk. I suppose I thought the worst would never actually happen because I knew he was always careful.' She dragged in a breath. 'But the worst *did* happen. And now the fear gets in the way.'

'What would he say,' Sam asked carefully, 'if he was here now and you told him that his job scared you too much?'

'Pretty much what you did,' she admitted. 'And I'm not seeing you as a replacement for Evan, or anything like that, Sam. You just happen to have some similar views on life. Only he didn't do all the risky stuff for fun.'

'I can tone that down, too,' he said. 'I admit, I did quite a bit more extreme stuff after I was suspended, simply so I had something else to focus on. Something that made me feel alive instead of just dragging through every day and waiting for someone to come up with a verdict. But I can tone it down now.'

She dragged a hand through her hair. 'I shouldn't expect you to change who you are for me. It's *wrong*.'

'But you lost Evan when he was doing his job in the emergency services. Of course you're going to worry yourself sick whenever there's a major incident, especially if I'm in the MERIT team that's called out—and even more so if that incident happens to be a fire. I don't want to put you through that.'

'So either you stop doing it and you'll start to resent me for holding you back, or you keep doing it and I'm frantic with worry every time you go out. There isn't a middle way,' she said miserably.

'There could be a kind of compromise. Maybe if you come with me to some of the leisure stuff—well, possibly not to go-karting on ice,' he amended, 'but to do something with just a tiny bit of risk. Then you'll see for yourself how safe everything is and it'll stop you worrying.'

'Kind of like immunotherapy? Building it up in little doses?'

'Kind of,' he agreed. 'So it's a compromise. We can work on this together.'

She grimaced. 'I feel horrible.'

'You're not horrible.' He kissed her lightly. 'It's because you care.' She wanted him to stop doing the dangerous stuff because she cared about him and she was worried he'd be hurt or killed—not because she cared more about her long-term goals and wanted him to spend the time sucking up to 'important' people instead, the way Lynda had.

Maybe he should tell her about that.

But he rather thought Hayley had had enough for today. He wasn't going to dump his own insecurities on her right now. 'Thank you for telling me about Evan,' he said. 'I know this must've been so hard for you. And I'm sorry if I made you relive some of the nightmare.'

'I… I should've told you before. Explained more.'

'I figured you'd tell me more when you were ready,' he said.

She swallowed hard. 'I'm sorry.'

'Don't apologise.' He kissed her lightly. 'You've had a rough day and you need food. Give me five minutes—it's fresh pasta and sauce, though I'm afraid none of it's home-made—it's from the posh deli counter at the supermarket.'

She gave him a wry smile. 'A tin of spaghetti hoops on toast would've done me.'

He looked at her. 'If you'd gone home on your own, you would have just made yourself a bowl of cereal, if that.'

'Busted,' she said.

'I can't promise you that things will always be safe,' he said, 'because even in the department something could happen. A drunk could swing a punch that accidentally connects with you and knocks you out, or you could get a needle stick injury while you're treating someone with HIV, or…' He held her close. 'But if you think about all the things that *might* happen, you'll drive yourself crazy. Think about how small the chances are of something bad happening—and how big the chances are that the worst *won't* happen.'

She swallowed hard. 'The bereavement counsellor I saw last year said something like that. But I can't seem to get the risks and the worries out of my head.'

'It's going to be OK, Hayley. We'll work this through.

We'll find some kind of compromise that suits both of us.' It would just take time.

And for her, Sam realised, he was more than prepared to wait. Because Hayley was special. And they had the chance of making their relationship into something really good.

CHAPTER SEVEN

FINALLY IT WAS the end of October, and Hayley finished her last bit of training with Sam on the Friday night, running the full 10K outdoors. They met up with Dani afterwards to have dinner and discuss strategies for the race itself on the Sunday. Saturday was a rest day, and then on Sunday morning at nine o'clock the three of them headed to Alexandra Park for the start of the race, getting Hayley set up with her numbered bib and the electronic tag for her shoe that would record her time.

Dani seemed a bit distracted, but Hayley put it down to the fact that her best friend was watching the race instead of running it. It was nearly three months since Dani had been diagnosed with the fractured metatarsals, and although the cast was off now she still wasn't quite back to her full mobility. Hayley knew that taking it slowly was driving Dani crackers, though at least she was watching the race with Sam—who would make her be careful, but without making her feel as if she was wrapped in cotton wool.

Which was ironic, because Hayley didn't feel as if

she could make Sam be careful without wrapping him in cotton wool.

Hayley was glad the weather was dry, cool and calm; the worst thing would've been running on wet roads with a bitter wind whipping through the runners. She would be happy if she could run the course in under an hour and a quarter. The route was lined with marshals, and some of the roads had been closed off for a couple of hours for the run. The course had two laps, partly along the streets and partly in the park; she'd also been told that there were two water stations, so she wouldn't need to take a water bottle with her.

It was the first time Hayley had done a race like this in a crowd, and after the first ten minutes she was surprised to discover that she was enjoying it. Plus running in a crowd meant that she didn't miss having either Dani by her side when she'd done the interval training on the treadmill at the local gym, or Sam by her side on the outdoor training.

She was flagging a bit on the second lap, but then she saw Dani and Sam near the finish line. They were cheering her on, and it spurred her to run harder for those last few metres. And then she was over the finish line, and a few moments afterwards she was swept into a hug by both Dani and Sam. Hayley found herself unexpectedly in tears with the emotion of it all.

'You're wonderful,' Dani said. 'Because of you, we've raised a ton of money for the new equipment for the ward.'

'People donated for you,' Hayley reminded her.

'But you're the one who actually ran it.' Dani hugged her hard. 'Thank you so much.'

Hayley hugged her back and then hugged Sam. 'Thank you both. I couldn't have done it without you training with me.'

He picked her up, swung her round and kissed her. 'You did brilliantly. I'm so proud of you.' Then he set her back on her feet and rested his forehead against hers as he realised what he'd just given away. 'Sorry. I know we were keeping this between us, but I kind of assumed Dani would know as she's your best friend.'

'She'd kept it sort of quiet, but I'd already guessed from the way you two look at each other,' Dani said with a smile, 'and it's a good thing.'

'Come on, let's go get your time,' Sam said to Hayley, 'and then I'm taking you both out for refuelling.'

Hayley was thrilled to discover she'd run the 10K in one hour, ten minutes and thirteen seconds.

'That's a personal best,' Dani said, 'and that's a really respectable time, especially for your first official run.'

'Seconded,' Sam said. 'As I said before, I'm so proud of you.'

'It doesn't mean I'm going to be a runner,' Hayley warned, 'because I'd much rather do dance aerobics. But I have to admit, I enjoyed it and I'm glad I did it.'

'Good.' Sam held her hand all the way into town, then found a table in one of the cafés on the high street and went to order pastries and coffees for all of them.

While he was at the counter, Dani said gently, 'You look happier than I've seen you since Evan died. You've fallen for him, haven't you? And Sam's lovely. I'm really pleased for you.'

'Yes, I've fallen for him,' Hayley admitted. 'It's not just the physical stuff. It's who he is and how he makes me feel.'

'But?' Dani asked.

Hayley bit her lip. 'I still can't quite get past the way he's not bothered about putting himself in danger.'

'Which is understandable, because of the way you lost Evan,' Dani said. 'But that was an accident, Haze. A horrible, tragic accident. It isn't necessarily going to repeat itself.'

'I know. I have to deal with the panic. I have no idea how I'm going to cope when Sam gets called out on a MERIT case—I'll fret the whole time he's away until I know he's safe,' Hayley admitted.

'Talk to him,' Dani advised.

'I already have. I told him what happened to Evan and he understands how I feel.' She grimaced. 'But I still need time to get my head round it.'

Later in the week, Hayley and Sam had a couple of days off duty.

'We could go to London Zoo,' Sam said. 'I'd love to see the lions and tigers. And I read somewhere you can walk alongside the canal from Regent's Park to Camden Lock—it looks as if it's going to be dry, so how about it?'

'Great idea,' Hayley said.

And she thoroughly enjoyed wandering hand in hand with him around the zoo, seeing the lions and tigers up close, along with the gorillas and the giraffes, although her favourites were the penguins.

Because it was half-term, there were plenty of children walking around with their parents, and at that moment Hayley could just imagine herself and Sam in the same position—taking a few days off together in the school holidays, and going to see the sights. The Zoo, the Aquarium, the dinosaurs at the Natural History Museum...

'Penny for them?' Sam asked.

She smiled. 'Just wool-gathering.' They were still in the relatively early stages of their relationship, and they hadn't even had a casual discussion about how they saw their futures. She had no idea how he felt about long-term relationships or children. 'So have you got any idea what to get for your Secret Santa present?' she asked instead.

'Ah, now—that's supposed to be confidential,' he said with a smile. 'I might cheat and talk to my mum.'

'So you've got someone older and female.'

'Not necessarily. It might be someone younger and male.'

'In which case you wouldn't need to ask your mum.'

'Enough with the detective stuff,' he said, laughing. 'So when does all the Christmas stuff start here?'

'Not until the first of December,' she said. 'Mike's strict about that. And obviously for health and safety reasons we can only decorate the reception area. But basically on the first of December the tree goes up and everyone takes a decoration from the box when they come on shift and puts it on a branch. That way we all kind of decorate the tree together.'

'That's a nice idea,' he said. 'I like that. And there's the Christmas meal.'

'Don't forget the dancing afterwards. Mike's dad dancing is not to be missed,' she said with a grin. 'I guess we're not quite as Christmassy as some of the departments—the children's ward always has Santa coming round and the Friends of the Hospital always buy a little present for every child who's in, as well as something for their siblings.'

'Whereas we're more likely to be patching up Santa when he's off duty and either ended up being hit in the pub when he's trying to stop a fight, or when he's put his back out from lifting a present that's too heavy for him,' he said wryly.

'Exactly. Christmas Day can be a bit grim in the department if family tensions have gone too far,' she agreed.

'Well, we've got six weeks to prepare for it. Though I think I'm getting a bit sick of the Christmas music and Christmas goodies in the shops already.'

'Bah, humbug,' she said. 'Are you telling me you don't like Christmas?'

'Oh, I like Christmas,' he said. 'I hate present-shopping, so the internet's been brilliant for that, but I love spending time with my family and playing silly games and eating too much rich food and watching all the old classic Christmas films. My mum always cries her eyes out over *It's a Wonderful Life*.'

'So does mine. And Dani and I always watch *Love*

Actually.' She bit her lip. 'Last Christmas was horrible. Dani's marriage was just about to collapse, I had to face my first Christmas without Evan, and even though we were busy at work I just...' She lifted one shoulder in a half-shrug. 'Well. This year will be better. I'm over that year of firsts—the hardest bit.'

'I think this Christmas will be better for me, too,' Sam said thoughtfully. 'I mean, it wasn't super-horrible, but Lynda's family is very different from mine and we spent Christmas with them last year. They don't like bad cracker jokes or silly games. And they wouldn't dream of making sandwiches from the left-over turkey and going climbing on Boxing Day morning.'

'To be fair, mine wouldn't either,' she said. 'Go climbing, I mean.'

'What about the silly games and the cracker jokes?'

'Oh, they do all of them. Board games are the best.' She grinned. 'Though the rules change halfway through. And there are forfeits. And you get made to sing Christmas songs really loudly, whether you can sing or not. No singing, no supper.'

'That,' he said, 'works for me.' He paused. 'So we might get to spend Christmas together this year?'

'We might.' And Hayley was shocked by how much she liked the idea. 'I guess it depends on the duty roster,' she said lightly.

'We need to promise mince pies and chocolate Yule Log to the duty roster fairy,' he said.

She laughed. 'We can try.'

'Ready to go and grab some lunch?' he asked. 'According to the website I looked up, it's about a fifteen-minute walk from here to Camden.'

'Sounds good,' she said, and walked down path by the canal with him, enjoying the views.

They'd been walking for about ten minutes when they heard a scream.

'My little boy's fallen in! Help! I can't swim!'

Sam ran off in the direction of the scream, with Hayley behind him.

There was a woman with a pram at the side of the canal, clearly frantic; when Hayley looked into the water, she could see a child floating face-down.

'It's too far to reach him from the side of the canal. Even if there was a pole nearby, it'd be useless because he's probably unconscious and couldn't grab it. I'm going in,' Sam said, stripping off his coat and shoes.

Before she could say another word, he'd jumped straight into the water, without a second thought of what might be beneath the surface. Part of Hayley was horrified, but then her professional training kicked in and she grabbed her phone and called the emergency services. Although the handler answered on the second ring, it felt as if time had slowed down massively. 'A child's fallen into the Regent Canal.' She gave their location. 'Someone with me is getting him out, but when we saw him he was face-down and I think we'll need an ambulance.'

'We're dispatching one now,' the handler said. 'Can you stay on the line and keep us informed?'

'Yes,' she said. 'Actually, I'll get his mum to speak to you, because she can answer any questions you have about him for the paramedics.' She placed her hand on the woman's arm. 'I've got the emergency services on the phone. An ambulance is on its way, but they want us to keep them informed with what's happening.'

'My boy. Oh, my God. My boy,' the woman said, her voice raw with anguish.

At that moment, the baby woke up and started to scream.

'I'm a doctor—so's my partner,' Hayley said. She rocked the pram in a desperate attempt to calm the baby. 'We'll do our best for your boy, but I need you to talk to the emergency services. They need to know about your son. Can you do that for me?'

'Oh, my God.'

She really needed the woman to get past her panic and help them. 'I need to help Sam to get your boy out. I'm Hayley. What's your name?'

'Alice.'

'And your little boy?'

'Jack.'

'All right, Alice. Keep rocking the baby for me.' She handed her phone to the woman. 'The emergency services are on the line. They'll ask you questions about Jack, things they need to know that I wouldn't be able to tell them but you'll know the answers because you're his mum. And I'll also tell you things to say to them. Is that OK?'

'OK.' Alice was shaking, her face white with terror, but to Hayley's relief she put the phone to her ear and used her other hand to rock the pram.

Hayley went to the side of the canal and knelt down.

Sam had just reached the side with the little boy, and Hayley leaned over and took the child from him.

It was very clear that the child wasn't breathing.

'ABC and CPR,' she said quietly to Sam.

He nodded, and while he was hauling himself out of the canal, she laid the child on the pavement and checked his airway. She fished water weed out of his mouth, then tilted his head back with one hand and lifted his chin with the other. She couldn't see any signs of breathing, and when she put her ear to the little boy's mouth and nose she couldn't hear or feel any signs of breathing, either. And there was no pulse.

She pinched the child's nose and put her lips over his mouth, and counted to two seconds in her head while she gave a slow full breath. She could see his chest rise and fall, and did a second breath.

'I'll do the compressions while you breathe,' Sam said; he put the heel of his hand on the middle of the little boy's breastbone and started counting as he gave the chest compressions.

She called to Alice, 'Tell them we've got Jack out and we started CPR ten seconds ago.'

She gave two more rescue breaths and checked for a pulse.

'Nothing,' she said quietly to Sam, and he continued with the compressions.

'Alice—do you have any clothes or spare blankets, anything dry?' she called.

'I've only got a change of clothes for the baby,' Alice said.

Thankfully the rocking had soothed the baby enough for the screams to die down to little whimpers.

'Is Jack breathing yet?' Alice asked, looking frantic.

'We're working on it—try not to worry, because this often happens when small children fall into very cold water,' Hayley said. Her own coat was dry; that would do to help cover Jack and keep him warm once they'd got the little boy breathing again.

Between her and Sam, they continued to do rescue breathing, checking for a pulse, and chest compressions. It felt as if they'd been working for ever, but neither of them intended to stop; given the temperature of the water and the little boy's age, there was still a good chance that Jack could recover.

And then finally he gasped and spluttered.

Hayley called, 'Alice, tell them Jack's taken his first spontaneous breath now.' She checked his pulse. 'And tell them there's spontaneous cardiac output now.'

Alice duly repeated what Hayley had said, but it was obvious to her that Alice hadn't taken it in. 'He's breathing on his own and he's got a pulse—tell them we're putting him in the recovery position.'

She stripped off her coat and covered Jack with it to help avoid hypothermia setting in. Alice was still shaking and tears were running down her face, so Hayley gently took the phone from her and spoke to the handlers. 'The ambulance is going to be here any second now,' she said to Sam.

Within a few moments, they could hear the siren of the ambulance, and the paramedics rushed up.

Between them Hayley and Sam gave the handover to the paramedics.

'The call centre told us the exact times you started CPR, his first spontaneous breath and his first sponta-neous cardiac output,' the lead paramedic said. 'Thank God you were able to get the poor little scrap out.' They carefully removed the wet clothes from the little boy and wrapped him in a warm dry blanket.

'This is Alice, Jack's mum,' Hayley said.

'Alice, we're going to take Jack to hospital,' the para-medic said. She glanced at the pram. 'We can take you and the baby with us, the pram as well. You'll see us hook Jack up to various machines in the back of the ambulance but don't worry, it's all standard procedure because we need to monitor his heart rate and oxygen levels on the way. At the hospital they'll continue mon-itoring him for a while and do tests to check that he doesn't have any injury to his neck or spine.'

Alice nodded. 'Thank you.' She turned to Sam and Hayley. 'And thank you both so much—without you, he would be dead.' She was clearly fighting to hold back the tears. 'He would have drowned. I don't know what I can do to thank you.'

'No need.' Sam waved away her thanks with a smile. 'We're both emergency doctors so this is our job—it's just we were on the side of the canal today instead of at the hospital.'

'Let us know how he is, later today,' Hayley said, and gave Alice her phone number.

Once the paramedics had taken Jack, Alice and the

baby to the ambulance, Hayley turned to Sam. 'We need to get you into dry clothes,' she said.

'We're hardly going to persuade a taxi driver to take us back to my place in this state,' he said ruefully, looking down at his soaked clothes. 'Do you know if we're near any shops?'

'There's Camden market,' she said.

He stripped off his top and his socks, then put his coat and shoes on. 'Hopefully they'll let me just buy the stuff and change in their changing rooms.'

'Let's get you some dry clothes, and then a hot drink,' she said.

It didn't take him long to buy a pair of jeans, a sweater and underwear; once he'd changed into dry clothes, Sam turned to her. 'Do you mind if we go back to my place for the hot drink?' he asked. 'I stink of canal water and I could really do with a shower.'

'Yes, of course.'

Hayley didn't say anything on the way back to Sam's, using the noise of the train on the tube tracks as an excuse not to talk. But inside she was a mass of seething emotions.

He'd jumped straight into the water. Not a single glance first to check if it was safe. And there was no way you could see to the bottom of the canal. He could have been caught in water weed and been unable to get back to the surface; or he could have been caught on rusty, twisted metal that someone had dumped at the bottom of the canal. If there were rats around—and there probably were—then he might have been infected by Weil's disease.

Worse still, Sam *knew* her fears. He would've known that she would worry even before he'd jumped into the canal. He'd said about trying to compromise, taking him with her to the adrenaline junkie stuff he liked so she could see it was safe, gradually overcoming her fears. Yet today he'd gone straight in without trying to find a safer way to rescue the little boy...

Then she was angry at herself. Of *course* he'd reacted by jumping in and rescuing the little boy. That was who Sam was. He saw a problem and he fixed it. He didn't hold back or wait for someone to take the lead. He just did it.

And she was holding him back with her fears.

He'd done a brave thing today. A wonderful thing. He'd saved a child's life. Instead of celebrating that and praising him, she was being selfish and thinking of the possible loss to herself. Fearing that she'd end up being lost and bereft again, the way she'd been when Evan had been killed.

Back at Sam's flat, she made two mugs of tea on autopilot while he showered. When he walked back into the kitchen, still damp from the shower, he looked at her. 'Do you need sugar in yours?'

'I don't take sugar.'

'Sweet tea's meant to be good for shock.'

'That's a myth,' she said. 'And I'm in not in shock.'

'You haven't said a word since we got on the tube. What's wrong?'

'I...' She blew out a breath. 'You saved that little boy's life.'

He shrugged. 'Anyone else would have done the same.'

No, they wouldn't. Not the way Sam had done it. The scary way. 'You went straight in without thinking of the danger to yourself.'

The critical tone in Hayley's voice touched a raw nerve. Right now, she sounded like Lynda. Sam hadn't lived up to Lynda's expectations; Hayley's tone made him wonder if he was making the same mistake all over again. 'This isn't about the little boy, is it?'

'No. Because now I've seen you in action in an emergency, Sam, and you lied to me. You don't even think of your own safety before you act.'

'What was I supposed to do—let him drown?'

'No, of course not.'

'There wasn't an alternative to going in there myself. Surely you could see that, too? Even if there had been a life-saving pole, he wouldn't have been able to grab it and hold on until I could pull him in. It was the only way to rescue him.'

'I know, and don't you realise how much I hate myself for this? I can't get past the fear, Sam, I just can't, and I hate the idea of losing you, and you *know* why I feel this way.' Her voice had risen almost to a wail. 'I've been here before.'

'So you're angry with me?' She was blaming him for making her remember Evan's death?

'Yes. And I'm even more angry with myself, because I know this is who you are and I shouldn't want to change you.'

Her words took some of the fight out of him. This wasn't another Lynda situation and he was overreacting. Hayley was as upset with herself as she was with him. He wrapped his arms around her. 'I'm sorry.'

'I'm sorry, too. It's wrong of me to feel this way.'

That was true. 'It's also understandable.' He stroked her hair.

'I worry that it'll be the same on a MERIT call-out. That you'll put yourself in danger—if they tell you it's not safe to go in but you think you can rescue someone, you're doing it anyway.'

'I wouldn't take stupid risks.'

'You just did,' she pointed out. 'So that doesn't re-assure me at all.'

He sighed. 'Lynda hated my mountain rescue work.'

'Your ex? She worried about you like I do?'

'Not quite. You worry that I'll be hurt or worse. She worried that mountain rescue work wasn't high-profile enough and I could have spent my time on some finance committee instead.'

She pulled back, frowning. 'Why on earth would you be on a finance committee?'

'To give my career a boost.'

'But you're a doer, not a talker.'

'It wasn't how Lynda saw things. She wanted to change me, too—to make me into someone I wasn't.'

Hayley bit her lip. 'I'm sorry.' Then her frown deepened. 'What did she want you to be?'

'The CEO of a hospital, eventually.'

'But then you'd spend your days in an office and dealing with admin and politics, not patients. And I don't think that would make you happy.'

Sam realised that Hayley understood him, and the rest of his anger dissolved.

'Is that why you broke up with her?' she asked.

'Yes. Though Lynda was the one who ended it. I guess I was a bit self-deluded. I thought she'd eventually realise this is who I am and I can't change.'

'I'm not asking you to change. Just to…maybe see the risks and think them through.' She looked at him. 'Do you want to be a CEO?'

'No. I'm not interested in managing staff and premises. If I'd wanted to be a CEO, I would have studied economics or law and gone into finance,' he said. 'I just want to work with patients. Though I'm not an unambitious wimp,' he added.

Hayley looked surprised. 'Of course you're not. Is that what she thought?'

'She thought I should have gone for promotion much more quickly than I did.'

'She obviously wasn't a medic, then,' Hayley said dryly, 'or she'd know that you can't cut corners on your training.'

'Actually, she's a paediatrician. And she's already a consultant.'

'Oh. Is she older than us?'

'No. But she's on several committees. She's a mover and a shaker. And very, very ambitious.' Sam blew out a breath. 'I guess she thought I held her back.'

'That's a shame. For both of you.'

'Maybe it's why we both dragged our feet about setting a date for the wedding,' he said. 'Maybe neither of us was prepared to admit we'd made a mistake. I wasn't what she really wanted, because I don't care about politics and power.'

'Was she what you wanted?' Hayley asked softly.

'I thought so, when I met her. But I know now that I want someone who'll support me instead of criticising me all the time.'

And Hayley had been critical of him—not just now, but ever since he'd been in London. She'd gone on and on about the adrenaline junkie stuff. And she hadn't been fair to him. 'I'm sorry. I wasn't trying to undermine you.'

'I know. You worried about me getting hurt. There's a difference,' he said.

'I was still criticising you.' She rested her head against his shoulder. 'I don't care whether you're a CEO or you're right at the bottom of the ladder, as long as you enjoy what you do. Life's too short to do a job you hate.' She swallowed hard. 'Though I can't help the way I feel about the risky stuff.'

'I'll try to think before I leap, in future. Literally as well as metaphorically.' He paused. 'Today made me realise how much I've missed diving. I was going to volunteer for the local search and rescue team—but I'm guessing that would be too much for you.'

'I'd spend the whole time worrying that you'd be caught on something at the bottom of the river and the air in your tank would run out, or a derelict building would crash down around you,' she admitted.

'The chances of that happening are about as small as being hit by lightning,' he pointed out. 'Especially when I've got a team keeping an eye on me. There are people monitoring a diver's air and depth and they'll spot the signs if something's wrong and get someone down there to rescue a stuck diver.'

'I know all that, in my head—but there's huge a difference between knowing something logically and knowing it emotionally,' she told him.

'I guess.' He held her close. 'I don't have any answers right now, but at least we're talking about the problem. We'll find a compromise. It'll just take time. And patience.'

And he definitely had patience—because he was falling for Hayley. Apart from his physical attraction to her, he liked her. She was sweet and funny and kind. And she was completely terrified of the stuff he loved doing... But they'd work something out. He was sure of it. It would just take a little time.

CHAPTER EIGHT

MICHAEL HARCOURT, THE head of the department, waited for all the emergency staff on duty to gather in the department, his expression serious. 'Everyone, we've got a major incident situation,' he said. 'There's been a big industrial fire at the other side of Muswell Hill in a clothing factory—at the moment the fire crew think it's likely to be an electrical fault that caused it. Obviously with cotton and other flammable material in the stockroom, the flames took hold very quickly. We need to triage all walk-ins, the same as we triage people coming in from the fire—obviously we need to treat the majors and the resus cases here, but refer all the walk-ins with minor injuries to local pharmacists, their family doctors or the next nearest emergency department. All our ambulances are on the way to the factory right now, and there's a MERIT coming in from Islington.'

Adrenaline surged through Hayley, mingled with relief. MERIT doctors were never used from the hospital that was receiving the casualties from a major incident because they were needed in their own department. So at least Sam would be out of the way of the fire. The very last thing she wanted was for Sam to be anywhere near a fire.

She pushed back the memories of the last big industrial fire they'd had to deal with in the department. The fire that had claimed Evan's life. *Not now.* She had to focus on saving the lives of the patients who were brought in by ambulance.

'We know we have casualties with burns and with smoke inhalation, but what we don't know is how many or how serious their conditions are. The burns unit is on standby, and I've called all the staff in. You all know the drill, so we're on code red,' Michael said. 'Any questions?'

When none were forthcoming, he read out the roster; Sam and Hayley were both rostered to Resus, dealing with the most serious casualties.

Michael took Hayley to one side before she headed to Resus. 'Are you all right, Hayley?'

'Yes.' As long as she focused on their patients and didn't think about the reason why they were being admitted, she'd be OK.

'Good. But I have a fair idea of how difficult this is going to be for you. If it gets too much, then you step out,' he said. 'And that's an order.'

'Got it.' She squeezed his hand. 'Thank you.'

'We always look after our own in this department,' he said.

The walking wounded were the first to come in— some with burns, and some still coughing after inhaling smoke. The Casualty Clearing Station had triaged them already; anyone who could walk was coded as a

Priority Three, meaning they needed treatment but it could be delayed until the more urgent cases had been seen, and they had green tags for easy identification. Priority Two were intermediate cases, more serious than P3s, and the patients had yellow tags; and Priority One cases were the most urgent and the patients would die without immediate intervention; they had red tags and were most likely to go straight into Resus.

But triage was always an ongoing situation, Hayley knew; someone who had a chest injury might be classed as a P3, but if they developed a pneumothorax they'd become a P2 until that was dealt with. So there would be a second layer of triage before they saw their patients, to see if anyone's condition had changed and become more serious.

Sam was waiting for her to join him in Resus. 'Are you OK?' he asked.

'I'm fine,' she said. 'As long as I'm too busy to think.'

'Do you want me to have a word with Michael and see if he can swap you to a different area, given that the cases we get in Resus—?'

'Thank you,' she cut in, pretty sure that he meant that the Resus cases were the serious ones, the ones where they were most likely to lose someone—and, given that it was a fire, this was way too close to the day she'd lost Evan. 'I appreciate your support, but Michael's already told me to step out if it gets too much. And I'd rather be in Resus, where I know I'm going to be too busy to think. Where I really need to concentrate on my patients.'

'OK. But promise you'll tell me if you need anything at all,' he said, squeezing her hand briefly.

'Thanks. But I'll cope.'

She and Sam helped to treat the minor injuries while they were waiting for the more serious cases to come in, cleaning burns and applying dressings and giving information sheets on how to care for the burns at home and when to seek further medical help.

Their first case was a man who'd been working in the stock room when the materials had suddenly blazed up, trapping him. The fire crew had managed to get him out, but not before he'd suffered severe burns.

'Peter Freeman, aged fifty,' Dev, the senior paramedic, told them. 'We've intubated him and he's been on high-flow oxygen.' He handed them a bag. 'We removed what's left of his clothing and his jewellery, and it's all safely in here. We've used a cling film dressing on his burns and put a cold wet towel on top of that to cool him down—he's been cooling for about fifteen minutes now.'

It was important to cool the burned area as quickly as possible, but at the same time they needed to be careful of the risk of hypothermia, Hayley knew.

'We've cannulated him and we started him on a litre of warmed fluid on the way in,' Dev said. 'And we've given him some initial pain relief.'

'Great—thanks, Dev,' Sam said. 'And I see you've got him sitting up.'

'Most of the burns are to his chest, arms and face,' Dev said. Sitting the patient upright lessened the risk of swelling—and it was particularly important to avoid swelling of the throat when burns to the head and neck were involved.

'Mr Freeman, my name's Hayley and this is Sam, and we're going to look after you here in the emergency department at Muswell Hill Hospital,' Hayley said. 'You've got a tube in to help you breathe, so you won't be able to talk, but if we do anything that makes you uncomfortable, please just lift your hand and we'll stop, OK? And we'll talk you through everything we're doing so you know what's going on. We're going to start with taking a tiny bit of blood from you so we can run some tests, OK?'

Mr Freeman managed a tiny nod.

She took a sample of blood and sent it for urgent haemoglobin, cross-matching and coagulation screen.

'And now we're going to take the wet towels and the dressings off so we can assess your burns, clean them and put new dressings on,' Hayley said. 'I know it's going to be uncomfortable, but we'll be as gentle as we can.'

Between them, Hayley and Sam gently unwrapped the towel and the dressings. The skin on his upper torso and the back of Mr Freeman's hands and forearms, which had clearly taken the brunt of the injury where he'd tried to shield his face from the flames, was dry and white, with no blisters; there was no capillary refill.

Working to the rule of nines—where you could estimate the body surface area affected by using multiples of nine—they assessed the extent of Peter Freeman's injuries.

'Over twenty per cent, full-thickness burns,' Sam

said quietly. 'He's going to need surgery.' Removing the burned skin and tissues would help to prevent infection and allow the wounds to heal.

'And we need to watch out for shock,' she said. The cling film dressing would have helped to stop leakage of plasma and blood—but the bigger the burn area, the bigger the likelihood of the patient sustaining hypovolaemic shock. This was where the circulatory system couldn't provide enough oxygenated blood to the body, so the vital organs were deprived of oxygen. The problem was that the most common signs of shock—pallor, clammy skin, and shallow breathing—were masked by Mr Freeman's condition and the fact that he was intubated. 'We need to put CVP line in so we can keep an eye on his blood pressure, I think.'

Sam nodded.

'Mr Freeman, we need to be able to measure your blood pressure, so I'm going to put a special catheter in your arm to let us do that. Is that OK?' Hayley asked.

He gave a tiny nod.

She explained the procedure to him and why they needed to do it, and then between them she and Sam inserted a central venous catheter. At least now they'd have an indication of his blood pressure and it would also help them to manage fluid replacement.

'We might need to do an escharotomy, too,' Sam said quietly. The burned skin could act like a tourniquet if there was swelling and oedema in the tissues underneath the burn, and cause problems with the circulation; where the chest was concerned, it could also cause problems breathing because the lungs couldn't expand properly. Putting an incision through the burned skin relieved the pressure and stopped the circulatory problems.

They cleaned the burns, then covered them with a pad and gauze bandage; covering the exposed nerve endings helped to reduce the pain.

'We're going to send you through to the burns unit, Mr Freeman,' Sam said. 'They'll be able to keep monitoring you and they'll be able to check your dressing and make sure there isn't any infection. You're going to need to have surgery and skin grafts on your chest and arms, but the surgeon upstairs will talk that through with you.'

Once Mr Freeman had been transferred to the burns unit, they had another patient in with burns, this time to her legs.

Sam introduced them both quickly. 'Mrs Marchant, we're going to assess your burns,' he said, 'and then we'll clean them and put dressings on. We'll talk you through everything we're doing, but let us know if you're worried about anything.'

'I… I've never been so scared in my life,' she said.

Hayley noted the hoarseness of the woman's voice. Was it because she'd been crying or maybe straining to make her voice heard at the factory, or was it an early sign of problems with smoke inhalation?

'Mrs Marchant, can I ask you to cough and spit for me?' she asked, handing their patient a tissue.

Mrs Marchant looked confused, but nodded, and coughed and spat into the tissue that Hayley gave her.

Hayley took a brief look at the sputum and relaxed. There were no signs of soot, which would've signalled potentially serious problems, and there was no sign of cyanosis around Mrs Marchant's mouth. All the same, she said, 'Just before we look at your burns, I want to double-check your breathing, because if you've inhaled smoke it can give you carbon monoxide poisoning.'

'Like the thing people get if they sleep in a house with a dodgy boiler, or in a tent with one of those disposable barbecue things?'

'Exactly,' Hayley said.

Her level of consciousness was fine; although her pulse rate and blood pressure were both raised, that was most probably a reaction to the terrifying event she'd been caught up in. Hayley listened to Mrs Marchant's chest; everything sounded normal, and her breathing looked normal, too. Mrs Marchant had clearly been crying, so the hoarseness was probably due to that. But, with smoke inhalation and carbon monoxide poisoning, things could change rapidly. She needed a blood sample analysed for carboxyhaemoglobin, to see how serious the carbon monoxide poisoning was. 'I'm just going to take a small sample of blood for testing,' she said.

'I used to hate needles. But they're like nothing after you've been in a fire and don't think you're going to get out in time,' Mrs Marchant said, sounding shaky.

Was that how it had been for Evan? Those last few moments, knowing that he wasn't going to get out?

She pushed the thought aside.

Not now.

Focus.

'We'll assess your burns now,' she said.

These were deep dermal burns: the skin was dry,

cherry red and blotchy, and there were blisters. There was no capillary refill, she noticed.

'We'd like to check where you can feel things,' Sam said, 'so I'd like you to close your eyes for me, Mrs Marchant. I'm going to touch the skin on your legs with a piece of cotton wool, and I'd like you to tell me when you can feel it. Is that OK?'

'Yes,' she said, and closed her eyes.

He dabbed the cotton wool lightly against their patient's skin; Hayley knew that he needed to touch rather than stroke, because a moving sensation was conducted along pain pathways and wouldn't tell them where she actually felt sensation.

By the time Sam had finished and said that Mrs Marchant could open her eyes again, she looked terrified. 'I couldn't feel anything. Does that mean I'm not going to walk again or something?'

'No,' Sam reassured her. 'It means that you have deep dermal burning.'

'What's that? Second degree? Third degree?'

'In between,' he said. 'It's not as serious as full-thickness burns—what we used to call third degree—so you'll recover without needing surgery. With this sort of burn, it's common not to be able to feel anything on your skin. It will heal within the next three to eight weeks, but you will be left with some scarring.'

She put a hand to her mouth, and a tear trickled down her cheek. 'My husband always said my legs were my best feature.'

'Your husband,' Hayley said softly, 'will just be glad you're alive. He won't care about the scarring. It's *you* that matters.' And she knew that from bitter, bitter experience. She wouldn't have cared if Evan had come home with scars. She'd just wanted him *home*.

Hayley's face had no colour in it at all, Sam noticed.

'Do you need five minutes?' he asked her quietly.

'No. I'll manage. The patients always come first.'

This must be so hard for her, he thought, remembering his own nightmare case. But it was typical of Hayley to put the patients before her own feelings. And maybe keeping busy and keeping her focus on her patients would stop her remembering the worst of the day that Evan had been killed.

They were in the middle of cleaning and dressing Mrs Marchant's burns, careful not to burst the blisters, when a middle-aged man came into the room. 'Brenda? Brenda Marchant?' he asked. 'The nurse said she was in here. She said I could come and find her.'

'Over here,' Sam called.

The man rushed over to them.

'Oh—Timmy.' Mrs Marchant burst into tears, and her husband hugged her fiercely.

'Oh, God—when I heard it on the news, I thought I'd lost you. I went to the factory and they told me they'd sent you here.'

'My legs,' she said. 'They're burned. They're going to be scarred. I'm going to be ugly.'

'No, you're not. And I don't care if you've got scars, as long as you're all right.'

Sam glanced at Hayley and saw a film of tears in her eyes. She'd been in precisely that position last year.

And he was pretty sure that she wouldn't have minded a few scars if her fiancé had at least made it out of the building alive.

'Sorry, am I getting in the way?' Mr Marchant asked.

'You thought you'd lost her. Of course you want to be with her. Give her another hug, and then if you wouldn't mind sitting to the side, that's fine,' Hayley said.

But Sam heard the crack in her voice. *You thought you'd lost her.*

She'd been there. The difference was, in her case, her worst fears had been confirmed.

Once they'd finished dressing Mrs Marchant's wounds, explained everything to her husband and sent her out into the department for continued monitoring from the inhalation risk, Sam turned to Hayley. 'Coffee break. Now.'

'We haven't got time,' she protested.

'Hydration's important,' he said, 'because this is going to be a long day. We're taking five minutes to grab a coffee, stick enough cold water in it so we can gulp it straight down, and maybe grab a sandwich.' He wrinkled his nose. 'Technically, you're my superior so I can't pull rank. But I can still nag. And I'm nagging now.'

'I'm fine.'

'You don't look it,' he said.

She lifted her chin. 'I'm fine.'

She was far from fine, he was sure, but maybe now wasn't the time or place to push it. 'OK, coffee and food.'

As he'd suggested, they grabbed half a cup of coffee

each, poured enough cold water in it so was cool enough to drink straight down, and shared the first pack of sandwiches they could grab from the vending machine.

Their next patient was a man who'd inhaled smoke and fallen unconscious.

'He was identified by one of his colleagues as Keith Cooper. We're not sure of his age—mid-forties, perhaps,' the paramedic said. 'His chest wall moved normally and symmetrically,' the paramedic continued, 'but the cyanosis was obvious so we intubated him and put him on high-flow oxygen. He hasn't regained consciousness yet.'

'OK. I'm glad you intubated him before the oedema caused by the inhalation made it impossible. Thanks,' Sam said.

He took a blood sample for analysis; if it turned out that more than ten per cent of the total haemoglobin was carboxyhaemoglobin, they'd give Keith some protein thromboprophylaxis as well as keeping him on high flow oxygen. If he'd inhaled carbon particles or toxic fumes, there was a risk of tracheobronchitis and pneumonia.

Between them, they checked Keith's pulse rate, blood pressure and circulation.

'There's some singeing of his eyebrows and around his nose,' Hayley said.

'We've got him on oxygen and a drip, and there's not much more we can do until he's conscious again and the blood results are back,' Sam said. 'I think we should send him up to the burns unit because he's going to need mechanical ventilation for a while.'

'Agreed,' she said.

They alternated between seeing burns victims and smoke inhalation victims for the rest of the day. Sam kept an eye on Hayley, ready to support her if she had the slightest wobble; but she was completely professional and focused on their patients' needs. Then again, he hadn't expected anything else from her. He'd liked her strength and calmness right from the outset, when he'd first seen her helping a middle-aged man with an asthma attack and no inhaler.

While they were between patients, one of the firefighters came in to see them.

'Haze! I heard you were in here so I've sneaked in for thirty seconds to say hello. You doing OK?' He gave her a one-armed hug, which she returned.

'Joe! It's good to see you.' She frowned. 'What happened to you?'

'The building collapsed on us,' he said. 'I got caught by a bit of falling debris. Bust my shoulder.'

Sam noticed that she went white again at the firefighter's words.

Wasn't that how Evan had been killed—the building had collapsed on him?

'I'm fine,' Joe said. 'Just cross that I didn't get out of the way in time.'

'Uh-huh,' she said.

'I know you're busy, and I'll let you get on, but I had to come in to say a quick hello. Don't be a stranger, Haze. We've missed you.'

'Give my love to the crew,' she said.

'I will. Take care,' Joe said, and walked out of Resus.

When they'd finally processed all the casualties from the fire and the waiting room had returned to just the normal kind of evening cases, it was time to go home. And Sam made sure he was waiting by Hayley's locker when she walked into the staffroom.

'Someone very wise once cornered me when I'd had a really bad day and she made me put one foot in front of the other,' he said softly.

She just looked at him and said nothing.

Yeah. He knew how that felt. 'I think,' he said, 'that's the sort of day you've had. So I'm taking you back to my place and cooking you dinner. Nothing fancy. Whatever I've got in the fridge, which could be anything from cheese on toast to pasta and pesto.'

She shook her head. 'I'm not hungry.'

And he knew that tone, too. Where you'd reached the bottom and you had nothing left to give. When you needed someone to take the burden of thinking from you.

'I don't care if you're not hungry. You need to eat. Get your stuff.'

Dully, she took her things from her locker. She let him put his arm round her and shepherd her out of the hospital.

'What about your bike?' she said when they went out of the hospital gates.

'It can stay here overnight and I'll walk in tomorrow,' Sam said. 'It's not a problem. Come on. We're going home.'

CHAPTER NINE

SAM TOOK HAYLEY back to his flat. Just as she'd done for him on the day when Pauline Jacobs had had a silent heart attack in the department, he simply got her to do a simple task to take her mind off things; he asked her to lay the table in his kitchen while he made them both an omelette.

'There's water in the fridge,' he said, 'and there's a bag of salad, a box of baby plum tomatoes and some dressing. You know where the crockery and cutlery are.'

She busied herself putting the salad in a bowl and pouring them both some water; by the time she was done, he was ready to serve up.

She picked at her omelette, and ate about half of it.

'I'm sorry,' she said. 'You've gone to all this trouble, and I...'

A single tear spilled down her cheek and she lapsed into silence, as if all the pain inside had grown so much that it blocked her words from coming out.

Sam knew what that felt like. When everything seemed hopeless and you were choking with misery. So he pushed his chair back, went round to her side of the table, scooped her out of her chair then sat down in her place and settled her on his lap. He held her close, stroking her hair. 'It's OK, Hayley. It was only an omelette—nothing fancy. It doesn't matter that you didn't finish it. You ate something, that's the main thing.'

'I just…'

Her shoulders heaved, and finally she began to sob.

He held her until she was all cried out, then reached across the table for a glass of water. She sipped it gratefully.

'Talk to me,' he said. 'Don't let it all stay in your head and your heart, where it'll destroy you. Let it out. Tell me.'

'The clothing factory fire.' She dragged in a breath. 'It just brought the day of the workshop fire straight back. Especially as it was Evan's crew dealing with it.' She gulped. 'His friends—*my* friends—I've been avoiding them because it's too hard seeing them without him. Today was the first time I'd seen any of them since the funeral. Joe was so nice about it. And I hate myself for being so selfish and pathetic. For being such a coward.'

'You're not selfish, pathetic or a coward,' he reassured her. 'It's completely understandable. It's hard to face people when you've lost someone.'

'If it had been the other way round, if I'd been the one who was killed, Evan wouldn't have avoided the social stuff, the way I have. He would've still come to the ward's Christmas party and the summer barbecue. I just…' She shook her head. 'Today brought back all the bad memories and I hate that I had to push myself through it. This is my *job*. I ought to be able to deal with major incidents—just as you have to face treating patients with heart attacks. I know we can't save everyone; but the next time you get a case similar to someone you lost, you're supposed to try and put it out of your head and just get on with it and help people—because that's what doctors *do*.'

'That's exactly what you did today. You got on with it and helped people.' He stroked her hair. 'I'm guessing this is the first big fire the department has dealt with since Evan died?'

'Yes.'

'It's really hard, having to repeat the worst day of your life.'

'And then you have to pull yourself together afterwards. You've got people asking you all the time if you're all right, and you know you're supposed to say yes even when the real answer's no, because it's the polite thing to do. Plus, if you admit how bad things are, people will start going silent when you walk into the room, because they simply don't know what to say to you. The next thing you know, you're the subject of the hospital grapevine, with everyone talking about you and suddenly changing the conversation and looking guilty when you walk over.'

He understood her aversion to hospital gossip. Even though he was pretty sure that the people in their department were all nice people and had only talked about her because they were worried about her and wanted to help, he could understand that it wasn't much fun being the subject of everyone's scrutiny.

'So did you live at your flat with Evan?' he asked.

She shook her head. 'We lived three roads away, in a slightly bigger flat. We were saving up for a place of our own. But I couldn't handle living there when he died, Sam. I hated walking into the flat and expecting to see him there, and for a second thinking that I *could* see him or hear him—and remembering all over again that he wouldn't be coming home any more. So I talked my landlord into letting me terminate my lease early and I moved here about a year ago.'

'Do you still see Evan's family?'

'No. They weren't close. Anyway, they lived miles away.'

Distance in all senses of the word, he thought. His own family would've made sure that his partner still felt included. They would've made the effort. But not all families were like that.

'I noticed there weren't any photographs of him with you on your mantelpiece or your fridge—they're all of your family, Dani or the department,' he said.

'I haven't put his photographs up in my new flat. It hurt too much to see them,' she admitted.

'Maybe,' he said, 'looking at some pictures of him are what you need to do right now. So you've got some good memories to get you through today.'

She looked at him as if surprised that he'd make the suggestion. 'I guess. There are a few on my phone.'

'You get your phone,' he said, 'and I'm going to make us some hot chocolate, and then maybe we can look through the photos together.' If he could make her feel better, if he could make the good memories outweigh the bad for her, then he'd be happier. He hated seeing her in so much pain.

By the time he'd finished making the hot chocolate and ushered her through to the living room, she'd pulled up the photographs on her phone.

'This is the summer he died,' she said. 'We'd decided not to have a holiday that year, because we'd got the wedding coming up in September, so we just had days out. We went to Brighton so we could paddle in the sea.' There were pictures of them together on the rides on the pier, with the sea in the background, and with Brighton's iconic Pavilion.

What Sam noticed was that they looked really happy together.

They'd thought it was their last summer before getting married; yet it had been their last summer, full stop.

How horribly, horribly sad.

'He looks a nice guy,' Sam said.

'He was. He got on well with everyone. And he put his life on the line to help people—just as you will with the MERIT team.' She swallowed hard. 'And it scares me, Sam, to the point where I can hardly function. I hate the idea of having to go through all that again.'

'Then it's simple. I'll give up MERIT,' Sam said. 'I can still make a difference to people's lives in our department.'

She shook her head. 'I don't think it will be enough for you. I know you miss the mountain rescue work. And I don't want to stop you doing something you love.'

'So what are you suggesting?' he asked, not sure where she was going with this. 'Because if you don't want me to stop doing the MERIT team but you also don't want to have to cope with me doing it… That sounds like you want us to go back to being strictly colleagues. That it's over between us.'

'No,' she said. 'I don't want that either. I just don't want to lose you. But I'm pushing you away and this is supposed to be the Year of Saying Yes.'

'And now you've really lost me. What do you mean, the Year of Saying Yes?' he asked.

'Dani and I made a pact in the summer, when her divorce from Leo came through. She said she didn't want to waste her life being miserable over someone who didn't love her, and she said Evan wouldn't have wanted me to be miserable and lonely. So we agreed we'd say yes to every opportunity to make our life better and happier.' She swallowed hard. 'Which was why I ended up going to Iceland on my own, after she broke her foot.'

'And why you and I had a holiday fling?'

She nodded. 'And then you turned up in our department. I honestly intended to be just colleagues, perhaps friends, but I just couldn't resist you.'

'Only you can't get past the rescue stuff.'

'I don't want to lose you,' she repeated.

'I don't want to lose you either. And if being with you means I have to give up MERIT, then I'm prepared to do that.' He gave her a wry smile. 'Which I think tells you how I feel about you, because I would never have given up the mountain rescue stuff for Lynda.'

'But you loved her, didn't you?'

'I did. Until I realised that she didn't love me for who

I was—she loved me for who she thought I could be,' he admitted. 'Then I was suspended and she worked out that I never would be the man she thought I could be.'

Hayley frowned. 'Hang on. She dumped you after you were suspended? But I thought you broke up before then?'

Even though he didn't want to make Lynda the scapegoat here, there wasn't any other way of putting it. He looked away. 'Yes. It was the week after my team was hauled in to see the head of department. When I was suspended, she thought that my career was over.'

'But why on earth would she think that?' Hayley's frown deepened. 'You're meticulous at work. You never cut corners. There's no way the investigation would've had any other outcome—of course you and your team were always going to be exonerated.'

Hayley's faith in him warmed him from the inside out. It was so very far away from Lynda's attitude. 'I have to be honest and say that she had a point. There was always the chance I might've done something wrong, or there was something I missed recording that could've made the difference. Nobody's perfect,' he pointed out.

'But you were exonerated.'

'That doesn't really matter. You know what they say about mud tending to stick? When it came to getting promoted, Lynda's view was that people would remember what had happened with me and then look a bit more closely at the other candidates, finding one of them more suitable than me.'

'That would be unfair discrimination,' Hayley said.

'And anyone who'd ever worked with you would *know* you're good at your job.'

'Even so. She had a point about people remembering and having doubts, even if they got past them. And if mud stuck to me, it would also stick to her by association. She was engaged to someone who was suspended—so, whatever the outcome, the investigation would harm her career.'

Hayley's eyes glittered with what looked like outrage. 'That's—that's...' She shook her head. 'I can't believe someone would be that selfish and shallow. She was your fiancée, for pity's sake! The one person you'd expect to believe in you and have your back.'

His thoughts exactly. Lynda's lack of faith in him had cut him to the quick. 'It didn't quite work out that way.'

'She didn't believe in you. I can't get over that. That's so horrible.' She blew out a breath. 'So when I went all quiet on you, I was worrying that you were going to end up the same way as Evan—but I'm guessing you've got similar worries about things repeating themselves, and you started thinking that I didn't believe in you, too?'

'I was probably being paranoid,' he said, 'and letting what happened with Lynda act as a kind of filter to the way I saw things. But you also said you didn't want anyone to know we were seeing each other,' he reminded her. 'I thought maybe you were ashamed of me.'

'No. I told you it was complicated. I knew it was time to move on, but I still felt guilty Plus you were the first person I'd dated since Evan, and...' She rubbed a hand over her face. 'I don't know how to put this. You would've been grilled to an inch of your life by half the hospital if they found out I was seeing you. And then everyone would be talking about us, and saying how pleased they were that I'd finally decided to move on—as if I was replacing Evan and scrubbing him out of my life. I just couldn't face that.'

'You can't replace a person,' he said, 'and you'll always love Evan. Of course you will. You were engaged to him for how long?'

'A year and a half,' she said, 'and we dated for a year before we got engaged.'

'Anyone who asks you to share their life will understand that you'll always love Evan,' Sam said, 'and that's fine—because love doesn't have limits like that. He was an important part of your life. Loving him and cherishing your memories doesn't mean that you can't share your future with someone else—that you can't love someone else and live a rich, happy life together.'

Love didn't have limits.

Yet she was limiting him.

'I can't make you give up MERIT,' she said. 'It's part of who you are. You're an emergency doctor. You save lives. And I can understand that it's important to you to use your skills to do that on the front line. To make a difference where you're really needed.'

He nodded. 'But you're important to me, too. I don't want you to worry yourself sick and remember how you felt when Evan was killed, every time I'm called out on a job.'

'Let me go through this logically,' she said. 'The Medical Incident Officer won't let anyone on the team

take unnecessary risks. A doctor at the site will have
to wear personal protective equipment, and will only
be allowed in the area right next to the incident if the
service responsible for safety at the scene says it's safe
to be there.'

'Exactly,' he said. 'The rule is not to risk your own
safety, ever—because as a rescue worker you're meant
to be helping, not adding to the problem.'

*But Evan risked his own safety. And then he was
killed.*

Though she didn't say it, he clearly guessed what
she was thinking, because he squeezed her hand. 'I'm
a doctor, not a firefighter,' he said. 'I know my limits
and I won't take unnecessary risks.'

She'd worry whenever he was on a MERIT incident.
Of course she would. But over time she'd become more
confident that she wasn't going to lose him.

'I love you and I want to be with you,' Sam said
softly. 'But I also want our relationship to be public. I
don't want to feel as if I'm the shameful secret you don't
want anyone to know about.'

'I'm not ashamed of you,' she said. 'You're a good
doctor. A good man. I'm proud of you. You've been
through an experience that would make a lot of people
walk away from medicine altogether—but you're still
here, doing your best to make the world a better place.'
She took a deep breath. 'You make my world a better
place, Sam. With you, I've been happy for the first time
since I lost Evan. And you're right. I'm never going to
forget him and a part of me will always love him. But

there's room in my life for another relationship—and I want that relationship to be with you.'

'I love you,' Sam said. 'I'll compromise and tone down the dangerous stuff.'

'You're never going to be able to talk me into doing mountain-climbing or even skiing, and I'm not even sure I can bear to watch you do it,' Hayley said, 'but I won't stop you from doing what you need to do. I'll trust that you won't take unnecessary risks. I'll worry about you—of course I will—but it's part of who you are. Part of why I love you. I won't stop you doing any of the stuff you need to do.'

He kissed her. 'Today's been a rough day. But it's going to get better, because from now on we're going to be right by each other's side.' He paused. 'It's probably the wrong time to ask you this, but I think we've already wasted enough time. And today's taught me that life is really precious, and you should seize it and make the most of it.'

'Seize the day,' she said. 'That's a good plan.'

He slid off his sofa and knelt before her on one knee. 'Hayley Clark, I love you and I want to spend the rest of my life with you. Will you marry me—and preferably as soon as possible?'

Given that it was the Year of Saying Yes, there was only one answer she could make. 'Sam Price, I love you, too. Yes.'

CHAPTER TEN

December 1st

IT WAS THE night of the departmental Christmas party, with a sit-down meal in the function room of the local pub and everyone pulling crackers and wearing the paper hats and groaning over the terrible jokes.

Michael Harcourt, the head of the department, presided over the Secret Santa, and everyone laughed when Josh's present turned out to be a miniature model of a go-kart and a home-made rib protector crafted from bubble-wrap.

'There is one more thing,' Sam said when Michael had finished, 'except I need to be the one to give this, not Michael.' He walked round the table to Hayley's chair, and held out a cracker to her.

She smiled, knowing what was inside; they'd agreed to go public on their relationship, and Sam was making it very public indeed. She pulled the other end of the cracker, revealing a velvet-covered box, and everyone gasped.

Sam adopted the traditional pose of going down on

one knee, and held out the box to her. 'Hayley Clark, would you please do me the honour of becoming my wife?'

'Yes,' she said, and he took the simple diamond engagement ring from the box and slid it onto her left hand.

'I think this calls for bubbles,' Michael said. 'Congratulations, both of you.' He shook their hands warmly.

'So have you set a date?' Dev asked.

'Christmas Eve,' Sam said.

'So we have a whole year to wait for wedding cake?' Melissa, one of the nurses, asked.

'Um, no. More like a shade over three weeks,' Hayley said.

'What—you're getting married *this* Christmas Eve?' Josh asked, sounding shocked.

'Yes. We'll be giving out the invitations to our wedding tomorrow,' Sam said. 'And we hope to see as many of you there as possible.'

'How on earth are you going to organise a wedding in three weeks?' Melissa asked. 'I mean, I know you two are efficient machines, but weddings...'

'We gave notice to the register office ten days ago and we have a venue booked nearby—and the venue's organising the bar and the catering for us,' Sam said. 'I'm hiring a suit and Dani's already taken Hayley shopping for a dress. Plus we've been making lists of people we need to call for everything else.'

'My aunt makes cakes,' Josh said. 'So if you can't get a baker, I can ask her to make the cake for you.'

'My sister does flowers,' Melissa said. 'I can ask her to do yours for you.'

'And my brother's a photographer,' Darryl said. 'I know he's not doing anything on Christmas Eve. I can book him for you.'

'What about a band?' Dev asked.

'Dani's asking Maybe Baby,' Hayley said. The maternity unit and paediatric ward had a house band between them, which often played at hospital functions. She smiled. 'I think you've all answered Melissa's question between you. It looks as if we're organising it by teamwork. And thank you, all of you, for being so supportive.'

'It's really good to see you happy again, Hayley,' Melissa said, and hugged her. 'I can't think of a nicer couple for this to happen to. And it's so romantic, getting married on Christmas Eve. This is going to be one of the best Christmases ever.'

Michael started handing out glasses of bubbly. 'Agreed. And I propose a toast: to Hayley and Sam.'

'Hayley and Sam,' everyone chorused, lifting their glasses.

Christmas Eve

'Turn round so I can check it's all perfect,' Danielle said when she'd done up the zip at the back of Hayley's dress.

Hayley dutifully performed a pirouette. 'Do I look OK?'

'More than OK,' Danielle said, and gave her a swift hug. 'That dress is perfect for you.' The cream dress had a sleeveless V-necked lace bodice and a full skirt with layers of tulle and organza that floated down to just below Hayley's knees.

Hayley stepped into her dark red high-heeled court shoes, which matched the spray of roses she was using for her bouquet, and also matched Danielle's empire-line knee-length bridesmaid's dress.

'Don't we look fabulous in our tiaras?' Danielle asked, standing next to her in front of the mirror and pouting.

But there was an over-brightness to her best friend's smile that worried Hayley. 'We do. Dani, are you sure everything's OK?'

'Of course it is. Why wouldn't it be? It's your wedding day.'

Which was precisely the reason Hayley knew Danielle wouldn't talk to her today about what was really wrong. She made a mental note to pin her best friend down the day after Boxing Day, when she and Sam were back from their brief honeymoon in Iceland, and find out exactly what Danielle was hiding. 'I love you,' she said. 'If it wasn't for you insisting on the Year of Saying Yes, I wouldn't have met Sam in Iceland, I wouldn't have given him a chance when he started at the hospital, and I wouldn't be here right now, getting ready to marry him.'

'Don't make me cry,' Danielle warned. 'I haven't got time to redo my make-up—or yours.'

And it was hard to make Danielle cry. Something was definitely up, Hayley thought. But she'd get to the bottom of it in a couple of days.

Hayley's mother called up to say the cars were there: a vintage black Thunderbird for Danielle, herself and Hayley's sister Joanna, and a vintage cream Rolls-Royce for Hayley and her father.

'You both look amazing,' Hayley's father said, blinking back the tears when Danielle and Hayley walked downstairs. 'Ready?'

'Ready,' Hayley confirmed.

All she needed was the deep red velvet cape that Danielle had borrowed from a friend to wrap round her shoulders, to keep her warm until they were back indoors again—and then she was sitting in the back of the Rolls-Royce with her father, being driven to the register office where Sam was waiting for her.

Sam waited at the register office, feeling sick.

'She'll be here. Dead on time, too,' Martin, his brother, reassured him. 'We're early.'

'I suppose so.' Sam blew out a breath. 'Why do I never get nervous like this at work or on the mountain rescue team?'

'Because you know what you're doing in the emergency department or doing rescue, and you're prepared for anything,' Martin said, clapping him on the shoulder, 'whereas this... You just have to be patient. She'll be here.'

'I guess I'm not very good at waiting,' Sam said ruefully.

At that moment, Hayley's mother and sister walked in, and took their places on the left-hand side of the room. Hayley's mother gave him a reassuring smile.

'See?' Martin whispered.

Anton Powell, the obstetrician who played lead guitar in the Maybe Baby band, had brought an acoustic guitar to the register office. At a nod from Hayley's mother, he began playing Bach's 'Air on a G String'. Sam heard the door open, then looked behind him to see Hayley walking towards him on her father's arm, with Danielle walking behind them. His heart skipped a beat: she looked so beautiful. And today she was joining her life to his. For ever.

When Hayley got to the front and sat down between her father and her bridesmaid, the registrar introduced herself as Camilla Fletcher, explained that the register office had been sanctioned by law, and added, 'If any person present knows of any legal reason why these two people should not be joined in matrimony they should declare it now.'

As Sam expected, there was complete silence.

'I now ask the bride and groom to come and stand before me,' Camilla said. 'Before you are joined in matrimony it is my duty to remind you of the solemn and binding character of the vows you are about to make. Marriage in this country is the union of two people voluntarily entered into for life to the exclusion of all others. I am now going to ask you each in turn to declare that you know of no legal reason why you may not be joined together in marriage.'

Sam repeated the words after her. 'I do solemnly declare that I know not of any lawful impediment why I, Samuel Price, should not be joined in lawful matrimony to Hayley Clark.'

Hayley smiled at him and repeated the declaration.

'I ask you now, Samuel Price—do you take Hayley Clark to be your lawful wedded wife, to be loving, faithful and loyal to her for the rest of your life together?' Camilla asked.

'I do,' Sam said, and smiled at Hayley—who made exactly the same answer to her own question.

Then came the contracting words. Sam took a deep breath and echoed Camilla's prompting. 'I call upon these persons here present to witness that I, Samuel Price, do take thee, Hayley Clark, to be my lawful wedded wife, to love and to cherish from this day forward.'

Once Hayley had made the same declaration, Camilla said, 'The exchanging of rings is the traditional way of sealing the contract that you have just made. It is an unbroken circle, symbolising unending and everlasting love and is the outward sign of the lifelong promise that you have just made to each other.'

Martin stepped forward with the rings.

'I give you this ring as a symbol of our love,' Sam said. 'All that I am I give to you. All that I have I share with you. I promise to love you, to be faithful and loyal, in good times and bad. May this ring remind you always of the words we have spoken today.'

Hayley mouthed, 'I love you,' as he slid the ring onto her finger. And then she made the same declaration, and slid the wedding ring onto his finger.'

'Today is a new beginning. May you have many happy years together and in those years may all your hopes and dreams be fulfilled,' Camilla said. 'Above all, may you always believe in each other and may the warmth of your love enrich not only your lives but the lives of all those around you.'

And Sam knew without a doubt that Hayley believed in him—just as he believed in her. The glance they shared told him that she knew exactly what he was thinking.

'It now gives me great pleasure to tell you both that you are now legally husband and wife. You may now seal the contract with a kiss.'

Sam didn't need a second invitation. He bent Hayley back over his arm and kissed her thoroughly, to the cheers of their family and closest friends.

'Now, ladies and gentlemen, please be seated while the register is completed,' Camilla said. 'As you have witnessed, a civil marriage is a brief, simple ceremony—but, Hayley and Sam, you are legally and solemnly joined together in matrimony and I would like to be the first to congratulate you both—and to wish you a very happy Christmas.'

'Thank you,' Hayley said, almost shyly.

Both their fathers signed the register while Anton played a love song on the guitar. Dani joined in with the singing, then Hayley's sister Joanna, then Sam's sister-in-law Robyn, and by the end they were all joining in with the chorus of the well-known classic hit.

'And it's right,' Hayley whispered to Sam. 'Love *is* all we really need.'

Once Darryl's brother had taken photographs of the wedding party outside on the steps of the register office, they headed across the road to their reception venue: a

Victorian gothic church, which had been turned into a community arts centre.

'Excuse me a minute,' Martin said.

A few seconds later, snow began to fall very softly.

Martin reappeared with a huge grin on his face. 'Well, hey—it's Christmas Eve. And you need to have snow at Christmas, don't you?'

'How on earth did you manage that?' Hayley asked.

'Snow machine,' he said, smiling. 'Don't worry—it's biodegradable and non-toxic, and I cleared it with the venue last week.'

Everyone in the wedding party burst into an impromptu chorus of a Christmas song about snow.

Hayley and Sam laughed, and thoroughly enjoyed having their wedding photographs taken in real snow on Christmas Eve.

Then they headed up to the top floor of the building. There was a canopy of fairy lights in the vaulted ceiling, and there were floor-to-ceiling lancet windows set within tall Gothic arches. At one end of the room, a large table was set up for the sit-down meal, covered in a white damask tablecloth. The arrangements in the centre of the table were holly and ivy, in keeping with the theme of Christmas; there was a large real Christmas tree next to the stage at the other end of the room, with a large silver star on the top; and there were sprigs of mistletoe strategically dotted round the room.

Sam's face actually ached from smiling, but he didn't care. He couldn't remember ever being this happy—and, best of all, that happiness shone from Hayley's eyes, too.

After the meal, Martin switched back into best man mode, and introduced all the speeches.

The first was from Hayley's dad. 'I'm going to keep it short and sweet,' he said. 'I want to welcome Sam to the family. And I'm so glad to see my little girl happy. Everyone, please raise your glasses and toast the bride and groom.'

'The bride and groom,' everyone echoed.

Sam stood up next. 'When I was whale-watching in the middle of the North Atlantic Ocean, I never expected to meet the love of my life. So I'd like to make a very special toast to our bridesmaid, Danielle. If it wasn't for her breaking her foot, I'd never have met a woman with eyes like an Icelandic summer sky and a smile that makes my heart beat faster.' He raised his glass. 'Thank you, Dani—for being an excellent bridesmaid and for being your wonderful whirlwind self.'

'Dani,' everyone chorused.

'I'd also like to thank everyone who's helped with the organisation of our wedding,' Sam continued. 'We've really appreciated it. Everyone in Muswell Hill has made me feel really welcome and I'm proud to be part of such a team—and I'm even prouder to be Hayley's husband.'

Everyone cheered.

And then it was Martin's turn. 'As the best man, I'm supposed to tell you scurrilous stories about my little brother. If I did that I'd be here all night and there wouldn't be time for cake or dancing, so I'll keep it brief. Given that my brother met Hayley while they were whale-watching and he talked the emergency department into doing go-karting on ice, I'm half surprised that he didn't talk Hayley into doing something insane for their wedding—like getting married at the top of an indoor snow ski-slope or in an aquarium among the sharks.'

Everyone laughed, especially when Sam said mournfully, 'Now, why didn't I think of that?'

'But seriously, Hayley's utterly lovely,' Martin said, 'and she makes my brother happy—which makes our whole family happy. I'd like to welcome Hayley to our family, and may I ask you all to raise your glasses in a toast to the bride and groom—the new Dr and Dr Price.'

'Dr and Dr Price,' everyone chorused.

After the meal, the venue staff cleared the tables and set everything up for the evening buffet. Hayley and Sam wandered hand in hand around the hall, chatting to everyone while Maybe Baby were playing Christmas songs that had people up on the dance floor.

When the hall was mostly full, Martin stepped over to the PA system. 'The bride and groom are going to cut the cake.'

Thanks to Josh's aunt, they had an amazing cake with four layers—lemon, chocolate, vanilla and fruit cake. There was a deep red ribbon around the bottom of each layer, the same colour as Hayley's bouquet and Danielle's dress, and around the sides were deep red and white poinsettias.

Hayley put her hand on the knife, and Sam put his hand over hers. Together, they posed for photographs and then cut the very first slice. 'And we'd like to say a special thank you to Josh for asking his aunt to make this wonderful cake,' Sam said. 'Especially after the go-kart incident.'

'You're just lucky she didn't ice that cake with go-karts,' Josh said with a grin.

And finally it was time for the first dance. Maybe Baby struck up their chosen song and Sam took Hayley into his arms, swaying with her in time to the music.

'I love you just as you are,' he said.

Hayley smiled up at him. 'I wouldn't change anything about you, even the dangerous stuff—because I love you and I trust you.'

He kissed her. 'Merry Christmas, Dr Price—and happy wedding day.'

'Merry Christmas, Dr Price—and happy first day of the rest of our lives,' she said.

'The rest of our lives,' he echoed. And it was the best feeling in the world.

* * * * *

MILLS & BOON

THE HEART OF ROMANCE

A ROMANCE FOR EVERY READER

MODERN

Prepare to be swept off your feet by sophisticated, sexy and seductive heroes, in some of the world's most glamourous and romantic locations, where power and passion collide.

HISTORICAL

Escape with historical heroes from time gone by. Whether your passion is for wicked Regency Rakes, muscled Vikings or rugged Highlanders, awaken the romance of the past.

MEDICAL

Set your pulse racing with dedicated, delectable doctors in the high-pressure world of medicine, where emotions run high and passion, comfort and love are the best medicine.

True Love

Celebrate true love with tender stories of heartfelt romance, from the rush of falling in love to the joy a new baby can bring, and a focus on the emotional heart of a relationship.

Desire

Indulge in secrets and scandal, intense drama and plenty of sizzling hot action with powerful and passionate heroes who have it all: wealth, status, good looks…everything but the right woman.

HEROES

Experience all the excitement of a gripping thriller, with an intense romance at its heart. Resourceful, true-to-life women and strong, fearless men face danger and desire - a killer combination!

To see which titles are coming soon, please visit

millsandboon.co.uk/nextmonth